Murder by Masquerade

by Camden Wyatt

DORRANCE PUBLISHING CO., INC.
PITTSBURGH, PENNSYLVANIA 15222

The contents of this work, including, but not limited to, the accuracy of events, people, and places depicted; opinions expressed; permission to use previously published materials included; and any advice given or actions advocated are solely the responsibility of the author, who assumes all liability for said work and indemnifies the publisher against any claims stemming from publication of the work.

Dorrance Publishing Co., Inc.
701 Smithfield Street
Pittsburgh, PA 15222
Visit our website at *www.dorrancebookstore.com*

ISBN: 978-1-4809-0906-9
eISBN: 978-1-4809-0768-3

SATURDAY MORNING

He was beaming with that infectious, mischievous Errol Flynn smile; the one that made men jealous and the one that prompted ladies on the film set to twist their heads or suddenly canter into his proximity. He was basking in this moment: a moment when his past seemed like a distant, foggy chamber in his mind; seemed like a fleeting, inconsequential line in his confessions; and seemed like an antiquated, insignificant moment in a lifetime.

As soon as Stu Givens waved, the applause for him commenced on cue and then bellowed. "Cut!" With that single word, he leapt over the white, ornate railings of the posh porch and landed in the billowy, artificial, green grass like a gymnast dismounting the parallel bars, waiting for the judges to flash— Ten! Ten! Ten! The multitude of cast members and crew parted, just as the sea that welcomed Moses and, as he slowly and deliberately strolled through the masses, Givens approached him and hugged him tight.

"One damn take! One! Ha, ha, huh ha, marvelous. You're a gem, Monty." Givens' brown, lunar eyes popped from their sockets underneath his mess of charcoal, disheveled hair, which randomly poured over his high, broad forehead.

Givens grabbed him by the shoulders and squared him up. "We're going to be on budget. We're going to be on target for the next summer's hot previews in the cinemas. We're going to be on target for a timely, lucrative, profitable Christmas opening next year. Who in the public will resist this classic, Monty?" Givens stood beside him now and placed his arm around him as they strolled together, while Givens' stomach protruded over his belt and swayed to their gait. He used his hands as a wand, while he leaned inward to speak to his star.

"Swept out of the pages of a *New York Times* sultry, grandiose, best seller," and, with another wave of his arm and hand, "and onto the big screen with Hollywood's latest, leading heart throb seducing three of the public's self-crowned sex goddesses in the roles of wife, mistress, and femme fatale. I love ya, Monty. I really do. I love ya. This is gonna be great!" Givens released him and watched as the throngs drooled.

1

Monty's sinewy physique swaggered, cutting through admirers, while the gracious, grey antebellum mansion façade dripped in humidity behind him. His cobalt blue shirt was open at the top, exposing a paucity of barbed, onyx chest hairs, and it was crinkled tight at the waist in a messy knot. He was Montilladan. And his legend seemed to grow with each new, weekly edition of gossip rags, celebrity magazines, entertainment events, and juicy internet news items. M, M, M, he imagined he heard in the chatter; or was he imagining it? Tom, the gofer boy, tossed him his towel and M wiped the beads of emerging perspiration from his royal, rectangular forehead. Then, as if emerging from a fresh shower, he briskly mopped his glossy, jet black hair, wiped his nape, and tossed the soiled rag down. *To savor this moment*, he thought to himself, while the crew assembled the grand, ballroom scene. He looked around. He was the center of attention. He relished it.

She slinked through the throngs of extras without drawing attention. Like a snake, she serpentined her way to a point where, for a second, they shared the same expelled, soiled air. Her disguise was perfect. Most importantly, he noticed her not. He was absorbed in himself like Adonis admired by his onlookers, like a hundred Aphrodites cooking fantasies around him. However, she was fixated on her mission. It was she who had taught him this arrogance, this rush of confidence, this bold prance, and now she would strike as an asp and use his hubris against him— fatally. It was so easy to win this part. It would be so easy to defeat him while he drowned in his repulsive haughtiness.

Her directions for the dance scene were simple. Move onto the ballroom floor to her assigned "X", pair up in the exact manner as this week's marathon rehearsals, and follow the simple, repetitive dance steps while allowing her male partner to take the lead. There were over a hundred extras reveling in this moment to share a scene with the great Montilladan and then to wait in anticipation for the release of the film to brag to their friends and relates who attended the opening, to come to see them as poetry in motion before Montilladan's grand entrance on the balcony high above. It was her only audition, her sole scene in the movie. It was so perfect.

The costumes were stunning with each member's garb a masterpiece. She had chosen a pink pastel, flowing gown, sculpted around her dainty waist with ivory frills, pushing what little breasts she had up and out. Dark red rouge plastered her cheeks. Then, to hide from him, a floppy, wide-brimmed white hat from the pre-Civil War period, the southern comfort adorning her curly blonde wig, hiding her natural, bristly, short, black hair. Her gown flowed over the floor, and yesterday's workout was taxing to keep up with the beat, while trying not to stumble, trying not to interfere and intersect with the outburst of lush, cascading garments just like hers. She played the shy one during rehearsals, going about her business with only plastic conversation to any of her peers during breaks and lunch, while brushing off any would-be male admirers. With her pay already in hand, her departure from the set was soon to be imminent. Not a soul would miss her, nor inquire of her. It was so satanically perfect.

The cameras were in place. The dancers stood motionless, all fifty-three pairs, waiting statuesque for their signal to glide into motion as Tommy Bee was hoisted to alpine heights in his mechanical chair above the waltzers. As eyes traced his skyward route, she was the only one on the floor with impure thoughts and distractions. There was a time when they called each other friends; and then they accelerated to lovers. She remembered the first time they had made passionate love all night, each tearing away the lead from each other, back and forth, top and bottom. He knew her craving to be dominant, so he wrestled it away from her, and she loved it. It had aroused her inner sanctum. She had never used that word before to anyone. Love. She had blurted it out to him that night. "Love. I love you." Why had she done that? Perhaps it was because no one, no one ever in her lifetime, including her parents, her aunt, other relates, past and present close friends, other lovers, ever made a fuss over her like he did. He directed their lives, their love, and threw boundless affection her way. They cuddled up as one, legs intertwined, shared affection. But love wilted quickly. She dug deeper into her mind and recalled. *No, not wilted. Vanished. Vanished as he became more obsessed, more vainly accustomed to his new role as a Hollywood celebrity, more comfortable with the moira of his new life.*" Now she despised his superfluous, ridiculous found fame. She was losing him. Then there were those lonely heartfelt moments late at night when she pondered, sat alone in the blackness, arms wrapped only around herself, gazing into a void, when she wondered if he ever thought of…murdering her…to keep their dirty, dirty, unscrupulous secret safe. *And now it was so perfect. He must be killed.*

She was different than him. She practiced life within herself, knew her gifts, comprehended her talents, and controlled the situation. *Setting goals. Deception. Scheming. Snaring the innocent. Using people. Spitting them out. Clutching power. These are my natural given strengths for my rapid ascension.* She smiled. Events were already set into motion. Nothing could stop it now. And yet there he was, only twenty feet distant, strutting, confident, smug, a phony! Unaware of what could and would strike him down. She thought to herself how she was the single individual in the throngs who knew his secret; the only one who knew. The only one in Given's script who knew where he had really risen from, and the only one who could reveal what he really was. And now his secret would die with him. Inwardly she screamed in her thoughts. *You are a nobody; a bum, an unwanted, unloved fake, beguiling the public, arousing them, pushing them into frenzies, begging them to worship you.* She exhaled and swallowed hard. This must end. It had gone too far. He knew what they had done. She knew from the beginning, and now they both were in deep denial. *It must,* she thought to herself, *end; it must come crashing down today. Oh, fate be true to me.* There would be no second chance. She understood that. No more complexities to this plot! If she failed, if he suspected, he might become suspicious and seek revenge on her. For a moment she closed her eyes, shut them hard and prayed. But prayed to whom? She did not know. She just prayed, paused, and prayed again, though she knew not a single God listened to her outpouring.

There was a momentary delay as one of the co-stars discussed with Givens where he was to be located in the ballroom while the waltz scene was played out. As they conversed, and he argued for a different vantage, she stole a memory of that time on the beach when they first met and her eyes met his, and his body chemistry exuded a male specimen of beauty, his eyes crying out, "I want you." She remembered standing there, benumbed at the sight of him. She was famished for sincere love in her life. She was always starved for excitement, even with her bevy of girlfriends, the business of acting, and the hectic pace she kept. He delivered. That first sighting, both drenched in sweat, clothes clinging to their physiques, a hot, Pacific sunset, the skyline torched, the steamy environment real. How could she betray him now? How could she do this to someone that she had uttered the word love to? And he, he had readily reciprocated. Yet here she was executing her demonic plan. But could she carry this to conclusion? Yes, it would be so perfect.

Now she changed her focus. *Givens. What a fool.* She knew him only too well as a weak director, and yet he had secured this lucrative assignment to direct Montilladan in this masterpiece. To her Givens had demonstrated time and time again his shortcomings. Always pushed back at her. "Good idea, but not for this particular setting and definitely not for this one scene." There was his usual, "Come at me again, some other time." She looked away. She firmly decided that she detested both of them. Montilladan's destruction would inflict pain on Givens, too. Underneath the shadows of her brimmed headwear, she smirked devilishly.

Reality check. He was one of only a handful of true lasting friends here in the fast-paced, highly competitive morass of Hollywood. Looking back at their relationship, his continual advances bonded them, but she had made the supreme, gutsy decision, and he followed her into this most dangerous game that they played. Greed. Fame. Notoriety. More greed. Those were their motives. And now she would have to look for another partner, one who could keep up with her pace. But there was this problem to deal with first, and she would need help. And who would she turn to? Perhaps in the end, only herself. She reflected as she gazed at him. *I wonder what really does motivate you.*

The debate was over. Givens won and the actor was vanquished into the side recess for the scene. Tommy Bee shouted directions. From his perch above, he saw only the tops of hats spinning around on the set below as he hung precariously out of his hoisted seat. The music commenced, taped, even though a string band mimicked the musical notes onstage. Her partner gave her a wide smile, and she reciprocated by locking her eyes on him. Her eyes, those radiant, dark eyes that could undress a man, slay an army, lure Tristan. Like a vampira, she glided after his lead falsely hungry for him, and thinking only of the scene to unfold above where she would devour the vulnerable. What a director she was. She was on a real Hollywood movie film set and the director, Stu Givens, was totally impotent, totally helpless to stop her play. He was unknowingly about to submit to her production. His directions were useless. So were Tommy's.

Montilladan opened the door and emerged on the balcony four stories above the carnival of dancers below. Now he wore an ivory, tight, tailored suit with a black bowtie in the lead role of Aaron Moss. While the cameras of Tommy Bee captured his elegance from above, the ground sets zoomed in, peering up, etching on film his boney chin, piercing, lustful eyes, and his lecherous smile. Montilladan stared to the scene below to accommodate, analyzing each belle, leaning over the balcony, expecting all below to recognize and bow to his superiority, submit to his role as Aaron Moss, host of the antebellum extravaganza. Then Bubby Childress, a brute of a man, burst through the French louver doors, storming onto the balcony above as the jealous lover, shouting, cursing, and hurling debasing obscenities at Aaron Moss for luring his sweet, naïve, innocent lover Giselle away from him and into his lustful clutches.

Jason Court was brilliant as Bubby as he shattered the eloquent environment, broke the rhythm of the dancers and orchestra with his yawping, wrestling away the gaze of all the audience below from Moss to himself as each of the dancers became alarmed with the bestial threat to their charming host.

The scene had metamorphosed. Court acted his part meticulously, the torso of Childress heaving in revenge as he spat his lines out flawlessly. Givens below reveled in his choice of the towering Court as the menacing adversary. Now the two sparred lightly, pushing, jostling, hatred drawing them closer together as the audience gasped. This was the cue for Tommy Bee to accelerate, his chair and lens drawing closer to the balcony, the camera fixated on Moss and Childress, Tommy Bee traveling to their sides to capture every raw look, every ringing syllable of malignant dialogue, while the cast below provided an adequate backdrop by shouting and acting out their concerns for Moss.

Childress pushed Montilladan and, as he did, she felt an anxiety creep into the pit of her body cavity; a tingling grip paralyzed her bowels. Only she knew. Only she could stop this. And why would she not stop it? She wanted to do the honorable thing. But this had all gone too far. The plan had spun out of control; their real plot was askew; recent deeds off path. She convinced herself. *This has to be done. Correction of course.* Maybe she would feel remorse later. Was that a reason to shout a warning out now to Montilladan? To Givens? To Tommy Bee? "No. No. Correction required." It was so hellishly perfect.

Court and Montilladan had feigned the motions of this scene seven times yesterday. One week ago, they approached Givens to comfort him and convince him to film the altercation while the cast was still assembled below on the ballroom floor and conduct the scuffle in the same frames, rather than separate films as planned. They were eager to capture this climax while the supporting cast expressed their reactions. Givens agreed to give it a try, rather than the frames he had envisioned. So the actors and cast were assembled onto the dance floor in the ballroom while filming Montilladan's soliloquy on the high porch, catching the dancers dressed and alert before the unusual midday heat, which suffocated those in formal wear.

The confrontation hastened. Childress grabbed Montilladan by the throat. He twisted his arm behind his back, M grimacing; and then Childress used his strength to overpower his opponent and jerk Monty's body toward the rails at one end of the balcony. Just as Montilladan arrived at the railing, he reached out with both hands, arms straight, to grab the rails firmly and break his momentum. But something went terribly wrong. The audience was aghast, as M's slightest bump sent the rails and supports flying, with the restraints dissected, splinters tumbling to earth, exposing nothing between Montilladan's momentum and an imminent fall. Only at this sole point of impact did the rails yield.

Montilladan was struggling to gain control of his balance at the edge, first teetering with nothing to grab onto, and then unexpectedly, and to the horror of all who watched, plummeting headlong, arms flailing, legs awkwardly kicking, now lungs screaming. The crowd was hushed; Montilladan not believing his fate, not realizing that his head would take the brunt of his fall onto the concrete seventy-five feet below, not believing that he was fallible, and not believing this was happening. In the blink of an eye, he thought of her. She was in his last thoughts. *No, it couldn't be her standing below, for there was no astonishment in her gaze. It couldn't be her. She seemed to be conjuring up a faint, hidden smile as only she could compose it.* Darkness followed.

Suddenly the ruby red contents of Montilladan's life spewed out on impact as women shrieked and men gazed in hot-held breath. His body was mangled, the chest and head thrust up into the torso as pounds of flesh like pudding intersected the cement floor. Givens collapsed, nauseated; Tommy Bee leaned over from his perch in disbelief and then slumped; Jason Court sank to his knees sobbing, petrified to look over the edge. A nightmarish scene unfolded. Numerous 911 calls were dispensed by cells on the set. What had happened? How could this structure lose its integrity? Not to Montilladan? This couldn't be real. Givens was in shock as he peered skyward. He had personally ordered the balcony set to be raised for effect; personally removed the safety mats at the request of Court and M. He choked back nausea.

Montilladan, arisen from nowhere to become a shining Hollywood star, now had crashed just like a meteorite, tumbling and burning in the Earth's atmosphere before a stark impact. Life's slate wiped clean into pieces askew. It had all happened so quickly. Sheer chaos ensued. It was so diabolically perfect.

She followed an onslaught of departing, distraught, tearful, frightened cast members as they scrambled from the set. There was no chaos in her plan. Reaching the women's dressing room, striding to her locker, she disrobed quickly, orderly, re-hung her gown on the rack, calmly placed her accessories into the black tote bag and hung them, too, on the rack, changed shoes, left the rouge in place on her face, employed a petrified solemn look, signed the ledger to signify goods returned, and dismissed herself to proceed down a narrow, dark, deserted corridor from the fracas. She made three turns before leading to an emergency exit at the back of the set. Following her designated escape route to a tee, stashing the wig into her oversized handbag before she entered daylight, pulling out a sports cap, the noise behind her fading into whispers as she walked gallantly forward, she was executing her escape. She had rehearsed this in her mind twenty times more than the dance routine. Forcing the heavy metal door open, once in sunlight, she donned dark, oversized sunglasses, exposed her shoulder flesh and legs in her short dress, walked briskly toward the exit of the grounds, brown shoulder purse rocking in sync, her bland, tan dress fluttering so slightly in the breeze. On her way out, she flashed her identification badge to the beleaguered guard, who was overwhelmed and preoccupied with an onslaught of ambulances and police vehicles demanding clearance. Her exit signature was readable. She wanted to leave no doubt that she had departed the grounds. She expressed her remorse about the rumor she heard to another employee who was also signing out and was also confused by the scene.

She strolled confidently, very slowly, oblivious to the turmoil, focusing on her vehicle, four blocks distant, leaving behind rhythms of sirens, ribbons of emergency personnel entering the lot. That stupid Givens. She won the part in her first audition. She couldn't believe her good fortune when she overheard the conversation between M and Court and Givens. "Okay, okay, we'll try it. I'll order the set construction crew to raise the balcony higher, position the dancers closer to the overhang and, okay, no need for the ugly mats to be in the scene as we shoot. As you've said, Monty, get those smelly tarps outta here. It's obscuring the ballroom floor of beautifully painted cement. We'll do the gala scene guys. Great idea."

She muttered. "Thank you Stu. Great idea."

Once inside her vehicle, she departed in an orderly manner. Traffic was light in her direction. Then it happened. An uncontrollable, silly laugh suddenly emanated from deep in her body cavity until it pierced the silence of her space, resounded off the interior leather, desecrated the weepy moments of tributes being cascaded at his death scene. She choked on her laugh until it waned. Now she breathed heavily, in and out, in and out, in and out, in calm, regular, deep breaths, feeling the rich oxygen entering her lungs. Now she bit her lower lip at the corner of her mouth in recognition of her triumph; a bad habit she had. No one could ever trace her. Her camouflage, her false identity would lead them down blind alleys if authorities ever sought to interview her. "Who? Oh, her, that lady in the flowing gown with the cute smile?" Gone. Vanished. With all the witnesses to his accident, with the fatigue of the props, it was perfect. The element of surprise—that was what she taught him today. "He was so goddam smug. But no more."

How did he feel as he plummeted to his death? Did he believe in miracles? Did he in that one second realize that...that...this was his last precious second of life? Did he perchance see her there? She certainly watched that magic moment, absorbed the terror in his eyes, and caught his bewilderment in his contorted face just before impact.

She panicked. Surely he must have died. Her fingers struck the on button and she surfed until she heard the breaking news. "Tragic accident at DelMar Studios in downtown Los Angeles just minutes ago, and there are unconfirmed reports through tweets; I repeat, unconfirmed reports that Montilladan has been involved in the accident on this film set. Of course, there has been much hype about the new movie starring Montilladan. I am talking about Sweet Sherry South, the nation's number one best-selling novel and, if you haven't read it, don't. That's right. Don't! Why? Because the Hollywood movie with our most beloved and most detested star, Montilladan, is bursting into theatres supposedly in one year and, if you keep tuned here, we will keep you informed of the latest developments at the movie set where there appears to be some sort of serious accident. A caller just a few minutes ago informed us of police cars, ambulances, and medics racing into DelMar's lot. Our caller was situated right outside the studio. It was only five months ago that Montilladan was on one of our local talk shows and informed us that he was holding out for this role because it was made for him and until George…excuse me, listeners, there is more information reaching us here at our studio; oh, no, wait…oh, my…my God. No, no, please." His voice fell to a whisper, his tone deadened. "Oh, my Lord. Excuse me folks." There was a whimper. He swallowed hard. He let go a heavy breath. "There are now confirmed reports, I am so sorry to inform you, our listeners, that an accident on the film set of Sweet Sherry South has…officially…taken the life of…Montilladan. This is an initial report; we will work to confirm details." She slammed her palm on the off button, veered off the road, sat on the shoulder, and clapped hard and yelled, "Yes! Yes! Yes! Yes!" She shook her head to and fro in rich triumph.

Driving further, in a furious fit of glee, suddenly a single tear rolled down her left cheek, dropping onto her dress and turning the tan to a dark brown spot. Rather than entering the freeway ramp, she pulled into a parking lot in front of a grocery store, hiding away from the gas pumps at the edge of the lot under a droopy oak tree and sat there, alone as reality stabbed at her. This emotion lasted only two minutes before she wrapped her arms around herself, and she regained her composure. After remorse passed, she checked her watch. Looking around and spying not a body in proximity, she peeled the thin layer of false flesh from her nose and cheeks, and rubbed off the rouge until she was clean faced. She expelled a sigh, shook her head, deciding that there was a new life to contrive and a new challenge to confront. The plan. She knew there was another victim, because the plot was already unfolding; a new plan, someone else to use. In her mind, she dispensed with the word plan. This was not a plan. This was life, and she was ready to act on life's stage again to accomplish her next quest, to perform in Oscaresque roles, onstage and off. But someone else would be required on stage with her, to accomplish her next daring and dastardly feat.

THE FOLLOWING SATURDAY NIGHT

It was another one of those gatherings of long-time female acquaintances—some single, several divorced, a few separated, an indefinite number seriously contemplating a split, and the remainder faithfully married. This bar, Fosse's Corner Tavern, was frequently the sight of their rendezvous. Situated on the northern perimeter of the downtown Los Angeles area, in a neighborhood of transition where the shops and business establishments grow thinner as apartments, condominiums, and middle-class, private housing appear more frequently as lofts, condos, and bungalows, this spot served as a landmark watering hole for young, budding professionals and longtime patrons of drink and sports.

As usual this group of females would tonight imbibe and, in parallel processes, share experiences of the arts, critique movies, allot time to hear the opinions of those whom had recently attended concerts and live theatre and, most definitely, magnify a flattery sometimes absent in the workplace and marriage. But, most importantly, to this group of twenty-somethings, the topic of conversation was never complete without running the gauntlet of new lovers, praising and chastising past dates, defending longtime hubbies and live-ins, and finally charting new possibilities. This territory blanketed all the other issues. Tonight, as in other gatherings, this was a time for each to play the role of comedian, critic, devotee, nurturer, champion, and friend.

Charlie Fosse never tired of this particular clan. It wasn't their money and his income that he relished. It wasn't the clamor that could be encouragement to lure new passer-bys through the heavy, red, oak swinging doors. It was their enjoyment of life, their genuineness, their pact to live life to the fullest through trials and tribulations and the fact that they had chosen his establishment to share their gospel on a regular basis. Perusing over the tables, he connected to Melanie's melodramatic appeal. Charlie leaned his colossal profile on his elbows on the counter, rested his furry face on one, up-turned hand, hoping to become engaged in Melanie's debate. They were always quick to ask, "What about it Charlie?" As if he were the local shrink.

Charlie maintained a mental record of their favorite libations, called them each by first name or nickname, knew their quirks, their traits, and which button to push to obtain a response. After these nearly three years of spirited conversations, Charlie often found an excuse to situate them in the alcove at the end of his bar so he could respond to their needs personally while his staff tended to the masses sprawled at the ageless, wooden tables in front of him. And so it was that this scene played out again tonight, in this two-story, red brick bar with the lead-paned stained glass windows, nestled under tall, old, deciduous trees at the corner of Market and Gibson Streets.

The chemistry of the night had just been established when she exited this corner tavern, her twiggy physique barging through the swinging doors. She had not bothered to make the effort to complete her customary round of "good nights" to her female comrades; not even offered excuses to anyone for her precipitous departure. She had rationalized only minutes before that her absence would not be noticed, with Annie and Denise stealing the show tonight with their surprise announcements of newly conquered, serious lovers. She chose the moment when all eyes were fixed on Annie, who announced her engagement, to turn her back on them, quietly lay her wine glass down at the end of the long table, and weave through a maze of hopeful suitors who, like sharks, were congregating, standing, examining her group, assigning each one of them a strike probability.

Her own contributions had been minimal tonight as her mind wandered into the bleak world of recent events, best left unspoken, best unshared with her friends—just left crystallized in her thoughts. The interest withered further as Lori spoke to her of unjust deeds at home. Would she end up like Lori, too? Trapped? "Can you imagine doing this to me, Zee? I run the damn household! I work myself to death. It doesn't function without me. How dare my family treat me like this?" Zoe wasn't listening.

Once outside, her deep-set, dark eyes darted from side to side. Her long, slender legs were firmly outlined in skin-tight, black denim jeans, her high-heeled black suede boots tapping each step on the pavement. She marched forward with conviction as her fingers fiddled the tiny key pad furiously, until eventually a single, piercing, high-pitched bleep broke the silence, signaling a letdown of security.

With her car headlights aglow, an illuminated path now designated the way in the darkened parking lot across the street. A sudden, brisk breeze rearranged her short, cropped, jet black hair, and she spread her fingers as a comb to expunge the small mop that had dropped onto her forehead. Ahead of her, the sleek form of her ebony Jaguar beckoned her, and soon she found herself engaging the engine, tugging her seatbelt snug, and adeptly maneuvering out of the lot.

Her prize possession halted. She felt remorseful that she had left Maggie in mid-story in a boisterous yarn about the advances that her supervisor was making toward her. She regretted that she had not remained to vote and pass judgment on Annie's new beau—a banker and fellow jogger. Annie respected her opinion immensely and would seek her out before the night was over. Annie was probably rummaging for her right now. *Should I turn around? Go back to appease Annie?* These were certainly reasons to do so.

This hesitation had served as a healthy interlude. It had pushed her to a decision, so she steered a sharp right turn into the roadway, navigating the vehicle down the narrow moist-laden path, momentarily glazed in brilliant, white moonlight. At the stop sign she paused again, peered skyward to notice the grey, sinewy clouds dashing across the sky in the aftermath of this evening's vigorous, early fall storm.

Identification reaction prevailed. She shifted gears and suddenly her Jag, with purpose, sped out onto the feeder road, soon to access the ramp to the interstate. Even at this late hour, the freeways of Los Angeles were still consumed by a grand prix.

The excitement within her swelled, this tangible elation directly connected to the acceleration. She and vehicle were as one, navigating through the onslaught of motorists. Undoubtedly, there were polarized emotions in all of these helmsmen as they sought to reach their destinations. But hers was clear.

The projectile shot out of the chute and into the foray of traffic with a confident, pleasing surge, so characteristic of its sole occupant. This was her escape! Units of exhilaration saturated her entire body. There was a complete focus on the task at hand.

Yet, just as quickly as this rush had satisfied her, she now struggled as a lingering somberness threatened to suffocate her pleasure. It stabbed at her mind. It was this same prick of sadness that caused her to decide to escape from the tavern gathering tonight, the gathering that she loved so much, yearned for, respected, and looked forward to with anticipation.

Even Charlie had yelled after her, "Hey, beautiful, you're not leaving so soon? Are you?" All she had signaled to him in return was a quick glance of pulled, taut lips, coupled with a sexy goodnight of fingers waving. She loved Charlie. She had spent many a minute at Fosse's Corner Tavern, pouring out her inner thoughts on life's crises to Charlie.

Now it grabbed her. How she wished that she could go back in time to rewrite the pages of her recent life. If only someone else had discovered the body. Why had she been so eager to lead the charge through the woods? Ahead of the police, the journalists, the official search party, her partner. Why? Who was she trying to impress? Or was it this desire to prove to everyone present that her deductions were correct? They would locate Heather's body exactly at the location she had prescribed, and alive.

She thought to herself, *Why was this incident so disturbing, when the odds of Heather being alive were so slim?* She knew these odds the day before; the week before. She was totally unprepared for the bloodied corpse.

Meanwhile, he stood attentive, perched in the gaping hole. His blue body suit accentuated every muscle, but especially his torso and legs. His six-foot-two body frame carried not an ounce of noticeable fat. Women frequently found themselves magnetized to his physique; his tanned, swarthy facial features were representative of his distant connection to an American Indian heritage.

Shamelessly, he had on occasions used his physique to his advantage to attract females.

Below the lights of the metropolitan Los Angeles area rhythmically blinked at him, intermittently hidden from view as the plane plowed across soft, snakelike pulses of clouds. The skyline of Los Angeles was barely visible in the distance; the cold, black tundra of the Pacific Ocean lay to his left; the chartreuse glow of the Hollywood Bowl pierced through the blackness on the horizon.

"Ninety seconds," the man with the tremulous jowls and khaki outfit shouted over the plane's deafening din of engines. Languishing in a tomb of cigar smoke, he was positioned directly in front of a monitor, his attention devoted to their coordinates, the images on the screen, the jumper at the porthole, and his glowing, classic cigar. The intersection, with a somewhat larger billow of cloud, caused both men to heave and sway. They resumed their positions, he at the open door by grabbing a guide wire, and he seated by grasping the fixed desk with both hands while biting down the cigar firmly with his brown, stained teeth.

The jumper peered back over his shoulder to the monitor inside. For a second, he made eye contact with the fat man but unlocked quickly less his true intentions be betrayed. Mentally he calculated the risks while weighing the consequences. Playing this scene out in his mind numerous times, he was convinced that this opportunity would never occur again. Any betrayal to the guide would create immediate disharmony.

In a split second, he pulled down his blue ski mask, positioned the goggles over his eyes, and inhaled a deep, prolonged breath, his chest swollen with ego. He fondled his apparatus one last time and jumped into the blackness!

"Thirty…goddam you! It's not time! Jesus! Hell!" In his angered state, the monitor slammed the headset onto the floor. As he did so, his cigar slipped out of his mouth and rolled under the desk. Muttering additional expletives, the man proceeded to crawl on all fours laboriously to retrieve his smoldering cigar before it had the misfortune to ignite any materials. This was not the first time that this specimen had been the recipient of his evident infuriation. This time he would be punished. Rising, moving to the open door, extending his head out the opening of the small plane, there was no sign of the jumper. He was anxious to record this disobedience in the nightly log.

It was too late for warnings and threats. The parachutist was away on his clandestine mission, and he could now only pray that the journey he had hatched could be executed, that he would arrive at his predetermined coordinates, since plan one had now been officially aborted. This scenario, this instance, could not be wasted.

He plummeted in free fall, his body spread-eagled in perfect symmetry, his arms stiff as cement, legs ferociously fighting friction to remain straight. He found the differential of air currents threatening to spin him out of control, but he found an inner strength to combat any pirouettes into chaos. Presently he was stronger than physics.

His eyes were wide open, his mind attentive and absorbing the arousal. The exhilaration of the gravitational pull provided tingling sensations in his toes, groin, and neck areas. Blood corpuscles tickled his veins in their frantic race as his body enjoyed all of this. He was oblivious to the danger of any obstacles. His infected mind had two intents—to retain free fall as long as humanly possible, to complete his mission tonight.

His heart continued to forge plasma in frenzy, the walls of the organ beating feverishly; so feverishly that he felt its exact location. His gut started to quiver as he continued his descent. This was his escape, and he languished in it.

Quickly he assessed his position, continuing the tumble, resisting a surfacing temptation to open the chute. Discipline. Focus. During these few minutes, he was divorced from all the worries of life and of his stressful, sometimes dangerous, occupation. Strange thought. For all his jumps, for all his risks, he never stopped to ponder his death once. For certain the chute would open. He had packed it personally. As usual, as throughout all his life, he had the absolute confidence in himself to manage danger.

The last remnants of an indigo twilight were barely visible in the west, even at this late hour. Now he thought of his self-serving goals, thought of the grief he would encounter tomorrow. Maybe. Only if they could locate and contact him. Was it worth it? Yes, no doubt. He would make it worthwhile. This was a loose end that had to be tied. It had to be tonight. He could not duplicate these circumstances again. "It has to be tonight." No one heard him.

His body passed safely through the base of cloud level. His vector of horizontal resistance was suddenly insignificant, so he opened his sail and momentarily jettisoned hard off course as the full bloom of the parachute corralled the night air, interrupted his acceleration, and terminated the uncontrolled phase of the drop. Now it was time to conquer the air waves. As one of many night creatures in Los Angeles, he used his twenty-twenty vision to quarry his prey. In his mid-thirties, he had perfect eyesight, a clear strength in his dangerous line of business.

On the ground, she was cognizant of her ultimate driving prowess; weaving in and out of traffic, exercising courteous subterfuges, dodging obstructions at breakneck rapidity, leaving a long line of envious clumsy admirers behind her. The hours of the past brooding had been vanquished by materializing a high out of her racing skills.

Suddenly a bout of paranoia surfaced. *What if I should crash? A solitary slick; perhaps an unexpected encounter with an intoxicated driver who couldn't hold his liquor or his lane? Statistics favored that scenario on this day of the week, and on this freeway, and at this hour. Perhaps an unpredictable brake of vehicles, resulting in total wipeout. Slow down. Slow down.*

She reconsidered. *Who would mourn for me? Were Annie and Denise serious close girlfriends? No frequent male lovers of recent. Twenty-nine, pushing thirty, and still searching for Mister Right. Distant from family in Lodi. I'm isolated. Alone with my Jag. That's my love, and I guess we both perish.*

"Geez, Zee, stop it!" she advised herself out loud, just as she sensed her drench in dismal thoughts. Now she arrested the steering wheel with both hands as the flick of the signals focused her concentration on the next exit ramp. Adeptly she charged across three lanes with little room to spare, while behind her, a blaring residue of horns sounded as a warning of her egregious tactics. "Sorry," she offered.

She altered her tempo, veering obliquely, decelerating to exit and, within seconds, the black four-seater comfortably approached her residential neighborhood of houses, condominiums, retirement lodges, low-rise apartments, and then finally, her street of executive townhomes.

As a laggard, she absorbed her street, lined with graceful palms; her street with a wide separation of driving lanes by a boulevard of elegant floral arrangements and flowering bushes; her street of rows of executive homes completed in adobe, stucco, and wood-frame, each finished uniquely to represent a time period or a distinctive style of architecture. There was the full package of amenities—including security.

The vehicle came to an abrupt halt in front of her two-story, red brick unit where she had two reserved parallel parking spaces. She roared the engine into one, last crescendo before meltdown, and then lingered, leaning against her vehicle, to admire her customized finishes. The windows on each level were adorned by bold, red awnings, in color harmony with tones of the brick. Deep, royal green accented the trim on each window frame. Multi-colored flowers adorned the entry, while her prize flower patch graced the small, front lawn.

Bouncing two steps at a time, her agile frame approached the oak front door, also finished in deep, green paint. She immobilized the security system upon entry, bolted the door behind her, and proceeded down the sparsely decorated hallway to a modern kitchen where she gleefully treated herself to a splash of sangria on ice from a pitcher in the fridge. She sat the tumbler on the beige, tiled island. Using a remote, she pointed into the adjacent dark room at the tall media unit and scanned until she stumbled onto her favorite soft music radio station, adjusting the volume to caress her soul.

Through the wide, double-glassed patio doors, the stillness of the night lured her into the living area, where she stood statuesque, appreciating how her unit gave her direct access to the expanse of park meadow in the rear. She unbolted the patio doors, slid both of them open, and there she stood, eyelids stickily closed, gripping her glass, savoring the gentle background vibrations that poured from the airways, pondering the next ten years, feeling each cold drip of glassy dew as it passed down the tall, cold tumbler to pond above her thin, elegant fingers.

Piecing the tragic case together, she punished herself by grappling over misinterpreted clues. But would it have made a difference? Would it have saved poor Heather's life? No, probably not. Her feelings for Heather were ever so genuine. She was not shocked at her death, but she was so deeply saddened.

The powerlessness of her profession was driven like a stake through her heart when she reached that muddy ditch to discover the nude, lifeless form.

Yet he was still on the loose, somewhere even in the Southern California area, hiding, surviving, celebrating the victory of his crime, saluting his escape, snidely rejoicing in her failure. She grew angry at these thoughts. She tired of this defeat.

Overhead he envisioned worlds colliding. The scenery was now becoming familiar to him. He had scoped the neighborhood earlier today from ground level and parked his vehicle at an inconspicuous spot, five hundred feet from his target's dwelling. With singular landmarks to guide him, a surge of confidence swelled as he thought about his weapon of surprise. Just as the rows of structures looked homogeneous, he strained his eyes to find the park and tipped the chute to realign the path with his terminus.

The descent was now rapidly becoming precipitous with every passing second as he exponentially closed the distance between him and his destination. Just as the tops of the trees were visible, the moon inconveniently hid behind a stream of marshmallow condensation. Interface was imminent.

On the tiled patio, she lobbed her head forward, reluctantly envisioning the angelic face of the sweet teenager, Heather, a motionless, white, lifeless form. The case had not been brought to closure. She shook her head and hair, thrusting her head back, controlling her breathing, the cool, moist air making her feel sultry. She was lost of this world on the large extrusion, exercising a ritual of controlled muscular movements so very common to her daily physical workouts. This routine, she hoped, would exercise the demons of Heather's death from her so she could find peace in sleep tonight.

She turned her back on nature, sauntering toward the open double doors, now positioning herself in the portico to her sanctity, the entrance to her world of microwave, plasma television, compact disc player, computer network, exercise bike, blender, and state-of-the-art air sofas. The arching of her toes helped carry her weight as she slowly slipped one step inside.

Meanwhile he spied her as a tiny, black molecule in an ochre ray of light. His ski mask was soaked in moisture and, inside his goggles, sweat beads now dotted his eyelashes, falling to cloud his vision. The air currents and turbulence and chute propelled him into fast forward and, for the first time, he tingled as her distinctive outline came into focus. Tall, leggy, slim, sexily clad in distinctive black, moving like a graceful ballerina, but he knew her to be much more deadly!

A plan was hatched. He would hit the ground running precisely at the target's residence, but with only four to five steps at most to establish the stability required to overtake her. God help him if she should close the glass doors. In his enthrallment, he now realized that it was too late. He had arrived! Impact!

She paused only for a second in the breezeway, turning to relegate herself to savor the calm of the night, the beauty of a bulbous, silvery moon emerging from cover. Now, mysteriously, blackness suddenly overwhelmed the moon's splendor. An eerie opaqueness. A mysterious, Shakespearean, fungible, black spot. An intergalactic wormhole in her space. Instinctively there was cause for alarm due to this unexplained event that had her brain spinning. Searching, eyes frozen open in terror, body muscles suddenly stretched in anxiety, mind soaked in inquisitiveness, a black apparition materialized literally feet in front of her. With all her special training, it mattered little, for this anomalous event of an opaque specter on her patio so stunned her that she lapsed into total confusion and paralysis and could only stand there to confront her intruder.

With three steps at high speed, the invader raced out in front of the parasail, his knees and ankles absorbing the impact of touchdown. His body bumped hers and, as he did, his strength grabbed her around the waist, using his enormous power to hoist her kicking, one hundred and five pounds up, the momentum carrying both of them into the living area of her abode.

They smashed full velocity against the back of her sofa; the force initially thrusting the sofa forward before finally turning the furniture over. They tumbled down the back of the sofa in a splatter of tassels and cushions; he ending up on top of her as they spilled onto the carpet in the middle of the spacious room. They were both tangled in a mesh of cord, rope, parasail, and flailing limbs.

She gasped for breath; the air of dear life expelled from her upon first the impact of the collision and upon his tight grasp around her waist. Using all her potency to push the intruder off, lest he regain composure and advantage first, she found her right arm bundled in twine, so therefore useless for her cause. Her martial arts training was of little value in her current horizontal position, especially with her most powerful arm pinned.

She fought to identify pressure points, areas of vulnerability of her assailant, but in the dim light, before she could organize her motor skills, he overpowered her to toss her up and over his body, just as she screamed. Rapidly he stripped himself of goggles, mask, and mesh, pulled a pocket knife to sever twine, emerging at once in the control position.

She panted frantically. He was gulping for air, exhaling with a jazzy beat. Body prostate, leaning on one elbow, he addressed her cockily as she finally became visible from under the messy bundle.

"You said if I was ever in the neighborhood that I should drop in."

"Damn you, Axel Hawk! Damn you!" Angrily she lurched forward and pushed him hard off balance as he landed flat on his back. Squatting on her bent knees, she inhaled intensely, expelled in short puffs, and barked at him.

"You could have crippled us, maimed us! Hell, killed us!"

"Hell, hardly; my landings include some of my best moves."

"You...are...crazy. Jesus mercy. And when did I ever invite you over?"

"Oh...this year, about...May...you said that if I was ever in the..."

"Stop it! Never mind. I can't believe that you did this. You trashed my living room."

"Well...when I saw you yesterday...you said that you were probably at home alone tonight and—what a rush. The roller coaster of emotions. First you relaxed in the night air and then the sudden onslaught of apprehension, followed by fear. The struggle. The climax of relief. To follow, the denouement, the embellishment of this evening into an award-winning tale at Fosse's." She was silent and sat on her bent legs with arms folded, clearly irritated, glaring back at him.

Axel continued. "And how about my entrance? Sensational?" No response.

"Come on, Zoe. Crack a smile! Admit it. This is a real rush moment." He tilted his head as he now sat on buckled knees. With this flurry of events behind him, he appeared composed. In a microsecond of contact, he winked at her.

But she forgave not easily, so she reached over, knocked him off balance with a single, spry blow to the chest and, in the ensuing moments, she mounted him, handcuffed his hands to the floor above his head, and positioned herself close to him, their noses now only inches apart, intensely competing for the same replenishment of air.

"You are mad, and this is madness."

In the background, the Eagles were playing,

"Take it to the limit,"

"Take it to the limit,"

As both stared at one another, the lyrics arrived: "Show me a sign." He heard it. She heard it. He lunged upward and stole a kiss. She had big, pouty, dark lips, especially the bottom one, and Axel frequently thought it to be one of her sexiest assets, as well as her rich, heavenly, olive tan. He closed his eyes on impact. She didn't. And now the Eagles were providing more encouragement as they lifted their lilt into, "Take it to the limit, wee, ee, ee. Take it to the limit, wee, ee, ee. Take it to the limit, one more time."

A strong gust of breeze burst into the room, chaotically rearranging the parachute, which eventually lifted over both of them. As it happened, the Eagles crooned their final notes, the parasail hid them, and he impetuously embraced her driving her body down onto him.

It was the first time in their four years of working together that he had established physical contact with her. His hand rested on her exposed back. She was smooth to the touch.

She had never thought about Axel romantically. Axel, on the other hand, had hungered for this moment. In recent times, he found himself and his thoughts on her. Daydreaming was very dangerous in their profession. But daydreaming had possessed him, and he had committed this night to expose his feelings to her.

So his mind was on her beauty, his emotions, her soft touch, and how much she had meant to him over these last four years. She tried so hard to find words of logic to dissuade any further actions to break this embrace. But her reasoning had failed her. For this moment, Zoe Burns was defenseless in the clutches of Axel Hawk.

SUNDAY EVENING

The note was scribbled in pink, her distinctive, inky trademark. It was clearly addressed to Axel Hawk. It spelled out eight-thirty sharp, yet many minutes had elapsed beyond, with still no sign of her. Last night he was performing acrobatic feats of aero-wonderment, trying to catalyze a new romance; tonight, Axel Hawk was on Venice Beach, waiting impatiently, pacing with a grinding knot in his stomach, debating his first choice of salutations, waiting for her, the recent past love of his life, a love now drifted far away

He halted, hands in pockets, gazed to his left. The sun was low on the horizon, the blue clear sky metamorphosed in the west into gold and crimson. He continued down the boardwalk. At sea he saw the crests of waves dancing in sparkling, yellow glitter, foam culminating on the beach, lathering the sands in white cream. At water's edge, two lovers strolled while holding hands, strategically bumping into one another, stealing an occasional peck, leaving footprints in the sands for only seconds before the tide reclaimed the territory.

He reminisced. *Somewhere on a breaker pile of rocks that ran perpendicular to the beach was etched Nikki Louden loves Axel Hawk. A scripture of days gone down; the sole, surviving journal to my Juliet. Perhaps like this past love, and the footprints in the sand, it, too, had been permanently eroded by time.* He stopped again, hands on hips to recall where the obelisk lies. No, this was not the location. It was not in these breakers. It was elsewhere further up the beach.

Lines of sailboats were just barely visible as darkness swallowed the sea, and with it devoured the last remnants of a glorious October day in Southern California. Lights twinkled, as the crafts were first thrown into a trough and jiggled on a peak. Now, he examined the waterfront, to his left, and now right. Axel pondered why Nikki had chosen this expansive section of white beach at Santa Monica to rendezvous at.

The lovers in front giggled. Soon a second couple joined them in romantic banter. But the view, the romance, the majestic sunset, these moments were all shattered. A ghetto blaster intruded and, as he looked to his left, he spied four contorting bodies gyrating in looping sexy rituals to a form of music that he had not connected to. He was wearing his Hard Rock Cafe shirt and faded denim cutoffs, but escape, not inclusion, was directing his mind.

Axel shuffled quickly down the beach and onto a broader expanse of sand. This stretch was cluttered with Sunday evening family strollers and picnickers. Now out of earshot of the annoyance, the hissing of the emerging tide suffocated his senses, the obtuse artwork of the advancing and receding tide stimulating a fanciful vision.

Again the moment was shattered. A sticky wad of purple gum firmly attached itself to the indentations of the sole of one of his antiquated Reeboks. From a nearby trash can, he located a metal pop can clip and proceeded to sit on his haunches, attempting to pry the disgusting substance free in an outburst of damning adjectives.

"Gumshoe. That's you forever—a gumshoe," she yelled as she paraded toward him. A smile encompassed his face at the sound of her voice. Axel looked up, chuckled, and deposited the biohazard into a trash can, wiping his hands on his shirt to greet her. It used to be a multipurpose kiss; tonight it was a limp handshake.

"Nikki, my dear Nikki." Her response was immediate. In an acidic, high-pitched tone, she spat at him.

"I am not your dear Nikki, Axel. Cut the bullshit lover crap. It's over for good. I'm here on business tonight. Strictly platonic. No! Shift to two gears lower than platonic." As usual, Axel's heart was not cooperating. He always melted in her presence, much to the opposite advice of his closest friends.

He inspected her. Ruby red, perpetually moist lips. Short, a little stocky, with firm thighs and buttocks. Curvy, tantalizing shape with pronounced breasts. Her thick, frizzy, blonde hair was plastically in place except for a single strand, which found its way out of the nest to reside over the side of her face, providing an extra sexy allure. Spontaneous reaction overwhelmed him.

"Nikki, your recent boob job has you busting out all over." The red straps of her bra created a defined imprint on her blouse.

"It is none of your damn business anymore, Axel." She removed her red shades and tucked them into her thick hair above her forehead. To break his gaze, Nikki tugged at the top of her blouse to remove any last view of her cleavage. Axel spied the pink, coral beads, which circled her stout neck. He dared to make eye contact.

Oh, those nights, and so many of them, when she had bewitched him to cast love spells by simply using her bejeweled hypnotic, blue eyes to exact her way. In the trance of her ravishing eyes, he had been rendered helpless. Suddenly reality returned. *How could two grownups in love, both thirty-five years old, act out the recent antagonistic scenes of malevolence? Conjure up such spiteful acts?* He felt like he had been confined to detox since the breakup.

"Your online gossip column is really quite popular." He had intended to compliment her but realized his mistake with his mawkish choice of vocabulary, the word "gossip."

"Correction, Axel, I pen a social column to acknowledge the accomplishments and social events of the citizens of our dear city. I acknowledge the significant achievements of our wealthy upper crust to create awareness and give credit to the contributions of our upper echelon. Upper echelon, that's high class. I rarely reference your associates. It is only gossip to my non-admirers." Axel's lips pursed and, unfortunately, he retaliated.

"Right. Since you redesigned your column online and in the daily papers to include that nifty little insert of you with your captivating cleavage, I bet that you have grossly increased the number of invites to functions, increased your number of sponsors, and even multiplied subscriptions."

Nikki shot back. "And you wonder why we broke up? I am more than flesh and bones. How dare you Axel! I'm really tired of this. I am a real human being with intellect, and I am having a damn good time now that I have my own column. I'm an excellent journalist as judged by my readers. Others in my profession grant that. I have also written and published short biographies. You have never given me any credit for my writing abilities. I majored in journalism at Southern Cal. You often forget that. Someday, Axel, I'm going to be a famous writer."

"Nikki." But she abruptly interrupted him.

"Even in high school, when I was editor of our high school yearbook, you figured that scoring one rushing touchdown or tossing a shutout was a helluva lot more important than crafting the yearbook."

Axel felt remorseful. Don't argue. Just listen. In a pause he interjected. "I'm sorry."

"My photo insert just aids the readers, allows them to connect to the author. If the public doesn't like what they read, they won't invest time in the product, Axel. Do you really think there are morons out there who spend time every day to get a minute glimpse of my cleavage by purchasing the local paper? Or logging online? And my photo is in black and white! Well, Axel?"

His mind was spinning. *Repair the situation, Axel. Do it. Quick response.*

"Sorry. My choice of dialogue was quite inappropriate. My use of the word gossip was insulting to you, and I'm sorry. How about a drink, Nikki? Our favorite bar on the strip is..." And, once again, she viciously interrupted him, her fleshy cheeks of a smile disintegrating into stretched, tight lips and stony muscles. Her eyes filled with steamy ire, her arms became fully animated.

"Regrettably, there is no *us* anymore, Axel. Words were exchanged that are now permanently recorded as a part of our destructive history." She continued. He stared back, so wanting to re-commence this rendezvous from the beginning, to go back five minutes in time. It hurt hearing her bitch at him like this.

"...can never be retracted. Actions were executed that bloodied my heart; yours, too. We can't go back. It's over, Axel. I'm not here to apologize nor express any regrets. We need to move on in our lives. The chapter of Nikki Louden and Axel Hawk is history." Her voice had mellowed; he fidgeted with his hands, hoping that other strollers were not nosy enough to overhear their awkward conversation or notice the redness in his cheeks.

"Are you still dating Moochie?"

"It's Murchie, James Murchie the third." She placed great emphasis on "the third" and threw her hands up in the air in disgust, turning her back and storming away from him, leading Axel down the beachfront, toward the water's edge.

Nikki proceeded hurriedly to a darkening, secluded corner at beach level, leaving Axel scurrying behind to keep up. "Deja vu." He recalled this from their past. She was always forging the way. She was always doing this—forcing him to follow her lead—to a boutique, to a restaurant, to say hello to friends, to a show, into a crowd. Axel suddenly recounted how many a planned date had rambled astray as Nikki issued new orders. Nikki was always one to lead. He didn't resent that; he just recalled it.

"Nikki, wait."

She deposited herself in the sands, twenty feet from the waterline, and there she sat, cross-legged, arms folded under her breasts, pushing them up and outward to accentuate her side sculpture. She stared out toward the Pacific Ocean, head postured up proud. Axel positioned himself next to her, mimicking her pose. There they sat stoically for over three minutes until he dared to speak first.

"Truly, Nikki, I'm sorry. I apologize. I won't toss any more barbs your way. I had truly forgotten that his name was Murchie." His tone was sincere. Would she notice? No response.

"I won't try to repair our relationship. I'll shift into the business environment if that's what you want. I promise not to reference your friend by any name other than Murchie. I won't even comment on your delicious physique. There. Okay? Please, let's at least still be friends."

A further peace followed, magnified into quietness until Axel took the initiative a second time.

"Now, tell me what is so important to bring Axel Hawk and Nikki Louden to Venice Beach on a glorious evening dressed in purple, gold, and ambience? And may I respectfully add beauty?"

It was as if she hadn't heard him. She continued to fixate on a point out at sea. Axel couldn't help himself. "And may I say that you look maaahhhvellus tonight."

Without turning her head, she replied with a smile and a response devoid of passion. "Thank you." The waves continued to break in unison in front of them. An accentuated body heave coupled her breathing pattern.

"Axel, a dear, dear friend of mine is in a horrible predicament. She needs the services of a private investigator in her darkest hours of despair and, with great reservation, enormous uneasiness," now she confronted him, "with much to be risked, much at stake, I recommended your firm."

Her voice rose to a squeakiness as their eyes locked. "Now, before you get too weepy-eyed, Axel, get too egocentric, in the end I feel that it was against my better judgment, but I kept thinking of you, even though it's over between us, and…I…I feel like you could be her best chance to elucidate this dilemma." Axel detected sniffles.

"Thank you, Nikki, for your kind words of confidence, and I love those big words you use, elu…cidate."

She snapped at him. "You are such an enigma, Axel. I still care for you and respect you, even though we have played bouts of debasement, over and over. It really was a hellacious journey as we broke up, but I will always have some lingering sentiment." Now her tone changed to nasty.

"But Axel, this is business. This is serious, deadly, gospel truth that I am about to lay on your shoulders. You and Ms. Burns are good at what you do; that is finding missing persons, conducting in-depth private investigations. That's why I'm sponsoring you." As she spoke, she lost her facial beauty that he frequently dreamed of in her absence.

"I'm a moron," he spouted.

"What?" she snarled inquisitively.

"Yeah, I sneak that peak at your column. It is damn good journalism. However, I'm the moron who spends a buck just to buy the paper some days to see your black and white photo and goes online, too. I still have a place in my heart for you. I figure that I must be responsible for that increased circulation, huh?" Nikki laughed, placing a soft slug on the side of his shoulder with her clenched fist. Axel maintained his composure.

"I am just jealous that it is Murchie who is there to share in your success and not me. He is by your side now that you are a true celebrity."

Her eyes were moist, so she wiped them with the back of her bare wrists, shuffled to position herself closer to him, locking her arm in his, knees touching, her thigh pressing firmly against him. After she had completed her repositioning, she whispered in his ear. "Down, boy."

Nikki proceeded to tilt her head so that it rested on his shoulder. Axel thought to himself, *From acidic to sentimental, this flow so typified their relationship.* Nikki spoke ever so softly.

"Let us be friends. Act as friends, like we did in high school. We didn't date in high school, but we were inseparable."

"Yes. Remember when we skipped school for the concert by the Grateful Dead in Anaheim?"

She responded in her raspy, high, sexy voice. "Yeah, too bad we were spotted on television by old lady Harding that night on the news. It always puzzled me. What was she doin' watching Grateful Dead highlights?"

"And the Dodger playoff game? Seats in the front row."

Nikki perked up. "What a blast, Axel. I also remember when you stood up against grouchy Robinson when he docked me unfairly on my math test. What did he say?"

He tugged her closer by positioning his arm around her waist. "The case, my dear. I want to hear about this case from you."

Nikki shifted as he tightened his grip on her. "It's much different, so far more difficult than any assignment you've tackled before. You need to get your mind straight. Your head needs to be clear. Lose your rough edges and concentrate."

"Nikki, I treat all my cases with the same focused intensity, a commitment to client, whoever he or she may be. So does Zoe. It is our responsibility to do so. So, who's your friend?" He resented her insinuation that he applied favoritism and that he exhibited uneven efforts. She countered her remark by repositioning once again and resting her stubby legs, bare below the bottom of her shorts, over his outstretched legs.

"I am telling you this under strictest confidence. And you! You must keep your mind straight. You must give her all your greatest efforts. She's so special, so important to me—and a V.I.P. to many others. Axel, this case is so unusual and so bizarre. You may even find it preposterous at times. But you must believe in her above all else, believe what she tells you in order to solve it. I hate to say this, but this case is bizarre and it may possibly lead to some danger."

Now she had Axel's full attention as he stared back inquisitively. "Nikki, I promise, I won't let you down. By the way, in case you hadn't noticed, the tide is higher, the waterline is approaching, and our rears may both get soaked before you tell me your client's name."

She pinched his cheek, in the process twisting his head to face hers directly. Their eyes were glued to each other. She clasped his hands in hers and brought them under her chin. For a moment, she searched into his dreamy, hazel eyes, observed his stately, handsome facial Chickasaw-like features, examined his wavy, dark, thick hair, admired his square, proud jaw with the tiny, little clef, and relished that gorgeous smile with straight teeth and full lips. However, she struggled for an urgency to kiss him again. They were sharing a locus of intimacy and, to any passerby, they must have been seen as two, dedicated romantics. He was anxious. "Who is your friend, Nikki?"

Whispering, barely discernible, replying, her outpouring was a stern delivery. "Lacey Sills."

The words stabbed at his mind. Was it right for her to be so cruel and treat him so, that she should utter the name of Lacey Sills? He had heard her erroneously. There was some running interference from the spitting tide. Yet the two words resonated in his head. No, maybe it was the ghostly murmurs of the tide that baked up this fantasy on this night when he was alone with Nikki Louden on Venice Beach. They were holding hands, touching and, in a remarkable rekindling of friendship, she muttered the name of Lacey Sills. All that he could clumsily think to say was, "The Lacey Sills?"

"Yes, the one and only. Get your mind straight. Now, you know what I mean when I keep harping at you to get your mind straight."

There was a sudden outburst of perspiration as beads of sweat rolled down his forehead, saturated his chest to intersect his shirt in strategic points to glue cloth to flesh. The silence in his mind was deafening. She, however, allowed him the courtesy to regroup his thoughts to prepare his inquisition. But Axel was stunned by this development.

"You never, ever, ever told me that you knew Lacey Sills. I don't recall you ever mentioning her name in any context when we dated."

"One of my life's little secrets. We were roomies for the first two years at university. She dropped out, went to Hollywood, embellished upon her acting capabilities, and set off to find a new life with all the God-given talent that she had for acting; not to mention her passions for improvs, which kept us up many a night watching the late, late show with Bette Davis, Kate Hepburn, and Meryl Streep." Nikki tossed her hair. "Man, she could do them all. She knew all the lines, the inflections, the drama, and the punch line. She captivated us with her one-woman show. What a performer. At university she starred both years in the university's showcase production and wowed the audiences. Now she is the heroine. Now she is the one that budding actresses fantasize about, even though her career is still in infancy." Nikki didn't allow him to interrupt.

"We've kept in touch all these years. How ironic. I see her at social functions frequently. She's a popular invite to everyone's gala, especially since she was nominated for best actress last year."

Axel retorted, "She should have won."

"She's been an excellent contact for me, as you might guess. Lacey has introduced me to key celebrities around town, secured the inside scoop on a few leads, verified certain rumors, obtained prestigious invites to dinners, placed me on gala invite lists, introduced me to charities, and secured invites to their annual balls." Nikki continued to expand on their relationship. Axel heard the sound of her voice, but he was already not keeping his mind straight. Her thoughts were not computing. Already he was groggy at the mention of Lacey's name. How could this be? Lacey Sills. Blonde goddess of all virile men. The center of the male universe. Second best stimulant for erectile dysfunction. No, maybe even a more powerful elixir. Men everywhere had undoubtedly created a virtual smorgasbord of sexual fantasies around her. Oscar nominee for best female actress for *Moonglow*; he had seen it three times and was justifiably convinced that she was denied her dues in that compelling, romantic epic. In *Moonglow* it was not just her sensuality, her sexiness, but it was her omnipresence that had captivated him. Former pin-up girl; a voice to inspire a thousand troops; a smile to melt a thousand foes.

"And, of course, she knows of your exploits from the Amanda Miller case; and, of course, from Heather Micks' case and Willie Doon. So she called me and asked if you could be trusted? Axel, dammit! Are you listening, or are you in Oz? Axel, dammit, look at me!"

"Yes, my cases...life...don't always turn out like Amanda Miller's case or Willie's. Unfortunately, it's the Heather Micks of the world who rest heavily in our conscience and expose the frailties of our profession. A poor, little, defenseless girl. But Lacey Sills!" Nikki touched his lips with her fingers to signal a silence on his behalf.

"Her lover has disappeared. Her best friend, Axel, gone, and without a trace! When you hear her story, you'll understand the complexity of this matter and perhaps sense the inherent danger. You'll see what I mean when I say without a trace. This romance has remained a locked box secret in Hollywood circles. Even I resisted the temptation to report it and respected Lacey's private love life when I accidently discovered the truth of this affair. When you are a starlet like Lacey, you need your sacred, private moments. I granted these to her, and now I come to ask you, as my friend, to help a friend of mine in need."

Axel bunched his bushy eyebrows inquisitively. "But the L.A. Police? Why doesn't Lacey report this?"

Nikki vigorously waved her arms back and forth. "No way. The police must not be involved—yet. I know you and Zoe have strong connections in the force, but you two must remain silent. You will understand why Lacey cannot go to the police when you hear of the strange, terrible, puzzling circumstances surrounding the disappearance of her lover. She arrives tomorrow morning."

"Tomorrow morning?"

"Yes, she's all yours at nine o'clock tomorrow morning in your office. And you had better hone your listening skills and deaden your male instincts, Axel." She emphatically threw the word "instincts" at him and coupled it with a poke to his ribs with her index finger.

Nikki bounced up abruptly, proceeded to brush the sand granules from her backside of her shorts as they splattered in all directions. This action prompted Axel to come to her aid until she stepped aside.

"Axel, Lacey Sills is in a very fragile emotional state. She has never experienced grief of this magnitude. You need to get your mind straight. Let logic and not infatuation guide you. Don't be impulsive. Don't get attached to her! Don't let her spring into your fantasies. I had better not hear of any advances toward our damsel in dire distress by you. This is strictly business, strictly platonic. Do you understand, Axel?"

Now that angry look reappeared in her eyes. "The events surrounding the disappearance of her friend are remarkable and would make a great, sensational news item. But we both now must swear to keep this information under wraps. Swear, Axel?"

His response was immediate. "I swear I won't let you down, Nikki." Axel couldn't help but key in his mind on some of Nikki's last words- danger, complex, remarkable, no police, fragile.

"I confirmed the appointment for Lacey with Lulu this afternoon. She just happened to be in the office when I called."

"Her proper name is Zoe."

"Whatever, she is the one who threatens to put the bra industry out of business."

"Zoe's very clever. She's a martial arts expert and a genius and, as my partner, she has held her own when danger has occurred, even physically saved my ass more than once. You are not fair to her."

"And you are not fair to me and Murchie," she snapped back. It had commenced again. Axel tried to apologize for his past behavior, but Nikki seemed suddenly wound up.

"I am on my own now, Axel. We don't live together anymore. Cherish the memories that are worth remembering. I see whomever I please, whenever I please. I please to give this case to you and, if you break any of the conditions that I have laid out, if you screw it up, Axel, I shall snatch it." She opened her hand in front of his face, quickly closed it as a fist, and withdrew it. "Away from you."

Axel felt horrible, as venom now dripped in her voice. "I promise that you will be removed from this assignment if you misbehave. I plan to check with Lacey frequently."

Without further conversation or an expression of goodbye, she trudged away from him, kicking up sand in her tracks, racing toward the boardwalk. She turned once to yell the word, "secrecy" at him. Meanwhile Axel stood dumbfounded. Lacey Sills. How many men on planet Earth had dreamed of this moment? Contact with the goddess. Contact with Lacey Sills. His love life was currently in shambles. Was she the chosen one?

The moment was shattered. A group of noisy teenagers encroached, complete with dogs, Frisbees, and were now in his territory. A Frisbee wavered precipitously over his head. Quickly he scampered away, running now as fast as he could to intercept her in the parking lot. Upon his arrival, there was no sign of Nikki Louden. He spied the exit just in time to catch a glimpse of her as she accelerated away from him.

He stood alone in his solitude to realize that Nikki Louden was lost forever. He turned about face to the Pacific. How prophetic. The last golden embers of the sun were about to be swallowed by the blackness of the night, just as the last hope of reconciliation with Nikki had died. But tomorrow would bring a new day, a new case, new hopes, a new client, a new life, and new challenges.

"How beauteous mankind is! Oh, brave new world that has such people in it!"

Axel Hawk stood leaning against the side of his vehicle in the parking lot, contemplating his synthetically controlled behavior tomorrow.

MONDAY MORNING

I am such a creature of habit, Axel Hawk thought. Yet, here he was, in full acknowledgement of his habits, breaking every self-imposed morning addiction: a shower in the morning instead of the nightly soak; a contrived selection of clothing instead of the random grab of garb; a wholesome breakfast instead of coffee and doughnuts on the gallop; a miss of the morning's jog and sit-ups; and a solitary, mental debate of well-selected crafted words to impress her.

He thought to himself how his alarm clock had only ever required a single setting since the day of its purchase two years ago; the same day that he had moved into this small, two-story wooden frame home on the north side of downtown Los Angeles. Today a five-thirty summons pierced the silence. Was his behavior so peculiar because changes were in the air?

He smelled each armpit of each shirt before singling out one that looked and fit of Maui, one that cast crisp vanilla aromas of the fresh beach, one that chose not to flaunt his muscles. This may be the only day in his life when he executed the inspection of the sock brigade. Following the effort to match tones in his shirt with the color of socks, he surveyed the line of trousers. *Wouldn't any man act this way for Lacey Sills?* he pondered and justified his behavior to himself as he stared into the bedroom mirror.

So, clad in tan slacks, a multi-colored bodacious shirt with sassy black shades to match, he splashed an extra dose of cologne on his cheeks, which burned after a super-close shave. Suddenly, reeking in his own stench, he retrieved a damp cloth to wash some of the smelly effects of the condiment away.

Now, a new debate confronted him. He queried if he should leave the top, two buttons of his shirt open to reveal manly chest hair. He stood there erect. "Why all the fuss?" Vanity wore thin. Axel opted for the more conservative look. The debates were over.

Axel seldom arrived before nine o'clock, never before eight, unless emergencies dictated it. With frequent night shifts, it paid to be well rested, endure a morning's workout, and casually make the scene at the office. However, today he would commence the vigil for her at eight o'clock.

So it was, in a state of raw anticipation, that Axel Hawk dragged himself from the clutches of sleep at five-thirty, dressed royally with thought, consumed a sit-down breakfast, and departed his neighborhood to arrive at the octagonal, brown, brick, five-story building on a nearside corridor of the downtown Los Angeles bustle. The building was dwarfed by more modern towers on the street. Small, adobe boutiques dotted the infill lots, but this section was distant from the serious shoppers of Rodeo Drive and Wilshire Boulevard. This corner had a distinctive, professional appearance with a resplendent, elegant, black and clear glass directory in front of the structure, the directory spelling out "A TO Z, Private Investigators," Suite 330. Their business to own, direct as they please, and of course he thought to himself, *with Zoe as my faithful partner*. Axel parked in the back lot, but pride encouraged him to stray to the front at street side to read the directory on this special day. Now, he eagerly bounded into the building and paced up the stairs immediately to their office.

"Good morning Axel," she piped cheerfully as he entered. Axel paused to absorb her glamorous smile. How he had grown to relish her qualities. Perhaps it was her intelligence, her humor, her mannerisms, her mystique that had pushed him over the edge to the adventurous episode of two nights ago. They had not seen each other since, nor spoken. As he stared back, his esteem swelled for her. Zoe bowed her head while cupping her hands in front of her thin figure.

"I'm sorry about Saturday night, Axel. I am sure that you wanted more than a sole kiss, a single cup of black coffee, and simple conversation."

"The kiss was inspirational, the conversation with you uplifting and the coffee...well, next time, I will make the coffee."

She raised her voice, extended her left arm outright, directing her index finger at him. "Next time you will ring the bell at the front door and abandon the showmanship. By the way, the instructors have suspended you from further jumps until you personally admit your guilt to jumping early and altering the landing target. Apologize to them in person, please." She presented him with an opened brown envelope.

"Well," he surmised, "no harm done, and it was worth it! File this. I'll deal with it later." Quickly he attempted to return the summons to her.

"No." Zoe was adamant. "There are some adjectives which, er, describe you such as..."

Axel took the hint, so he waved his open hands at her. "Okay, okay, I will deal with it as soon as time permits. I'll set up my attendance at the next meeting of the club to apologize." He paused and pleaded. "But, what will I say? How can I possibly tell them that Zoe Burns made me do it? Her beauty and persona drove me to the edge of romantic anxiety until I had to have her. They're all males. They've got to understand."

She stood arms folded. "Bullshit." She broke into her contagious broad smile to reply. "She's here."

It registered. Axel was crushed.

"No! She can't be here! It's barely eight o'clock." He eyed his watch. "I arrived early to tidy up."

Like a sports official, Zoe used her hands to signal a time out. "If Lacey Sills is to be our client, then she must reconcile herself with the real Axel Hawk, his quirks, his habits, and his habitat."

"The half-eaten pizza on the cardboard plate? On my desk?"

"Sorry. Still there."

"No, Zee! The priceless collection of half-empty pop cans? Curdled cups of coffee?"

"There. There. Sorry. Sorry."

"Ah, my socks smelled like ten-day, unwashed armpits. Surely?" He leaned forward on the desk that separated them.

"Reluctantly I removed your socks and sprayed them with a killer fungicide. I am just playing mind games, too, just kidding with you, for I burned the pizza, tossed the pop cans, and disposed of the antiquated coffee. I applied the antifungal fumigant yesterday after Nikki called."

He moved behind the desk to plant a solid kiss on her high cheek while sneaking his arms around her thigh. Axel whispered in her ear. "Zee, you are a goddess, too." He took notice that today she was dressed in a shiny, bold, black leather pantsuit, which outlined her reedy athletic physique.

She broke his hold by spinning free and moved to confront him by standing opposite him, leaning on the other side of the bureau. "Get your mind straight."

Axel sighed. "You've been listening to Nikki."

The floor vibrated as Thumper entered from a dark room behind the front reception area. Axel turned and acknowledged him. "How's my favorite overweight computer geek?"

"Boss, she's dy-no-mite. Look! She autographed my shirt. I'll never wash this shirt again!"

"No one believes you actually do laundry anyways, Thumper!" Zoe quipped. She thought to herself that, behind those wiry, reddish-brown whiskers, the spindly moustache, those overbearing sideburns, the full head of static auburn hair, was a face that she had never seen.

"You've seen her?" Axel jealously inquired.

"Yeah, and she wanted a cup of coffee. Naturally, I obliged her. Neat, huh. Now, I can tell all my friends that Lacey Sills asked me to oblige her in my Black Sabbath shirt. Observe. Good 'ole Stephen's bare arm now bears the John Hancock of Lacey Sills."

Axel was insistent. "Thumper, you are to tell no one that Lacey Sills visited here and is our client. Client privileges prevail. Understand, Thump? You cannot wear that shirt in public."

Thumper turned, shuffled his three hundred pounds back to his computer dungeon, dragging the cuffs of his black jeans on the floor, his massiveness creating displacements in space, Richter measurable. In his deep voice, he was heard saying, "Rules. Chill out boss."

Axel in jest retaliated. "The Adams Family is alive and still searching for new members. They are envious that we keep you. That can all change."

Zoe chimed in, "I say, Axel, that we get a divorce from Thumper and toss him to the Exes." While they both chuckled, Zoe positioned herself to intercept Axel as he approached the door to the inner office. "I think you need to check your hormones. Here is a claim check." Indeed, she handed him a claim with the number thirty-five engraved on it. Axel grinned, recognizing it as the number that he wore on the sports jersey at his last birthday bash. He seized the mock ticket and deposited it in his shirt pocket.

Suddenly Zoe recognized the silly contrivance. "Oh, my goodness!" She cupped her hands over her cheeks. "Don't we look pretty today?"

"What?"

"Axel, you have never shaven so close, dressed so neatly. This is the only day that the fashion police can rest on your case! The unmade bed look has vanished." She looked down.

"Egad, you blew it. What are those?"

"Those, my dear, are my vintage running shoes."

"They do not go with the rest of the outfit, Axel. Are you insane? They are old, discolored, and disfigured. Yuck." He had had enough of this kibitzing, so he stepped past her into the inner office and Zoe in tow with her laptop.

Lacey Sills immediately pushed back from the desk upon Axel's entry, stood, turned, and stepped briskly to him. The light shining from between the slots of the window coverings behind her created a hallowed silhouette around her. Axel stood bedazzled in his tracks. She extended her arm and hand toward him. "Good morning, Mr. Hawk. It is a pleasure to meet you." Axel had already melted.

"The pleasure is all mine." He felt her soft, fleshy hand, warm to the touch. Her blue eyes were two, bright eternal beacons. Suddenly, he recalled the scene from the movie *Frame Seven* when, in the ebony twilight, she turned her head to peer over her shoulder as a narrow shaft of streetlight intersected those brilliant, azure eyes afire with life. Her thick, blonde hair was perfectly combed, cascading down shoulder length to rest on her bare, white shoulders, which were speckled with delicate, tan freckles.

She had unusually high cheek bones, stood at about five eight, taller than he would have guessed, had thin, delicate lips, today carrying a soft pink pastel color. She had a long, distinguished royal nose, a slender dress that pulled in at the waist before it continued its descent to her knees. The dress was cut to subtly expose her distinguished breasts, which had never been fully exposed to a craving male audience but had teased the public in her scantily clad outfit in *Move over Rex* and again in her debut movies, a bedroom scene in *Gilda Loves Thomas and Comedy* and...

"Earth to Axel, come in Axel." Zee had cupped her hand over his ear and was whispering while pinching him firmly on his butt. He finally broke the hand contact.

After Zee greeted Lacey for a second time, Zoe moved past him to take her customary place at the end of his expansive, maple-sycamore desk. While she set up a new file, Axel hurriedly stepped to slide a chair to accommodate Lacey and proceeded to behind his magnificent desk to assume the command position, the goddess in front of him, Zee, at the end to his right. He thought the desk looked so oddly clean and organized.

"This is an immaculate piece of furniture."

"Thank you. I purchased it four years ago at an auction. I showed little foresight, as the movers claimed it was their most daunting challenge of the year to deliver and position." Somehow, he had to resist staring at her. Her posture was letter perfect. Square shoulders, an ever so pleasing shade of skin. Now she broke into a smile to reveal those incredibly straight, ivory teeth, looking as a queen on her throne about to address her loyal subjects.

Hawk noticed a slight scar on the right side of her chin and a small, brown mole (a la Monroe) to the left of her mouth. She spoke again with a slight effect of hoarseness in her tender voice, a tone that conveyed her present drench of grief.

"Mr. Hawk," she began, and he quickly interrupted her respectfully to reply. "Ms. Sills, please call me Axel, and this is Zoe, who goes by Zee to all her friends. That includes you."

"Axel, Zee, I am so grateful for this hearing." She reached for her tiny, gold purse to extract a delicate, white hanky. Lacey dabbed each eye. Axel was star struck. "Wow," he thought to himself, "just like the scene from *Sir Starbucks*."

Lacey spoke up. "And I absolutely insist that you address me as Lacey." Axel and Zoe nodded in agreement.

Silence prevailed. She spoke: "I must first thank you both for seeing me on such short a notice. Nikki insisted that it would not be an inconvenience."

Axel reassured her. "This is our business, and we receive clients as soon as problems arise. It pays to react quickly before clues become cold and stale and then disappear."

"Thank you. I can't begin to tell you how much sorrow has consumed me. I can't sleep. I can't eat. Every second I pray to wake up and live the last weeks of my life over again. I am in a constant state of dolor from the loss of my loved one. Nikki informed me that she had at least conveyed this much to you, that I have lost a lover. That I need the services of someone experienced to find my beloved, who seems to have disappeared." She closed her eyes. The room was silent. She reopened them to continue as she laid her left hand over her bosom. *Lights, camera, action*, Axel thought. The show was hers.

"For the first time in my life, I find myself taking a prescribed drug, an anti-depressant, to make it through each day of misery. Oh, forgive me, I am babbling. I had best start at the beginning for your benefit."

Axel situated himself to a more comfortable posture: legs crossed, chair tilted back, eyes glued on her, and arms on the arm rests. Zee sat upright, posed, and ready to record Lacey's testimony on her laptop.

The inner office room was large, walled at opposite ends by bookcases. A third wall, where the entrance resided, was fully decorated in sports memorabilia and photos, documenting many of Axel's exploits and athletic highlights and Zoe's accomplishments on the police force. Behind Axel were ceiling-to-floor veneer window treatments, slightly open. Oddly, yet not coincidentally, he realized the room looked very professional, so he stole a glance of admiration at his partner. Surely she must have patience extraordinaire to put up with his sloppiness. Lacey began her oration.

"For the past two years, I have conducted a discrete love affair. Not even our precious Nikki, with all her resources and dexterity, was able to analyze clues and uncover Hollywood's most prestigious couple...until recently. When she did, she confronted me, and I begged her to maintain silence. She honored my request." Her voice was as an outpouring of smoothly delivered grief, ripe with silky overtones that established immediate bonding with Axel.

"I...er...we...kept our love a secret to protect both our acting careers. I think that you will agree with me when I say that any serious romantic linkage exposed to the public about me would seriously erode some of my current sustained fascination, which is largely built on my availability for every man's fantasy and desire." She looked at each to gain approval for her logical excuses. Axel acknowledged; Zoe simply captured the zealous comments with a hint of envy.

Now Lacey shifted uneasily, brought her elbows onto the desk top, leaned forward in a dramatic moment, a la the classic black and white Bogey scenes, or maybe from one of her own movies as Zoe thought. She lowered her voice, glancing at Axel first, then Zoe, and then robotically stating, "My lover was..." and Axel hung on every syllable until her last expelled particle of air revealed, "Montilladan."

The very sound of his name created shock waves in the room. Zee stopped typing the oration. Without moving her head upright, she extended the side reach of her eyes to analyze Lacey. On surface she appeared so delicate; a poster girl with an innocent image. Thus, by looking at Lacey, Zoe missed the expression of astonishment that Axel gave as Montilladan's name continued to resonate. In the ensuing silence, the two postured to respond. Axel fumbled the response with a weak riposte.

"Incredible that Hollywood's leading esteemed starlet should be involved with Hollywood's most...er...controversial male actor."

Axel attempted to visualize the twosome. *So, unlike each other, at least on the surface. Lacey Sills, gorgeous, composed, exquisite, a work of immaculate beauty, always so articulate in interviews, so fluent, so responsive to the press, so sought after by an admiring public craving to see more of her, an ever-present smile. It seemed that every tabloid and periodical these days was graced by Lacey Sills on the cover.*

And he, Axel perused as he winced, *Montilladan. What could be said of his performance to date in Tinseltown? Very popular with the ladies who drooled all over him and his body. However, overbearing, a publicity hog, outspoken, forever promulgating his image, gregarious. He certainly suffered from overexposure. The male public prayed for a rest from Montilladan's presence. Now Lacey Sills wished him and Zee to accept that she found a way to love this—this—creature, this plastic contrived icon of Hollywood?* Axel just didn't get a women's fascination with him. Axel just didn't get it.

Zoe expressed her sorrow first over the death of Montilladan. "Lacey, I am so sorry for your loss." And, as she reached across the corner of the desk to caress Lacey's hand in support, their eyes met, Lacey obviously was choking back tears.

"His death is seen as a great loss to our entire industry," Lacey was heard to mutter. She once again dabbed her eyes with her hanky.

Axel was confused. He sat astonished at this development. "Excuse me, Lacey. How do these events make a case? Montilladan passed away...ten days ago?"

"Yes," she blurted immediately.

Axel struggled. "Excuse me, Lacey, but help clear up our confusion. This lover that Nikki spoke of to me, this lover that you spoke of, whom you seek with Montilladan gone is...then?" Axel looked for direction. "I think we are confused."

Lacey shook her head vehemently, waves of blonde hair blocking her face. Using both arms, hands with her palms exposed, she signaled for them to restrain themselves from further interrogation.

"This story gets very complicated. Please let me finish my story of love. Please, no more questions until I have laid out the facts. You have to hear my tale." She bowed her head to sob softly. Zoe was bubbling with questions but retreated.

"I attended the wake the evening before the funeral. After everyone had left, I asked the funeral parlor director for permission to steal a few private minutes with my Montilladan. It was not an unusual request, for we had starred together in two motion pictures. Although not romantically linked, we had attended many functions together, and we were often witnessed in each other's company. The director thus granted my request to stay after normal viewing hours."

Unanticipated, Lacey stood up, turned away from Axel and Zoe, and positioned herself in the very middle of the room. Now she began to pace, deliberately, step by step, back and forth across the length of the office in front of them. It was wide enough for twelve paces, bookcase to bookcase. The dress she wore was knee length, had large yellow flowers on a white background, and each petal shifted in unison to her sway. She stared alternatively at Zoe, and Axel, and commenced her prologue, preacher-like.

Axel felt uneasy for the first time, not knowing what she would say next. "You have to understand. I loved Montilladan in a way that I never thought about people before. Oh, I know what you are both thinking about him—how crude a person, how pompous, how cocky and insolent. But you only witnessed Montilladan the actor and observed his combat with the press. And don't forget how charming he was in the presence of ladies? Excuse me, I am rambling, so let me return to my plight. I want you both to know that to be alone with Montilladan aroused a fire within me that I thought not possible in a lifetime. For this aroused passion, I will always be grateful to Montilladan."

After a loud sniffle, she continued, "Back to that night of the wake. All the mourners had departed. The parlor was empty, very dimly lit. It was a few minutes after ten. It was quiet; I was alone. The casket was open, elevated, perched at the end of the room in a sea of blazing floral arrangements. I approached the casket." She did not break stride as she talked. "A glossy red robe lay over the body. I...I...I positioned myself beside the casket. I...I was shaking, just as I shake now as I regenerate that moment. I wept openly. My vision was clouded by tears. Slowly, gently, with purpose I lifted the robe. The look on Montilladan's face was uneasy. Most of the architecture of his face was reconstructed poorly because of the severity of the accident, which disfigured his face. To most, it must have seen to be unrecognizable."

"My dear, dear...ah...Montilladan, I had to see my Monty once more in the corporal flesh." She stopped dead in her tracks. The room became eerily silent. She pivoted to face Axel. Her eyes had lost their allure, somehow taken on a slight bulge while migrating into a glassy haze. A distinctive crease accented her forehead, cutting horizontally from one side to the other. There was no charm in her stare.

Axel sensed a swell of hysteria as he watched her fidget with her hands and shuffle on the same spot with her feet. Barely loud enough for them to hear, with her head bowed, she whispered, "That was not Montilladan's body in the casket."

Axel's neck muscles tightened, goose bumps bolted from shoulder to shoulder causing him to twitch. He moved in the chair but couldn't retard the icy shivers in his legs. Zoe sat calmly in a steady state of discipline, hands clenched, not exposing a hint of her disbelief. She motioned to Axel to be silent with a slight wave of her hand. He heeded not the warning. Unable to gain eye contact with Lacey, he called her name.

"Lacey." No reply. "Lacey, please sit down." Reluctantly she moved back to her seat, inhaling, slowly releasing air. Shivering she wrapped herself in her arms tightly and began to stroke her bare arms up and down with her hands while crossing her legs, moving her head in awkward jerks. Axel decided to confront her.

"Lacey, please listen to me. I have a great deal of experience in my line of work with people whom have lost loved ones. In a state of shock and grief, the mind, sometimes, can play cruel tricks. It can make you believe the impossible. It can make you believe that which is not real. It can also block the truth." But that was as far as he recited.

"No!" she screamed, causing Axel to jerk in his seat, as she stared wild-eyed to confront him. The outburst caused Axel and Zoe alarm. Feverishly she shook her head, the beads around her neck bouncing to and fro. The chemistry of the previous minutes had completely evaporated.

"That was not M in the casket!" she blared as she started to cry. Axel tried to remember when he had been so moved, for her outburst, and now her emotions, were garnering a clogging in his nose and a blockage in his throat.

He cleared it with an "ahem," just as Zee passed Lacey some tissues and poured her a glass of water. Zoe continued to study her. Lacey was married to her script. Axel waited until her sorrow had subsided to open again his line of logic.

"Lacey, I am not trying to upset you, nor trying to discredit you, nor trick you. I apologize sincerely, but I just want to remind you how powerful the human mind can be during times of heartbreak."

She gazed at him. Her blue eyes fluttered. "Understood." She continued to swallow gulps of water, wiped her face of tears and, with another vocal blow, emphatically stated, "I swear it to both of you, as true as I sit in front of you corporally now." She sounded with fanfare. "That...was...not...Montilladan's...body...in...the...casket! I swear to you!"

Axel made a decision to take charge. He leaned on bent elbows toward her. "Did Montilladan have any distinctive scars on his body?"

"No."

"Tattoos?"

"No."

"Birthmarks or deformities?"

"No."

"Hair or skin discolorations?"

"No."

"Something abnormal in his reconstructed face?"

"No."

Zoe interrupted to say it bluntly. "How can you be so sure Lacey that it was not Montilladan's body in the casket? Convince us, Lacey. Axel and I both want to believe in you because you now are our client. However, I am sorry, Axel and I need convincing."

Another onslaught of weeping consumed her, a series of bodily heaves heightening as moisture glazed her cheeks. Her arms exercised an occasional flail, as bound in double joints. Axel retained his position behind the desk; Zoe stood and slid her chair to move beside her, placing her arm around her, attempting to cradle her head. Lacey initially cooperated, but then resisted. Axel waited impatiently. Zee was determined to have a response to her query.

Lacey fixated her eyes on him. Axel became alarmed as he recognized the fear in her gaze. "I lifted the blanket over his body a second time." Rhythmically, as if doped, she moved her head, wiggling it as if her neck bone be broken into multiple pieces.

"And I touched the genitals. They were real. It was not Montilladan's body in the casket, for...you see...the person in the casket was definitely a male, and Montilladan and I were..."

And he prayed and prayed that she would not say it. Even though he was not a religious man, he somehow tried furiously to contact God in his thoughts; to seek God and direct him to instruct her not to say these words;

to stop life so that he could correct her; and to recommence this charade and go through these introductions again. She was not permitted to tell him this. This was the ultimate minute of time-frozen terror. She could not make him feel this way. To sink him into a state of confusion. And he saw her lips move and knew that her words were spoken and it was too late, and he heard, "Monty and I were female lovers."

Life as he wished it was instantaneously disrupted. The implications were surreal, outrageous, and to him, personally, disturbing. Axel slumped forward, head buried in his hands, arms bent and resting on the desk. He thought of all his investments in her, the posters, the rented videos and DVDs, the subject of discussions with his soul mates at Fosse's or his time spent at the movie theatres. Like any other normal male, he wanted to reject her testimony. He felt compelled to challenge her statements on her sexual habits on behalf of the entire male population, everywhere since there had never been any mention of female tendencies in Lacey's history.

There must be contradictions. There must be lies in this menagerie. This must surely be a glass house. The most gleeful day of his life had plunged into bewilderment. Lacey Sills first in love with someone he disdained; now to discover impossibility that Montilladan is a female, a male impersonator. It was reality. Lacey had walked out of the closet. Lacey took up conversation while he still reeled.

"You see my dilemma. Don't you realize all the innocent people who will be disappointed if this news were to leak? The millions of public adorers crushed, furious, frustrated, when they discover that their favorite Hollywood female sex idol is," and now she sobbed while her voice quivered, "a fake goddess. And the people in Hollywood and all movie fans everywhere, when they discover that they nominated a woman, Montilladan, for best male performer of the year, two years ago. Montilladan pulled off the greatest hoax ever witnessed in Hollywood with that nomination. Montilladan deceived a nation of actors."

Axel connected to Nikki's warnings that this case was very complex. For the first time, all of Nikki's dialogue made sense. He definitely had to get his mind straight. In the middle of her soliloquy, he had experienced a bout of prickliness on the back of his neck. He continued to swallow batches of saliva, but still she had to be challenged.

"Lacey, please. Zoe and I require further clarification on some issues. First I'm having difficulty understanding how Montilladan could dupe an entire movie industry and an entire world of movie goers, an entire group of gossip mongers and millions of female fans." Lacey affirmed by nodding and was eager to reply. As she spoke of Montilladan, sorrow fled from her expression, her heart lifted, and her voice became inspirational.

"Don't you see? Montilladan is perfect to play a man. She is flat-chested, with a deep, husky voice, large, sexy, dark eyes, a head of marine-cut hair, and slight body hair, which she shaves on her legs and arms to enhance growth. She has big bone structure, big hands like a man, an unusual muscular physique because of years of exercise and bodybuilding. She was an avid weight lifter...I mean *is* an avid weight lifter and has a private gymnasium in her house. She never skipped a day's work out. And, of course, she had that powerfully hypnotic speaking voice; the power of her presence; and her command over an audience. Need I go on?" But she did.

"Boy, could she act. Her act of supreme arrogance was the crowning event to every public performance, ever meeting with the press. Her powers of persuasion kept everyone off-balance and made them believe the impossible— that she was a man!"

"She is the perfect man. She is the perfect man in every way. In public, in the movies, she took charge, and you felt it. Men loved to hate Montilladan or, with no in between, just love her. She was, excuse me, I mean *is*," and she beamed with pride, "the greatest male impersonator the world shall ever witness, and it culminated with an Oscar nomination. Do you believe it? She didn't win, but she should have." Lacey Sill's eulogy cried out for support from Axel and Zoe but, instead, they just stared back in disbelief.

"Look, I know what you're thinking." She was excited. "That this was a damnable act of deceit, but just look at her achievements. To act twenty four-hours a day and convince everyone in the whole world that you are someone else of the opposite sex! Montilladan was, I mean *is*, an award-winning actress on the set and off."

She smiled at both of them. Axel returned the gleam. Zoe was not amused. "Producers, directors, fellow actors, make-up artists, journalists, television talk show hosts, friends, all were converts, all believed. She made everyone believe that she was masculine." Astonishingly, Lacey began to applaud exuberantly by herself with a series of singularly loud claps of her hands and launched a smile as Axel and Zee sat stunned. Lacey gazed from Axel to Zee and back whilst she clapped, waiting for their approval. It failed.

She exhaled a deep breath. "When I discovered that M was a female, when she divulged this to me on that stormy night at her residence, I couldn't resist my admiration and love for her. Her feats of accomplishments overwhelmed me. I became engrossed with her, captivated by her achievements, enveloped by her outpouring of sensuality. Eventually I fell in real love with her because of private, tender moments we shared. I swear it!" She raised her right hand to testify. "I love men first. Montilladan is the first time, and only time, that I ever fell in true love with a woman. But to be with her, to experience her, to touch her, just made me feel so special."

Zee motioned to Lacey to halt. "So, can I ask you, Lacey, did you ever fantasize about women or have a previous fascination for women?"

Oh, Zee, thought Axel, *please don't ask that! What the hell are you thinking?* He would confront her later.

"No, actually," and she made Axel the clear recipient of her comment, "I guess I am a one-time bisexual. I told you, I like men, and I guess so much more than women. I swear again that my singular, female encounter has been, and only will be, with Montilladan, as I stated. M made me love her. I mean when I discovered that secret that night, and the way she pitched it to me, so tender, I fell in love with her instantaneously. Her feats are unparalleled. Think of who she is. She made me do it. The person whom she is, the female titan that I know her to be, deserves incredible respect for her grandiose achievements. By being her lover, no one else in the whole world could share her. She made me love her. It was she who made the first advance. She told me of her secret that night and disrobed, and...I...I...couldn't help myself, which told me something about me. I love M! I love her. I don't think I shall ever fall in love with another female again." Axel elected to remain silent. With Zee and Axel charting out endless complications, the room was eerily silent, so Lacey continued.

"She is so sensuous, so powerful, so in charge, so like the roles that M plays. The beating that her character takes in the press and in the public domain is totally unjustified. It is just part of her charm. She is irresistible and...she is still alive! Don't you see? Don't you get it? She's alive! That wasn't her in the coffin! It was a male! Now you both understand."

Axel and Zoe noticed how confused Lacey was in her grammar, skipping back and forth from past to present in her references to Montilladan. Did she truly believe her alive? Or was there a doubt? Foul play?

Zoe was curious. "Did Montilladan love you with the same passion, affection, and respect that you have just spoken of her?"

Lacey was adamant. "Absolutely!" Her voice filled the room with a strong, soprano level. She stood and twirled around. "We have a very deep, true love for each other. It has propagated for two years. You just don't build that kind of relationship we have without commitment, certainly in lesser time. Of course she loves me, now and forever."

"Then," and it was Zoe who still dared to venture into uncharted territory, "why hasn't she contacted you if she is still alive? It has been ten days. Surely Montilladan would not want you to suffer if she cares for you."

Lacey returned to stir in her chair, trying to determine how to address her solace. She pushed her chair back, arose again, wiped her face of perspiration, draped her arms around herself, and commenced to grind out a new trajectory around the room, this time oval in shape.

"I don't know. It has all happened so suddenly. I'm going out of my mind thinking about her. I miss her so. Knowing that she is not really dead but hasn't called is driving me crazy. I can't conduct a public sweeping crusade to locate her. I need a discreet, private effort. I can't go to the police with this incredulous, sensational story."

Lacey hollered in anger, as she looked upward. "Where are you, M? Where the hell are you?" Lacey stood with her back to them as she shouted these last questions.

"Maybe, Lacey," Axel dared to explore, "you will have to face the facts that if she is alive, hasn't contacted you, that maybe she will learn to live without you, that...for some reason she doesn't wish to be found."

Axel was the subject of a new, vehement outburst, about to receive one of the worst tongue-lashings of his life. She turned to face him; she turned cold. She skewered the air between them with her sharp words. "No! No! No! Don't you ever, ever say that again!" Now the conversation had turned sour. "I am about to engage you to find her. I'm paying you to find her. I know that she's alive. I looked in the damn casket and discovered that Montilladan is still alive. She still loves me, and I love her. She still wants me, and I want her. Our love can't possibly end on such a sudden, unpredictable, disastrous, sour note. You," and she pointed her finger at both of them alternately, "are going to find her. I have shared these solemn secrets with you, and no one else and you will do it!" She shouted at them. "I don't intend to tell this story to anyone else! You have to do it. You have to find her! Nikki promised me. I have risked all by exposing these sacred facts to you two. I am not crazy. These are the facts as I know them to be. Look at me both of you!" She stared at Axel and Zee alternately.

She startled Axel and Zoe by moving to the desk and slamming her left fist on the table in an act of scolding them. "You must do this for me! Look at the bonding of secrecy that we three now share."

A look of desperation swept across her face. It was so out of character that Axel was convinced that she needed special psychiatric care to assist her through this emotional abyss. Zoe, in her silence, had similar reservations of Lacey's mental stability.

Axel's new bout of tingling, rising from his knees to his torso, was entirely due to this deteriorating situation. He was being chastised. Nikki was right. Lacey was on a roller coaster of emotions. Axel struggled on how to connect to a meaningful dialogue, one that could sooth Lacey and regain her confidence in them. In his hesitation, and Zoe's, too, Lacey dramatically, as out of one of Axel's beloved Shakespearean tragedies, knelt beside the front chair to plead with them in an upwelling of tears.

"You have to find her. I have no one else in the whole wide world to turn to. You have to do this for me, now that I have shared these sacred thoughts with you." Her voice was quivering, fading. "Please, I beg of you."

Zoe stood immediately to come to her aid. She planted her hand on her elbow and tugged at it until Lacey rose. Zee stood in front of her, grabbed both arms until they shared eye contact. Axel restrained himself and sat. Zoe addressed her, "You need not beg, Lacey. It is not necessary. Axel and I will help you. Honest, Lacey. Now, please sit down, so we can continue."

Two minutes elapsed as Lacey repositioned herself and cogitated. Zoe led with an obvious thought. "Do you think that Montilladan has also met with foul play? Is that a possibility as to why he, I mean she, hasn't contacted you?"

Lacey sunk into a deep trough. She suddenly seemed distant, drained of all energy. She slouched in her seat, her posture, jelly-like until finally, she whispered, "Ah...ah...perhaps, I don't know...maybe...I don't know. I believe she is alive."

"Did she have any enemies that would want her dead?"

Lacey responded to Axel. "No, that's preposterous. Besides, you two are not listening. I told you. She is still alive. I mean, some people disliked her intensely but not enough to kill her. She was—I mean is—argumentative, but no one wished her dead. That's an absurd thought."

Axel shared his thinking. "Lacey, if she is hiding, maybe she's doesn't want to be found."

"I told you. She can't come out of hiding, come forward after the accident that supposedly claimed her life, even if it was meant for her, which is a ridiculous thought. There would be too much explaining to do; too much embarrassment about her ruse. Her deceit would be a huge burden to carry the rest of her life. She might get backlisted in the profession she loves."

Zoe persisted. "Then why has she not contacted you if she trusts you? To put your love back in place?"

Lacey remained silent. Both Axel and Zoe awaited her reply, but it came not forth. Instead, she offered another line of thinking.

"Funny thought; a lot of people disliked her. That is a huge part of her charisma. In private, she was warm, thoughtful respectful. In public, she actually got off on pissing people off. It was all part of her act, her captivating image, her karma. She just never found peace unless she was at odds with someone. In private, she and I were so compatible."

Axel took a chance. "Speculate, Lacey. If for some reason she doesn't wish to be found, and she hasn't contacted you, what's driving that decision?" Axel's passion for Lacey was still crushed. *Lacey Sills in a serious love affair with another woman*, he thought. A foreboding silence to his question allowed him to think further. Zoe stared at her, wondering what of this incredible tale to believe. Lacey avoided answering the question.

"Help me, please. You have to. I can't turn to anyone else. I'm helpless. With every day that passes, the trail of M grows colder, just as you stated Axel, and I plummet into a deeper and deeper malaise."

Axel resisted the urge to race around the desk on cue, to take her in his arms, to declare himself the white knight. A little voice in his head that sounded much like the sound of Nikki's voice kept saying, "Keep your mind straight; don't get attached." It wasn't his alter ego. It was Nikki's ghost. Against the background of shattered dreams, he boldly knew his next line of questioning.

"Lacey, I must know ask the obvious question to you. Whose body is in the casket? Who is buried instead of Montilladan? You must know! Or else you would not be so sure that Montilladan is alive. You would not have stated with confidence, and with such conviction, earlier that M lives. Let us assume that your mind is not playing tricks. Let us trust you. Therefore, Zoe and I want to know. Who is buried in Montilladan's grave?"

Zoe and Axel allowed her to respond in her own time, as she sat as frozen, trying to find the proper words. "Yes, well, I mean, the words are very difficult for me to say to you, that I...that I...that I...I think that it is someone...a man

I know as Roy Spiller, a California beach bum, part time, low-budget film stunt man of no real renown or big movies and not very well-known. At least that's what I think, unofficially." She paused. Axel thought, *Now we're getting some facts.*

Lacey was flooded with grief in her voice as she addressed them. "Montilladan and I met him a few years ago just after M and I began to see each other seriously. We made his acquaintance on a deserted stretch of beach in Southern California when we were out for an evening's stroll. M was mesmerized by his appearance, and so was I. M and Roy were the same height, although he was a little scruffier in appearance. They had similar voice tones, inflections, but Roy could imitate her voice perfectly. They were kindred in age, similar builds, and they were unbelievable clones of each other. At that time on that night, they both had identical, marine-cropped haircuts. The resemblance was freaky. No, I recall, it was downright scary." Lacey sat up and regained her composure. Her voice had begun to return to normal.

"I may as well tell you: You need to know these important facts. Montilladan and I befriended Roy and eventually they, they being Montilladan and Roy, played their first deception, as she recruited him to blindly substitute for her in movies, in action shots with limited dialogue that required no close-ups. Roy was great."

"I told them they were crazy, out of their minds, they would get caught, cause a scandal. M asked him again, and again, and again. All of this was performed without anyone on any set even suspecting that Montilladan was really in absentia. Roy Spiller was playing the part of Montilladan beautifully. So beautifully that Roy and I acted in a scene together in one movie, and I couldn't even tell until the end that Montilladan was elsewhere, gone AWOL."

"Zoe, Axel, I am scared. Just think of the coincidence of Roy's death. He just happens to be subbing for M on the set on that fatal day and coincidentally involved in the faulty apparatus which leads to his death, instead of M's. Don't you see? M can't come forward now! She can't come forward and expose the big lie. We have to go out and find her. That's your mission. Don't you realize it? Your mission? The search for Montilladan!" She looked at Zee and then Axel.

Axel and Zoe were by no coincidence cogitating the opposite idea to Lacey that there was a possibility that Roy's death may not have been an accident and that someone may have targeted M as the intended victim, and now Montilladan was in hiding for fear for her own life. Axel continued to jab Zoe with his foot under the table to signify their harmonious symmetry.

Zoe was curious. "Lacey, tell us what you know about the accident?"

"Not much. I received a phone call from the studio from some administrative fellow. I intended to have late lunch that day with M. This caller told me that there had been a terrible accident on the film set. That they were shooting...involving Montilladan on a high balcony. He provided no details, except to say that Montilladan had died in a freaky accident on the set. I cried my eyes out believing it was M who perished. In retrospect, we now guess that Roy showed up and participated. I don't know where Montilladan really was; she certainly wasn't with me." Lacey stopped to reminisce.

"Anyway, I later discovered from another call that a railing that was supposed to be secured splintered, accidentally causing poor Roy to fall to his death. Of course, this person that called conveyed to me that M had died, so how was I to think differently, so I immediately raced to the hospital in grief, as did other friends of Montilladan." Lacey spoke loudly.

"From that moment until that night at the funeral parlor, I believed M to be deceased, which precipitated my melancholy. Actually, now that I know that Montilladan is alive, I am still suffering from mental anguish but relieved at the same time. It's kind of a topsy-turvy world in which I exist."

She became melodramatic. "M was dead for all the world and Hollywood to know and died in front of over a hundred witnesses on the set. A news crew next door rushed to the scene within minutes of the fatal event and informed the world." Now, she took an interlude.

"And now look what I have done. By a complete fluke, by an urge, by fate I think, I have discovered that Montilladan is really alive. We three and Nikki now share a dangerous secret." For Axel's benefit and morale, she flashed that famous smile, fixating it on him.

Zee was still confused. All of Lacey's commentary was spinning in her head. She had found it so stunning and, at times alarming, that she now realized that there were gaps in her testimony. She noted how Lacey had just used the word dangerous. Lacey must personally believe a cause for alarm. Lacey recommenced.

"I mean, no one has questioned Roy Spiller's death. They all witnessed M die. They all witnessed what they believed to be the death of Montilladan. They witnessed his head take the brunt of the blow upon landing. His face became mangled. They all shed real tears. They all attended a funeral and wept with real tears."

Lacey elaborated. "At the funeral home, they did a pathetic job restoring poor Roy's face. Poor Roy, poor Roy. As far as everyone knows and believes, it is Montilladan buried in that grave."

"I know you referenced this previously, but how often did Spiller fill in? Can you quantify this charade?" Axel retorted.

"I can't quantify it. I can only state that the two of them performed this fraud often. At first, they—M and Roy—experimented in situations where Roy's exposure was short and where the action scenes were short. They expanded his role. Montilladan and Roy celebrated every time they pulled this trick. I personally was scared to death that they would be found out. M just laughed, as usual, dismissed my concerns, shrugged it off, and continued with the risk taking. I guess it became habitual. She loved the thrill of getting away with this deception. As I said, she wanted to take these risks and so did Roy. In that sense, they were two of a kind, extreme risk takers. They played a dangerous game, didn't they?"

When neither Axel nor Zee replied, Lacey swallowed hard. "No one ever doubted her. The imposter was perfect. She and Roy made everyone believe that she did her own stunts because Roy was so talented. They never came close to getting caught or slipping up. Montilladan played the world's greatest male impersonator; Roy Spiller performed the greatest impersonation of Montilladan."

Zoe drilled deeper. "Was Roy the type to become jealous and perhaps wanted more credit, possibly demanded either fame or more compensation, more money? Did you ever witness that conversation between them?"

Lacey scowled at Zee. "I don't care for that insinuation. I am sorry to refute you. M and Roy were friends, until the end would be my guess, and I was her lover."

"I am trying, Lacey, to determine the relationship between M and Roy, and if Roy felt like he was being cheated out of recognition due him for an outstanding performance."

Lacey was further irritated at Zoe. "I just told you that they were friends. They got along famously. The three of us hung out together, so I saw them interact a great deal. You will need to believe me when I tell you that Roy was paid handsomely, much more than any stuntman could have earned. Put any petty theories of blackmail and jealousy behind you."

Axel played it straight. "If Zoe and I are to work together with you and investigate this matter, then we will start by investigating the possible death of Roy Spiller and the background of Roy. It may give us some clues to the whereabouts of M. We promise that we will work on your behalf and for your interests, but you have to concede right now to us that you may not like the consequences of our findings. This is one of the possible realities."

Lacey streamed tears onto her bosom. "I pray that you will find her safe. She means so much to me. She's been such an important part of my life recently and an inspiration to me."

"Where is Montilladan's gravesite?" Axel inquired.

"Forest Haven Cemetery, off Grant Road."

"Yes, I know the place. Now, Lacey, this is a very, very important question. Other than you and me and Zoe and Nikki, does anyone else know that M was a female—a male impersonator? Please answer us truthfully."

Lacey signified a negative with body language by shaking her head. She opened her purse, extracting again the hanky to wipe away tears, while placing a check squarely in front of Axel with the other hand.

"Fifty thousand dollars now to take this case, followed by another one hundred thousand above all your expenses, when you find her and deliver her safely to me. Just keep the receipts for your expenses. I'll give you the balance check as soon as you find her."

Axel politely interrupted her. "We have a standard, legal contract, which outlines our terms."

"No!" she barked. "No contract; I will not sign anything." Her tone severely distorted the environment.

"You have my money. It's a simple deal. I'm paying you big dollars to find her. Find her! Got it? And when you do, whatever the circumstances, do not harm her, do not inform the police, detain her and just let me see her first. I want the chance for reconciliation and for the truth of what has occurred, no matter what the circumstances. Understood?" Axel looked at Zoe and found approval.

"Understood." He accepted the check. "What is his, sorry, I mean Montilladan's real name?"

"I don't know. No one knows. The journals were correct in reporting the past. M was a street kid who grew up in Miami. Her parents were Brazilian, immigrated when she was eight, tragically died early in her life. She told me she was raised by an aunt in a destitute Miami neighborhood. She also conveyed to me that she took to a life of petty theft and panning. She conducted mime, acted in amateur plays, played musical instruments on the streets of Miami to earn wages for her next meal, as well as being part of a teen gang who conducted petty theft." She was anxious to explain further.

"She learned all the tricks to avoid being placed in a foster home. She frequented the dumpsters of classy restaurants for her next meal. She was sixteen when her aunt became frail and couldn't take care of her anymore, so she relocated to California. Would you believe it? She either stowed away on train cars or hitchhiked the entire way, from coast to coast. Other than what I have just told you, she never talked much about her life in Florida." Lacey decided to stand and pace again.

"Once here M frequented the freeboard playhouses where she took acting lessons. There's a small diner near Manhattan Beach where she worked to garner extra money—shortly after she was discovered as a male actor. I think it is called The Green Thumb. It's a salad joint and bar. They know her as a male there. Anyhow, she secured infrequent roles in plays, played television as a filler, sometimes as a background stroller, a waiter, once played a policeman. Nothing too serious, no big payoffs in sight. Her first roles were inconsequential, although her tutors thought her to be a hidden talent." Lacey became animated.

"Here's what she told me. About eight years ago, before any serious friends had been established, she was mistaken for a man during casting for a play in Downtown Los Angeles. Her short hair, husky voice, the way she filled her clothes were exactly what the producers were looking for. Montilladan told me that she felt so comfortable and powerful in the role of a man. There was always more work according to her, so the transformation began, and it gripped her for life and lasted these eight years. She changed her name at that point."

Zoe was curious. "What was she called back then? I mean before Montilladan?"

"Zee, she told me Christian, however that wasn't her real Brazilian name."

Zoe probed further. "Why Montilladan?"

"It just popped into her head when she tried out for that leading male role and she needed a catchy, male name. She secured the lead male role, attracted rave reviews from local critics, and the rest is history. She was scouted by a movie director who saw the play and presto, she vaulted her transition from playhouse into the movies. Christian and Christian's history were dead. Montilladan was alive. Maybe it's also Brazilian. I don't know. When asked she told everyone that Montilladan was her first and last name, her only name."

Lacey suddenly became disinterested in this line of questioning and did not volunteer any more info as she sat facing both of them. Axel needed to know if Lacey was aware of other relations. "Did Montilladan ever mention the existence of any other relatives living in the United States?"

"No, she told me that after her aunt passed away there were no other known relatives. Montilladan was an only child. She told me on numerous occasions that she had no one to turn to other than the people here in California."

"You mentioned that she was an avid weight lifter, that she enjoyed physical workouts. That she had her own private gym. Did she ever engage any private trainers?"

Lacey answered Axel. "Not that I am aware of. I guess that I should tell you that one of the reasons we became so close is that we frequently shared workout sessions at her facility. She needed a close friend. I mean she loved the cameras, the fame, the lights, action, and the publicity, but she treasured her private moments with me as a woman. We challenged each other in fun, you know, sit-ups, chin-ups, tumbling, even some wrestling although I was no match for her. No one was as fanatical about exercise as M. I mean, is as fanatical."

"Do you know where Roy Spiller lived?"

"No, only that he was a frequent resident of all the beaches in Southern California. Most of our meetings were at M's house or my apartment."

Lacey reached across the desk grabbing Axel's hands, locking them with hers, dragging them to her soft warm skin under her chin. "I am counting on both of you. Help me. Please. Believe all I have said to you this morning as truth to signify the foundation of our relationship, ever so difficult parts of this tale seem. I deeply regret this life of deceit and that I haven't been honest with all my fans, but it has happened, it is reality, and now I must turn only to you to explore a new chapter of this incredulous tale- the search for Montilladan."

Axel smiled at her, broke the hand lock, and confidently strode to the other side of the desk to assist Lacey as she rose. She hugged him tightly and he felt her firm breasts press against him. Over her shoulder, he caught Zoe's consternate look, arms folded, eyes glaring back at them. Finally, Zee respectfully shook her hand.

"I must go now. I am so very tired. I look forward to some results. You can reach me anytime at this private number," and she gave a card to Zoe who issued further plans.

"Lacey, why don't we plan to meet in two days? Axel and I need to build some traction around the clues. I'll call you to set an appointment."

She was flustered again. "Fine, call me. I will forever be in your debt if you find her alive. Please Zoe and Axel, bring her home to me."

With those words her exit was abrupt. When she reached the outer office door, she turned one last time to wink at Axel. He strode forward to the open doorway to absorb her free flowing form amble down the hall to the elevators until the steel doors encased her. He turned to find Zoe leaning against the inner office doorway, arms folded; Thumper, heart a pounding, was breathing heavily as he sat behind the reception desk.

"Calm, down big boy," Axel said, brushing by Zoe and returning to the inner office to sit behind his master desk, to rationalize what had just transpired. Zoe broke the pensive mood.

Zoe inquired. "Was that Lacey Sills, sensual person extraordinaire? Or just another one of her characters? From an award winning scripted performance?"

Axel was stunned. "Zee! Shame on you. I don't believe that we are having this conversation. You doubt her. You think that she went to all this trouble to concoct a fabrication about M being alive. For what possible purpose Zee? I can't believe that you are proposing this!"

Zoe moved into his proximity behind the desk. "Axel, I believe that we have the foundation of an investigation. The facts are incredulous. You have absconded with her check, so we are obliged to investigate on her behalf. Call it women's intuition. Call it Zoe's foolish sense. Call it my experiences in life, but we are in for one helluva ride, Axel. There are more surprises in store for us if what she says is all-true. And how much should we believe? Suppose it is all fabrication. If I called up a gossip rag and try to sell this yarn, they'd give me a buck."

"You doubt her! Why?"

"Well, I do and I don't doubt her."

Axel was not discouraged. "Zee, I need a more definitive answer than that please."

"Axel, it still seems perplexing to me that Montilladan could keep her true female sex such a secret from an industry rife with so many inquisitive minds and so many tell-all snoops, and so many prying journalists."

Axel sighed with an exaggeration. "Zoe, listen to me. What possible intent and motives could Lacey Sills have to fabricate this tall tale? Flush away thousands of greenbacks," and he waved the check, "to support the fabrication?"

Zee quipped. "Axel, all that I am saying is that surprises breed more surprises, lies breed more lies and deceit flourishes in deceit."

Axel nodded. "If we find the subsequent disappearance of Roy Spiller, will you give Lacey more credit?"

Zoe stared back at him, causing Axel concern. Axel pressed her. "Zoe, I need your help. I need your buy-in on this one. The faith of our client is a prerequisite if we are to succeed."

"A love lived through lies has many faces," was her rapid response. Axel felt crushed. First the revelations of Lacey Sills; now Zoe playing skeptic. He stared at the ceiling as she resumed her place and typed some of the testimony.

Eventually Axel and Zoe sat closer to converse, drawing pathways of assignments, charting a course for Thumper on the internet. Zoe added checks to the list. "We have to probe M's background, Lacey's, too."

Axel stated. "I'll visit the funeral home first, and then the cemetery plot after I interrogate the Forest Haven's director about any unusual events during the ceremonies or wake. Zee, I'm still stunned by your skepticism."

Axel sat back to admire Zoe. She stood without responding to his comment, departed into the reception area, moving so fluently with a sexy gait. He called after her. "Nice."

"Keep your mind straight," she snapped, added, and rotated to lash sternly at him. "Give this some thought Axel. If Nikki, Lacey, you and I know, who else knows? I know you asked Lacey that question, but she answered it from her point of view only and with the knowledge she has. It doesn't address who else might know. There may be others who know Montilladan's secret and may also want it protected, or are already engaged in blackmail with her." She shouted from the outer office back to him, "Think about it."

"I need you to believe Zee." She appeared in the doorway.

"Okay, I believe. I'll give her the benefit of the doubt. This tale of Lacey Sills is an age-old tale, of lost love, of perhaps, one lover losing interest in the other without disclosing this betrayal. I firmly believe if Montilladan is really alive that there are bountiful more tears to be shed by Ms. Lacey Sills."

"You are concerned that M hasn't initiated contact?"

"Absolutely. I suppose that you gave her the benefit of the doubt when she squeezed you with her sexy bod?"

"Nope, I did that when she stared at me with those big beautiful blue eyes that bedazzled me when we first met."

"That's your criteria for belief?"

"I need you Zoe. You are my strength, and I am yours. You know that. We feed off of each other." She didn't feel like responding. She was still reeling from Lacey's eulogy, so she left him alone with his thoughts as she once again tuned the testimony that she had just recorded. He could hear her in the outer office shuffling around.

Axel leaned back into the spongy grasp of his chair. The excitement of a new case was upon him. "Start from base zero, build facts, uncover new clues, and magnify the confidences that the case was solvable." These thoughts ran over and over in his mind.

The Lacey Sills. Who could have ever guessed that this incredulous tale would be spun into their lap? How many males would be envious of his position? The reality of her double love life devastated him once again but that, too, was an accepted fact of modern society. Her only guilt was to disappoint male fans. He pondered, *Did Montilladan know of Lacey's discovery at the funeral home? If their love was true, why had she not contacted her?* Those questions ate away at him.

It was time to shift gears. Zoe reappeared to break his daydreaming. "Here is your copy of Lacey's testimony. If I send it to you by e-mail I know it will sit there forever in your inbox. Therefore, I printed it." It landed with a thud in front of him.

"Thanks," he motioned as she stood in front of him. She turned to retreat rather engage in dialogue. Axel could wait to read it. The client was real; the case materializing; he sensed the evenings of quiet twilights were to be few. The thrill of the hunt was upon him.

MONDAY MIDDAY

Peter Blevens was animated as he spoke. In vivid techno-color and with un-canny voice inflections, he described six eulogies in monotonous detail for Axel. Axel tried desperately to move on by changing the subject.

"Oh, the patronizing; it never ended. That day was the most stressful day I have ever experienced here. The funeral home was overpopulated with celebrities, press, adoring fans. Eventually, I had to summon extra security, even call the local constables in order to restore control, not from the guests but to restrain disorderly fans at the gates who wanted access to the grounds. Mostly misguided females I think. Unfortunately, we couldn't allow admission to all the populace that desired entry. In all my fifteen years here, I have never experienced anything like it. All for a man that I thought had blemished relationships!" Blevens, as onstage and perhaps before a sellout audience, emphasized the word everyone as his brown eyes grew open wide and the multiple creases on his face contorted.

At this point in his dialogue, he launched his large frame across the desk toward Axel with bitter disgust, and on one elbow, recited, "Our special showy flower beds were ruined. Some hooligans inside the grounds victimized our landscape just as we had planted the fall bloomers, beautiful multi-colored varieties. Our snazzy flora fell prey to people who wouldn't honor the system of trails throughout our sanctuary. We pride ourselves on the beauty of our haven." Blevens ranted on.

"I don't think it was the celebrities. I have a hunch that most of those were fans at the gate might have been autograph seekers, were imposters to the real theme of reverence, the real event of paying homage, and showing last respects. They also littered the lawns outside the gates with cigarette butts, showed no respect for the pinnacle of our landscape, the floral corner. It's been restored however. You must view it before you leave, Mr. Hawk, the floral corner, it is just outside as you exit- to the right."

Axel consented to walk by it as he nodded. Blevens continued his tirade. "This funeral cost my business thousands of dollars personally beyond what Constance and Lieber paid from the estate."

"Constance and Lieber handled all the arrangements?"

"Yes." He addressed the rest of Axel's inquiries. "Yes, I recall Lacey Sill's request to spend private minutes with the body in the chapel. I thought it not unusual. I thought it odder that so many people should now appear to worship and pay tribute to Montilladan in death. They were all clad in such grief over their loss. Montilladan would have been deeply touched," Blevens added in satirical jest.

Blevens remembered Lacey's abrupt exit about ten-twenty, or thereabouts. "I was deep in thought when a shrill sound from the direction of the funeral parlor disturbed me, so I bolted down the hall in confusion from this office just in time to see Ms. Sills scurrying down the dimly lit hallway. I called after her to wish her a good evening, but she ignored me. No. Perhaps, she just didn't hear me. Whatever, she did not acknowledge me."

Axel wanted to know about any peculiarities. "No, Mr. Hawk, there were no abnormalities about the funeral nor the burial. Everything went as planned. The estate paid for all the expenses promptly except our damaged flowerbeds, which in time, they may also respond to. Some new sod was also ruined."

Blevens reflected. "The stars largely behaved themselves. The mood was somber, although many of them took this time to reacquaint themselves in side conversations. There was an overabundance of journalists. Some of the guests had drinks; I mean hard liquor, before they arrived. I heard that Montilladan had that effect on the press in particular."

It was the only hint of humor from Blevens, so Axel hooted to connect to his little joke. "The only oddity for my staff was traffic control, as limo after stretch limo entered the premises." Blevens used his outstretched arms to emphasize his commentary.

"Why, Mr. Hawk, some of these people traveled in limos long enough to seat eighteen to twenty. Upon opening the door, one might discover only a single couple in occupancy! You can imagine how my parking lot became congested."

Blevens chatted, in great detail, about the limousines: the different types, the colors, the shapes, the lengths, the sparkling interiors including the bars, "and some of them had sampled liquor wares, too!" As previously, he displayed his disgust for libations by shaking his jowls and pointing his stubby index finger at Axel.

Blevens finished with a blow by blow of the glitzy occupants. Axel politely interrupted. "Can I have a copy of the guest list?"

"Absolutely. From the signed guestbook we produce a master list for posterity." He proceeded to spin away from Axel to face his computer. In less than thirty seconds, with six commands entered, a list was printing. He spun around.

"Presto, even our business is in the computer age." He presented it across the table to Axel as he rambled on. "It was difficult to distinguish between the Oscars and this ceremony. Each star had a contrived, staged, timed entrance. Each had a dramatic role to fulfill. I adored the outfits, well, most of them. Some ladies just don't know when to stop flaunting it. You must know what I mean." He tilted his head and smirked.

Thirty minutes later, Axel had extracted all he could from Blevens, although Axel was sure that this event was a shoo-in for chapter one of Blevens' memoirs. Blevens conducted his work passionately, a professional right down to the minutia. For that he should be commended. Axel had hoped that this interrogation would reveal some clue, some oddity, a single fact out of place, but no such luck. Even a precursory glance at the list of attendees, as he stopped to examine it, revealed nothing extraordinary.

"Do you need a lift to the gravesite? We have golf carts available for the convenience of our visitors."

"Thank you for your courteous offer. If you'll provide directions, I prefer to walk and enjoy the stroll."

Axel raised his right hand as to testify and pledged, "Scout's honors. I promise to stay out of the flowerbeds and stay on the trails Mr. Blevens."

"Ha, ha, it is quite a stroll, Mr. Hawk. Forest Haven is an expanse."

"No matter, it is a glorious day. Please." As they walked together, Blevens sketched a crude drawing on the back of his business card, outlining the pathways, their names, followed by the series of turns. They shook hands, Axel offering a final "Thank you for your help." He locked the guest list into his vehicle and waved a goodbye to Blevens.

Fifteen minutes later, Axel found himself in the back lots of the acreage, deep in a section of dark woods. This abruptly ended in a clearing, which led to a majestic pink granite epitaph on the far side.

It was a most imposing tablet, towering eighteen feet high with golden letters of Montilladan etched across the base of the column. Flowers were strewn everywhere, and a strong breeze dispersed the faded petals further to litter the scene.

Axel absorbed the ambience of the locale and commenced to read aloud. "Born Rio de Janeiro, Brazil. No reference to any other name than the eight-inch high bold etchings M-O-N-T-I-L-L-A-D-A-N. Died in the thirty-third year. How convenient. Not his thirty-third. Not her thirty-third. Just *the* thirty-third year." He sat down on a white marble bench situated about twenty feet in front of the epitaph.

There were two lines both with religious references. He scribbled the words in his pocket journal. He made a note to himself to inquire who wrote the words on the monument. He noticed how down in this lowest point of the dell, an eternal flush of fresh waters forever would congregate to replenish the afterlife. But would it purify M's soul? The soil was spongy here, a sea of wild flowers sprouting in the soggiest spots to provide a delicate scent, pleasant, uplifting, and alluring. This flashy piece of masonry dwarfed all the other plot designations casting cool shadows on the bench at this time of day.

"Be yet not afraid of greatness.
Some are born great.
Some have greatness.
Some have greatness thrust upon them."

After he spoke, he thought to himself that those words, in simple terms, described it all. Here amid the firs, pines, shrubs, in these rolling hills, this seemed to be the single most grandiose location. Hills on two sides converged behind the tomb. The front of the column faced a clearing of impressive tombstones leading to the woods he had traversed. A few stately pines were to his left. He concluded that this was one of the highlights of Forest Haven. Even he had seen the top of this royal protrusion rise above the gravesites when he had turned the corner out of the forest to enter the clearing.

Suddenly he became startled. Out of the corner of his eye, Axel was frozen by a slight of movement up the hillside to his right. He became galvanized on the spot where he stood. His palms grew greasy; his throat and neck encountered a prickliness.

Should he turn abruptly? Confront the spatial disorder? No. He knew the first rule of his profession was to check his rear, so he wheeled to face the clearing of gravesites with no one in view. It was restful although he conceded that there were multiple hiding spots behind larger tombstones. Now courage was summoned.

He rotated ninety degrees, daring to penetrate his look up the hill to the right of Montilladan's stone- and there it was! A sole figure, maybe five feet and a half in height, witchlike, totally clad in black, small in stature, standing at the highest point of elevation but dwarfed on both sides by memorials. Without moving, it was projecting an ominous fear within him. The figure stood with an unobstructed view of Montilladan's gravesite and naturally himself, obviously spying. Staring directly at the spot where he stood. Obviously close enough to overhear his outburst from Twelfth Night. The next move was his.

So, he climbed the hill slowly, maneuvering amongst the gravesites, epitaphs, the high shrubs. Slow-footed, carving his path up the steep incline toward the figure, constantly checking his flank and rear, weaving left, and right to honor Bleven's flower beds. He lost sight of his target numerous times behind thick foliage, frequently peering around to intercept any accomplices of the watcher, or screened ambushers.

Moving cautiously, steadfastly, the distance between him and the figure in black was diminished. Now as he stopped to catch his breath, bent over, the figure was completely obstructed from his sight, so he leapt from behind a full conifer to re-establish contact with the intruder. There it was, standing faithfully to receive him, standing at the apex of the cemetery like a black clad anti-Christ.

As Axel approached closer, he could see now upon inspection that it was an elderly woman, slight of build as he had originally perceived from below, an icy stern face peeking out from beneath a black bonnet. She wore a charcoal long dress, black laced up shoes, black high-necked collar, arms folded across her crotch, standing as stiff as all the tombstones themselves. Axel was now within thirty feet of her. He stopped.

"Good morning." She totally ignored him. She continued to stare unflinchingly past him to the marker he had just vacated below. Her eyes blinked not.

"Death was not too good for him, Mr. Hawk." Her voice reeked of hatred. It was cold and gravelly. A sudden breeze intersected the sight, and under his short-sleeved shirt, Axel felt a chill.

"You have me at an extreme disadvantage, miss..."

"Whitehurst!" she snapped. "Mrs. Kathleen Whitehurst." As she introduced herself finally, she impaled his confidence with her cold steely eyes. They were as frigid as a soulless angel. She finally extended her hand. Upon contact, her touch was of cold rotten flesh accompanied by boney protrusions. It left him wondering if he had just discovered a cold-blooded species of homo sapiens.

Her presence was creating an anxiety within him. But why? Were there other accomplices hiding undetected? How could someone so small and thin in stature threaten him? He thought, *All she needs is a broomstick to complete her garb.* How should he respond? He struggled. She overpowered him with a malevolent outburst of revenge.

"He was evil. He brought a life of debauchery into our lives. Sin abounded. How many others did he pollute? Well, we may never know, Mr. Hawk, will we? Sex. Drugs. Foul-mouthed. Low morals. Devoid of ethics. A diabolical fiend." She stopped to catch her breath to reload.

"How could our Lord possibly be the creator of someone who broke so many commandments and pierced so many hearts? It made me sick just to be in his presence, to hear his filthy ideals about life. What is it Mr. Hawk that we should live life for?" Axel was not allowed to respond.

"Had God the Almighty come to Earth to search for an anti-Christ, he should have looked no further than Montilladan and his life of deceit and immorality, and his irresponsible actions. They should have ground his remains into pieces and let the vultures feast on his flesh, bones and dung." A very pleasant soliloquy, Axel thought. He noted that she used the word deceit in her outburst. He was wrong. According to her, Montilladan was the anti-Christ. Now he was in her grip to be judged.

Mrs. Whitehurst spoke with so much venom that he now realized that every word that he would speak would be scrutinized to determine if he were ally or enemy. But he was having trouble making the connection from her to the gravesite below.

"First hand experiences?" Axel inquired of her. There were liver blotches on her hands; deep indentations lining her throat; crinkles ran parallel on her forehead.

"Yes. The Colonel and I, that's Colonel John Whitehurst and myself have spent far too many restless nights worrying about our poor dear helpless Lacey in the clutches of such a malignancy."

Zoe had warned him, "Surprises breed more surprises." Another shock to the body had just catapulted through his system. At this rate, it would be time for his annual physical- yet he had just completed it! How could this creature be the mother of Lacey Sills? Impossible! Axel inspected closer as she blurted out more of her hatred.

"The two of us were glad to see him dead." She emphasized the two Ds in the word dead with so much accent that congregating birds in a nearby tree suddenly scattered on cue, fleeing from the scene to leave him alone with her. No witnesses. Just silence.

Were the surprises never to stop? But the mother of Lacey Sills? Not even a flicker of resemblance! How could a creature like this bear such a beautiful innocent pure likeable child? Was Lacey a product of rebellion? Or perhaps, adopted? Did she turn to a life in Hollywood to defy her parents? Mrs. Whitehurst stared at him, moving into his space step by step. He intersected her mint-laden breath.

She surprised him. "Yes, I am the natural mother of Lacey Sills."

Could she read his other thoughts? He best be careful about his recurring image of a witch with a broomstick. Before he could regroup, she barked at him. "Walk with me."

She motioned to him to depart the current setting, descending on a pathway, which cut through the woods on the backside of the hill that he had just ascended. In their traverse, they encountered numerous family plots as they held true to her destination. Suddenly, the forest closed in around them, the pathway was not wide enough for their previous side-by-side strut, so she briskly led the way with Axel, as follower, watching over his shoulder, not a word spoken. As he digested her previous comments uneasily, he hoped that this murky dank stretch would end soon. He felt like he was in the haunted woods of Oz.

At last the woods terminated; they walked alongside each other across a wide expanse of carved tombstones. "You mentioned drugs. Did you have reason to suspect that Montilladan was a frequent drug user? Maybe had enticed Lacey to experiment with them?"

She was sharp on her return as she stood to block his way. Axel halted rather than collide. "He had the audacity to use drugs in my house directly in front of my face one evening while he was visiting. I lectured him, but he disrespectfully talked about his experiments with other harder substances."

"How often did Lacey and Montilladan come to visit you and the Colonel?" Axel reminded himself not to let a false gender slip.

"When they first started dating, they visited frequently. It became difficult to get them to accept an invite. Lacey became negligent. She even skipped her first Christmas with us last year. She said she was too busy. Busy. She was with him. I verified it." She was entrenched on her spot in front of him.

"Can you imagine? She spent every single Christmas morning of her entire life with us until last year." Axel felt his first pang of sympathy, felt sadness replace anger in her voice.

"We taught her values, gave her a decent childhood, gave her an honorable purpose in life. Slowly, deliberately, he eroded all that. The Colonel and I shall never forgive him." They entered onto a perfectly flat area enclosed on all four sides with juniper clusters. Ahead he spied a long ebony shiny limousine, complete with black tinted windows. Naturally, a chauffeur, completely attired in black, stood at attention with his arms folded across his crotch. *What is it with these people?* he thought.

Like a guard at Buckingham Palace, the chauffeur dare not move. He wore a black hat, black vest, an unbuttoned overcoat. Axel saw that he played his part well with a slender face coupled with beady eyes. Upon the snap of her fingers, the chauffeur opened the rear passenger door. Mrs. Whitehurst entered first, waving vigorously at Axel, beckoning him to follow. Reluctantly, he climbed into the vehicle for he had lost his bearings.

"We will drive you back to your auto in the parking lot."

"Thank you," he obliged. He felt like Hansel. The air inside seemed muggy, fully saturated with a foul humidity. There was enough seating for eight comfortably.

"Mr. Hawk, let us get down to business. Your time is valuable and so is mine. The Colonel and I will pay you two hundred thousand dollars cash, right now," and she displayed a certified check payable to A to Z, "to end this tomfoolery on this absurd quest of Lacey's."

"What absurd quest might that be ma'am?"

"Stop it!" she snapped as if threatening a subordinate and turned her face so her nose was but inches from his. Axel stiffened. "Don't you ever play games with me, young man! The Colonel and I know very well of Lacey's foolish ideas that the death of Montilladan is somehow suspicious, that she has confided in you to investigate this absurd theory of hers that Montilladan's death is not as it…it seems!"

Axel pondered her words, *it seems.*

Now she raised her voice to him to fill the container of the car. Her wicked pitch penetrated all the pores of his body. "Montilladan is dead and dead he'll stay. His name shall never grace the halls of our house and decent people again. His memories are all damnable. He converted our Lacey to dark side. If there is an afterlife, a hell, and he shall eternally lie in unrest every second, chained to flames that scorch him, so he may never know a moment's peace." She changed her demeanor, her tone turned sensible, passionate.

"Our Lacey is an impressionable girl. She seems to believe that the circumstances surrounding the accident are suspicious, mysterious, that the film set needs more scrutiny. Well, the Colonel and I know what is best. I am here to tell you to stop this farcical charade. I don't beg of you. I order you to come to your senses. This is a complete waste of everyone's time. Plus, I feel that you are personally taking advantage of her while she is in mourning."

Axel decided to be a smart ass. "And money. You left out money. It is a complete waste of everyone's time and money." She was not amused. Now it was his turn. No doubt she would not accept his counter argument, but he felt compelled to set the record of A to Z straight.

"Mrs. Whitehurst, I have already accepted compensation from Lacey. She is our client now, so we will not betray her. If you had intercepted me earlier today, perhaps, you might have had a small chance to convince me to abort this mission. Instead, we will give our honest efforts to Lacey. She is depending on us."

How much did she really know about Montilladan? What was she withholding? Did the Colonel share her views? What specifically had Montilladan done to pollute Lacey? And her earlier reference to irresponsible deceit? What did that mean?

"You spoke earlier of deceit. Could you share with me what you meant specifically?"

"As long as we disagree about these matters, no, I will not. It would serve no purpose. For us to engage in specifics we must be working toward the same purposes. We must be on the same side." Axel remained composed.

"I believe that we are, Mrs. Whitehurst. It is called doing what's best for Lacey." Her thin purple lips tightened and he withdrew inside her mouth.

"I am sorry, Mrs. Whitehurst; I cannot accept your charity." Calmly, he placed the certified check on her lap. Her face reddened. As a witch, she raised her arm, and Axel thought for what reason? To cast a spell on him? To strike him dead? She held it there, just inches below the roof, and loudly tapped on the glass partition. As she did the door unlocked.

"Such a mistake, Mr. Hawk." Would she spit out nails next?

"Is that a threat?"

"Just a warning to you and Ms. Zoe. You have absolutely no idea of the journey that you are about to embark on."

That was probably a truthful statement, he thought.

"And you do? If you are in possession of information vital to our success, then you should act as a responsible citizen, act accordingly to share the future with us."

"The future holds only surprises and disappointments ahead for you and Miss Zoe. Some perhaps, very nasty." Their eyes were glued to each other. She was scaring the hell out of him. She was trying to suck all the confidence out of his life as she inflicted her wrath.

"We seemed to have arrived at your car, Mr. Hawk."

He wanted to pry a rise out of her. "It is said that the greatest terror man faces is when the dead don't die."

"And what does that silly, silly saying mean?"

"Think about it. Here is my card." But she pushed it aside before he could position it on her lap.

"Get out," she yelled.

Thank God, Axel was cogitating. *I am released.* He slowly opened the door to emerge in the daylight, looking back intently inside the limo one last time.

"Looking forward to meeting the Colonel."

"The Colonel is a very busy man."

"I'll bet he is, Mrs. Whitehurst. Good day." At the instant he closed the car door, the vehicle powered up, spraying loose gravel behind. They left him abruptly alone standing in the pebbly lot. What did she really know of her daughter's love life? Of the accident? Of he and Zee? Of Montilladan? And she surely believes M to be male. Or does she know the secret? A lady to be reckoned with.

The sun shone brightly directly overhead, the noon warmth restoring his circulation. He placed his hand on his chest. Yes, his heart was still beating, but very rapidly.

"Screw your courage to the sticking place, Axel, and we'll not fail!" He looked around. He was alone. Not even Macbeth to hear his last outburst.

MONDAY AFTERNOON

Axel believed that there was just no other place like Los Angeles. Born in Southeast Oklahoma, he recalled his youth there but blessed the day he and his family arrived in Los Angeles where his father's trade landed their family. Why was he here? For the third day in less than three weeks and situated on this corner? Sitting in his sport car, staring at this ugly, one-story mall. He exhaled, shut his eyes tight, and thought to himself.

How lucky to reside here in one of the world's hub of sports, entertainment, commerce and trade. Now my Nikki is completely immersed in this relentless pursuit of news. He opened his eyes. In his heart, Axel wished her well. In his heart he felt a somberness of what could have been. Somehow, he had to disencumber himself from this sea of disappointment, a disappointment that he had to take full responsibility for. He had known from the start of their love that she would be the dominant one and he would have to be subservient. In the end, it just didn't work.

He remembered his mother. "God bless her soul" he muttered. It was almost three years ago that she delivered a stern lecture. "Nikki is not the right girl for you." She oscillated her arms and raised her voice. Even though she lived in their L.A. home until her end, she had met Nikki only twice but was strong on advice. "You will be just a fleeting romance in the long list of broken hearts on Nikki Louden's ambitious road to her pinnacle. Axel Hawk is not and never will be as high reaching as she. Listen to your mother, Axel; you'll be the wounded one when it ends."

He summated. Nikki was truly gone; his parents both passed on; his sister Loretta now residing in Phoenix; his brother Palmer returned to Chickasaw roots in Oklahoma; the recent target of his affection, Zoe, rejecting him. "Things are not looking up."

He had exited from highway sixty, drove south half a mile to park on this cement field. Aloud he affirmed. "So, this was the best that the city of Los Angeles could do? Demolish three city blocks of one-story houses, early fifties' motif, with charming front porches, my old homestead included, to construct a super strip mall that quenched the delight of takeout addicts. At one end, a dry cleaners, at the other a national cell phone chain, coupled in between with a hodge-podge of today's most popular places to blow your money on hamburgers, books, vitamins, more hamburgers, submarine sandwiches, game rentals, electronics, pizza, donuts, and kolaches." As he stared, he almost expected the Chickasaw ghost of his father to materialize in front of him. His cell phone chimed to a jazzy version of William Tell overture to interrupt his ugly thoughts.

"Hello, this is Axel."

"Axel, my man, Harlan here. How the hell you doing?"

"Harlan, believe it or not, I am parked where the old Hawkman's homestead used to be. It has been replaced by the Rolling Meadows Shopping Center. Know the place?"

"Hey, stop and get a burger. They got tasty burgers at Opie's House. They also got super pizzas at Maria's. But I got great news for you."

"I need a boost. There may be some high moments in the cuisine, but this sight is depressing me."

Harlan interrupted. "It is a sign of the times, Axel, people crave all that stuff. Hey, our advisory board met. You, my man, get to play Shylock in our next production."

"Alright! I am forever grateful." Axel shuffled gleefully in his driver's seat. "You know that I have always owned a hankering' to play a heavy, one which will showcase my real acting abilities and a vehicle for my talent at long last."

"Man, you can't bullshit me; your whole life's been one acting job, Axel." Harlan was incessantly smearing his private eye career, convinced that Axel was perpetually acting to pry information out of witnesses.

"Hey, Harlan, I owe you one. Thank you, pal."

"You are my friend, Hawk. You owe me nothing. I have got other calls to make to notify people of their assigned parts." Axel delayed to disconnect with a sample of his wares.

"Fair sir, you spat on me Wednesday last,
You spurned me such a day, another time,
You called me dog; and for these courtesies,
I'll lend you this much money?"

"Bravo! Bravo! But Hawk, save it for the audiences, the critics, the talent scouts. Don't waste such pristine performances on friends like me! And remind me never to borrow money from you. But remember my motto, Axel. A man's best friend is an actor." Harlan was no longer there.

Axel clutched his cell phone under his chin and tightly pursed his lips. He was ecstatic at securing the role of Shylock and shouted a gleeful *yes*! to himself. But he returned to wonder how his sister, Loretta, felt when she signed away the property to a developer who would erase all childhood memories. Maybe this was how his ancestors felt when they were told they would be relocated from Alabama to Oklahoma.

He reminisced. *All his co-acting peers said, Oh, Axel, he's such a nice guy. What a swell guy. What hero can you play next time?* Well, with a role like this, he would seize respect for his acting abilities—finally. Now his thoughts turned to another subject as he veered disgustedly away from the mall.

Zoe. It was wrong to jump early. But he grinned, he had really surprised her. Recently his strong urges for her were at play. He started the engine and slowly drifted down streets behind the plaza. He recalled Gloria Kimball as he drove by the old Kimball residence, still standing, a block behind the plaza, but reflecting its age with peeled paint and a rotting stoop. Gloria's father had called his dad by the time he arrived home. He was ready for his first father-to-son talk about the facts of life. His dad was always there for him. The phone rang again. It was Charlie Fosse. He pulled over and parked.

"Hey, Axman, You called?"

"Charlie, Zoe and I need our private nook reserved tonight. Can you do that for us?"

"You got it. Anything for you two. You know, Zoe busted out of here last Saturday night as if something is bothering her. You didn't propose to her again, did you?"

"No, I did not. She's probably just still upset over the Micks' case. She'll cleanse her mind eventually."

"Hey Axel, your favorite lawyer, Pena, is buying half my interest."

"No kidding. Great. However, I thought he was looking for a good investment?"

"Now that I didn't need."

"Just in jest, Charlie. You will enjoy Marco's great sense of humor and keen business skills. He sharpens his pencil on the overhead. Charlie, I was glad to make the introduction to you and now, even more elated that it has worked out."

Charlie expressed his sentiments. "The place is picking up more business, but with the improvements that Pena and I have planned, it ought to stand another fifty years. Fosse's will always be the friendly watering hole forever. Marco agreed to let my name stand. No Pena and Fosse."

"Good luck Charlie. See you tonight." By no coincidence, he had parked in front of the old ball field. It was dilapidated when he was in his teens. It hadn't changed a bit. It was dilapidated now. He recalled the greater city championship high school game when Don Drysdale had shown up to throw out the ceremonial first pitch. He threw a straight ball, and looked at Axel to say, "How selfish of you kid. I coulda made it dip if you had offered some Vaseline from your hair." The photo of he and Don was proudly displayed in his office. So, was the miniature replica of the city trophy which each player had received for their victory.

He recalled the night his team all sought shelter under the leaky bleachers while a freak storm passed through and dumped rain and rattled the wooden structure with gale-force winds.

Now, for no other reason, his mind flittered and he remembered sitting next to Cher at Formaggio's. He slipped her noticeable glances until finally, she put her cutlery down, broke conversation with her friend, leaned over to Axel to inquire, "Why do you keep staring at my pasta primavera?"

It opened a dialogue with Cher, her date, Nikki and himself. But she was ecstatic when she discovered Nikki's identity. His remembrance suddenly stabbed at him. It was Nikki's charisma that carried the conversation with Cher; her dexterity that guided them through two hours of frolicking conversation. Why had this memory surfaced? Enough. To the office.

Just as he was about to pull into the street, a group of baby-faced ballplayers paraded in front of him, slapping the front of his vehicle, as if to say, "Hey man, you're going nowhere until we pass." He wondered: *Did they have the same commitment and passion for this game that he had at their age?* It wasn't for him to pass judgment.

Turning onto the next street, he passed a series of vacant lots where other memories of stolen kisses with Gloria surfaced. It was this same field where he got his first, serious bloody nose playing tag football. "Axel, get a grip. Why are you exploring the past? What is causing this bout of nostalgia today?" He thought further. *Searching for sanctity after the spooky encounter with Mrs. Whitehurst? Cher now was just a blur; Nikki lost; ball playing days over; the old house gone. Crows in the elms overhead squawked out a symphony, which bit his eardrums. He knew what they were barking. Get your mind straight, Axel.*

He sped back to the sanctity of their office, galloping through thin early afternoon traffic. The day had cycled through a California metamorphosis. From the cool of the midmorning when he first arrived at the cemetery, where he had had his first close encounter, it had now transformed into a blistering hot early fall day, complete with unbearable humidity, one of those days when the distant images of the Los Angeles skyline creeps through veils of orange cider smog.

Parking four blocks from his office beside a solitary vintage palm tree and a vendor, he partook in the gnashing of two chilidogs with a quaff of lemonade. Somehow they were not finding a comfortable resting place in his stomach. He attributed the indigestion to the residue of the morning's events.

Lacey's oration had severely impaired the vestige of his manhood; her mother had stepped into his proximity to shake his confidence. As a result of this morning's interface with Lacey, he now carried a burden on behalf of Lacey admirers everywhere to keep a secret. Shylock suddenly seemed like a consolation prize compared to these troubles.

Axel pressed his pedal to the floor for the last leg. Impatience was driving him to Zoe as she became more of a constant in his life. Sifting through her attributes, he had come to respect her uncanny research abilities, admire her dependability, and oh, such a fierce fighter. Mm, that slinky sexy physique, in combination with her appealing personality. Who would have ever guessed her to be so tenacious? Who could have ever guessed her such a superior combatant? And he thought, *That was it! Her mental and physical strengths. Those were such comforting factors.*

Navigating into his parking spot at the rear of the office, his agitated mind was creating paranoia. Or was it? Hadn't he spied that steel-gray Mitsubishi Eclipse earlier on the way to Forest Haven? Again pulling into the strip mall behind him? He placed the lemonade in the drink holder so he could dash to street-side, just as the vehicle vanished into the jungle of traffic up the hill. Frustrated, he was anxious to return to the one human whom could lift his spirits.

Proceeding up the elevators and into his sanctum, he found her in the inner office at the oval table deep in research.

"Hi, I am glad to see you back, Axel. I checked with the police and there are no dead unidentified bodies adrift in the Pacific, nor in the glorious smelly sewers, none unclaimed. No missing persons that answer the description of Montilladan. No recent back alley finds either."

"How did you verify all that?"

"With Tinker's help." He felt uneasy at the very sound of his name, so he changed the topic.

"Tinker?" He was annoyed for a second time as he heard his name. "No police Zoe. What were you thinking and without conferring with me? No wonder you didn't want to hold hands. No wonder your hands are cold."

Axel was animated. When angry, he had this habit of lowering his voice. "How is the frequent contact search progressing?"

"Slowly." She lowered her head and, as he sat across from her, she slowly made eye contact. "Do you ever stop to think about Heather Micks?" She expressed a hint of tiredness. Axel rose, and placed a chair next to hers and looped his arm around her back, tugging her closer.

"I talked to Charlie earlier. He sensed that you were not your exuberant self with the girls last Saturday night."

"The ghost of Heather Micks haunts me."

"Do I think of her? Yes, all the time. The memories are fleeting instances during the day when I speculate about how close we were to finding her alive. I remind myself that she had been dead for two days and that there was nothing that we could have done, Zoe, nothing; absolutely nothing. Look at me, Zee. Two days before her death, we were struggling to piece the evidence together. She was probably dead by then. So I stop speculating about how close we were because we weren't. You have to remember there were official agencies which didn't unearth clues to her whereabouts."

Zee finally turned her head into his space. "She was so angelic, so pure, her death so sudden, so final."

"Zee, it's a casualty of our business. It's the worst part. We have each other to thank that we haven't experienced it more." They each reflected about the case until Axel removed his arm from around her, placed it on the desktop and squeezed her hands tight. She came into a moment of reality by breaking the grip.

"Okay, back to business. Thumper and I had a hell of a time constructing a list of the friends of Montilladan. It's like Lacey spelled out previously- M doesn't, or didn't, have all that many close recurring acquaintances. There are lots of intersections, but no one jumps out as close. Thumper gave us a start. Look." She positioned her chair three feet from Axel, turned it to face him, reached for a computer printout, and cascaded it from the middle of the table down onto the floor as the pages unfolded, revealing a list of names with corresponding profiles of individuals.

"Here is a list with bios from public data. Montilladan jumped from producer to producer, and studio to studio. Here on the printout is a list of films that M acted in and observe, not a repeat of even the makeup artists. Stu Givens was one of a few people that seemed to put up with his shenanigans."

Axel studied the volumes of paper by sifting it through his fingers. "I note that Lacey checks in at number six by frequency."

"Yes, frequency defined by the interfacing with M from press clips, news clips, films, rags info, public data bases, and internet sites. Montilladan circulated when she was off the set; friends are scattered from greater Los Angeles, one resides in Frisco, a number in Sacramento, one in Dallas, even a dentist in San Clemente. Rather a well-known dentist."

"San Clemente? There are hundreds of dentists in Los Angeles. Why go to San Clemente for your teeth?"

"Observe the dentist's picture. The bio spells out that he is available, handsome, wealthy, a little on the gray side, but I will perform hardship duty to check him out tomorrow. I'll get to the root of the problem."

Zoe's presence was soothing to his soul, so he comforted her with a ha-ha on her little pun. Axel shifted to a seat now across the table and before she could withdraw her hands, he grabbed both. "This could be a bumpy ride. Let's make certain that we share information soonest and remain in constant contact. Keep our cell phones fully charged and with us at all times. I don't want you taking unnecessary chances."

Zoe withdrew. "Here is the public file on Montilladan's accidental death. Corroborates Lacey's comments." Sheepishly, she added, "Tinker will be here soon."

Extending his forehead and pushing his bushy eyebrows over the tops of his eyes, Zoe spied the signal, so she motioned for a time out. "Axel. Calm down. This is Zee talking. Hear me out." At least now he had explained the even neater state of his office since he had left, and the positioning of chairs around the oval table. "Not to worry Axel. This is Zee, your pal. I trust you, you trust me, and we're a happy P.I. team."

Axel appeared frustrated. "Et cetera, et cetera, ya-ya, ya-ya, but this is damn important. You should have consulted me. Teamwork."

Zoe moved her chair beside Axel sitting sideways in it to create an intimate interface as they knocked knees. "You are going to listen to me. When I called Tinker this morning to seek his help to inquire of any unidentified corpses down at the morgue, I discovered that he investigated the fatal film set in which Montilladan died. The clues at the film set are cold now Axel. They're gone. The set was dismantled since the case is officially closed. The ruling is accidental death. But Tinker was there. This could be invaluable to hear his version. He knows nothing of the nature of our client, nor what we are investigating, except what I told him."

"Which is what?"

"That we are conducting an investigation on behalf of a client and the incident of Montilladan's death has surfaced in our investigation. This incident may or may not be vital to the case. However, we need to talk to him personally to clarify some points of the fatality."

Zoe pleaded her case further by raising her voice. "Axel, I had to make this move. He's coming here to tell us about the incident. He was there, we weren't. This is a worthwhile development. We are sure to learn more from Tinker than reading old news reports. You know that Tinker's eyes see more than anyone. I informed him that we would not be divulging our client's identity."

"All that I am saying, Zee, is that this is an important development on an unusual case, and that you should have consulted me first." His tone was awash in displeasure.

"But Axel, the moment was when I was on the phone. Tinker is a busy man. There you were the other night at my place telling me how much you trust my judgment."

She continued her logic. "You conveniently forget. I know Tinker. We're soul mates. He has always been very special to me. When I joined the L.A.P.D., he was my mentor. You know that, Axel. I served an apprenticeship under him. Tinker will keep this conversation confidential. We need to hear him out! Tinker is special. You know that. Come on Axel, don't just sit there! Give me some words of support!"

It didn't take long for reconciliation. He purred as a cat, leaned across the table to peck her on the cheek, and agreed. "Okay, I will pardon you." Inside, he resented Tinker's affection for Zoe.

"Pardon?" She wacked him on the shoulder with a rolled up segment of the report. "Pardon me?"

"Alright I overreacted. You made the proper decision. But you should have called me to confide in me. Graveyard or not! This was an important decision."

"Pals?"

"Sure." They shared quiet eye locks of mutual respect. Zoe scanned her watch and elected the business discussion.

"Quickly, before Tinker arrives. Here is a biography of Montilladan. Not much turned up until eight years ago when she, he, whomever it is, burst onto the scene just as Lacey said. That is, catapulted onto the scene and shot like a rocket to the top of her profession, um...his profession, whatever."

"However, in all this reading, there are some common themes. Theme one: not very well-respected by the peer group of actors. The word arrogant keeps re-occurring. Some biting commentary from fraternity. Theme two: loved and idolized by the ladies at almost—sort of—a cult status. Many of them would be surprised if they knew what we know. Here are testaments to this. Theme three: disdain is glued to M, over and over. Look here. There." She circled quotes in red ink.

"Pissed off talk show hosts by grandstanding on stage or not in sync with the scripts. Equally despised by journalists." She leafed through the printout to various spots to highlight them for Axel's benefit. "We are all familiar with the confrontations with the press."

"Here's some interesting reading I was unaware of. Look, mysterious regular absences from film sets that led to costly delays. Wanted to be pampered. All documented here, and here, as supporting commentary from directors." She pushed the dossier closer to him.

"Any references to doctors, lawyers, operations, girlies, accidents, hospital stays?"

"Only the dentist."

"Urologist?"

Zoe chuckled. "N-no! But endless dates captured by the press and fans."

Thumper entered the room and proceeded to dump a quantity of leaflets onto the table. "Here: further history of Montilladan, another cross-reference of most frequent directors, co-stars, friends. Not much of a pattern. Surprisingly a real loner. Smells deliberate if you ask me."

Axel inquired of Zee. "Did you inform Thumper?"

"Yes, and he took the news like a very, very large man."

"Don't give me that look, Hawkman, I will keep quiet. I told you that I would never wash that shirt again. This devastating news now proves that I am a man of my word. I disrobed, not in front of the lady, naturally, to retire that shirt. Replaced it with Iron Maiden. A classic. Look, it has multiple autographs of the members emblazed on it. However, I was somewhat relieved when I heard Zoe say that she is a bi but loves men more and has had only one female affair."

Axel knew that he could trust Thumper. He countered with a sharp order. "Next step, see what you can find, big guy, on a Colonel John Whitehurst and his wife Kathleen. Reside in the Los Angeles area. I want a thorough background check."

Zoe squinted, "Connection to our investigation?"

"Most definitely." Axel thought how difficult it was to put into words his encounter this morning with Mrs. Whitehurst. It was still gnawing away at him.

"I had the singular most unpleasant experience, as Dr. Watson would say, of meeting Mrs. Kathleen Whitehurst at the cemetery this morning. That was, after I interviewed the director of Forest Haven. The meeting was not by chance. She was spying on me as I visited Montilladan's gravesite. Mrs. Whitehurst is a lady of relentless revenge, all directed at Montilladan. She tried to interfere in this investigation by buying off you and me, Zoe, with... a couple-a hundred thousand dollars. She wants this investigation aborted."

He had her attention as she sat straight up. "Don't tell me that you spoke for me and turned down those dollars?" Axel knew that she was kidding him, so he did not respond. "Why does she want the investigation discontinued?"

"Montilladan is dead and will stay dead. She wants the world rid of him and she wants our efforts terminated. She wants Lacey's imagination curtailed.

She wants the memories of Montilladan erased from Earth forever. She wants all of this done immediately and if she had her way she would have ground M into bits for vulture feedstock."

Thumper quipped, "Hell, that all sounds reasonable."

"I don't mind telling you two in private that she scared the daylights out of me with her witchlike appearance, her gestures mimicking black sorcery, and her piercing, impaling voice and penetrating beady eyes."

Zoe was quick. "Damn, to think I missed all that to stay home with Thumper and cuddle up with him in front of the computer in the cave." Zoe added, "You promise to share all the fun with me from now on?"

"Zoe, I think this woman is dangerous."

She inquired, "The Colonel and Mrs. Whitehurst are?" There was a silence. She repeated, "You were going to say something. Are?" Zoe situated her elbows on the table. Thumper expelled an irritating grunt to convey his impatience while locking his thumbs in the front of his jeans above the buckle. Axel bit his lower lip, sipped the final remnants of his lemonade to extend the melodrama and articulated. "They are the parents of Lacey Sills." Before either could respond, Axel continued.

"Mrs. Whitehurst must have had me followed. She was determined to execute an encounter. You know the song, "Ding, dong, the witch is dead, the wicked, wicked witch is dead?" Well, I got news: she isn't. The song communicated falsehoods in our youth, and led us astray as adolescents."

He directed his next comments to Zoe. "A most unlikely parent-sibling combination." He finally finished his drink and completed a three-point play by burying the cup in the trash bucket on the other side of his desk with a hook shot.

"I am very disturbed by this meeting with Mrs. Whitehurst. Chance or deliberate? I say deliberate."

He stood to address Thumper. "You need to re-gear into cyber-action. The Whitehursts. Immigration files on Montilladan. Here's some one-liners I noted from Montilladan's tombstone", and he ripped the page out of his notebook. "See if you can find its origin, and, finally, a list of attendees at the funeral. I want all these people identified as to, occupation, residence, relationship to Montilladan, etc., etc."

"Yeah, yeah, yeah, boss. I know the routine."

"We also need to find the documentation of a young girl who emigrated from Brazil to America through Miami, Florida, thirty some years ago. Call your computer geek amigo in immigration."

"He works Tijuana only."

"Well turn on your thumping charm. Offer him for the love of country and apple pie to purge Florida files." Zoe piped up. "And Roy Spiller. We need a profile of Spiller."

"Yes, ma'am," and Thumper stood at attention, clicked his heels, saluted them, and marched out. Zoe shouted after him. "And we need Montilladan's social security number, driver's license number, personal health care program."

Thumper returned. "A cool four days of work, plus overtime."

Zoe quickly retaliated in a booming voice. "We don't have four days. And how is it that the Worldwide Wrestling Federation hasn't discovered you?"

"No way, I am staying right here to torment you two." The kibitzing ended as Thumper disappeared into his cave. Axel turned to Zoe.

"Speaking of Roy Spiller?"

"Nothing yet, Axel. Thumper and I conducted a penetrating search on different public sites with no luck. We may have to visit beach haunts randomly to track him down. He doesn't have any recorded public addresses. All I found were very sparse references to movies where he was listed in the credits, most of the time for his work as a stuntman, sometimes for small bit parts such as a waiter, teacher, bellman, valet."

Axel responded. "I'll start that physical search in an hour." There was a disturbance in the outer office as Tinker emerged at their door, Felix Dunne in tow. Axel's spirit was suddenly crushed. Zoe quickly amassed their research records in piles, quickly stashing them behind Axel's desk.

Tinker bellowed, "Hey, how's my favorite little lady?" His massive, six-foot-six black hulk sprung forward, swept her off her feet, twirled her as heaving and catching an agile cheerleader, hugged her from behind as her feet dangled, kissed her on the back of her neck voraciously. Axel, envious, observed the chemistry between them as she adored his attention. Tinker prolonged his grasp and released her. They stood admiring each other, Tinker beaming and exposing his massive tongue during a prolonged smile.

Axel looked up, way up, to his ominous presence. He'd never seen hands that huge or biceps so bursting, or such a shiny lacquered black head, not even on the court at basketball games. Tinker's pistol looked like a peashooter strapped to his waist.

In contrast, Felix was a weasel, complete with dense curly burnt almond body hair on his arms, neck and sideburns, chiseled jutting jaw, skinny, and a face resembling a fox from a character in Alice in Wonderland. Felix greeted Zoe first when she landed, and extended his boney hand to Axel. Axel recounted their last meeting when it took four police officers to restrain them from tearing each other apart. Felix scratched out his cigarette over a prolonged minute as Axel and he watched Zoe and Tinker share extended courtesies; Felix sat down at the table beside Axel, bending his body away from him. Meanwhile, Tinker expressed his sentiments toward Zoe as they positioned themselves together.

"Hey, we still miss you down at the station, the arm wrestling, the crazy twisted sense of humor, your irrefutable logic. Sometimes, we a little short of humor down at the station." This glorification by Tinker caused Zoe to break out into a wide smile, exposing her gorgeous white straight teeth.

Axel cast a disrespectful glance at Felix until Tinker finished. "Now, guys," bellowed Tinker in his normal bass tones, "what is all this shit about Montilladan's death? Why you two want to go poking around that incident?"

Zoe took the lead cautiously as they now positioned themselves around the oval conference table. Felix avoided eye contact with Axel, instead, taking the opportunity to ogle Zoe, which irritated Axel at length.

Zoe endeavored to convince them that there was no cause for alarm to the L.A.P.D. "This investigation on behalf of a client, and the death of Montilladan has surfaced, as an event that we need to know more about, one that demands our attention. Axel and I need to understand more about the circumstances to satisfy our client, and what better way to do that than to interview the men who were there."

"In particular," as Axel let her continue, "were there any abnormalities surrounding the accident? Anything unusual at all? Can we interview some selected persons whom were on the set at the time the accident occurred? Talk to witnesses? Is the case officially closed? Ruled accidental? Officially accidental?"

With the last two questions, Felix suddenly sprang upright in his chair. "That's all? Geez, that's it?"

"If not closed," Axel added, "why not?"

Felix barked in his usual gruff voice. "Who's the client?"

Axel retaliated, "Felix, you know that we can't divulge the identity of our client and especially in an impetuous moment without the consent of our client."

Now for the first time, Felix turned to face Axel, his tangy garlic-laden spiked breath suffocating Axel's near spaces. "It's really goddam simple Hawk. You and Miss Zoe here spend a lot of time in missing persons. Now, I don't seem to remember too many fuckin' cases where you did anything else. So, who the hell are you trying to find? Who's the goddam client? In particular, how the fuck does this dead dude Montilladan fit into your case?"

Felix stopped to catch his breath, and leaned over to Axel. "Look at me. Do I look like a dope? Do I? I want straight answers." Zoe was regretting this invite as Axel cast a glance her way. But Axel remained calm by allowing Felix to finish before responding. "Our client and the nature of this case are confidential at this time."

Felix was furious as he snarled and grunted. Tinker played referee before Felix could open wounds again. The sparring was over. "We'll share information with you two, but we're gonna need to know if you find evidence contrary to official police findings. That's the deal. That's what Felix is trying to say."

Axel nodded affirmatively. "We'll keep you informed." Zoe, with body language, agreed accordingly.

Felix was not satisfied, so he belligerently raised his voice. "Yeah, just like the Miller case. We got hosed on that one by you two personally. Is that your idea of cooperation?"

"Felix, we made a mistake. It's old news. I solely take the blame. Look at me, Felix, not at Zoe. I admit it. We screwed up. We should have informed you earlier. But Zoe and I make extra efforts to cooperate with your people, in particular, detectives reporting to you. We were furiously chasing clues leading up to the climax of that case. We had no time to update you. I have apologized many times over. Can't we clean the slate on the Amanda Miller case Felix?" The blood-shot beady eyes of Felix stared back.

Axel continued to present a plea. "Let's cooperate. We need to know what happened on the set. Otherwise, we will have to conduct our own investigations. We are not trying to go around behind your backs. We're trying to be honest here Felix. Let's bury the hatchet and work together."

"I'll stay close to Tinker on this one." It was Zoe's pledge. She nodded her head as she spoke to Felix.

"Boss, Zee's word is good and she speaks for Axel, too." Tinker was carving out a route to bond. "Now chill out man! Chill out, too, Axel! Felix, give these dudes another chance."

Felix massaged his knuckles, fixed his citreous gaze on the ceiling, lit up a smelly cheap cigarette in defiance of the no smoking sign on the door, and responded methodically.

"Okay. You tell the lady and Axel what we know, Tink."

Felix sat back.

Tinker began his recital after two *ahems*, which cleared his throat.

"Well, the investigation was messy. I mean when I arrived at DelMar studios, the ruddy liquids of the man's skull were strewn all over the floor, and were saturating the cracks and permeability of the concrete. There was yucky yellow brain matter splattered two feet away and pooling beside the corpse. It was a disgusting site as the man's skull was thrust into his chest. It took me a few minutes to realize that it was the film star Montilladan that we were about to examine. But it was a routine case in many ways. There were a couple a things unusual, but most facts not so unusual."

"Like?" Axel was impatient. Tinker piped up. "Chill out Axel. Like I said, I will tell this in my own time." Tinker felt he had to put Axel in his place to appease Felix.

"The set is a very large studio, up on the northeast side of downtown called Georgia Pines studio, owned by the DelMar group. They were filming a ballroom and fight scene from a new movie that Montilladan was starring in. The movie was based on that best-selling book Sweet Sherry South. The set was built to resemble the grand foyer of an old southern antebellum mansion. There were over a hundred dancers engaged in the scene, plus an orchestra on the ballroom floor. According to Stu Givens, Montilladan performed his own stunts. You know, I was surprised. I never knew that, but I never stay for the credits in the theatres."

"Okay, so in this scene, Aaron Moss, played by Montilladan, is on the balcony of this four story New Orleans style mansion, a long balcony which overlooks the foyer. Montilladan emerges onto the balcony and examines the festive site below him while the ballroom dancers are in motion. Then Jason Court, you know the strongman type of action films, who has played the burly villain more than once in action movies, bursts onto the balcony. Supposedly, this Aaron Moss has stolen his gal. The witnesses all testified that the two men shoved each other around just like in the script. Well, Montilladan got pushed by Court up against the railing, against the leading edge so all below could see, so the camera had best advantage. So, he's supposed to bounce off the secure railing, see," and Tinker stood, using the back of the chair and his hands to illustrate how Montilladan made contact by bracing himself, "and turn and proceed to leap across the balcony, tackle his foe, Jason Court and jointly bust back and roll through the French doors."

"But that's not what happened." His baritone voice expressed regret. "Stu Givens told me that the two of them rehearsed this fight scene to perfection over the past two days. Coincidentally, tragically, the rail on the secure side gives way when Montilladan hits it. Because of the angle that he hit it, because of the element of surprise, because of his momentum, why he hits the concrete floor face first. Smashes his skull wide open." Tinker shook his head. "Not a pretty site. No time to turn his body in mid-flight to allow another part of his body to absorb the impact. It all happened in just seconds according to witnesses who observed him flailing his arms and legs as many screamed and shouted. He was dead on impact in front of one hundred and sixty three witnesses. We interviewed most of them and took their names, and while they were on the set, took recorded statements. You are welcome to come to police headquarters to examine the file, Zee."

Tinker sat down. "Montilladan's momentum just shot him to his death. I mean Montilladan was gutsy, gory dead. I understand that pandemonium pursued. Females broke down and cried and some were still wailing when we arrived. Jason Court told me he couldn't bear to look and was on his knees on the balcony for fifteen frozen minutes, feeling sick to his stomach from the chaos below."

"Now for the strange part. Two technicians on the set swore to me and signed in a deposition that they witnessed Montilladan inspecting that very particular section of railing just hours before they commenced to filming that day. Apparently, talking around the set, Montilladan ritually examined all his stunt sets before he participated to check the safety. So, that was not unusual. That is exactly what he did here on that set, that day, that balcony, that section, earlier. Examine the integrity of the set he was going to work on."

Tinker felt the need to expand on his comment. "What is strange is not that he examined that section of balcony, but that somehow he overlooked the flawed holdings and supports that were loose on that side of the balcony. I also discovered from these two technicians that this particular balcony set had been used many times before, so it may have just given way because of fatigue, but these two technicians were surprised. They informed me that they inspected it as recently as the night before filming, when they were told that they were not going to use any fall mats. The railings passed their stress test."

Axel wanted clarification. "I want to make sure I understand. The rails gave way exactly where the two technicians saw Montilladan inspect it earlier?"

"Exactly. The two testified to me that Montilladan examined the entire set but seemed to spend more time at the front overhang. In the testimony

Felix and I took from observers, some stated that he may have hit the rail somewhat harder than called for." Felix grunted a confirmation.

Axel was curious. "Why no mats for safety at that end? Look at the consequences. Surely the union must have safety regulations."

Tinker bobbed his head. "Good point. The balcony was over seventy feet high, but there was no chance of falling over the rails according to the technicians. No one guessed its integrity would be compromised over a hard hit. However, a fatal mistake was made by Givens and the production staff. They gave the order for no mats. I interviewed Givens and no one feels worse than he. He claims the mats interfered with the paths of the dancers given the size of the dance troop. He also stated that Montilladan and Court convinced him to film the dance and balcony scene contemporaneously, so the mats were removed to give the dancers more surface area below, more lavish appeal to the floor, and to record both the balcony and dance scenes simultaneously."

"Can I talk to these two technicians who witnessed Montilladan's inspection earlier on the set?" Zoe requested.

"No harm, I see, Zee. What you say Felix?" Dunne nodded in approval.

Zee continued, "Is the investigation closed?"

Felix shifted awkwardly, his body shuffles giving clues to Tinker to reply but, before Tinker had the chance, he blurted out. "I want to set the record straight. I don't trust you two. I don't like you two. You buzzed me once—no, twice. I'm still toting' burns around with me!"

"So, what does that mean?" Axel followed on. "We haven't buried the hatchet. The case isn't closed?"

Tinker interrupted. "The case is officially closed, man. What Felix is trying to say is what I said before, that if you two discover evidence to the contrary, you better inform me soonest. You help us. We help you. Cooperation. That's what the boss wants, and Felix is the boss."

Tinker turned to Zee. "I got me no ambitions to come and rescue you, Zee, once you have been put in a no-win situation. I want to be there if the situation around this case gets dangerous and ugly!"

The temper of Felix flashed. He vehemently began to extinguish his cigarette, crumpling it into bits on an ornamental plate on the table, scattering the ashes. "Look, I demand cooperation Hawk. It's bad enough that Tink and I got to associate with someone who acts in Shakespearean productions."

This was personal to Axel, so he interrupted Felix. "What's wrong with you, Dunne? Just because you have no talent for acting or the art or interfacing with people?"

They traded insults for the next twenty seconds, trash talking over each other until Felix let go of the Shakespearean references, stood to finish with, "Real men drink beer, watch sports, not talk goofy in a language people ceased to speak hundreds of years ago." Tinker had had enough, so he intercepted the lances and placed his massif between them.

"Okay, boss. This is Tinker talking to you. We need to maintain a business approach in this matter, and that means no more bad language in front of the lady and no more personal insults to Hawk about his recreation. Now, Hawk here apologized for the Miller case. That's history. I don't see how he can do much more than that. His personal choices of recreation are not on trial here Felix. Now, calm down! Keep this conversation focused on business."

Felix was breathing heavily, his bursts of expelled air sounding like a spastic breeze blowing through leafy shrubs. "Okay, I will settle down. But since we are engaged at a business level, I would calmly like to raise an issue once again. One of your specialties in this firm is locating missing people, or so you advertise. Not investigating accidental deaths of movie stars on film sets in Hollywood, especially, in my territory. So, mister bright private investigator, who the hell is missing? Eh? Tell Captain Dunne. Last I heard Montilladan was buried, so who is missing? And how does he connect to Montilladan?"

As Felix raised his voice to fill the room, the echo of Dunne reverberated in Axel's ears. Meanwhile, an expression of ugliness filled Felix's expression as deep parallel furrows contorted his brow and his short red hair blended with the color in his cheeks. Axel was muscularly fit compared to Felix's thin frame.

"I want the name." After the word *name*, he blew a prolonged wave of nauseating breath into Axel's face.

Axel, meanwhile, standing, extracting himself from the table, restraining himself, replied. "I can't answer that question truthfully. Zoe and I are only hours into this investigation. I will tell you honestly that there is the chance that no one is missing. We have not proven if foul play is a factor. We are at an extreme disadvantage to other players in our investigation. Spending time at the film set may turn out to be a wild goose chase, Felix, so we seriously can't answer your question right now."

Zoe wrestled the conversation from him. "We can't reveal our client's identity Felix. We are checking into circumstances. In them, Montilladan's death surfaced. I would like access to the police report, too, as Tinker suggested. Will you deny us, or help our case? That's all we wish to know from you. We'll share any revelations once confirmed."

Axel struggled to remain calm in the aftermath of Felix's biting criticism, but a look at Zoe told him that he had just exhibited great discipline. Felix circled Axel three times, and halted to address him. "I am gonna bust your balls if you screw me this time. Make it my mission to suspend your license."

Taking the chance to intersect his nauseating nicotine aroma, Axel taunted him, "I relish the opportunity to cooperate."

"Look, smart ass," Felix waved his crooked index finger at him, "you inform Tinker when you need his help. Personally, I choose not to assist you two, but I will assign Tink, only because of the past relationship between him and Ms. Zoe and Tink's one of my best." Felix expelled additional expletives as Tinker immediately came between Felix and Axel and with force-marched Felix away, grabbing his arm by the elbow.

"Boss, I already asked you. We have a lady present. She and I don't appreciate your choice of language."

Felix tugged his arm free as he received Tinker's remarks. "I will talk to the little lady, boss. She'll keep me abreast of developments. Right, Zee?"

"Deal."

Felix stared at Axel with a look of disgust. Axel stared back, pondering, *Where did you get those awful clothes, Felix?*

Today Felix wore a solid orange shirt, crumpled, khaki pants, a cheap, black tie, and feet adorned with war-zone, scuffed shoes. Every time that he and Axel had met, Felix appeared to have missed a section of whiskers upon shaving. Today, it was an obtuse set of rosy brush bristles under his chin.

He was just an old man, dressed in drab, brown clothing that fit his slender frame. He entered the street and hobbled along through four blocks. He spoke to no one and no one acknowledged him as he kept his head bowed. Shoppers and businessmen passed him as his gait was half of theirs; at one traffic light he hastened his pace slightly, while his black ebony hardwood cane, which was ordinary, which had experienced better days, which was chipped in numerous places, which was eroded on the bottom, kept his time with a perfunctory tapping beat. He wore a faded gray goatee, which protruded downward, from his chin; his eyebrows were neatly trimmed; his black shoes needed polishing; steel wire-rimmed glasses were not a perfect fit and slipped on his nose, so he pushed them back in place.

He stopped in front of a tobacconist; the shop advertised SMOKES-TO-BACCO-PIPES. He pretended to inspect each pipe in the window. The shop-keeper moved to the window to motion him in, but he cast a faint smile and looked away. Now he turned with one block to go. In front of him, three young ladies emerged from the luring confines of a day spa, remarking on their manicures and tans. Absorbed in their banter and self-compliments, they passed in front of him without a side-glance as he came to a halt.

Finally, crossing the street, reaching his destination, he feigned the need to pause and wipe his brow. So very, very slowly he extracted a large kerchief from his front pocket and proceeded to wipe his forehead and cheeks while staring down at the black square monument in front of the building. His photographic memory needed only one glance to record the display. It appeared that there were two to three businesses for each of the five floors, except for floor two, which the executives of a construction design company occupied the entire floor. One by one he eliminated each entry except two. Possibility one: A life insurance and casualty insurance company on floor five. *Is he an insurance investigator? And why as he stared at the magnificent tombstone, did he suddenly appear startled, cast a glance my way, and scamper up the hill out of sight. I certainly didn't scare him. He most certainly didn't see me. I was deep in the woods out of sight. Or were my eyes playing tricks? And was that really the Whitehurst limo that exited the cemetery in front of me? Probably not.*

The only other possibility. A detective agency, A to Z, never heard of them. Perhaps worth checking out. "But why would a detective visit my gravesite. A fan! That's it. Better be careful today. But what startled him?"

The old man looked around. "So far, so good." Ambling on and turning at the corner, a circular lazy route was carved out five blocks, leading back to the bus stop. No hurry. Keep true to form.

He was just an old man, faded into the street environment. Nobody noticed him. They had other things to tend to. He came. He gathered information. He departed unnoticed.

Zoe presented their case. "With Tinker present, Felix, I would like to visit the studio this afternoon, as well as Montilladan's dressing room on the set." She added, "Montilladan's residence soonest, like this evening." Felix thought to himself that she was not bad for a skinny broad.

"You got spunk, kid. I admire that. Great tan, nice buns."

"Keep to business, please," she retaliated.

"Anything develops that we should know about you better call Tinker. If this becomes a criminal investigation, Tink's in it and in charge."

"So," Axel wanted to confirm, "we can examine the police report on Montilladan's death?"

"Tinker, you set the appointments up. Keep a tight leash on these two." He adamantly stated this as he pointed his long crooked index finger again. Felix had had enough. "I'm going outside for a smoke. You summarize Tink."

He stormed out of the room into the outer office and out of the building while Tinker remained to chart a course of action. He reassured them about Felix as he closed the door to the inner office to address them privately.

"Guys, he ain't so bad. He's still pissed that you two solved the Miller case before he did, that you got all the credit," he whispered, "that you got to go on television instead of him. That's really it. Now, you and I both know that events developed so hastily that you couldn't wait for the police, so you rescued the victim. I say excellent job. Felix, he calls foul on you two!"

"You gotta work for the man for a while. He's smart. He's tough. He is brutally honest. He's a damn good cop. I like him as a boss. He plays by the rules. You probably heard that he suspended Bobby Lake for his unauthorized leaks with the Miller case, but that's Felix. By the book. I sure hope he isn't listening out there, because he desperately needs a woman to dress him up, and take him out on the town and for an occasional roll under the sheets." They laughed heartily. Tinker continued after the din died.

"He had his fiftieth birthday last week. He didn't celebrate except to get plastered with a few of us guys. I'll manage Felix. We will be okay if you work through me."

Zoe summarized. "So, I will come by later to view the police report."

"Fine. If I am not there, I will make arrangements for a security clearance for you. Check with Barry on level three when you arrive."

"Tinker, you'll call the two technicians to inquire if they are available? Insist they cooperate when I arrive?"

"Sure. I send you their names and contact info when I return downtown."

"And Montilladan's dressing room? I want to have a quick look around. With or without you Tink?"

"I don't need to be there. Just don't suddenly get a bout of sticky fingers."

"Can I take photos?"

"Sure."

"Inspection of Montilladan's residence?"

"Ah, now that I will need to arrange. I definitely need to accompany you, or Felix will have my badge. How about we rendezvous there tomorrow evening? I will send a locator map to your email Zee. Confirm a time tomorrow evening. Is that soon enough, Axel?"

"Tomorrow night is just fine. Thanks for your assistance, Tinker."

Tinker peered down with an intense stare. "What are you two lookin' for at Montilladan's residence?"

"I wish we knew ourselves, Tinker. Something unusual. Something mysterious. Something that doesn't fit. A photo. A mysterious black book. By the way, any insurance claims?"

"Not that I am aware of. That who you two looking for? An heir? An inheritor."

"Can't say. What about the film company, did they carry any insurance?"

"Speak to the victim's lawyers, a law firm called Constance and Lieber."

"They're already on my list."

"Tink, did you personally examine the shattered rail? Were they wooden or metallic?"

"Yeah, you know, they were wood and what was left splintered when they hit the concrete. But there weren't any signs of tampering, like, ah, marks they had been altered to bust. They were held tight together by a dowel system."

"No metal screws?" Axel continued.

"No, just dowels which were screwed tightly into each piece and post, and one rail fitting snuggly over all of them to hold it together. I tested the balcony that remained in a number of spots and it was solidly together, held firm against my weight."

"Did the movie camera catch the scene? Close up? Anything unusual?"

"Felix and I watched that death scene over and over. It was tough to take, real hard to find any evidence of tampering as the camera zoomed in. The rail and dowel system just blew apart in one place where Montilladan made contact and the rest failed in that section. Simple as that. That dowel system is supposed to take the weight of four hundred pounds according to the technicians, but it flat-out failed."

They exchanged courtesies, as Axel blessed Tinker's refereeing skills. Tinker placed his humungous arm around Zoe as they strolled to the door where he leaned over, embraced her with both arms locked around her, kissed her firmly on the cheek and whispered pleasantries in her ear, to the jealous gaze of Axel and the amusement of Thumper. Zee cooperated fully. She waved her fingers flirtatiously to culminate a friendly goodbye and turned to find a crushed Axel.

"It is not what you are thinking Axel. Tinker means a great deal to me. We respect each other immensely and I enjoy his companionship. We are just very close friends."

They each retrieved cold colas from the fridge in the butler's pantry before retiring into the Axel's office to sit across from each other at the oval table. In silence, they sifted through the facts of the morning, she sipping quietly through a curly plastic straw, while Axel poured his diet cola into his gigantic Bob Dylan mug.

"Tell me, Zee, how does Felix ever get a date dressed like a clown?"

"Yeah, he kills me. He's a hoot. When I was little girl growing up in Lodi, my mother used to pin the wet laundry out on the clothes line in the back yard where breezes could carry away the moisture. I often picture Felix walking up to the line, unpegging some crumply uncoordinated clothes and dressing up in them."

"Most women don't like the f word especially in public. He does have definitive strikes against him. He is forever shrouded in a cloud of nauseous gases just like some cartoon character." The humor was short lived. "Axel," Zee seriously stated, "there is that possibility that the person who inspected the studio set hours before the take was the real Montilladan, setting up the murder scene of Roy Spiller."

"Great minds think alike for those are my sentiments exactly. We have great syncopation, you and I. She tampered with the set to design his death. Bingo! Roy Spiller performs as Montilladan hours later to act out his own real death scene, his own personal deathblow for... her. Possibility number one, premeditated murder by Montilladan. Lacey won't like that."

Zoe took a turn. "A set occupied by real witnesses, who can lay claim to the death of Montilladan. No one to know any different until the unsuspecting Lacey Sills inspects the naked corpse at the funeral home and ruins...a perfect escape, sabotages a perfect murder."

Axel piped up. "Possibility number two Zoe that someone else disguised as Montilladan loosened the bolts, intending the real Montilladan to be the victim. In that case, Montilladan is either hiding for fear for her life, or took the opportunity of Roy's unfortunate death to build a new life."

"If we can prove that Roy Spiller has vanished," Zoe spoke, "we have very strong evidence of who lies in the gravesite."

"Ah, so, Zee it sounds to me like you are changing your tune from this morning, awarding Lacey more credence. You are beginning to believe in this whopper."

"Not necessarily. Possibility three. The fact that two witnesses saw M inspect the stage is condemning. The other possibility is that the stage was not in prime working order and Roy Spiller met his death as a true accident to allow M to take the opportunity to escape from her life of fame and manhood. The devil is in the detail."

"Okay, but where does she want to escape to?"

"I don't know, Axel, but if she was involved at all in possibility one of plotting and executing Roy Spiller, some dramatic event must have transpired for Montilladan to scheme this, to suddenly decide that the glitzy life of a rich movie star had to be eradicated. She hasn't even included Lacey in her future plans."

Zoe didn't allow him to reply and she straightened up. ""Don't you see? She just drops out of sight, leaving behind lucrative financial paychecks with the job security of an acting career. I think some drastic situation has occurred Axel."

"I absolutely concur. But what inspired this diabolical murder?"

Zoe interrupted him. "And why now? Why plan her escape from Hollywood stardom at the pinnacle of her career? Lacey thinks we're to be engaged in the search for Montilladan. Me, I think," and she paused for effect, "that we should search for the impact event. This person was pampered in her Hollywood life. We need to uncover the event that disrupted it."

Before Axel could reply, as he seemed anxious to do, she stood, circled the table, arms folded, her body swaying with a sexy swagger, pacing on the balls of her feet. She turned on him.

"Zoe's intuition. She has panicked because of an event. We have got to find out what that event was Axel, the event that reached out and touched her deeply and broke her rhythm, forced a dramatic change in her lifestyle. I hate to say it, but I have a strong hunch that she has killed as a reaction to it. Or she may be in hiding because of what you alluded to earlier, Axel, that Montilladan really really was the intended victim."

"Whatever has happened, it is like Lacey told us, Zee, she can't come out of hiding now to face the embarrassment of her double life."

"Yes, and just like the web of deceit she spun through Hollywood, now she continues her master deceit in a new role by duping the whole world into believing that she is deceased. What a script!" Axel offered a somber note.

"Think of it, Zee. It's inevitable that we be drawn into her web if we pursue this investigation. This script is right out of an award winning mystery novel. Felix is gonna hate us if we prove that Montilladan is still alive."

She scorched him. "This time we had better include Tinker earlier in our plans." She sat beside him. "Oh, gee, the fatality is ten days old, so we have to put our cumulative mental abilities together in haste before the trail gets any colder."

"Speculate, please, Ms. Zoe."

"Well, as we said earlier, Roy may not have been the intended victim. Maybe Montilladan really was the intended, so now she is undercover because her life is in danger."

"Okay. Rack it."

"Financial woes. Gambling. Spending into oblivion. Over extended credit to zealous creditors. Maybe borrowed from unscrupulous types."

"Who are her bankers?"

Zoe was quick. "We have that. Thumper found it. She dealt with three banks. It is in the dossier. I will add that to my list."

"Keep going."

She was about to expand when she stared at him. "Oh, no! I've seen that look before."

"What look?"

"That one!" She pointed her finger on her outstretched arm at him. "The goofy look that always infers that you are conducting a fantasy, engaging in private thoughts of lust."

"What?" he protested.

"You have it Axel. For years I have noticed it and endured it."

"I don't," he pleaded.

"Yes! There it is again."

"Stop it, Zee. Get serious."

"Aha, your eyelids are raised, like maybe you are planning a romantic assault. Your lips part slightly, you pull up your cheek muscles, on the right side only mind you, and presto. Axel's goofy look! The prelude to a fantasy!"

Axel decided that denial was useless, although he was embarrassed that she should uncover his thoughts. He startled her by mounting a chair, standing upright, towering over her. She gawked back at him. He kept his legs straight together, one hand over his heart, the other one outstretched in front of him. His face now changed to reflect a dire appearance. Unexpectedly, in a high-pitched squeaky but sexy voice, he lamented.

"Oh, Romeo, my Romeo. Wherefore art thou, Romeo?"

Zee grimaced while continuing to stare up at him. "Oh, I like this. We have just embarked on perhaps the most challenging mission that we have ever been confronted with, a complex tale of master deceit, and you are trapped in a Shakespearean moment. It really is time for your annual checkup, Axel. You may even require a shrink. You need to get on medication."

But strangely Axel maintained his balance, ignored her wit, her biting sarcasm, kept his pose, and in a fraction of a second Zoe connected to his line of thought, suffering a shake of rapidly developing thorny goose bumps up and down her back. She rose slowly, walked to the other side of the room to cogitate. She was astonished at this development. Her body shivered in a cold state. She challenged him.

"A man? A man! You think that Montilladan has left Lacey and killed Roy for a man! This is your idea of an impact event? A man? A new boyfriend? A new male lover? Murder Roy and jolt Lacey?"

"Why not?" He gleefully dismounted from the chair, walking to stand in front of her, expressing extreme pride in him. He turned, sat down, and with a motion to her to do the same across from him.

"As you yourself said, we are searching for an impact event. What root causes are there? Old Willy Shakespeare knew. They were the inspirations for all his writings. Love, money, revenge, fear for one's life, love, murder, self-defense, self-preservation, jealousy, love, hatred, greed, love, murder, and sex. I prefer love, murder and sex as the motive for this plot, especially since it has maintained its number one ranking throughout the ages and especially since we are dealing with a deprived, and possibly depraved, female for many, many years."

Axel was on a roll. "You remember what Lacey said. She said that Montilladan changed to a man because of the job market, not because of any sexual preference. I prefer to think that she has discovered after eight years or whatever it was as Montilladan, that she finally wants to be a woman again, a real live sexually active woman. She probably discovered that real sex abstinence ain't worth it. I vote, and seriously ask you to consider, that Montilladan has abandoned her manhood forever! She killed off Montilladan, her supreme character, in front of hundreds of witnesses, and she did this for her new lover! She had to. Zoe, she is in love."

Zee sat back stunned to meditate. This thought had not crossed her mind. She was engaged in her own debate to rationalize this development. "Ah, I don't know Axel. This is a very committed lady, as committed to her mission as anyone I have ever heard about. As Lacey even said, she performed flawlessly for years without a single solitary slip-up! And think of the scads of money she made in the movie business. I wouldn't walk away from millions of future dollars per performance for a man."

"But, Zee, here's how I rationalize it. She finally meets the man of her dreams, and it obviously ain't Roy Spiller because she killed him off. It obviously ain't Lacey she wants. Considering how long that she has waited to meet this beau, and how long she has played this deceit, she is desperate for the love of a man, her man, her paramour. If she remains as Montilladan dating this man in public, she'd really complicate Hollywood's life, and hers, and her beau's. She would be seen as a man dating another man. She can't do that."

"Conversely, she would have to come out of the closet to reveal to the world that Montilladan is a female with gargantuan embarrassing consequences, and admitting to her fraudulent habits and her duping of an industry. Either scenario, she initiates burning scandals, causes extreme personal embarrassment, incites more unpopular venom against her, loses credibility with Hollywood. Montilladan places herself in a lose-lose situation, unless she can convince everyone that she is dead. If she is dead, she can assume a new identity as the lady of her lover's dreams." Zoe did not respond. Granite-like, she stared back, arms folded, legs crossed. No comment.

"Plus, Zoe, once all this scandal is inked in the public domain, she would never know a moment's peace again. The fascination around her life would exponentially rise. The rumor rags would make millions. This will be one of the greatest scandals ever and journalists everywhere would hound her for years. Not to mention potential charges against her by the guild and…think about sponsored products and endorsements. They would sue." Zoe still fixed her deep dark eyes on Axel. He hadn't been able to solicit a response yet, so he just rambled on.

"So, she plans her death of her alter ego, using Roy as the sacrifice. Or, perhaps, she sees the inopportune accidental death of Roy as an escape route. But whatever the scenario, in one dramatic moment, M dies. Then she re-emerges with Romeo on her own time and they flee into the night, to spite William Shakespeare, living happily ever after. Tragedy is denied. Justice is denied."

Zoe was now motioning him to stop. "That makes six people who know the secret—Nikki, Lacey, Roy, you, me, and Romeo. I am very, very impressed that you thought of this line of plot Axel, but I am not yet convinced."

"Why?"

"Difficult to execute all that!"

"Exactly! That is exactly why we will find her. That is exactly why we will find Romeo. There is no such thing as a perfect crime Zee, there is always flaw. Now I ask you, are there detectives up to the challenge of revealing these flaws? Of course! Us!" Axel extended his arms outright as a prophet. Zoe frowned and muttered.

"Okay, so I'll go along with this crazy idea. It is one of the scenarios to be considered and investigated. So, how do we find Romeo?"

"Good question. Honestly, I haven't got the faintest clue. Hm, perhaps, as heir to the insurance policy." He gave her a demonic look. "Perhaps, the lovebirds intend to flee with Montilladan's fortune into the night. Maybe, he's a dentist in San Clemente. All we need is one detail left unattended by her, and him." He waved Lacey's check in front of her face. "We are motivated to find Romeo."

"Long shot, Axel. I think my ideas of financial woes are valid. I'll visit the banks tomorrow. Besides, Axel, maybe she just suffered a flood of guilt and decided to terminate this charade."

Thumper burst into the room grinning. "Hey, look what I found surfing the crime net." He slammed an enlarged color glossy photograph in front of them. Axel picked up the eight and a half by eleven, color print to express elation as Zoe positioned herself behind him.

"Creepy, isn't it? I mean this guy Roy Spiller really, really, really looks like, and resembles Montilladan!" Axel was curious.

"On what sight did you find this?"

Thumper spoke proudly. "Spiller almost did time. Got off but not before this picture was taken. Petty theft, four years ago. Only blemish other than one dropped vagrancy charge. Anyhow, Clarissa, that's two ton Clarissa down at the police records, my kind of woman, checked police files for me on Spiller. We got lucky."

Zoe perked up. "He is younger-looking but, no doubt about it, he could pass for Montilladan facially and physically."

"Did Clarissa see the photo?" Axel wanted to know.

"No, way! She transferred the file to me instantaneously as I disconnected. She's not suspicious Hawk. She has helped me before." Axel didn't look satisfied. "It's routine for her to assist us." Thumper added.

"Does she log the retrievals?"

"Who's going to notice?"

Simultaneously they replied, "Felix!"

Axel stood and gave him a pat on the back. "Terrific job, big guy! You are a gem. We will have to take our chances now. The file has been downloaded, so let's hope Felix doesn't get a line on it and don't contact Clarissa again. A hearty thank you, Thump."

Axel reflected on his previous dialogue with Zoe and lamented. "Unfortunately, we now can assume that Roy Spiller won the Montilladan lookalike sweepstakes contest and paid with his life."

Zoe recited. "Montilladan is going to disappear across a rainbow to her pot of gold with her lover, maybe. If her life is in danger, she may have already left the country. Only reason to stay is if Romeo is still here or…if there are other loose ends to tidy up."

"I like this. You are warming up to my Romeo theory. Thumper, get me an address, phone number, and background check on Constance and Lieber law firm. We were just joking earlier. The Adams Family can't have you."

"Yup, this is a beer moment."

"Not on these premises. Settle for lemonade." Thumper departed, his body frame creating huge spatial shifts in his baggy blue jeans, the back pockets swaying to the beat of his flip-flops pounding the floor.

Zoe summarized as she opened her laptop. "The police reports, the film set, M's dressing room, interview the two technicians, M's bankers, current events, the dentist, Montilladan's residence. Wow."

Axel realized that it was his turn. "I will spend the rest of the afternoon combing the beach. No pun intended, but I will drift around the surfing and beach haunts looking for signs of Roy Spiller. Meet you at Fosse's at seven o'-clock? I'll tackle Constance and Lieber tomorrow. Don't forget Zee to confirm the visit to M's residence tomorrow night. Plus nail Lacey down for an early Wednesday morning meeting."

Zoe regrettably speculated. "Axel, I'm scared. Let's suppose that Montilladan killed to protect her secret; she would consider murder again, if we get too close."

"To us?"

"Why not? If she finds out that we are investigating her, she could get pissed off. Promise me that you will remain alert, not take unnecessary risks, run from danger, watch your back for any tails on the beaches, on the roadways and finally check in with me often."

"How sweet that you care about me."

She barked. "I care deeply about you, Axel, but I am not sleeping with you."

"Whoa, I just had a thought. To follow your line of reasoning, if we are in jeopardy, what about our girl, Lacey? We should alert Lacey. With the knowledge she has, she could be categorized as a loose end. Any ideas for a bodyguard, Zee?"

"I'll call her. Let's allow her to select her own. I don't think she will receive our idea too well, plus I don't think that Montilladan will harm Lacey." She emphatically raised her voice. "No chances, Axel." Axel was prompted to promise.

"Which reminds me, keep your eyes peeled for a silver and grey Mitsubishi Eclipse, new model; it may have tailed me this morning."

The phone interrupted their dialogue. It was Nikki. Axel politely asked Zee for a private conversation, so he waved at her to depart. When she had left and sealed the door shut, he replied.

"Hey, Nikki."

"Axel, I promised you high drama. Will you believe me now when I say to you to get your mind straight?"

"Definitely. I need no more convincing of the matter."

"This is a very complicated case, Axel; you have to be alert and responsive."

"Agreed."

"She is in a volatile state emotionally."

"You need not convince us." There was a pause. He dared to venture, "How long have you known?"

She didn't reply immediately. He stayed on the line for an eternity hearing each pulse of air at the other end of the line. "For some time. I took an oath not to disclose the revelation. I was at Lacey's place when Montilladan showed up one night, where she created a spontaneous scene by taking Lacey into her arms to kiss her. They explained their love for each other. I vowed to keep it a secret. At that time, I knew Montilladan only as a man. I swear."

"Then, a few days ago, why, Lacey showed up at my place, wild-eyed, disheveled, a basket case mentally. She was being driven crazy by this problem. She poured her soul out to me. She told me about Montilladan and about M's double sex life. She explained how this crazy thing had all happened, how they fell in love, how love grew, and what she witnessed when she lifted the blanket at the funeral parlor and saw M's nude body. It was her first and only female love affair. I sympathized with her as she poured her story out. She needed help. As we conversed further, I recommended you. Enough said about this affair. It troubled me at first, but there is no one else to turn to other than you and Zoe and we three have to guard this secret."

There was a pause. With zeal, she ordered, "If this story breaks, it's mine, you understand?" Axel confirmed with a curt "Yes."

"The reason that I called is to tell you that Lacey just called me to convey that she has confidence in you and Zoe. She said that you were both good listeners, excellent interrogators, so she is committed to you. I would have to say from her tone and comments that she really is dedicated to you, as I hope you are dedicated to her."

Abruptly, she added, "I have a report that is overdue. I'll call you later." Before Axel had time to develop the dialogue further, she hung up. He was upset that he had been abandoned so quickly, left alone with his pressing inquiries that only she could answer. He hungered to converse with her further, but she obviously didn't. Slowly, he replaced the receiver, sat back in his sea of displeasure. No matter, the beach was beckoning.

And Shakespeare's great question of "Romeo, Romeo, wherefore art thou Romeo?" suddenly had taken on a new modern meaning.

MONDAY, LATE AFTERNOON

It was ironic. The station that he had tuned in was conducting a day's tribute to the oldies' beach music on the very afternoon that he was chained to the sweaty beach roads and Highway One. From San Clemente to Dare Point, Doheny and onto Laguna, it had been a fruitless bundle of hours. He knew all the beaches where the gods and goddesses of the sun and waves resided with their equipment and napkin-wrapped accoutrements. A very patient disciplined approach was summoned in light of the scanty public information about Roy Spiller.

"Clues just don't fall into your lap," Axel muttered to himself. Roy's photo had been flashed to countless bathers, surfers, bartenders, lifeguards and even a few local law enforcement officers. Through experience, his profession had taught him to conduct a well-paced thorough and patient investigation. His sweep of the area along the coast south of Los Angeles could be followed tomorrow by the inspection northward. After eight beaches, three bars, four diners, and even the interrogation of four vagrants, he was no closer to Roy but running out of time if he was to rendezvous with Zee at Fosse's at seven o'clock.

The top was down on his fire engine red Mustang sports car, so his dark hair shuffled to and fro across his head as the currents dipped into the automobile. Between stops, he pondered about his next move with Zoe. Would she reject him outright if he continued with these approaches? He certainly wouldn't want to damage their relationship as partners. A retrospective moment absorbed him at a red light.

Gunther Magnus, the previous subject of a past kidnapping investigation, had his berretta focused on his forehead behind the Hollywood Bowl on a pitch dark night, three in the morning. It was almost two years ago to this day. Suddenly out of the darkness she darted air borne, caught Magnus under his chin with a swift whip of her right leg, while extending her arms, as lances, outright to relieve Gunther of his weapon. It had all happened so precipitously that to this day, as that night, these were burning memories of Zee's bravery forever etched in his mind.

On that early morning, life as he had known it had come to an end. He remembered as he lay prone and helpless on the ground, that Gunther, whom had killed many before him, devoid of feelings, was boasting of his latest triumph, Axel Hawk. When she materialized into view to save him, he was lying helpless and in awe of her prowess. Before he had a second to aid her, Zoe had Gunther's right arm in a most uncomfortable position behind his back, while Gunther plead to Axel for assistance in the absence of his uncle, lest Zee dislocate his shoulder or break his arm. He chuckled to himself. "Only Zoe Burns could have reduced Gunther Magnus to a quivering heap of jellied flesh."

Axel pulled his vehicle over. The sign read Huntington State Beach. This would be his final trek for today. He perused the street map focusing on an area one half mile ahead. Sand granules like sticky foreign substances had attached themselves in his scalp, onto his twiney chest hairs, even somehow in between his toes. "Fun, Fun, Fun," was blaring on WKBW, the rocker's world. But today had not been fun. Previous stops, accompanied by brisk strolls had been arduous as he endured a vigorous brisk workout.

Now he drove the last few blocks to position himself in the parking lot of the Golden Parrot Bar, a distinctive, low-class beer and gin joint for drifters, vagrants, beach muscle, surfers, and beach meat. It was located three blocks from the oceanfront, away from the beach strollers and transitory fishing crowd. He had been here various times before in assisting law officers make an identification, leading up to an arrest. However, he recognized his disadvantage as the bartender changed frequently and so did the inhabitants. A glance at his watch signaled him to hustle.

Before departing the office he had changed. Now, in his Bermuda shorts, blue Dodger tank top, sock-less sandals, his look blended with the environment of the liquid docks. The door squeaked on rusty hinges, there were holes in the thin metallic screen, and the bar inside was empty, except for two scantily clad skuzzy looking women sitting at a table in the corner, suddenly ogling his body, toes to head to toes. The bartender was a stranger to him. However, luck was on his side for the first time as the bartender recognized Spiller from Thumper's glossy.

"That's Roy Spiller, alright. Somewhat younger, a bit more flattering, but that's him. He's a patron here. It's bin weeks since I've personally seen him."

The bartender continued to use his soiled rag to wipe beer glasses, soldierly lining them up for the anticipated rush as he and Axel conversed about Roy. "Is it unusual for Spiller to not be seen or not be present for weeks?"

"Nope, sometimes I don't see him for longer stretches. He just doesn't come in for some time. And then you see him a whole lot. Roy gets around. He re-locates up and down the beaches."

"You wouldn't happen to know where I could find Roy or where he resides?" Confidently he pointed to a group of young men sitting outside under a picnic table awning sipping tall alcohol coolers. "You best ask them about Roy. They're some of his best buds."

Cautiously, Axel moved outside onto a weathered wooden creaky patio, decked in wooden chairs and reinforced plastic tables with sweeping bodacious umbrellas. As he approached the group, silence suddenly swept over them as they each took time to inspect him. After a perfunctory assessment, greetings were ventured to the group of seven. Axel identified himself.

"Please excuse my intrusion. My name is Axel Hawk. I'm urgently trying to locate a Mr. Roy Spiller to resolve an important personal issue. I want you to know that I am not an undercover policeman and Roy is not wanted for any crime. Roy has not broken any laws. As a matter of fact, I can honestly state that finding Roy Spiller will precipitate a joyous event for some individuals. I'd appreciate some help."

They confessed, as they exchanged banter amongst them, that Roy had not been seen for two weeks. They cast suspicious glances toward Axel but, above all, sought approval for their actions from a brazen-haired muscular young man in his early thirties, as if he were the leader of this pack. His body language was the cue for each of their participation and responses to end.

One of the men casually remarked, "Roy stashes his possessions at a homeless hangout under a beach bridge up the coast road. You might check there." At this remark, the one that Axel perceived as the leader displayed an expression of disapproval on his face, obviously at the apparent blunder of the other male. So the brazen Aryan stood up, feeling suddenly compelled to take charge and intersect Axel by the arm, to lead him away from the others. So he did.

"My name is Katz, with a K and a Zee; an abbreviation for Katztritus."

"Axel Hawk, pleasure to meet you." His grip was firm. Katz directed him back through the bar and out to the parking lot. After a coaxing, Katz admitted, "Yes, I know Roy Spiller real well. We all do, but I am closer to him. Now, you are sure this conversation isn't going to land him in trouble?"

"Not at all Katz. I need to find Roy for a friend. Trust me, I am representing his best interests. When I locate him, he will be darn relieved to see me and I will be ecstatic to see him. That's all that I can reveal right now, except to emphasize the absolute urgency to locate him. I sure would appreciate your assistance and presence to inspect his hangout. Perhaps, together we could find some clues to his whereabouts." Katz inhaled heartily, peered skyward, giving the request some thought. Axel remained patient.

Katz's voice was high-pitched. "Okay, I'll escort you to our outdoor hostel. But I need your word that you won't reveal Roy's living place, nor bring any authorities, nor direct any authorities there. They hassle us you know. We have nowhere to go. They'll get tough until they eventually evict us. We're not troublemakers, I promise. I don't think that Roy is there now, but we'll go together to be sure."

"You have my word, Katz. I mean no harm for Roy. I'll state again that I only have his best interests at heart."

They sealed their trust without returning to make further introductions to the remainder of the group. Axel noted that the fingers of Katz were adorned with multiple rings and he had a sole tattoo of a multi-colored serpent on his right shoulder. He guessed that he frequently lifted weights from his perfect muscle tone in his arms and bulging chest. They departed, with Katz seeming eager to show the way and end this. There Axel was, back in the familiar setting of his vehicle, riding up the Pacific Coast Road again, only this time with Katz as guide to the first clues of Roy's whereabouts.

Katz had two-day-old, blonde bristles dotting his cheeks, was well dressed in a brief Khaki shirt and tight pants. He was basking in the limelight, enjoying the thrill of the ride as Axel darted in and out of traffic, the turbulence rearranging Katz's thick bleached blonde hair. With music reveling, the prestige of occupying a seat in a red Mustang Cobra impressed Katz, his right arm out the vehicle, head held high speaking fondly about Roy to Axel as they glided.

"I have known Roy for over two years. We are soul mates, and we have shared an overabundance of life expanding experiences together. I can say that of all Roy's friends I'm about the closest. He disappears for lengthy periods of time, but there is always one constant, and that is that he returns," and now he surprised Axel. "Roy always comes back with a big payday that he graciously shares with all his friends." Katz motioned to a parking lot a few hundred feet ahead. Axel took the left turn toward the ocean and propped the top up on his convertible as he espied sultry types observing them.

Katz was in motion and seemed eager to cooperate. From here they hiked hundreds of yards along the beach, behind dated buildings and warehouses, their path sometimes intersecting the lather of breaking waves, until they reached a bridge and cement embankment, which was more of a preventive measure to control washouts, than to provide access for a stream into the Pacific. They shimmied down an unconsolidated, silty bank into a mucky depression.

Axel noticed the foul odor here as he spied heaps of rotten seaweed, shredded litter, and refuse in shallow standing water in puke colored pools. They proceeded under the bridge where the stench proved to be a relief in comparison to the outside depression. Katz led Axel around a maze of shopping carts, traffic cones, metal refuse, blankets, hampers, large cardboard boxes, eventually to the deep belly of the cave. Here the pounding was deafening, as the backside of the cave was sealed and exposed to the constant buzzing of traffic overhead. The entire adit ended against this steep sealed embankment.

Katz sheepishly stated. "Here they are. It is not much, but these are Roy's total possessions. We are all very modest here, as you can gather. He's got no permanent place to call home, just like the rest of us. We go to the local shelters to shower and to attend to our personal hygiene. You get used to the pounding background traffic noise and to the assortment of odors. When you are down on your luck, it's the simple things that count. Friendship counts the most."

Axel got on his knees in the grungy moist silt to untie the first pile of belongings. It was marked as "Roy's" with a note clipped to a pair of black jeans, which were on top of the pile. There was an abundance of varied sundries. Newspapers. Binders. Plastic bottles, some filled with what appeared to be water. Beside the heap, was a surfboard, adorned in the colors of red, white, and blue, marked with the letters R.S.

In a second pile, there were crumpled stained shirts, two pair of seasoned running shoes with grossly soiled laces, and a third pair with significant holes in the soles. Gingerly, he felt inside each shoe. Nothing. Axel saw a shaving kit. Upon inspection he found that it had bandages, some cologne, a toothbrush, and a dozen dull razor blades. Turning his attention to a large stack of paperbacks, noting each title, Katz provided commentary. "Our communal library. Roy owns them but shares them with us. We use the honor system when we borrow them."

Axel picked up a weather-beaten backpack. He rummaged through it to find only more soiled clothing with abundant greasy socks. How could people possibly exist like this? He turned his attention to the literature again, thumbing through each book. They were largely mainstream mystery and adventure novels.

"His money is not there."

"Pardon?"

"His money. Roy's money. He usually stashes it in one of his paperbacks. This time I am holding it for him."

"Oh." Axel drew a start. A scantily clad muscular drifter appeared at the entrance to the underpass. Katz's body movements conveyed disappointment. Slowly he made his way to intercept the intruder to draw his attention away from Axel. Axel realized that his position, deeply submerged under the bridge, was disadvantageous. The twosome seemed engaged in intense conversation and Axel was unable to overhear the dialogue with the incessant buzzing of traffic above. The second man was now waving his arms at Katz, seemingly unhappy. He placed his hands on hips as Katz obviously scolded him in return.

Axel turned away. He had to work quickly. A shoebox behind all the other contents beckoned attention. Inside were more paperbacks but in better condition. He leafed through the top one, flipping the pages. Nothing. Now a second one. A piece of paper with the name Jenna and a phone number was in the third. He slipped the paper into his pocket.

In a small black book with numbered unlined pages, was a page with three seven digit numbers; phone numbers perhaps? He removed the page by carefully ripping it out. Just as he pocketed it, he saw a set of photos clipped together, obviously capturing sudsy highlights of a festive evening. Roy was in all the photos; Katz in most. They were sharing pleasant social contact at what he guessed might be the Golden Parrott Bar.

He deposited two clear prints of Roy and Katz in his shirt pocket making sure not to bend them, but sealing them by closing the button. Further examination of the books was fruitless; nothing else of interest in the shoebox. Accidentally, he dropped the box and it tumbled over. Presto. A white hard plastic card key was taped to the underside of the box. He dropped to his knees and removed it and buried it in his pants pocket. Quickly, he stood and moved out from underneath the moist stinky adit. Katz and his friend were sitting on a cement plug in the middle of a slim stretch of sand a hundred yards away, sharing a what Axel perceived, by odor, to be a joint.

Axel approached. "Katz, how much money did Roy leave you?"

"Eighty-seven dollars."

"Can I see it, please?" He stretched his hand out as a sign for Katz to place it in his palm.

Axel played a hunch. He had dealt with vagrants before in his business. Axel's face lit up. On one of the ten dollar bills was another seven digit number, so Axel committed it to memory. "Thanks," and he returned it to Katz. He had a name, Jenna, her phone number, and perhaps four other phone numbers and a card key. He had waited long enough for Katz to introduce his pal.

"Hi, I'm Axel Hawk."

"My name is George," the husky man replied in a surly slurred tone denoting his displeasure with the search. George was clean shaven, late twenties, long wavy brunette hair in place behind a receding hairline and tied into a bun. Displaying a rich creamy tan, he wore pressed shirt and shorts. Bodybuilding might also be his specialty.

"Friend of Roy's?"

"Yes, we all are. We like Roy. You need to find him?"

"Immediately. I told Katz that I sure could use some help. Do you know where he might be?"

"No." George was not cooperating. After a silence, Axel ploughed in.

"Maybe you could give me a list of Roy's other friends and his other hangouts?"

"He could be anywhere up to thirty miles north or all the way to Sandy Point in the south, so take your pick."

"Anywhere else?"

George looked at Axel curiously. "Are you with M?"

Axel was excited. Another clue. Was M a co-incidence? Or not? "Pardon?"

"You are not with M?" Axel looked puzzled but pleased as Katz pried his elbow forcing him away from George and insisting that they walk together back to the parking lot. The expression in Katz's face told him that George had just completed a faux pas.

Out of George's earshot, Axel interrogated. "Katz. I need your help. Obviously, you didn't want me to know of M. But George let it out, so I'm going to ask you and I want an answer. Who is M?"

"Oh, George shouldn't have said that. George's man of the week. He is enjoying himself. Did you notice his new shirt?"

"Now, you've really lost me. You're the one that informed me that you are all down on your luck. But George has a new shirt. I also noticed that you were on your third round of libations back at the Golden Parrot. You have some explaining to do. Best start at the beginning."

They finally halted out of sight from George. "I'll cross into your territory. I'll believe that you are trying to locate Roy for his best interests. So, I will inform you that Roy has a mysterious benefactor. We, his friends, are beneficiaries. We all refer to the benefactor person as M. Once and awhile, Roy ups and treats us to a damn good meal. Corrals everyone on the beach, the homeless that is and we go and have a seafood orgy. Sometimes we check into a decent motel if the weather is rainy." He laughed gregariously. "Not for an orgy. Don't get the wrong idea. For rest and relaxation and cable television and comforts we cannot afford, like say a soaking hot shower."

Katz's tone denoted his ultimate respect for Roy. "Roy, he has a big heart. He's our most respected and most valuable resident on the beach. Everybody knows Roy; everybody loves Roy. Always a smile, always generous, always willing to share his new loot with us, that's Roy. What's his is ours. We can't argue with him. He shares his good fortune with his friends and we're all so close. But lately there are more friends, so he initiated Man of the Week, or as two months ago, Lady of the Week."

Axel wanted the bottom line. "Meaning?"

"Rather than treating us all, why ole Roy would just chose one of us to bestow his good fortune on. That way no one gets insulted if they miss out on a feast or a motel room. This is George's week and he is excited. Actually, until Roy returns, George is Man of the Week and that's been for two weeks now."

"Roy gave him money for new clothes, new shoes, food, and a motel room for four nights at the BeachComber," and he pointed to a rundown mauve colored motel barely visible to the north. "Roy also bestowed extra cash to treat his friends. Roy set this all up before he went away last time. He finalizes all the arrangements before he disappears."

"Disappears? You don't know where he is?"

"Nope."

"Take a guess."

"Honestly, I don't know and nor does anyone else."

"Has anyone seen him over the last two weeks? Think hard."

"No."

"Roy sounds popular."

"He's a god. We miss him when he is away because he is the only one with a steady source of substantial income," and he clarified, "substantial by our standards, that is. The rest of us wash dishes, do seasonal work in stores, mostly in the backrooms like unpacking, sweeping. Don't get me wrong. I keep mentioning Roy's income but, to be honest, Roy has a sincerity about him, and an aura of intelligence that is absent in others. It sets him apart. When we have the tiniest chance to re-pay him, we do."

Katz was on a roll. "He shares his wealth, what little he has, and for that we are all in his debt. When we earn wages, Roy is the first one that we look to treat. Payback time. You know. Keep your brethren happy."

"Tell me about M." Axel made the connection from M to Montilladan, rightly or wrongly. Katz needed a prompt. "Please. I can't reveal my true motives, Katz, but you have to believe in me when I tell you that I am representing

Roy's best interests. I am determined to locate Roy Spiller." Katz peered up and down the beach before he replied.

"We don't really know that much about M and that's because Roy never tells us much about M and we never ask. He only referenced her a few times. He specifically asked us never to repeat "M". We took an oath. George shouldn't have done that."

Axel caught Katz's slip. "You just referred to M as her. M is a woman? Perhaps a girlfriend?"

"Probably, well, yes, well, no, I mean that's what Roy leads us to believe that M is a woman. But never referred to her as his girlfriend. Well, I guess I should, I can trust you; tell you that Roy did tell me once and only once, and that M and he had become intimate. Since Roy is not gay, like some of us, I inferred M is a female." George was suddenly in sight so Katz yelled and motioned to George. "George! Come here!"

George sauntered down the beach, hands in pockets, feet dragging, kicking up sand more than once until he reached the twosome. He definitely had an attitude. His inflection, his hostile facial expressions, his long pauses between words, his lack of eye-to-eye contact all irritated Axel. Reluctantly, George recited his account about Roy's other life, after a second scolding from Katz.

"Roy had a few too many drinks one night and informed me that he was earning more money as a stunt double and some rich broad, name of M, and some studio was funding his jobs, getting him the work with her connections in the film industry. Roy even told me that he travelled to sets in New Mexico, Texas, and Vancouver, Canada. He told me that he was being compensated for performing dangerous feats."

"On a movie set? Correct? Not television?"

"Yeah. A couple of times he mentioned a film set and movie making."

Axel was elated. "Where do I find this rich broad, M?"

Katz spoke up. "Honestly don't know. Somewhere in the vast network of Hollywood. I want to go on your record of stating how much I appreciate Roy's generosity." George rambled on and came to some pertinent information. "Hey Katz, remember the night at the BeachComber Motel when Roy got seriously drunk—we all did—and he was not lying around or passed out but, in his drunken stupor, got mad at us, stood in the middle of the motel room, and screamed that if anyone of us ever dared to follow him, to see where he went to, to identify the location of his gigs, he would sever all our relationships? And he kept saying, *Got it? Got it? Get it?*" It was the only time I ever saw him irritated."

Katz interrupted George. He turned deadly serious. "We spread the word about what Roy said. Didn't we George?" George agreed. "Nobody tails him when he heads off; don't inquire about M from Roy anymore. Katz and I sometimes insure that no one else trails him either."

"Does Roy ever mention any family?"

"You are looking at them."

"I mean outside the cave? Outside California?"

"No!"

"Ever mention that he lived in Miami?"

Katz was quick. "No, Roy Spiller was born, and raised here in California, mostly in Orange County and Ontario. Is Roy in some kind of trouble and you're hiding it from us?"

"I hope not, but I need to find him. You must put the word out on the beach discreetly. Can you do that for me? I'll check back with you, say, in two days."

George asked, "You a private eye?"

Axel decided to be honest. "Yes."

"Just like on television?"

"Not exactly. In my line of work real people can get killed. Plus I don't carry a gun." He handed George and Katz each a business card. Katz was curious. "If you are A for Axel, who is Z?"

"Zoe Burns, my partner. Look guys, if Roy returns, it is imperative that you ask him to contact Zoe and me soonest about an important personal matter. You two also have to promise me, that if anyone else comes a calling or snooping for Roy, anyone, that you will obtain their names, get their business cards, and contact Zoe or myself right away. This is very important. If I'm not there, you have to confide in Zoe. Do we have a deal?"

George grinned. "For a coupla' twenties." Katz scolded him, but Axel was already reaching into his pocket to reward them with forty dollars each. "Consider this a small token of my appreciation and a small price for bonding." Axel shook George's hand and turned to Katz.

"Katz, let's talk privately." Katz followed in tow as Axel made his way back to his Mustang where he dared to venture into more dangerous territory.

"Katz, you have to trust me even though we just met. I keep telling you that I have Roy's best interests at heart. Can you believe me? Because without George's faux pas, I would have never have known of M."

Katz hesitated, examined Axel head to foot to head but submitted. "Okay."

"I need some answers. Can you tell me if Roy had any permanent or occasional lovers?"

"I can answer that one conclusively. Roy Spiller does not have any male lovers as I stated previously. He has plenty of male friends, some gay friends, like me and George, but old Roy leans toward women. He is definitely a lady's man! He treats women with respect." He looked to the heavens. "As for female lovers, he only had one interest of permanency and that was with Debbie and she split."

"Last name?"

"Smith."

"Great. Where to?"

"San Francisco, to live on the streets, about um…six to eight months ago."

"Do you think that Debbie found out about M? About Roy's intimacy with M?"

"I can't say. I kept out of Roy's love affairs."

"What does Debbie look like?"

"Oh, she is tall, thin, average body, extremely dark tan, very low key, very uninspiring, a low talker. Hmm…she has three tattoos on her left ankle and lower leg."

"Why did she relocate?"

"Found some other guy; first name of Bart, I think. She has choppy, brunette, long hair and always wore bulky metal earrings, usually gold or brown or copper colored."

"Age? Born here?"

"Oh she was about twenty-five or twenty-six, and I don't know where she was born. I can only tell you that she had a crush on Roy and then—boom—she left without saying goodbye to him. She blended in with the crowd here, but we never knew she would suddenly lose interest in Roy." Axel had an idea shoot into his mind.

"Did she ever get any acting jobs? A long shot, but do you think she ever had film set gigs? Or acting out other persons on a set?"

"Not that she ever mentioned to me. If she was connected to the film industry she kept it a secret. The only jobs she ever had when we knew her, was here in Huntington, at fast food places."

"Did Roy ever mention any out of town shoots other than the three mentioned previously? Like overseas? International travel to Europe?"

"I think he mentioned New Orleans twice and San Diego in addition to what George said. There could be others, given that he was gone for a month but never mentioned sets in Europe."

"And you were led to believe that M paved the way for his stunt gigs?"

"As far as I know."

"Did Roy drop any clues as to where he might have met M? Any ideas at all where I can look for M? Let your mind run wild."

"Sorry, Axel, I don't have a single guess or idea."

"Thanks, Katz, you have been a great help."

They shook hands, Katz left, and once Katz and George were out of sight and walking into the city blocks, Axel scampered up the beach and under the bridge to take one last look, noting the litter, the ugly collection of personable belongings, trying not to overlook any item of significance outside Roy's piles. By the time he re-emerged, the beach strip was cluttered with a group of surfers eyeing the ebbing tide.

He scaled the culvert solo, running away, entering his Mustang to speed down the beach road heading south. No sign of the two. He intersected the east bound expressway heading toward Fosse's. On his way, he left a message for Nikki to call and surfed the dial until he found a modern rock station where Bruno Mars was crooning.

Zoe was just departing the police station when Axel reached her on her cellular. "I hate to say this to you Zee, but I almost wished I had found Roy to prove that Lacey is an out and out liar. Roy is everyone's friend on the beach, a regular hero, verging on cult status. But the truth is that there is no trace of him. He hasn't been seen for weeks. His pals confirm that he has been earning some significant money from working as a stunt double on film stages, and involved with a mysterious female, known as, get this, M. Intuition tells me that M is Montilladan; intuition tells me that Roy is lying six feet under. What a shame Zee. He's next to sainthood in this beach nation."

"Do we tell Tinker?"

"Hell, no, we require absolute proof of Roy's death or M's crime or someone else's crime. Hey I've got to pull over." He reached into his pockets. "Can you call Thumper for us and ask him to trace these local telephone numbers. At least, I think that they're telephone numbers." He proceeded to call out each one out to Zoe as he searched for any signs of a Mitsubishi Eclipse in his rear view window. He finished and hung up.

Meanwhile, it was apparent that the rush hour of L.A. was going to be a problem to return to the office, so he stuck to his original plan to head to Fosse's Bar. On the radio, Sugarland was belting out the warmth of "Tonight" but, inside, he felt cold and thought he had better tighten security.

Soon, he was moving at a constant five miles an hour in condensed sardine-packed traffic. He emitted a snort as a chuckle. Surrounded by women on this case and not managing any of them very well. The affair with Nikki was over. A recent hormone attack was diverting energy toward Zoe, with their relationship stuck in neutral. He had a lifelong crush on Lacey Sills. Experiencing her in the flesh had first stimulated him before he was surprised by her sexual tendencies. Yet, he found her overwhelmingly magical, even in possession of the new information.

M was a perplexing character. A trickster extraordinaire, half man, half woman. Even if Roy was in that grave, was Montilladan M? Then what of Mrs. Whitehurst, a witch for all seasons. What did she know of Lacey's love affair? And M's disappearance? Could Mrs. Whitehurst really turn him into a toad? How would he win her over? Axel was disappointed. He knew in the end Mrs. Whitehurst had to be converted to an ally. He was anxious to meet the Colonel. Now two new names, Jenna and Debbie Smith. Was his mind running too amuck to believe that Debbie could have been in disguise as Montilladan on that fateful morning? An act of jealous revenge? Such a collection of woman in this case. All different; all memorable; perhaps some, dangerous.

At a red light, he tapped his fingers on the top of his steering wheel in syncopation to the jazzy beat. To his right, a soft blue convertible pulled up and the women, blonde hair tied up with a scarf, adorning snug dark sunglasses, directed the faintest smile at him without breaking her lips apart, and looked away. Axel drew a chill from her smirk. "But why?" he pondered.

So, you are Axel Hawk. What a pleasure to meet you. I will stare directly into your eyes, but you cannot see mine. They are not for you to see. I see your hazel colored peepers, notice your tanned skin, feel your confidence and aura shining into my space. I suppose you think you are an indestructible male specimen. What are you up to? What has that bitch got you doing? Why are you traversing the beach roads? Why are you snooping around Roy Spiller's former haunts? What are you up to? You are so naïve.

As the light turned red, she discontinued her examination; she exited into a right turn and broke contact.

Surfing the airways again, he stumbled onto Frank Sinatra bellowing out, "Luck be a Lady Tonight." Just my luck.

MONDAY NIGHT

Just as the chili dogs had reigned in a fit of indigestion, so now the pepperoni pizza was suffering a similar fate. Bountiful excuses had been self-created to justify a deviation from his healthy diet. "Tomorrow," he reminded himself, "I gotta return to the health kick."

The liquids he had consumed all afternoon had not been adequately retained by his bladder, so they passed through him in a sea of expectorant at the first stop at Fosse's Tavern. This case was in infant stages but already complex. There was a sea of tender twitching muscles in his stomach.

It was now a little past eight. Since the encounter with Lacey earlier, there had been further complications with a few quick wins. He wasn't praying for Roy's death, but Roy's fate was quickly becoming inevitable. The fact of confronting the Whitehursts was inescapable, perhaps on their own turf, perhaps tomorrow. There had to be more gleaned from another private conversation with Nikki.

Zoe and he were at an extreme disadvantage. All of these thoughts were causing him to be absorbed in mental gridlock. They needed to launch an intense offensive in a quest for facts in order to try to gain an equal footing with the dark forces omnipresent in this mystery.

Begrudgingly, Zoe and he would soon have to confide in Tinker soon as some of the conclusions in Tinker and Felix's report became falsehoods at the expense of their thorough investigation. Once again, Felix would be pissed. They needed to bring Kathleen Whitehurst into their confidence. What was she hiding? What did she know?

Sitting in a dimly lit corner table of the tavern tonight, he continued to mull over all of these details, revisiting some of them as many as three times. Some of Charlie's customers, new to the pub, resented the fact that they could not penetrate proximity to the alcove, speculating what made these two people—she, thin, dressed in black blouse and tight black leather pants, and he, looking like a handsome relic of the Beach Boy era—so special that they could command a presence of two at a choice table for six, and in the alcove, and on a busy evening.

Axel analyzed Charlie at work. Such a smooth operator with a personality fit for exactly this role. Zoe noticed his gaze and probed. "How and when did you first meet Charlie?"

"Many years ago, Zee, so long that I am not sure that I recall the exact year. I was wrapping up a case for a client, before you joined forces with me, driving in this neighborhood, and stumbled in for a solo drink at the bar. Coincidently, the Dodgers were playing a big pennant deciding game. Charlie and I discovered that we both played high school baseball here in L.A., both grew up loving Dodger blue, although I spent my early youth in Oklahoma, and it took off from there. The conversation that Charlie and I had that evening inspired an everlasting relationship. By midnight we were challenging each other to Dodger baseball trivia." As he made eye contact with Charlie, Charlie himself was reminiscing about all the business that Axel and Zoe had secured for him and the fun-loving respectable types and young professionals they had lured into his establishment.

Charlie thought, as he returned Axel's stare, *This is one of Axel's domains. Here at Fosse's, he is respected, even on the verge of being idolized by some of his friends. Any investigation referenced in the press or in the news has provided a huge opportunity for embellishment at Fosse's. Back in their office he could candidly converse with Zoe over moments of frailty or weaknesses in their cases but not here. This is Axel's kingdom.* Charlie was summoned to the end of the bar by a stranger.

"Over the years, Zee, I have regarded this establishment as my second home. Female friends often seek me out at this bar; male friends chose to argue over vital sports trivia with me or analyze the latest game. As you know, I am always eager to participate in any debate of sports, politics, current events, and entertainment, a reflection of my voracious appetite for current events. I especially love to beat up Sparky mentally."

But while speaking the right words to her, he knew that changes were in the air. He was breaking rules again tonight, for he was sitting in Fosse's Tavern examining his insecurities prior to her arrival. His mood tonight was one on the verge of brooding. There was so much to make sense of, so little time for catching up to the defining truths, so little precious time to find Montilladan. He tilted his stein and sipped the pale amber ale of Fosse's microbrewery.

On the other side of the round table, Zee tasted her Californian Cabernet. Her velvet voice tones soothed his anxiety as they sat in this dim recess. Staring at her, he was reminded again of how appreciative he was of her efforts, her astute contributions to the firm. In the past, he had hogged all the press interviews, attended functions on their behalf. Now it was her time to shine. Just as he had changed the name of the firm to A to Z one year ago by incurring legal fees, it was time to relinquish more responsibility to her. He hoped that she would recognize it as a vote of confidence and not as another attempt to win her feelings.

Or was he kidding himself? he pondered. He had to reconcile how honest his intentions really were. Was it her affection or her abilities that had earned these step changes? Somehow he knew that he was going to have to present business arguments to substantiate his position.

Zee reached across the table and tugged his shirt. "Hey? Are you listening? Earth to Axel. I look into your dreamy hazel eyes and I can't help but believe that you are ignoring my speech of the last minute. It was a helluva great oration following your tale of bonding with Charlie. Tell me what I said."

"Did you know Zee, that most men have up to forty sexual fantasies a day? They obviously don't participate in my line of work where daily mental frenzies occupy the mind not sexual dreams. But I have a much easier routine. I save up my fantasies. I come to Fosse's with you to have a singular focused fantasy about you for forty minutes. It's so much easier to fit it all into my schedule. Easier on the mind, the body and a great time management tool! One fantasy for forty minutes."

She slapped him hard with the backside of her hand on his forearm, as she leaned over the table.

"This is not healthy for our relationship, Axel."

"What?"

"You know damn well what! The fact that you keep giving me the hints that you are falling for me. The timing is all wrong. We are business partners. This is the most perplexing and challenging assignment that we have ever undertaken. We need to be as focused as we have ever been. Not to mention the fact that we need to operate at light speed. I'm giving you some great advice, Axel. Burn calories on the solving the mystery, not on admiring me and fantasizing about us!" Axel prepared a rebuttal but to no avail.

"Axel, I am serious. We need the company of each other more than any previous case, but not for love and sex, so switch gears, Axel Hawk, please. I mean it! I feel dreadfully insecure about our new undertaking and your recent advances grossly complicate matters. This Montilladan case gives me the creeps. You and I both know this could be a premeditated murder case."

"What? No love and sex?" She reached over with a Manila folder to clobber him again. At the bar, Charlie noticed the interaction, interpreting Zoe's reaction to mean that Axel was once again making unsuccessful advances toward Zee. He chuckled out loud. Since Axel was facing him, Charlie read Axel's facial patterns. It was not going well for him. It never did.

Charlie recalled the night of three months ago, same table, same night of the week, same play. On that occasion, Axel slyly positioned his arm around Zoe. He observed the master in motion, capturing Zoe's attention, encroaching into her territory until she nailed him with a black binder. He loved them both, his two dear friends.

Zoe was animated. "We need to be alert, responsive, and smart! Analytical! Energetic! This case is overwhelming and it's only the first day. The data that

Lacey spewed out for us this morning defines a caper never been accomplished in Hollywood's history."

"Keep your voice down. I concede, Zoe. However, I want to tell you something. I don't want you to take it the wrong way." She relaxed.

"My appreciation for you has blossomed. I depend on you, I trust you and you have flourished into someone that I love and respect. You've matured right in front of my eyes these last four years. You are so very special to me, why hell, you've even gained a whopping three and a half pounds. I see you every day and I don't even know where you've put it!"

Zoe interrupted. "Remember the first time we met, Axel?"

"Larry's Roadhouse, July fourth weekend, I think six years ago. I asked you to dance."

Zoe laughed. "And you also said that I probably had to run around in the shower to get wet."

"Oh, don't remind me. I'm surprised that you considered even talking to me after that doozy."

"I must admit, you were a challenge. A reclamation project extraordinaire however, I am always up to a challenge, so I joined forces."

She turned her head to look back toward the end of the bar, "Speaking of challenges, I've noticed that you have had your eye on that hot little platinum number at the end of the bar since she entered."

"I have not."

"Oh, yes, you have. The evidence is conclusive because you flashed that goofy look more than once since she arrived."

"Zoe, gimme a break with the look. She's not my type."

"So, you have spied and analyzed her and so have I; and physically she is bloody spectacular, and she is every man's type, Axel Hawk. No matter what her name or shoe size is, hormones spring into action when gals like that sit alone at Fosse's bar."

"Did you read the police report on the accident?"

"Go ahead, change the topic." Zoe reached into her monstrous black leather tote bag to withdraw a small brown envelope and tossed it in front of him. "I captured notes on the flash inside this envelope."

"Axel, Lacey won't like how this case is progressing. M is being implicated in a crime of murder. When do we tell her?"

"Zoe, our job is to locate Montilladan. When we do, we will divulge to our client first, and then Tinker and Felix. We accumulate any evidence that makes M guilty or not. If and when there is overwhelming conclusive evidence of murder, and then we inform Tinker. Until then we have nothing to report since it is all circumstantial."

Zoe embellished on her activities of the afternoon. "There is nothing in the police files that we don't already know. I also found time to venture to the studio to interview the two technicians. It was just as Tinker conveyed to us. They both swear that they witnessed Montilladan inspect the balcony hours before the shoot commenced, early in the morning." She directed Axel to the testimony.

"They both got an excellent unobstructed view at the individual and both swear that they were close enough to the person to conclusively identify him as Montilladan, the actor. Montilladan even waved a good morning at them. Later, they both witnessed the fall of Montilladan to his death by smashing his skull on the concrete. They witnessed him die instantly. The testimony of these two witnesses looms large in the police verdict of accidental death in that, number one, they inspected the balcony and found it firm, and number two, Montilladan inspected it subsequently."

"Did either of them see Montilladan with a wrench or any kind of tool?"

"No, they both agreed that he appeared to checking and not tampering, although you and I suspect differently. Everyone on that set, according to the statements that the police took, believes that it was an accident. There are sworn statements from all of the witnesses, including dancers, extras, prop men, producers, cameramen, et cetera, et cetera. Everyone believes that Montilladan is buried at Forest Haven Cemetery. Case closed. The police report is very mundane reading; the interviews that I conducted likewise. I prepared an executive summary for you of the police report, but it has no great revelations. Take time to pop the flash into your computer soon."

As Axel absorbed her summation, Zoe continued. "The two technicians are still in mourning, since they were directly responsible for the safety on the set. I interviewed the co-star of the film, Jason Court." Zoe perked up. "I kept it strictly platonic dear Axel, no rush of female adrenaline. Poor Jason, he is on a guilt trip since he pushed Montilladan. The director Givens was coincidentally at the set today, working on another project. He sobbed as I heard his recount of that dreadful day. The status of the film is in jeopardy since they had only shot fifty percent of the scenes with Montilladan's required presence. Everyone at the studio is still drenched in sorrow. It was a very depressing site. The physical investigation of the set has been completed by authorities, so the set was disassembled." Zoe continued.

"While I was at the studio, I also took the liberty to delve into something that has been bothering me about Lacey's testimony."

"Which is?"

"In our attempt to reconcile the facts of this tale, I wondered how Roy got away with imitating Montilladan's voice. Did he deliver it perfectly?"

"And?"

"Lacey was right. The times when Roy substituted must have been during scenes of restricted dialogue, such as the ball and fight scene. In addition, both technicians and Givens confirmed that Montilladan on the set was a specimen of very few words. Socially, he opened up, but Givens swore to me that M was an introvert at the studio. So, I guess with voice coaching by Montilladan, Roy got by imitating M's voice."

Axel opened the envelope and deposited the flash into his shirt pocket. "Okay, so the police report is boring. Did you uncover anything that Tink and Felix didn't? Anything startling? Anything unusual?"

She smirked. "I was waiting for you to ask." She leaned into him. "Stu Givens and I met in his private room." She lowered her voice. "He told me that Montilladan's death couldn't have been more untimely."

"Why?"

She leaned over and whispered. "Axel, Givens conveyed to me that the studio was so sure that Sweet South Sherry was going to be a blockbuster hit that they had already commissioned the author, Florrie Greene, to write a sequel. And, get this! The production studio had already offered Montilladan and Givens some outrageous monetary contracts, loaded with bonuses, to star in and direct the sequel, one of the greatest cash packages ever afforded to any actor-director team. This a result of their sure fire first hit."

Axel was puzzled. "No kidding. So, if M really did commit the pre-meditated murder of Roy Spiller, she did so wittingly and knowingly that she was walking away from one of the biggest pay days ever in Hollywood. Are you sure M knew of this package? Or only Givens?"

"They both knew. Givens confirmed it to me. The studio presented the offer with both present at a meeting a few days ago. So, kind of makes you believe that our theory that she murdered Roy might be flawed. Surely, M could wait for one more bonanza. It scares me, Axel. Reality check. Why would M do that Axel? It doesn't make any sense to walk away from guaranteed millions."

"I don't know. Givens' comments sure complicate the situation don't they? Logic, greed and ego would dictate that she didn't murder Roy. Just like you said. Who in his right mind walks away from a short term future payoff of guaranteed millions? What else?"

"Found out another tidbit of info." She winked at him and raised her thin black eyelids. "One of the two technicians took me aside before I left. He claims that Montilladan showed up late for filming two weeks ago and blamed it on nausea. The investors of the film and the production chiefs of Sweet Sherry South were on the set, and they accused M of showing up drunk, and disorderly, again; one of the investors of the studio even accused Montilladan of being under the influence of drugs. A heated, verbal altercation ensued until Stu Givens arrived to disentangle the mess and bring cooler heads to bear. The technician overheard Givens warn Montilladan to get control of his drug and alcohol problems or he would ruin the future for both of them. How's that for juicy gossip?"

"I'd say interesting enough to say, rack it. So, the question Zee becomes, was it Roy or Montilladan who was showing up incapacitated on the set?"

"What about Spiller's habits?"

"I'll have to give it a few more days. We need absolute proof of his death, which can't be concretely proven by his absence. But the indirect evidence is mounting."

After a sigh, Axel admonished, "I was very moved by the testimony of two of Roy's friends, Katz and George. Spiller is a very precious commodity on the beach. I never heard of someone so generous toward the vagrant movement."

"Tell Felix to exhume the corpse!"

"No, Zee. Find Montilladan, that's the answer. We don't have enough evidence yet to ask for an exhumation."

"I knew that you were going to say that Axel. We already have strong suspicions, so I say dig him up!"

"No." She was disappointed, so she announced to Axel more good news. "Tomorrow night we visit the estate of Montilladan in Beverly Hills. It has been sealed since the tragedy, except for a police search and investigation. The lawyers for the estate are preparing an estate sale, per the instructions of the will according to Tinker, so we will need to conduct our examination before the trail grows cold."

Axel grew excited. "I am ready. Thumper has to join us. He can photograph the place while we conduct our thorough search. A tour of Montilladan's sanctuary, mm, how exciting."

In a soft voice, he probed, "I might be distracted with you these days, but somehow, even after our abundant previous talks, I sense that you still aren't letting go of Heather's death."

Axel felt magnetized as he looked into her dark satin eyes, encompassed by those long slender lashes. She whispered. "No. Why do I keep thinking that we could have saved her life? That we were so close?"

"Zoe we weren't! That's the whole point! I've told you over and over. There were no short cuts to her rescue. We did the best that we could. Our best efforts couldn't get us to the scene of the crime any faster. The kidnapper panicked and strangled her. We could not have shaved time from our course of action. You know that!"

"She was so young and beautiful. I close my eyes and see her as one of God's graceful creatures."

"Zee we did our best. I think about Heather, too. When I do, it drives me to the conclusion that this is where I belong- to fight crime and evil wherever it may be, to be contracted by whomever needs to engage our talents. Here we are again. New case; new client; new request; and new villain. It is time to fight evil again. With clear minds and with a clean slate. Zoe and Axel on the trail of evil."

Axel added, "With you by my side, Zee, for I can't do it without you. That's what I was fumbling to say earlier. You and me, we are the A team. No, apologize, I mean, we are the A to Z Team. Partners."

Zoe's dark moist eyes gave away her sadness. "Tinker informed me today that they are no closer to capturing him than two months ago. A monster, a cold-blooded murderer on the loose. Gives me the shivers."

"Our duty to Heather is over. It's the responsibility of the F.B.I. now since his last sighting."

"So, does that mean that you and I have been exorcised?"

"Zoe, you were right earlier when you stated that we need to find focus in this investigation or we perish."

"Right." There was a sniffle as she said that. "For me, I will depart for San Clemente early tomorrow morning to visit the dentist, a Dr. Sorbet."

Axel interrupted. "Sorbet? For real? Hey, do you think that Montilladan could be French derivation?"

"I will ask Sorbet. See if I detect a rise. Next, I have to return to inspect Montilladan's dressing room at the studio. It was locked today with the key conveniently misplaced."

"Aha," Axel retorted, "as Holmes would say, a singular convenient event. Be careful."

"Honest error, my guess. Three, visit Montilladan's bankers. End up with you and Tink and Thumper at M's residence at seven tomorrow night. A full agenda."

Axel felt compelled to reveal his itinerary. "I will pay a visit to Constance and Lieber, M's lawyers in the morning. We had better make sure that we refer to Montilladan as he, and not she. No slips ups. Think before we answer. I came precariously close to blurting out the word her today to Mrs. Whitehurst."

Zoe was animated. "Axel, what great bait! Drop a she here, and a she there, and detect the response. And," she extracted papers from her satchel, "take your pick from this expanded list of frequent contacts that Thumper diligently constructed. It also has the bios of the attendees of the funeral, per your request."

"Hey, this does look different than this morning."

"It is. Thump's been busy. Got it all super organized. There are twenty-two new names of connections. What suits your fancy Axel?"

Axel perused the report for five minutes while she quietly read. He looked up in time to see her graciously hold the wine glass by the stem and take a small sip.

"Why did you ever decide to take such an interest in California wines?"

"It all started many years ago when Annie and I did the road trip through Napa and Sonoma. The stories behind the wines and vineyards captivated me. You know? Soil types, geology, climate, types of grapes and their blends and of course, the history of the families and their vineyards. It's sort of a social thing that binds me to the wine clubs I frequent. I like the great cerebral conversations with the connoisseurs. Plus, I am on the mailing list for wine tasting events that lead me to guys. Ooh, if only you knew about the sophisticated handsome types I meet, like Tom and Emery and Lyall and Jacob and Merrill and…"

"Okay, okay, I get the message. Back to business." Axel zeroed in on one lead in particular. "Wow. I don't believe it. Dr. Renee Montoya, psychiatrist. Wow! Now this I gotta see. Visit this doctor for myself! Montilladan was getting help from a shrink?!"

"Darn you, Axel. I want to interview her. If you hadn't selected her, I would have. I talked to Tinker about her this afternoon since he already interrogated her. Apparently, M was a regular patient. But Tinker turned up very little evidence of use from the doctor. She played the old doctor-patient privilege card more than once with Tink. He discovered Dr. Montoya by finding her business card in M's residence. Dr. Montoya did not reveal anything to Tink about M's treatments. You know as I stated- patient to doctor private relationship."

"Hmmm. But Tinker doesn't know that Montilladan is two people and we do. I'll bet money that Dr. Montoya, the psychiatrist, knows that Montilladan is playing two people." Axel was animated. "How did Thumper find her?"

"Firstly, Montoya and Montilladan sit together on a board of directors of a research firm, medical research that is. I noticed the reference in Tinker's police files. Her card was listed in confiscated belongings."

Zoe laughed hysterically. "She's going to be putty in your hands once you give her that goofy look."

"Will you stop it? Stop embarrassing me. I don't have the goofy look. Even if I did, what the hell would I give it to a psychiatrist for?"

"To break her down, Axel. An intro, Axel. And once you gave her that look," and she contorted her face as she aped it, "you have introduced a powerful conversation piece to break the ice, given her lifelong reasons to analyze you." Zoe mimicked Axel's look this time with severe flinching contortions. Charlie was examining the twosome but had no idea what was transpiring.

Axel was hysterical. As he bellowed, she found it was contagious, holding her hands over her chest. Axel tried to speak.

"If you can't do the look any better than that, don't try it at all. That look should be outlawed. Either you do it correctly as I do, or you Zee, are forbidden to do my look. That's it, I forbid you to do it." He snorted at her.

"I have it down to perfection," she drawled. "It is you that needs more practice," and she posed again for his amusement.

"Oh, behave." Axel regained his composure. "Zoe, back to business, a sobering thought, including you and I and Thumper and Nikki and Lacey and Roy and now possibly the shrink, the list of people who know the secret grows. I think we are going to have to put the hard charge into Dr. Montoya. We've got to find out about Montilladan's instabilities and insecurities."

Zee postulated. "Maybe M was lamenting to her shrink about Romeo. If so, maybe Dr. Montoya is sympathetic. Maybe Dr. Montoya is an accomplice? Maybe, together they are hatching a plan for her to escape from bondage of her male persona and Hollywood career? Maybe together they devised a scheme to unleash her from her male sex character? Either way, Zoe Burns' intuition says watch out."

"Where is her office?"

"In Beverley Hills. While I think of it," and she handed him a small piece of paper, "here's the address for M's residence, and the address for Dr. Montoya's practice. Why don't you let me visit Dr. Montoya? Or let us go together. I really want to meet this doctor."

He was curt. "No. Anyone else catch your attention on this list?"

"Movie producers, artists, chefs, philanthropists, let's split it right down the middle." She proceeded to tear it in half. "You take these eleven. Thumper has constructed excellent profiles, contact information, even emails and cell phones and Facebooks where available."

In a moment of weakness, he blurted out, "Are you seeing Tinker?"

"Axel, it is none of your damn business." She decided to reply as she searched his inquisitive eyes.

"If you insist, I am not dating Tinker. We have lunch on occasions and once a month, we meet for a game of billiards at Crespo's."

"Crespo's? Billiards?"

"Yes, I handle myself very well, thank you."

He felt foolish. "You never cease to amaze to amaze me. I suppose you buy a round of Merlot for the guys at the pool hall."

"I can drink and handle beer if I have to with the guys."

"The guys? Once again, I am sorry I pried into your private life. If you had said yes, though, I would have been extremely jealous of Tinker but, as it is, just foolish."

"Axel, did you not hear a word that I said earlier today? Get focused on this case."

He reached into his pocket to extract a small box, gift wrapped in royal green glossy paper. He placed in the middle of the table, slid it over to her deliberately.

"Axel, have you not heard a word that I have said?"

"It is not what you think, Zee. Go ahead and open it."

Sheepishly, she tore the paper, opened the box, and expressed a pleasant smile while extracting a dainty light onyx necklace.

"Please accept it from me. Happy Birthday, partner."

She moved beside him to the same side of the table, hugged him tightly and smiled with a courteous thank you. "It would mean a great deal if you would wear it for me." She did so, and as he placed it around her neck as she spoke to him.

"I am staying out late in two weeks, on the weekend with some dear girlfriends. We are having an old fashion pajama party to share frustrations, indulge in make-up and wine, re-visit old romances, critique movies, and spin old hits. They're treating me to a birthday dinner first. Annie's organizing it."

"Thirty-one?"

"Don't exaggerate. Thirty years old. I can't stand getting older."

"Older? You are thirty. You have your whole life ahead of you- the most satisfying years, the part that delivers your greatest achievements. What an exhilarating experience for those share it with you."

"That's what I like about you Axel, you are always so upbeat."

"Your thirtieth birthday is one of jubilation. Put Heather Micks' unfortunate death behind you. Be empathetic but not guilt-ridden. You don't deserve to blame yourself."

She quickly changed her tone. Somberly, Zee spoke in a low voice, "She doesn't want to be found, Axel. She has abandoned Lacey. I feel this is all part of a master deceit that she has planned to the nth detail, and the wild card is us, if we dig too deep. Be careful with Dr. Montoya. She may know a great deal more about Montilladan than she would ever want to tell you. She may very well be an accomplice of M's. Her profession by nature commits her to secrecy."

"And you be careful with the dentist, Zee, especially if he is handsome. For me, I think Dr. Montoya ought to have secrets about Montilladan or why else would M seek help, if not to reveal her dilemma to someone who cannot speak of it? However, the doc might inadvertently point us in the correct direction."

"She might also, Axel, pick up the phone and call Montilladan as soon as you leave, exposing our entire operation, thereby, threatening our lives. Lacey's, too. That's what scares me. As long as M doesn't know what we are up to, we have the edge. Lose the edge, lose any element of surprise, we lose our advantage. Promise me that you will be careful."

"Oops," she exclaimed, "I must call Lacey to confirm our next appointment. Oh, darn." As she pounded buttons on her cellular, he guessed that the modern age gadget had failed her.

"My cell is dead. I'll have to go outside to use the charger in my car. I'll lock the police file in the glove compartment at the same time. Be right back. Order me another glass of Cabernet, will you, sweetie?"

She stood, pausing, staring, and admiring him. "Thanks for the necklace. It was very thoughtful of you." She walked over to his chair, leaned over him, put her arm around his shoulder, pulled his head back and toward her, his head now bent up into her smacking wet lips. She held this position with a kiss for ten seconds until the applause in the tavern, initiated by Charlie, reached a crescendo. She posed to let him admire her new adornment, before strolling out with an exaggerated swagger in her hip movements. She stopped to chat with Charlie, show off her new jewelry, pointing to Axel with admiration.

When she kissed him, the burst of day long perfume emanated from her to arouse him. He followed her trim delicate body, swaying to the tavern's blare of the jukebox, "You drive me crazy. Oh, oh, I'm stuck on you." Her mid-section, thin waist as it was, particularly accented the curvy rear end, clad in tight black leather pants. Axel followed her until she passed the platinum blonde visitor, perched alone at the end of the bar. Axel broke for the goal line.

As he approached her, she ignored him, instead fixating her gaze on the icy drink in her hand. "Good evening, I'm Axel. Do you live around here?" Axel positioned himself on the stool next to her.

She inhaled deeply, dragging the smoke from her sweet smelling thins into her being, exhaling with a prolonged jettison of an aromatic cloud hurling toward him.

"I am very sorry, but you won't obtain my address or attention that easily." Two luminous blue eyes popped his way. She had two large freckled breasts on display in a low cut brilliant blue dress, business attire. Adorning her head was clunky jewelry of silver earrings. Her hair was Cleopatra style with a spray to hold every strand of platinum hair in place. At last, she extended her bare arm to him.

"I am Kelly Burston. I just moved into the neighborhood from Chicago. I dropped in here because I heard that this was the place to come to get a great kiss." They touched; he laughed. Her hand was so warm and spongy, her arms a hint of flabbiness. Her eyes were attempting to beam directly to his heart.

"That was Zoe Burns, my business partner."

"I'm sure it is. A lot of kisses are expended in business environment these days. I think a lot of ladies in here envy your business partner. I'm a salesperson for a very large computer software firm. It provides job security these days. I am caught up in the internal cyber revolution and my friends accuse me of being a computer geek, although you might not know that by looking at me." She butted out the cigarette in a tray in front of him, giving her a reason to lean over and move closer.

"It is my pleasure, Kelly. I am Axel Hawk, a private investigator."

"Ooh, really?" She seemed surprised and placed her hand across her breast to exaggerate her reaction. "A real life private investigator? I have never met a private investigator before. I always thought that they existed only for the purpose of selling novels and making hit television shows. However, based on shows that I've seen on television, this is the place to investigate- California! Oodles of people to be investigated here."

"Can I buy you a drink?"

"Axel, it is a pleasure to meet you, but I am nursing this one—see," and she placed a half glass of contents before his face, "and I really have to depart soonest." There was an impish tone in her voice accentuating her alluring mannerisms.

"Will you come here again?"

"Slow down." Kelly laughed before crossing her legs to expose a well-tanned, slim, sleek leg.

"I like you. You are so strong, so handsome, with pitch black hair, a square confident jaw, and oh, that commanding voice. I like dominant men." She leaned over closer and pinched his exposed bare curled enticing bicep. "Wow, that is one, solid, arm muscle."

"Former jock, but I still work out a lot."

Regrettably, the lady apologized. "I really am sorry. I have a commitment tonight. I'm a divorcee, in case you're wondering, and I am expecting company tonight. No males. Just two ladies, local interior decorators, are arriving to assist me in choosing some materials for drapes in my new pad." Her head tilted sexily at an exaggerated degree to stare at him.

"Tomorrow night I should be right here on this bar stool in this same location after work if you are still interested." Kelly Burston rose, slung her oversized purse strap over her shoulder, sipped the remnants of her drink, and bade him farewell. "Same time, same stool."

"Okay, Kelly, I'll perhaps see you tomorrow." As Axel watched her saunter down the aisle in front of the bar to depart, Charlie leaned over to parallel process Hawk's analysis.

"Those hip movements are illegal, Hawk. Arrest her."

"Just hit Zoe and I up for another round Charlie. I need to visit the facility."

"Yeah, go and cool down, Hawkman. By the way, good taste. I mean Zoe's jewelry, that is."

Axel made his way along a dimly lit corridor, turned right, proceeding to the men's room. With only two urinals, two stalls, a sink and trash can, it seemed overly congested when two other large male specimens entered behind him. Axel was just zipping up and turning toward the sink to greet them, when the first blow hit him solidly just below the ribs in the upper part of his stomach. He recalled only the stupid leering grin on the huge man's face as bare white knuckles made swift impact.

A further glance at his assailant registered him as husky, Caucasian, broad shoulders, an ugly scarred face with a black, thick, lousy manicured moustache. No matter what the occasion, Axel's mind had been trained to analyze appearances first.

The pain was excruciating. Before he could recover, a hairy sinewy arm clamped around his neck from behind him, preventing him from a collapse to the floor while at the same time leaving just barely enough space in his windpipe to pass precious oxygen.

Axel wanted to yell but was smothered in pain and extreme suffocation as the arm around his neck tightened to choke him in a paralyzing grip. He opened his eyes to see the fluorescent ceiling lights spinning, and just in time to see the husky one launch his boney fist at the side of his nose.

Blood furiously gushed out over his cheeks, lips, and chin, staining his shirt, the taste of fresh plasma in his mouth. It splattered onto his shorts but was camouflaged in the multi colors. In these last five seconds, he had been transformed from a strong date candidate with sexy Kelly Burston, ex-Chicago, to a helpless cripple. The thug behind him released his grip and Axel, strong as he was, felt as if on a carnival ride of immense G-force with gravity collapsing him downward.

He was unable to retain his balance, so he spiraled onto the floor on his knees. He tried desperately to regain mental composure as nausea swept up his esophagus. He fell, free fall from his knees, to prostrate on the tiled floor. In a microsecond as he fell, he did manage to exhale his first audible plea for help. The third assault arrived. A very large boot crushed his already tender abdomen, rendering him totally debilitated.

Zee left a message for Lacey and followed up with a phone call to Tinker to confirm the time to meet at M's residence tomorrow evening. She was about to place a third call when suddenly the creep of gooseflesh engulfed her shoulders.

Paranoia? Maybe not. As a suburban exited the parking lot, the headlights of the vehicle intersected, panned, and outlined, a silver-gray Mitsubishi Eclipse. The car was inconspicuously setback under an elm tree. It beckoned her. In a second, she dashed toward it, leaping an obstructing metal rail landing directly in front. Quickly, she extracted pen and paper from her purse, jotting down the license plate number. Nervously, her brain sent pangs of distress, as she recalled the scene that she had witnessed in Fosse's a few minutes ago from her vantage point outside. Through the windows into the tavern, Ms. Platinum had pinched his bicep. Zee had noted it, recorded it. *Why would a lady, five minutes from introduction do that? Purposefully move closer and pinch Axel's bicep.* Inquisitive as she was, her detective mind assimilating facts, Zoe rationalized that she could be a sentry and her pinch, the signal for the inhabitants of the Mitsubishi. She had found and identified Axel Hawk for the assailants.

She raced through the swinging doors, toward the bar, bolting in, stern faced, with a look of concern. Ms. Platinum had departed. Where was Axel? With a tilt of his head, Charlie motioned toward the restrooms. She ran hard down the hallway, heart pounding, turning the corner in time to hear the unmistakable plea for help from her dear friend, Axel Hawk.

Instinctively, she knew what had to be done. Dropping her satchel, removing her high-heeled boots, she took a deep breath to regain control of her body. She focused on her combative agility, deciding that an ambush was her best chance, perhaps the only arsenal to save Axel. She reminded herself, "Don't look at the faces. Concentrate on the limbs and soft spots."

She backed down the hall, took seven running steps, as a track artist would in the long jump, snapped the men's room door open with one foot, charging in like a starlet from a Kung Fu movie, leaving the corrugated, bloodied, tiled floor and, in mid-flight over Axel's prostrate body, jerked her right leg into the most vulnerable apparatus of the husky one so hard that her foot ached on contact. While the hulk was on the verge of popping out both his eyes, he grabbed his aching crotch instinctively to protect him from further damage and waved his tongue in the middle of a scream.

Axel saw her as a supernatural spirit, an elixir of rheology, first disabling the larger one in flight, and landing, turning, pivoting immediately into the second, smaller assailant. But this small strongman thrust a punch toward her face. With split second reaction, Zoe in an ideal stance caught the fist confidently, and using both her hands, bowed his arm behind his head, before crashing his head into the tall metal trash receptacle with a crack.

As he turned to face her, crippled, she thrust two taut fingers into a pressure point in the soft, fleshy part of his neck, causing the stout ruffian to appear as if he was choking himself to death, as he grasped his throbbing neck, falling to his knees, gasping for air, unable to converse.

Axel now observed the larger thug on his feet wielding a knife. Zoe had not an advantageous position after her attack on the second one, standing in the far corner with no room to maneuver. Axel was painfully helpless. Or was he?

He noticed that the elbow of the arm that held the knife was perfectly positioned to receive a blow from the closure of the bathroom stall door if he could reach it. From his prone position, he rolled into the adjacent stall, rolled again under the partition, kicked, and drove the door as hard and as swift as he could against the assailant's back of his elbow, causing him to release the knife. Axel knew of their victory as the culprit shrieked to convey defeat.

Zoe exploded. She proceeded to a state of airborne again, kicking the disarmed villain in the ribs with a thrust of her leg as he protected his tender region. The bloodlust expression, from when he had first appeared to Axel, had been wiped clean off his face.

The other one, scurrying sideways as a crab, conceded defeat, departed. Meanwhile, the hulk groveling, hands paused on his knees, growled, and fled. Breathless, Zoe chose to remain behind to comfort Axel as Charlie and others suddenly descended down the hallway. She wiped the bloodied mucous from his face with paper towels until his flesh appeared. There was wheezing in his oral discharge, a glint of hope in his eyes, there were bloody rags on the tiles; red zinfandel stains in the cement grout.

Axel hung onto a state of semi-consciousness. Where his right cheek was, there was an inferno. An incessant throbbing dominated his stomach; his ribs would not show mercy to a dull pain that felt like split bones. The crowd was silent, hovering over him, Charlie the most concerned.

Zoe cuddled his head in her arms and said, "I was the homecoming queen at my graduation."

To which Axel replied, "Bullshit."

To which Zoe responded to the concerned onlookers, "He's going to be okay."

He vaguely heard her words over the din of ringing in his ears. Zoe hoisted him up to his feet, and just as he stretched his legs outright, very unmanly like, vertigo arrived. Axel fainted, a tumble earthward until Charlie caught him in mid-flight, dragging him to a cot in the adjacent storeroom.

Later, he had surgery. There was no alternative. The surgeons debated whether to remove all or part of his throbbing damaged stomach. It served no purpose anymore in its ripped state. Intravenous methods were so far advanced in technology that he could at least remain alive on fluids and plastic forever. The debate was short lived.

He could hear them as they argued how to render him unconscious. He would be alive, thank the Lord, though. He recognized her touch, smelled that same aroma as when she had smooched him earlier in the evening.

"Zoe," he begged in a whisper, "Don't let them do this to me. I want to eat food again. Zoe, are you there? Can you hear me? Save my stomach."

"Axel, Axel, you are hallucinating. It's the drugs. You're delirious." She squeezed his hands in hers.

"Zoe, don't let them."

"You've not been to the hospital for surgery. You are dreaming. Wake up Axel." She gently shook him. The ceiling was vaguely familiar. This was not the dark woods of Mirth, nor the floating wagon wheel chandeliers of Fosse's, nor the white sterile ceilings of St. Mary's Hospital, but some other vanilla, grainy-textured ceiling of recognition that portrayed a sensation of comfort.

"You've not broken your ribs. You do not have a broken nose. You do have a badly skinned cheek, a bloody, sore nose, an award winning cherry red stomach, which in time will turn to passionate purple. That, Axel, is the good news."

Axel ran his hand down his chest to his stomach and over his head. Zoe talked to him. "You are delirious. At least, you were."

"I want to sit up straight, Zee." She grabbed him under the arms to wrestle him to an upright position where he rubbed his eyes and recovered. "Axel, I have some bad news for you."

"What?" He was groggy but computed her voice.

"Take this like a man, Axel. I strongly suspect that the greatest damage to you tonight is the injury to your ego!"

"What? Does not compute." He was still woozy.

"Your ego, Axel. You lost five points on the scoreboard."

He wasn't following her logic. "I think you have had a bump on the head, too."

Zoe rotated him, placing him into the sitting-up position and moved to sit beside him on her sofa while stroking his forehead to recondition his hair. Before she had a chance to speak, he said foolishly, "I've never been mugged before." That comment drove her to a hearty bout of mousey laughter.

"Sorry. Mugged? You? Axel Hawk? There has to be transparency in this case. Honesty first. Since we are smothering in deceit that leaves you and me to be honest with one another, we can never lose that or all is lost on this quest."

She continued. "You still have your watch, your antique shoes, your wallet, your money. They could have fled with all of those after the first crippling blow. At two to one with surprise assault, they overpowered you, could have robbed you and left."

Axel was hearing her clearly now, reconstructing the setting and the painful events. But a new issue arose to distract him. "Where am I? I recognize it, that ceiling texture… or do I?"

"You are at my place. I know that you feel like you parachuted in, and this time the sail didn't release to save you and you splattered over the patio. Actually, Charlie and I dragged you in through the front door."

"What…were you saying?" Axel could not connect to her reference of ego to this situation.

"Your ego," she quipped. He nodded in recognition of the word but not the connection yet.

"I said that you have to face the facts, Axel Hawk. The truth is that your ego got pulverized tonight. Firstly, the platinum blonde, the one that you so eagerly sought after to impress, after I paved the way to the parking lot, she played the part of the lookout for the gang. Was she convincing?" Axel stared back at her inquisitively.

"She found you. Secondly, she confirmed your identity and relayed her findings to the waiting thugs with a signal- that sexy, self-serving, self-satisfying pinch of your bicep."

Axel thrust his head to and fro, difficult as it was to do so. "You are hallucinating now. You can't be suspicious of her?"

"Axel Hawk, I am your friend. I am your partner. I wouldn't lie to you ever. I saw her execute that nifty move from my vantage point in the parking lot as I glanced through the windows of the bar. As I did, I mumbled to myself at the time, 'Nice move, lady.' Axel will love that."

Expressive hand motions of doubt greeted her. However, Zoe was determined to convince him. "Axel, you languished in that moment, a moment of purposeful deceit, while the two thugs targeted you. Thirdly, the assailants tailed you into the washroom, they found you alone, and they beat the hell out of you. They fled with only the bruises and cuts that I administered."

Now Axel noted the gravity in Zee's tone as she restated her dramatic version. He had made such a fuss over her Saturday by parachuting into her house ala macho man, Axel Hawk. He purchased her a birthday gift today, expressed sincere feelings of trust while offering a full partnership. Surely, he must believe her. He was not in the mood for one of their frequent great debates that sometimes lingered for hours. Should he submit? One last attempt.

"She is Kelly Burston from Chicago. She just relocated here. I am supposed to meet her again tomorrow night at the bar, Fosse's."

"Gentleman's bet?"

"Come on, Zee. You are wrong."

"I take great offense to what happened tonight Axel. Somebody wants to hurt you and that greatly offends me." She was stern in her delivery.

"Axel, it was a setup. While I was outside in the parking lot, I noticed a silver-gray Eclipse. I checked that spot after the incident and the vehicle was nowhere to be seen. No one else departed after the raucous started. It is human nature to stay to see what all the excitement is about. But the occupants of that vehicle vanished." She let him absorb her logic and waved a stub of paper in front of his nose.

"Luckily, I copied down the license plate number, local, California, phoned Tinker and as we speak, he is conducting a check."

"Oh, geez." Axel cupped his head in his hands feeling some embarrassment. "I was dazzled by her. She touched me. She promised me. She bonded with me."

"All primary male weaknesses: touching, promising, and bonding. Weakness, weakness, weakness. I am deeply sorry for you, Axel, but she played you. You were the prey and she was the hunter. I told you earlier, it is your ego that got mugged tonight!"

"How long did I black out for?"

"About forty-five minutes. Lucky for you that your pal, Dr. Jim Gieske, was there at Fosse's tonight to accompany us back here. He examined you. You can thank him for bandaging your wounds and providing these painkillers." She rattled the bottle of pills in front of him.

"His conclusion is that you are badly bruised, bloodied, but the pain should recede in two days. You will look like hell but be back in the real world sooner than your appearance. Jim says that your obvious bruises the next few days will be a character builder." Axel shook his head in disgust.

"Thanks, Zee, for saving my ass. Through the red mushy pulp on my eyelids, I witnessed you in action. You were magnificent. The way you moved like a female wrestler, depositing singular perfect blows into strategic locations. You know the male anatomy well. What a business plan you executed! Numbing their strategic muscles. Neutralizing their weapons. A real Joan of Arc in battle."

"Axel, the best offensive move of the evening was by you though, when you intelligently figured out how to kick the bathroom door shut to disarm the bad guy's knife. One for the police assault training books. It blew the knife right out of his hand, right to me."

"I learned that one in assault one-oh-one. Always look for a bathroom door to surprise your assailant." He was feeling better so tried to ascend vertically but quickly was consumed with abdominal pain so collapsed back onto the sofa. Zoe intercepted him to position a soft landing.

"Save your strength; you will need it. I've covered my sofa in plastic tonight in case you drool, sweat, or re-open any wounds. You do remember this sofa? It's the one that you tried to mangle Saturday night."

"Zee?"

"Yes." Eye contact was established with her.

"I've been a fool tonight. I won't make that mistake again. I compromised our investigation, drew you into harm's way. I truly am sorry. I placed you in a more dangerous position than I. Thank you for bailing us out!"

"It's our asses, Axel, not just yours. If someone wants to hurt you, you can bet they want to injure me, too. It's our firm. Won't be much of a firm if I have to rename it, to Z. Not catchy at all." The laughing hurt. She positioned herself on top of the sofa looking down at him, combing his hair back as he broke into a tune.

"Zee, I know I'd stand in line with you,
If I think you have the time to spend,
An evening with me."

She would not hear any of this tonight, so she commenced her retreat down the hallway turning out banks of lights as she receded. "Axel, get some rest." He remained tenacious.

"And if we go someplace to dance,
I know that there's a chance,
You won't be leaving with me."

"Shut up, Axel," she chirped in tune to his melody.

"And afterwards, we drop into a quiet little place
To have a drink or two,"

"Please, Axel, please." She turned off all the lights in the living room and hall. He vaguely recognized her outline now as she stood to receive the next lines at the end of the hallway and perched to ascend upstairs.

"And I'd go and spoil it all,
By saying something stupid like,

I love you."

She darted forward. Surprisingly, Zoe returned in the dark, leaned over him to deposit a quick strike kiss on his swollen lips. In his weakened state, he closed his eyes to lavish the experience, absorb contact, but he couldn't retain her. As he opened his eyes, she had vanished. All that he could hear were her footsteps, quietly fading away.

"Good night, Axel."

"I do, oo, oo, oo, oo."

"Pleasant dreams Axel."

"I do, oo, oo, oo, oo."

It was suddenly murky and quiet. He heard her climb the last few stairs to her bedroom on the second floor and seal the door. He was alone with his thoughts in the abyss of love and pain. Sleep outran him into a coma.

But a terrible uneasiness, about what evil waited for them, haunted his dream…and her dreams, too.

TUESDAY MORNING

"Two pain killers, orange juice, and a bulbous, red nose, swollen to Bozo's size without bursting. One helluva bruised cheek. You look like shit, man." Tinker snickered as he basked in this rare opportunity.

"Thanks, Tink."

"Axel, this is a photo op moment, but I'll be danged if I didn't bring my camera. If only Felix could see you now, it would lift his heart or at least cause him to crack the first smile I've ever seen him wear in all the years since I've known the man."

Zoe entered her living room dressed in a fire red top, ivory tennis pants with spanking white shoes and oversized jet-black shades. Handing to Axel the instructions for dressing his wounds, plus the directions for administering his medicine, she pulled up Axel's shirt to reveal the blistered brilliant magenta stomach muscles to Tinker.

Zoe teased him. "Keep your shirt on today, macho man; you are a real turn off above the belt." Tinker bellowed, and sarcastically added, "Axel Hawk, fighter extraordinaire." He was giggling while his large black arms waved about.

Axel retaliated. "I can hardly wait until you two leave. Ouch," he grimaced, as he navigated around the kitchen by himself. He stood somewhat unsteadily as he addressed Tinker. "I know that I can identify that big jerk. He was tall, Caucasian, muscular, thick neck, untrimmed moustache, gangly arms. Most importantly, I never forget an ugly face. His square menacing jaw was riddled with mischievous guilt. He had at least three small scars around and above the chin. Bushy eye brows, too."

Tinker opened an attaché case to extract an official police photo and pass it to Axel. "This him?"

"Tinker! You are so boringly efficient. That's the brut." Axel stared back in bewilderment. "How did you identify him so quickly?"

"Your lady friend got an excellent look at him, too. More importantly, she got a license plate from the escapees. It didn't take ole Tink long. The Eclipse is leased to Herman LaForge, alias the Appleman. He is an enforcer. He makes people turn apple red through punishment; hence the nickname. It's pretty easy to see that he caught up to you. Only business he knows is brute force." Axel was not amused.

"Axel, this dude has served time in Peoria, also maximum security in Kansas and is always in trouble. He has twelve lifetime charges with four convictions; eleven of those charges are for assault of some sort, and one for possession of narcotics. He was released from prison seven months ago."

Axel inquired. "And he found time in his busy schedule of crime to fit me in?"

"Listen up, you two!" Tinker's voice was raised and demanded attention as he dually addressed them. "Dude's a muscle man, meaning if somebody's got the money, he's got the time, and he's got the battery. He was charged twice already since his release for assault, but it didn't stick. If he's guilty of this beating, he is breaking his parole. He's never killed anyone, but he's come close."

"Where is he now?"

"Last known address is Detroit, but that can't help us much with where he is in California. The address he gave to the car rental agency was a phony. We gonna find him Axel before he comes at you and the little lady again. He never leaves a job unfinished, so beware. He ditched the Eclipse to a midnight used car lot for cash after the incident last night, and used phony papers to sell it. Probably has already bought himself another set of wheels."

"How about the squat one?"

"Sorry, Zoe only got a glimpse of him. What can you say?"

"Not much. Medium height and stocky. He has a scar on his left leg, deep and long. Overweight but strong. Pear-shaped body is misleading since he's also a brute. Stereotype weightlifter I would guess by his upper muscle development. I had blood in my eyes when I finally looked at him."

Zoe confirmed, "Brown marine cut, with a tattoo, small, on his upper arm, mid-thirties, thick fingers, but it all happened so quickly."

Axel lamented to Tink. "I would be grateful if you nail the Appleman before he finds me again."

Hoisting her black satchel over her shoulders, stuffing more paper into it, she informed them. "I am off to San Clemente guys. Date with a dentist. Wish me luck."

She gave Axel a gentle hug; and then Tinker. "My two main men. Axel, don't forget to lock up when you leave. I left an extra key for you on the hallway desk. Thumper drove your car here earlier and placed your car keys on the kitchen table. Tink, see you tonight at M's residence."

After she had departed, Tinker stood in front of Axel, towering over him, big grin, beaming down. "You and I have known each other a long time, Axel. Is there anything that you want to confide in, ole Tink? Given our relationship of mutual respect throughout these years, you know I am a good listener." Before Tinker had completed his pronunciation of the word listener, Axel had blurted out, "No."

"Fine. I will respect that for the time being. I'll be moving on, too. I got real police work to conduct. Mind you, I'd like to tag along with you today to find out what you two are up to. Seems to me that whatever you two got in mind, somebody else in L.A. got a great deal of objection to it. Now your beating last night could be interpreted to be one of two things. Either, they are trying to scare you off this case early; or, maybe you are getting too close to the truth, and you needed to be punished to remind you of that. You just remember that Tinker's your friend. I care about you and Zoe."

"Tinker, we can't disclose anything with you now because we don't have any absolute concrete facts. Plus, we have to respect our client's wishes. Zoe and I will keep you informed as necessary. When the time is appropriate, we'll call you."

Tinker raised his voice. "Axel, the Appleman is serious muscle. He hurts people. That's his business. He is an armed assassin. I do not like the idea that my gal Zoe has got to keep her eyes peeled all day to keep one step ahead of the Appleman. If you need my help, you better abandon the macho shit and come calling Tinker. I love that little lady. I do not want to get a call that Appleman caught up to her and she now looks like you. Understand?" Axel vigorously nodded in affirmation even though his neck muscles hurt.

"I understand. I feel better. Zee and I will rendezvous with you at Montilladan's residence tonight. I appreciate your offer to assist. This is a private investigation Tinker until we deem otherwise. We have to protect our client first. If we absolutely confirm new evidence we'll call you. I promise."

"I hate that. I hate it! I hate it! Don't call me, I'll call you. That is not the remark of true friends. However, it is your cheeks at risk and your tummy at exposure. The beating of your ego last night makes that event police business."

"So, Zee told you about Kelly Burston?"

"We put an A.P.B. out on Ms. Platinum. Charlie gave us an excellent description of her right down to her beautiful assets. It appears the musclemen and his friend waited outside with a clear view of you two, and entered through the back door since Charlie didn't recognize them as drinkers. If she returns to Fosse's tonight, Charlie's going to call us pronto; we gonna nab her before you do, unless you can tell me anything more about Ms. Burston?"

"No, you know what I know."

"I am going now, Axel."

He strutted to the front door, turning to face Axel down the hallway, shouting, "A lot of criminals got pretty faces, Axel. It's a great weapon and Ms. Platinum used it well. I don't want to receive another call from you today. Even strong guys like you got your Achilles heel."

Axel pondered when he should bring Tinker into their confidence, but that could not be accomplished without Lacey's approval. "Last comment. The Appleman doesn't work cheaply. He commands a big salary, so whoever is employing him here in LA got lotsa money for crimes. Behave yourself today." Tinker slammed the door shut before Axel could deliver a sincere thank you for his efforts and concern.

He called Constance and Lieber to confirm the appointment that Thumper had scheduled for him. He marched into the bathroom to inspect the damage. In the mirror, the reflection of himself shattered his confidence momentarily until he came to the realization that the show must go on, that he must wear a brave face as people stared at his bandaged nose. After all his lectures to Zoe about security, he had been the one to let his guard down. "How bloody embarrassing." He shook his head.

Probe. Be naturally inquisitive in our business. Challenge. Interrogate. Don't let your guard down. He recalled those words of advice to Zee on many a case. In front of all his friends at the tavern, he had let her down. It was just like he had advised Zoe. "We have our whole lives ahead to learn from our mistakes, to become stronger, to fight evil wherever, whenever."

In the next hour, he showered, re-bandaged his wounds, gingerly dressed, ate only toast, and sipped strong black coffee. The swelling was beginning to recede on his cheek. However, there were bound to be wise cracks, inquisitive looks, cutting jokes accompanied by glares, all about his appearance. Within the next hour, he found himself in the upscale offices of Constance and Lieber. Within minutes of his arrival, he positioned himself across the desk from an imposing figure clad in an expensive European suit, silk pink bow tie, and thick black suspenders. This rather plump individual introduced himself to Axel as Mr. Raymond Hartwig. He spoke rudely with an arrogant air.

"I really don't have to disclose any information to you Mister, ah, Hawk. I am obliged to execute the last wishes of the deceased, Montilladan, and execute the will, that is all. This intrusion is very inconvenient." Hartwig paused to open a gold cigarette case without offering Axel one, and lit a custom rolled cigarette, puffing vigorously, the cigarette dwarfed by his stubby fingers. He blew smoke toward the ceiling, raising his head to watch it rise in an obtuse halo. Hartwig cast a suspicious glance to Axel.

"Now that I have observed your ruffian sewn-together appearance, I am even less inclined to converse with you when your assistant confirmed on the phone. From a distance, your firm seemed much classier. So, I would prefer to keep this conversation short. Considering your appearance and motives, we should strive to get right to the point. Let us not protract this meeting. Also, I have Montilladan's interests to protect."

Axel was being scolded; first by Lacey, then by Tinker, and now by Mr. Hartwig. "I will attempt to be brief, Mr. Hartwig. Honestly, I do appreciate the time in your busy schedule to see me. I apologize for what you described as a ruffian's appearance, but it is a casualty of my profession. I intersected some criminal elements last night."

"Please, Mr. Hawk, get to the purpose of your visit. Your internal affairs are no concern of mine."

"I understand that the reading of Montilladan's will is later today."

"Yes, that is correct."

"As my assistant conveyed to you yesterday, my partner and I are investigating the accident of Montilladan on behalf of a deeply interested party."

"Yes, I am aware of that. Get to the point, please."

"Do I have your promise that our conversation can be held in strictest confidence?"

He paused and examined Axel with a studious gaze. "Yes, you do."

"Thank you. Under the terms of the will, would the distribution of the proceeds of the will to heirs and heiresses change if the cause of death were to be changed?"

Hartwig pushed his cheek out with his tongue as he squinted at Axel with hollow dark eyes. Hartwig reframed the question. "Does the disbursement of the proceeds to inheritors alter according to how the victim died? That seems to be the question that you are posing. The answer is emphatically *no*."

"Do you know the identification and location of all the beneficiaries in the will?" Hartwig paused to answer while he stared at him again.

"Yes."

"Can you tell me who the principal beneficiaries are?"

"Specifically, no. However, in general, there are fellow movie directors, fellow co-stars, and close friends, all who receive generous payments. Montilladan left behind no living relatives. The identities of the recipients will be disclosed later today." Hartwig was animated as he described the answers to Axel, fully engaging his hands, changing flabby facial features and thrusting his upper body in jerky movements.

"Some local playgrounds and parks will be delirious of their gifts, as well as certain specified orphanages. There are some charities which will receive generous contributions from the estate, as well as, naturally, actor guilds and local amateur playhouses." Hartwig had barely smoked his cigarette, but he chose to grind it out as with an act of twisted vengeance. He leaned back in his chair with his hands gripped behind his head.

"There are some individuals whom Montilladan felt compelled to give monies to because of the influence of them on his acting career. They will be pleasantly surprised. Of course, there are the two research laboratories." Axel perked up, trying not to be too surprised. He played along.

"Right. They are in California as I recall?"

"Yes, local. Montilladan was active in some bio-research organizations."

"Can you tell me the names?"

"I don't see why not since it was common knowledge that Montilladan resided on their boards. Peculiar that you don't know this, Mr. Hawk. The labs are MUREX Laboratories, that is capital M-U-R-E-X. The other is deMox Labs, small d-e- and then capital M-O-X. Both of these organizations received donations in the past from Montilladan." Axel now recollected the past reference by Zoe and the investigation of Thumper to the board positions.

"What do these labs research?"

"I don't know Mr. Hawk and I don't think that it enters into the equation of our discussion. That is neither my charge nor the purpose of my firm. They are responsible, legal, existing, legitimate corporations with charters and credible credentials. They will receive their grants as specified. I seem to feel that suddenly you are asking me to do your leg work. You claim to be a private detective and yet are unaware of the two bio-med boards that Montilladan gave free time to."

"Do you have contact names?"

"No. Their funds are simply to be paid out to the legal entities. Probably, they anticipate this and will have a representative attend the reading of the will."

"Did Montilladan have any large debts to pay?"

"No he did not, except for the mortgage on the residence. This has already been paid out through mortgage insurance thus providing the estate clear title to sell. Montilladan had an accidental death clause in his will."

"Any persons identified as creditors?"

"I have already answered that with no."

"Are there any other encumbrances?"

He was growing impatient. "No."

"Couldn't you at least check for a contact name at the bio labs to help me on my way?"

Hartwig shuffled through a file with impatient sighs, while Axel, in agony from the throbs in his cheek and stomach sat patiently. Finally Hartwig scribbled something on a piece of stationary and passed it to Axel. "Larry Bartlett is the President and Chief Executive Officer of both of these companies. There is the address which appears in our files."

"Thank you very much. Is Ms. Lacey Sills mentioned in the will? I am not asking of her amount of inheritance, only if she is mentioned."

"In confidence, Mr. Hawk, yes, as a minor inheritor. No more, no less than other close friends of Montilladan will receive."

"Did you personally oversee Montilladan's affairs when he was alive?" He had to go fishing. If Montilladan really was alive, there may be foreign accounts to tap into.

"Yes, I did."

"What about the out of country bank accounts? Are those also administered by you? Do they figure into the will?" By his expression, Axel figured Hartwig to be surprised by this inquiry.

"Any out of country foreign accounts are administered by following the directions of Montilladan." Bingo. Now, where from here?

"Will they be administered now? Frozen? Or left to the co-signees to resolve overseas? Or is there some legal vehicle that frees those funds to co-signees?"

"Do you represent a co-signee? Is that your client? Is that the basis for these queries?"

Axel needed the information. He played it coyly. "My client's identity is confidential because of the amounts concerned. However, any information on the offshore accounts is appreciated."

"The proceeds of the bank accounts in Andorra are clear of any creditors and will be excluded from the reading of the will at this time. Co-signees are free to exercise their administration according to the will and I will instruct the banks, as Montilladan's executor, to do so."

Axel was ecstatic. Offshore accounts. Co-signees. Andorra. "To your knowledge, did Montilladan have a financial, personal accountant?"

"That is none of your business. Montilladan's account will be settled for proper taxes according to the law, and the true up will be calculated by one of our accountants at Constance and Lieber. Any due foreign taxes will also be paid. If Montilladan had a personal tax advisor and personal financial advisor, we are under no obligation to divulge them. I believe the time has arrived to end this meeting." Axel needed to play the Andorran angle again.

"Please, Mr. Hartwig, you have been so helpful. Did Montilladan make any recent changes to his will, or their distributions, or recent changes to co-signees in the accounts offshore? This is important."

Hartwig wasted little time. "Not any of your business."

"Last question. I promise. How much money is in the bank accounts in Andorra? Confidentially. Promise. I'll leave. If you cannot tell me exactly, just approximately. Please."

"I shall only state that there is great deal of wealth in the accounts." Axel let go of a deep breath. Following Hartwig's answer, he bore the brunt of further sarcasm about his scarring. Leaving the premises, he ambled down the hallway, admiring the original watercolor paintings between six foot high oriental vases, while drawing a fit from the gazes of paralegals to his dismay.

Despite his sore stomach muscles, the agony to walk erect, he felt elated as he left the law firm, moving outside, and if he had had a hat like Mary Tyler Moore, he'd have thrown it into the heavens. Two great leads. Larry Bartlett. Offshore bank accounts in Andorra with great wealth. The biting jabs were worth it after all.

He elected to make one more stop before lunchtime since he was in the neighborhood but first, a cell call to Zoe, which proved fruitless. She must still be engrossed with the dentist. Axel stopped to think. They must beat other sources to the bank accounts in Andorra. He mumbled, "Especially before Montilladan liquidates them; or if any accomplice is directed to do so." He knew just the man in France to assist them but needed Zoe to pitch the request. He reasoned further. "If in her new disguise, she shows up as the heiress, withdraws all funds, closes the account, and disappears with Romeo, all would be lost. Or maybe Romeo is a co-signee? That stash could buy a new life anywhere in the world," he muttered.

He was anxious to put Zoe on that trail, but she did not answer again. He also needed help to find out how Montilladan could obtain new passport papers for a new identity. Axel left a phone message on that issue too for Speed. Soon he was elsewhere in upscale Beverly Hills. It was mid-morning and there was a bustle of activity on this swanky street as female shoppers buzzed from boutique to boutique while caffeine seekers packed the numerous coffee cafes that beckoned by way of outdoor extensions and wafting odors.

Dr. Montoya's office was a small, remodeled, older home, now painted in light copper pastels and capped by a red tiled roof. She occupied the entire first floor of the three story building according to the plaque in front. Entering into an exterior waiting room, Axel discovered that it was a small space with four high back chairs, and a round pink granite coffee table laden with today's trendy magazines of fashion and medical journals. The mood lighting was in shades of a soft gold.

The table was decorated with a collage of colorful fresh fruit. There was, distressingly, no sign of a fresh cup of coffee, which he hungered for. There was, however, a water cooler to one side, with goldfish bowl pillars adjacent. Behind a large glass paned-partition, a very, very tall young attractive receptionist, dressed in warm bright shades of cream, had been observing him.

"Good morning," she lauded and now, upon inspection, she stared aghast at his face.

Axel tried to force a smile. "Good morning, my name is Axel Hawk." He saw from the sign in front of the pane that her name was Lillian. She was twenty-five-ish, well groomed, pink rimmed glasses, thin graceful eye brows, a dark makeup in contrast against her resilient pale skin and creamy garb.

"Lillian, that's a pretty name. I don't believe that I have known a Lillian before. That's a very attractive chic suit you are wearing."

"Thank you for the compliments. Are you a boxer?"

"No," Axel replied with a laugh, "I had some trouble with some rowdies at a tavern last night. I usually don't look this bad. Do you always look this good?"

"Where is all this flattery headed, Mr. Hawk?"

"I'm a private investigator. I know this is an impromptu request, but I'd like to briefly converse with Dr. Montoya."

"Do you have an appointment?" She annoyingly searched the appointment log on her computer while knowing his response, and playing a mind game with him.

"No, I don't."

"I am very sorry, Mr. Hawk. I cannot accommodate you today. Dr. Montoya is very busy. She has an extremely popular practice. I could give you our card. That way, you could call back to schedule an appointment with me, but I must inform you that Dr. Montoya is not taking any new patients at this time. It's a very small practice and she deals with only select clients." Lillian said all this with the greatest regret in her tone.

"You don't understand. Excuse me, Lillian, I don't need to see a psychiatrist for treatments." She was quick to reply.

"Well, that's just your side of the story." Her remark broke the tension as they both imbibed in laughter, she in a mousey lilt, as Axel pleaded again.

"Excuse me again, Lillian. Let me restate my request. I need to converse with Dr. Montoya on an urgent matter regarding one of her patients. I wish to pose a few questions around an investigation I am conducting. It won't be an inconvenience and it is urgent. I promise I won't be an imposition."

"But, Mr. Hawk, how can you possibly say that? It will be an inconvenience. It is already an imposition. Firstly, the relationship of patient and doctor is confidential. As a private investigator, you should know that. I doubt Dr. Montoya can answer questions about this individual. Secondly, Dr. Montoya is very busy these days. In order to squeeze you in, it would create an inconvenience to cancel someone else. You must realize from my comments that I can't assist you."

"Lillian, please. This is an urgent matter. I'm sure that Dr. Montoya would accommodate me if I had the chance to explain my predicament to her."

"Well, you are persistent. For someone so wounded, you do go down fighting, but it is easy for me to deny you access because Dr. Montoya is not here. I don't know when to expect her today. She has appointments outside the office."

Axel's hopes fell. He moved forward to slip his card under the glass. As he did so, he observed Lillian's elaborate computer system on the back desk. "Please at least inform her I called by personally. Please present my card. Please ask her, or you, to call back at the earliest convenience as this is a rather delicate, urgent matter."

Lillian replied in a stern voice. "Your use of the word urgent grows weary. I shall give you no promises. I shall mention your visit when she arrives and deliver your request. You should not expect a timely response due to her schedule."

"Thank you, Lillian."

As he hobbled out, she remarked behind him, "I hope you feel better soon." He nodded to acknowledge her pleasantry and promptly descended the steep incline into street level. Axel had never felt so hopeless. The more he walked, the more his stomach ached. The more he forced a smile and talked, the more his cheeks and beak throbbed. He stood at attention at curbside to admire the well-manicured neighborhood. Across from him, a lingerie shop with sensational mannequins beckoned strollers. Beside it, a corner kitchen with open air seating in rustic green wrought iron furniture, complimented with the sweet aroma of fresh coffee, hailed him.

He crossed the street and ordered a medium latte with a scone. The customers were smartly dressed here, so he hid outside at a corner table, peering street-ward where he had an advantageous view of the comings and goings of Montoya's building. There were other smartly decorated homes up and down the avenue occupied by art galleries, small businesses, tea houses, and antique furniture. He had never been on this route before. Twenty minutes later, just as he had left the cafe and was standing street-side, just as he was about to abandon this sortie and move on, a black BMW convertible, two-seater, decelerated in front of him, signaled, and slowly turned into an alleyway between the fashion shop and Dr. Montoya's office and disappeared behind the doctor's building.

Axel received an unobstructed view of the sole occupant- female, long dark hair, black shades matching the automobile's sleek color, and a chic wide brim hat in a light shade of red. Haggardly, he limped down the alleyway on a prayer and a hope. Reaching a brick wall at the end of the property, he looked to his right behind Dr. Montoya's offices, locating the vehicle in a covered carport.

She emerged, untied her hat and spied Axel. Startled she withdrew a small hand pistol from the glove compartment to gain advantage. She aimed it straight at the center of his body. Armed only with rhetoric, he tried to overwhelm her with apologies.

"Please, forgive me. I didn't intend to startle you. I am, indeed, sorry for the intrusion. I can't overpower you in my present state as I was in an unfortunate fight defending my honor last night. Please, miss...I mean, Dr. Montoya. You are Dr. Montoya? Aren't you? I see you are parked in her parking spot."

"I do not schedule any appointments in my carport."

"I apologize profusely. I am sincere. I did talk to your receptionist earlier and Lillian did her job as she explained how busy you are. She is very efficient. I was about to depart when I saw the vehicle drive in here, so I took a chance that it might be you."

Axel introduced himself further, walked cautiously forward to present his credentials by way of his business card and driver's license and withdrew five paces while she patiently completed her examination of them. As she did so, he rambled on about the urgency to converse with her regarding a present case concerning one of her patients. She resisted his logic.

They exchanged further arguments and counter arguments until she realized and stated, "Better to meet with you now, rather than to be pestered by you later." They entered her office from the rear, passed through a small kitchen, she signaling Lillian of her arrival on her desk phone and her desire to not be disturbed. With courteous new exchanges, they revisited his rude approach, selected cold beverages from a small, but well-stocked, wall bar, and sat at opposite ends of a very large low standing polished tan marble table, he on a love seat, she in a high back chair that dwarfed her.

He absorbed the surroundings. They were immaculate. There were small copies of French Renaissance paintings occupying every space on the walls. He idolized the camel clothed sofa and love seat and the ecru chaise she occupied. Her desk was enormous, four times the size of his. He pondered the secret of how she maneuvered it inside.

There were sienna colored drapes. Small high circular earthy vases proudly stood on display on high stands everywhere. This office was terribly over decorated. He turned his attention to her as he caught her eyeing him. She looked like a high class model adorned in very expensive jewelry as long, opal ear rings peeked out below her long pitch black hair.

Black satin pearls embraced her neck in a four choker set; sapphire rings were on each middle finger. Now as she removed her glasses, he came into contact with two deep brown eyes. Axel sat frozen while she completed her inspection before she turned to her side view.

They conducted brief banter about the weather, a recent breaking banking scandal, and the upcoming fall mayoral election. He opened the serious dialogue with a head-on assault.

"Dr. Montoya, was Montilladan a patient of yours?"

Her left leg, which lay across her right, had been engaged in a rocking ritual. Her left hand had been undergoing a clenching and unclenching ritual. At the sound of the word Montilladan, there was an abeyance of both rhythms, so abruptly noticeable that it became an awkward moment for both of them. A minute passed. He decided that he would not repeat the question. After another minute, it came.

"Yes." Her answer was soft but deliberate.

"For a customized therapy?"

"Yes, he came frequently at first when the treatments commenced. From there, it increased in intensity as our relationship grew. He started skipping sessions until the visits became infrequent and he became very delinquent in arrival times." Dr. Montoya pronounced each syllable slowly, succinctly, deliberately, perfectly.

"I was visited by the Los Angeles police. I told them all this and more. They have my comments on this matter. May I ask what interest Montilladan is to you and what different ground we will cover than the police queries? I presume that the police have furnished a thorough investigative report." She was so assertive, so smooth.

"There are certain irregularities surrounding his death, so on behalf of a client, I am investigating the nature of the accident."

Her left leg twitched before the oscillation recommenced. "On behalf of the studio?"

"No."

"Insurance company?"

"Maybe." Now Axel found her incessant rocking motion to be a distraction; now her entire body was engaged in the motion. Was this designed as a diversion to keep him off balance?

"Do you represent inheritors?"

"Quite possibly I do. Can you divulge the nature of Montilladan's appointments? In generic terms?"

"No, that is privileged information." She changed her composure to scorch him. "What nerve you have, Mr. Hawk." She raised her voice when she delivered the comment. "I can't understand why you, a professional investigator, wouldn't already know and respect this privacy between doctor and client. You are a real private eye? Correct?"

Axel decided to play tenaciously. "Yes, please, without violating your professional conduct, can you tell me generally what his ailment was?"

"No." She was conducting an optic examination of him, fixing her eyes on his old runners, moving up to pelvis level, now scanning through to his face. Axel pressed the issue.

"Insecurity?"

"Who? Montilladan? Hah, ha, ha, you jest! His confidence reduced gladiators of the press to jelly; he commanded legions of movie goers to flock to see him on the big screen and all this with utmost confidence." Axel sat waiting for her peculiar giggle to subside, wondering how much of this comical folly could also be a distraction.

"Financial woes?"

"No comment."

"People problems?"

"No comment."

He made a bold decision. "Sex life?"

The distinctive sway of her leg halted. Uncrossing her legs, discontinuing her clenching of fists, hands now resting comfortably in her lap, body stiffly upright, raising fingers to delicately wipe a hint of perspiration from her eyebrows, she fixated on him. He thought perhaps that her face had impregnated cheeks. She was a very attractive lady. Was he going through a male bout of hormonal assault that he should look at every woman these days only to discover beauty? Nikki, Lacey, Zoe, Ms. Platinum, Lillian, Dr. Montoya. Mrs. Whitehurst. "Well, not her," he thought.

"What are you muttering, Mr. Hawk?"

"Nothing."

"Do you have native American blood in you, Mr. Hawk?"

"Hmm, how perceptive you are. My great grandmother was a European immigrant; my great grandfather a full blooded Chickasaw Indian from tribes in Alabama, later relocated to Southern Oklahoma. My family can be traced back over hundreds of years. I know of my family origins, roots, linear history. Modern times, however, seemed to have absorbed me, but my family is one of the first inter-racial marriages of our tribe. I often think of it as the precursor of peace in America."

But Axel didn't want to get sidetracked. "Is Lacey Sills a patient of yours?"

"No!" She snapped. "Is she a client of yours?" She raised her right eyebrow a la Spock as she beamed back at him. Axel had fallen with regret into that suggestion. They were sparring. He was losing. He chose not to reply just as she had not replied to his earlier questions. In the silence, she attempted to end their meet as the rocking started again.

"Any other questions?"

"Was there anything out of the ordinary at all that Montilladan shared with you? That caused you alarm about his behavior recently? An act purely out of character?"

"Such as?"

"Well, suicidal tendencies?" Now she took her laughter to new levels that rocked the room with joy, expelling her high-pitched giggle. Lillian must surely be inquisitive as to this incident, for her laughter must surely resound outside her office.

"Montilladan? You obviously never met the man. That suggestion is so preposterous that you have brought laughter into my soul today with that remark.

How silly you are. Come, Mr. Hawk, these fishing expeditions of insecurity are tedious. Your bait is weaker than worms. You know nothing about Montilladan or else you would ask not these choice foolish queries. I cannot determine whatever you want of me! Montilladan tragically died in an accident. He is mourned by many who knew him, including me."

"How about an existing anger within Montilladan, one enough to evoke actions that were, say, out of character?" She was blunt.

"I cannot discuss Montilladan with you. I have already told you that! The police have questioned me. I gave them appeasing answers that are in an official report. Our conversation has come to an abrupt close."

Axel had absolutely nothing to lose. "How about a deep dark secret of his life? Let's say, a secret so evil, so nasty, so consuming that it was destroying him, unless of course he take steps to remedy it with your professional assistance and skill. A secret turned obstructive to a normal life; a secret, which prevented any future of prosperity. One that demanded your help, Dr. Montoya!"

Not a muscle flinched. She was so cool, so calm, and so unflinchingly collective. It was impossible to detect even a sigh, a sign that she was breathing. It is said that a person blinks their eyes thousands of times per day. But not Montoya.

She broke her own trance. She put on huge pink-tinted reading glasses, just like Lillian's. The lenses exaggerated the size of her pupils. "Such as?"

An opening. Incredible. So, she didn't want him to leave. She wanted to spar some more. She didn't want to bring this interview to a close. Why? Was she a co-conspirator of Montilladan's as Zoe had postulated and warned? Was she attempting to drag info out of him before plunging him into the danger zone? Arrange another beating?

"Well, a secret that might hold a clue to the settling of Montilladan's estate." She was perfect. Her lips hardly moved. "Such as?"

"A sexual matter, perhaps?" There it was. He had laid it out a second time, played a trump card. Or maybe the joker? She acted thoroughly annoyed.

"You keep returning to sexual matters. Are you secretly and trickily trying to engage me, so that you become one of my patients? Perhaps all these references to sex are to amuse me? I must admit that I am lost for words on this silly issue. What are your secret motives?"

Axel was silent. While he was contemplating a response, she probed further. "Why do you continue to connect Montilladan to sexual problems? This is really bizarre. A stranger walks into my practice to press me on Montilladan's sex life?"

Axel stared into her dreamy eyes, now veiled in a transparent sexy pink. She could very well perform hypnotherapy on him without him even knowing it. He had to keep his wits about him, ward off any spells and keep his guard up. Look what it had cost him last night!

Axel checked his watch. He mentally recorded the time. If she were to perform hypnosis to deprive him of precious minutes of his life, he would know! Dr. Montoya was rude.

"Your time is up. My time for you has expired. I am a very busy lady. This has been a complete waste of both our efforts."

"As is time with the Colonel!"

"What? What foolishness do you ramble on about? What Colonel?" There was a scowl on her face.

"Nothing." She stood, moved beside him to shake his hand. Axel squeezed hard. "I specialize in locating missing persons. Perhaps, we could consider you assisting me in certain special cases, where I might require construction of the psychological profile of the criminal. I live in L.A., and so do you. Let's get together one evening to discuss the possibility."

"Mr. Hawk, you have been extremely intrusive into my world. You have interrupted my day to pose ridiculous questions about Montilladan, which have no substance. You have no further business here." Her tone was sinister. Axel was silent. "I have accommodated you for longer than was necessary, than even you begged me for. I have important patients to tend to, so please leave."

"Coffee, later, after work, so I won't be intruding."

"Be thankful for the previous twenty minutes in my hectic life. There is nothing more to say. Whatever your quest, I wish you luck."

"I would like to see you again." She remained silent. In his state of optimism, he manufactured this as a yes response. "Is Montoya Spanish derivation? Is that your maiden name?"

"Yes and yes."

"Any Brazilian in your family?"

"No. Brazilians are largely Portuguese origin. Just plain ole Spanish origins in my life line."

Axel played one last gamble. "If I expose to you exactly my true cause for investigating Montilladan's accident, will you in return agree to tell me what you were treating him for?" What a risk he was offering.

Dr. Montoya studied him. She didn't take the bait. No sign of life as she stood as a statue. No blink of an eye. Nor any detected vital signs.

"Think about it for the enrichment of both of us. I'll call you." Not a response. He must depart before her drop dead eyes make him drop dead, or she hypnotizes him to become her slave. *Well, there were worse ideas,* he thought to himself.

"Out!" she ordered and opened the door.

Lillian jumped as he entered into the reception room by way of her office. She was in the area rearranging some periodicals and stood upright with a start as he passed her.

Axel addressed her in a loud voice. "Ah, Lillian, so good to see you again." Axel walked up to her to check his watch.

"Ten-twenty to ten-forty Lillian, but Madame assures me that there will be no charge. But log the minutes anyway. Pleasure to meet you both. You have my card and number if you need to contact me."

Lillian grimaced as Dr. Montoya glared at him. Axel felt better. He had won a few rounds. To only be a fly on the wall now to see if she would call

Montilladan. There was a glimmer of hope that she would want to satisfy her curiosity, or maybe, M's curiosity. He had offered a plausible trade. Fifty-fifty chance he calculated.

He phoned Zoe once he was out of sight of Dr. Montoya's building until finally she answered. "Zoe, I have just visited Dr. Montoya. I'll brief you later. More importantly, we need the help of that French detective, you know, the one who helped us out in the Landray case, the one that you went gaga over."

"I didn't go gaga over him. You're the one that keeps insisting I went gaga over him. I just admired his extreme professionalism, his gentlemanly style, his groomed looks, his savvy, sophisticated approach to problem solving..."

Axel terminated her commentary. "Yeah, yeah, this is no time for debate. What was his name?"

"Jean-marc Farand."

"Right. That's him. A Mr. Hartwig at Constance and Lieber informed me that Montilladan has significant funds stashed away in a bank account in Andorra. It is not subject to the terms of this will except to instruct the bank to honor co-signees and pre-agreed terms. He led me to believe that there might be co-signees. While Constance and Lieber will insure that the Andorran bank follows M's instructions, I think the co-signees could very well know of Montilladan's existence and empty the account. That co-signee could be Romeo. It could be Montilladan reborn in her female persona. We need Jean-marc to locate that account, find out who has signature over it, and determine if anyone has been making significant withdrawals from it, or if anyone has contacted the bank with instructions since the fatal accident. Are you there? Can you hear me?"

"Oh, Jean-marc, Jean-marc. Wherefore art thou, Jean-marc? Oh, those dreamy eyes."

"Knock it off Gigi!"

"Loud and clear. What about Montoya?"

"What a classy dame; what a classy office. She is all pro, all the way. By the appearance of her office, I suspect she has a very wealthy clientele. She could have hypnotized me for life and I would have never have known it. I'll brief you later. I didn't get a rise out of her, but we may meet again. I planted some dangerous seeds. Let me recite the total incident later. I'm on the move."

"Good. I'm on my way to the office, Axel. Inform you later about the dentist, except to say that I extracted, no pun intended on the word extracted, M's dental records which include full mouth X-rays."

"Great work, partner!"

"And I discovered some other valuable info from Dr. Sorbet. Got to run, I'll send Jean-marc a text mail soonest from my phone. How are you holding up?"

"Wounded, sore, alert. If I even see Ms. Platinum today, I will set my own record for the hundred yard dash in the opposite direction."

Zee snickered. "Anything else?"

"What day is day, night, night, and time is time,

Were nothing but to waste night, day, and time,
Therefore, since brevity is the soul of wit,
And tediousness the limbs and outward flourishes,
I will be brief. This noble case is madness."
"Ah, ha, ha, ha, ah. You spent time on that for me?"
"Tis true. This case is madness."
"Good bye, Axel." The line went dead.

Immediately he dialed Thumper and gave him the names of the two re-search laboratories, specifying complete profiles. Within fifteen minutes, he was climbing up the steep hills north of Los Angeles, navigating winding roads that hugged the hillsides that embraced small communities.

Amongst the multitude of hair-pin turns, he was obsessed with the ab-solutely stunning image of Dr. Montoya. It was haunting his mind. She must know a great deal more than she revealed. He had interrupted her rocking routine, first at the mention of Montilladan's name, and then at the insinuation that M had some deep sexual problem. She was so cool. It will be a challenge to extract truths from her.

Thumper had given him the address of the Whitehurst residence. That was where he felt compelled to go. He passed a cozy restaurant on a hair pin turn. Food and drink would be welcome, so he decided to revert back to a planned healthy diet of tossed salad and ice tea.

Just as he was about to turn off the ignition, Robert Palmer was blaring out one of his personal classics, Addicted to Love. He thought to himself, *Yes, I am Robert, you're right dear Robert. But to whom?*

TUESDAY MIDDAY

"**G**reat work, partner!" It was a deliberate conveyance of confidence directed at her, as Axel emphasized those words. Zoe entered the freeway, foot hard on the pedal to accelerate. With insubstantial traffic heading into the city, she would reach the office in one hour. She reflected to recall Tinker's advice from years ago.

"Your voice is one of your greatest tools, Zoe. Use it to your advantage. It provides a calming influence over whomever you are conversing with, whether it be the victim's friends or family, a witness, a suspect, the chief himself. People will automatically feel confident in your presence, Zee, so never mislead them, but always remember what a powerful tool you have."

Dr. Sorbet took an instant shine to her and she recognized it. "Yes, it is French derivation. My parents immigrated to New York City when I was in my late teens. I came west to California after I graduated from high school as an ambitious young man, looking to capture an acting bit and rise through the ranks to Hollywood stardom. When directors kept reducing my parts and writing me out of their scripts, ultimately asking me if I could play a corpse, I finally took the hint. I made a hard decision. I figured if I couldn't infiltrate Hollywood by acting, maybe I could hobnob by fixing their teeth and building them Oscar winning smiles." His droopy moustache straightened as he laughed by pulling his cheeks up. "And, so here I am in my niche: a star in my own right after many years at dental school."

She reciprocated at first by describing her only trip to France in which she didn't leave Paris. "You must believe me when I tell you of my genuine enthusiasm of the impressions of the Louvre, the Eiffel Tower, a dinner cruise down the Seine, Sunday ceremonies at Notre Dame and the vibrant nightlife. Where were you born in France?" Sorbet informed her that Paris was only thirty miles south from where he grew up, immediately launching him into his childhood memories.

So, it was that Dr. Sorbet was easily drawn into dialogue. He was approaching seventy with a forty year old practice in San Clemente. He had played cosmetic dentist to some of the great stars of Hollywood, some of whom had resided on the expansive acreages in the vicinity. "Saved some of my best lines for them, but it never won me a screen test." Their outburst of tittering must have caused others in the office to question what was occurring in the cubicle. He spoke briefly of his apprentices as plans for his retirement had arrived.

Within minutes, she had coaxed him into describing Montilladan the patient. "I met him one Christmas at a local gala. It was one of those invites afforded me because I attended dental works to the entire family who was hosting the affair. To my amazement, he chipped a tooth right in front of me on a cherry pit, you know, one of those cherries covered in dreamy hard dark chocolate. Well, the host was incredibly embarrassed and took me aside and begged me, respectfully begged me, if I could possibly conduct the repair right away given Montilladan's pain and inconvenience, and the jolly season upon us. So, off we went to my offices. Montilladan spent the next two hours in my dentist's chair in extreme discomfort as I rebuilt his tooth. Apparently, my work won him over. The next day I received a luxurious Christmas package of wines, fruit, cookies, chocolates, even," and he roared with ha-ha, "chocolate covered cherries! I took it as his sense of humor."

Sorbet spoke further, "After that first encounter, Montilladan always was calm in the chair. He never fussed and he spoke very little. He always came on time and then departed with compliments of the day, babbling on of how gentle I was with him. Montilladan was very complimentary of my dental work and appeared to me to be much different than his image in the public and on news casts. He was so placid, so polite, and so accommodating. I felt a genuine sadness when I heard of the accident for I admired him so. He was a regular patient."

Zoe asked if the relationship went further than dental work. "There were a few social engagements between us. The singular times that I saw him in San Clemente were for dental work. We had dinner in Los Angeles, oh, I'd say three times and it was purely social and I might add, enjoyable. Oh, it must have been great for him to be up there on the movie screen for all his friends to see," Sorbet chimed. Zoe coaxed him into releasing the dental prints when she revealed her practice to him, and their close association with the L.A.P.D.

She added. "I wish that I could inform you of my mission, but professional confidentiality prohibits me."

Dr. Sorbet was adamant. "These records must be returned to me within a few days. That is the sole condition that I insist on. If you personally deliver them on return, inform me. Maybe we could have lunch and recollect additional adventures in France." Sorbet had elected to trust her. Zoe was bursting.

She had absolute intentions to copy them immediately and to compare them to the autopsy findings. She also knew that the dental work of the victim was severely damaged by the catastrophic fall. She thanked Dr. Sorbet profusely, left him with fond memories of her rich smile, and headed up the Pacific coast road. As she peered in the rear view mirror, she spied on the closest vehicle, a white van, loaded with children and what appeared to be a haggard driver. A close watch was ordered to observe who followed her onto the exit ramp. Meanwhile, she relished her contribution while gleefully patting the brown envelope beside her.

Thumper's directions to Axel were somewhat ambiguous after he left the main thoroughfare. With five confusing snakelike turns behind him, in an upscale locality of wooded acreages, he was about to contact Thumper when he eyed the swaying wrought iron sign that spelled 5097, Whitehurst. Hesitating in front of a towering Victorian style mansion, set back over three hundred feet from the roadway, with two ebony bulging ominous turrets dominated the residence of earthy colors. From street level, Axel noted how all the window frames, and even the front entrance, were trimmed in dreary shades of shale gray.

He chose to park not in front of the house, nor out in the roadway, but turned ninety degrees toward the property, rolling and slinking down the enclosed treed driveway, which skirted the acreage, deserting his red Mustang eventually on a rare shoulder between two lofty stately pines.

From here, he could announce his arrival by strolling onto the vast expanse of lawn between street and house while proceeding in open view to the front entry. This was the option that he chose. He checked his watch. It was twenty minutes to one. Springing out onto the front lawn, now in the middle of an open lea, it smelled as if freshly cut, resembling the texture of a well-groomed, par-five fairway he had recently double-bogeyed.

Soon five, magnificent, blue granite rock stairs confronted him. Customized flower boxes on each side abounded with vivid shows while a gloomy dull marble statue of a saddened Atlas peered down from the top center of the stairs. Ascending, Axel was now perched underneath a massive courchere where the driveway circled. He gazed up to find an elaborate chandelier with at least forty hanging lights. He momentarily retreated down the stairway, shaded his eyes, cast a long glance skyward to six menacing gargoyles, two atop each turret, another four clustered above the overhang of the front entrance. According to folklore, gargoyles protected the residence. In his current position, they all seemed to be focusing their glares on him. Naked before them, he was suddenly anxious to navigate under the cover of the canopy once more.

Upon re-establishing his position, this time the front doors were slightly ajar. Multi-colored stained glass windows graced each side of the double opaque doors, with a burst of blood red glass in a half moon over the top of the entry. Before he had even a chance to approach further, one of the doors wheeled wide open. Totally dressed again in sinister black garb, she stood blocking the way with an arrogant smirk on her face.

Axel conceived a plan, spoke first, drawing immediate attention to himself with a blaring resounding salutation. "Good afternoon, Mrs. Whitehurst. I was just in the neighborhood and thought that I should respectfully pay my kindest regards to you and the Colonel."

"You insolent ass," she whispered as she hunched over. "The Colonel and I are quite busy. We don't have any time for you. We just don't sit and wait all day at home to receive visitors." She continued in the hush-hush voice, her pointy face leaning in toward him. But in the background Axel clearly heard the cue for him to crash through the barrier as a deep voice inquired.

"Kathleen, who is it?" The voice was fortified, husky, penetrating, discernible, emanating from the bowels of the deep hallway, which bisected the mansion.

Here it was, his only chance of a sole excuse to enter. Axel scampered through a narrow opening that she had quite unintentionally left, gliding across the foyer, pacing down the hallway, Kathleen Whitehurst shuffling desperately in pursuit. The hallway was lined with grandfather clocks all ticking loudly. Reaching an open doorway, the voice called out, "Kathleen? Kathleen?"

At once Axel was in an expansive den. Behind him her hot breath garnished his neck as she gained on him at the last steps. Bracing herself, she sought to explain. "This is the impertinent young foolish man of which I spoke to you about yesterday! The one whom is blindly following Lacey's ill-created whims."

Colonel Whitehurst rose from behind a burgundy lacquered desk. With a head of trimmed army cut gray hair, a shriveled thin face with high boney cheeks, he stated the orders in a commanding tone. "My dear Kathleen, please leave us."

"But John, this…"

"Kathleen!" She endeavored to seek Axel's attention so she could show disrespect with her frown, but Axel stared at his feet with lips sealed until she had departed. In disgust she smacked the door as she closed it.

Axel had moved to the desk to shake the Colonel's hand while taking note of his strong confident embrace. John Whitehurst immediately made Axel feel at ease with a shower of pleasantries as Axel perused the den, which gallantly displayed an array of civil war antique swords. Watercolor paintings of Civil War scenes, each bound in grainy leather frames, dotted the wall to his left. There was also a glass case with muskets from a bygone era. A tall ceiling to floor bookcase, adorned with classic novels bound in rich leather and embellished with bookends of civil war characters, stood behind the Colonel's desk.

"Sit down, young man." Colonel Whitehurst steered Axel to the large bay window where two high back chairs were positioned on opposite sides of a hand crafted chess table, whose warring sides were appropriately blue and gray. Axel politely waited until the Colonel was in position. This was truly a military man's sanctuary.

Suddenly Axel saw it! It was behind him as he had entered; again in the rear as he and the Colonel had conversed. It was positioned so that the most spectacular view was from sitting behind the Colonel's desk. For all the memorabilia in the room, the den was dominated by a large watercolor portrait of Lacey Sills, which hung over a fireplace.

Upon noticing Axel's stare, the Colonel prompted him. "Come, young man, take a closer inspection at the canvas."

As Axel stood at attention in front of the masterpiece, the Colonel moved to his desk, lit a cigar, offered one to Axel who declined, and then moved to stand adjacent to Axel at attention. Both men now fixed their gaze upon the painting. It was the best depiction of Lacey that Axel had seen or could ever imagine. It captured her indomitable spirit, her outgoing personality, her charisma, her pristine beauty. The Colonel exhaled as Axel suddenly became the prisoner of the sweet pungent odor.

"It is not polite to barge into one's home like this, Mr. Hawk. If you had telephoned me, I would have cooperated to grant you an audience."

"I apologize, sir." Axel knew that Mrs. Whitehurst would have attempted to thwart his efforts, just as she tried moments ago at the front entrance.

"Apology accepted. You appear to have injured yourself."

"Yes, I was the unfortunate victim of a brutal assault last night."

"Sorry to hear that! I hope you have been examined by a physician?"

"Yes, I am feeling somewhat revived. This painting is such an extraordinary likeness of Lacey. Although I have just made her acquaintance, it captures so much of the essence of what is your daughter."

The Colonel exhaled. "Lacey can be many things to many different people. This portrait brings to life that which means so much to me. That is what counts. That I am satisfied with the artist's rendition."

Now Axel saw the artist's signature- Col. J Whitehurst. Such artistic talent. The Colonel walked to the window seat. Axel followed. John Whitehurst was small in stature, but Axel had already passed judgment that he was a large man. They sat down simultaneously.

"God, I hate that woman. She upset me every time we interfaced." She clenched the steering wheel as she spoke to herself.

"Why the Hell is this no name detective visiting the Whitehurst's? What valuable information could he possibly get out of them?" She breathed heavily.

"Nothing, you fool, they know nothing of my master plan." She closed her eyes and sat back in the driver's seat. Her passenger spoke.

"So, do we make a planned attempt on his life? No more beatings. Arrange an accident just for him?" She looked in the rear view mirror to see the roadway was empty of traffic and pedestrians. She sat, rationalized and responded.

"No, that would draw further attention to us. My intuition tells me that Axel Hawk and I will interface in the future and it will be fatal for him; just not right now. He and that skinny broad won't stop digging though. Let's leave. You return to base camp. I'll switch garb, my appearance and use another vehicle and tail him."

She started the van and slowly cruised by the Whitehurst residence as the Appleman leaned over for a better look at the residence. Inside he was willing Axel Hawk and Zoe Burns to cross paths with him again, so he could exact revenge on both of them. Tinker was correct, the Appleman had never killed but his fee for this assignment had enticed him to cross into more treacherous deeds.

"I was in the military for most of my life, Mr. Hawk: amphitheaters in Europe, and in Korea, and on U.S. bases. After many encounters with the enemy and training troops for readiness, it is difficult to remove the army from the man." Axel noted how the Colonel was in polarized contraposition with the outward meanness of his wife.

Axel changed the subject abruptly to business. "Colonel, about Lacey, do you share Mrs. Whitehurst's view that Mr. Montilladan was a detrimental influence?"

His gaze drifted out the bay window onto the examination of the vast expanse of backyard. He became pensive. Axel studied him, remaining rigid, giving the Colonel the courtesy to reply. As the Colonel broke into a smile, a great revelation appeared to Axel. Immediately in that light, he recognized the uncanny resemblance to Lacey that was so distant in Mrs. Whitehurst. John Whitehurst had given her the best of his looks. It was all there. The distinguished nose. The royal clef of the chin. The resilient eyes. High royal cheek bones. Genetically, he had contributed this to her.

"She is my pet, my angel, Daddy's girl. This was our private playground. Yes, we lived here once before for many years during Lacey's youth. This house and acreage has served us well. Once, we moved away, overseas, and to our surprise upon return, this estate was for sale. By the fortune of our great God, he provided it for us a second time." He commenced his tale.

"We had a pony. His name was Fathom; light brown, a very docile, warm creature. Lacey loved it, so until one day in her teens she just informed me that she tired of it. Over there, see where the grass is slightly discolored, that is where the great sand box resided. We had so much fun with the assortment of plastic toys, and of course, a sand mover, and a large battery operated bulldozer with shovels…" In this pause Axel remained with the discipline not to interrogate.

"Swings, slides, a playhouse of epic proportions, this yard has played host to all a young girl's dreams. She had a passion for soccer. Lacey and her girlfriends would beat poor Kathleen's roses to a pulp." He laughed jovially recalling the incidents. The Colonel continued as Axel sat. Speaking of Lacey he seemed contented, totally immersed in his tales of his young daughter. Axel admired him as he locked in on his past sanctities.

"Look!" and he leaned forward excitedly. "I can still see her ghost out there chasing Fathom- prancing running, even quarreling. Yes, young girls had their spats, too, and sometimes, even inappropriate language."

Axel felt that he should not interrupt until he was sure that the Colonel had finished. "All gone now. Just the visions of what was, just the poltergeists sprinting across the lawn at dusk and dawn, cruelly reminding me that for all the moments I shared with her, that I plead guilty to also being absent from some of her greatest triumphs, being negligent in some of her vital moments of parental need. This imbalance was squarely my fault." Now he turned to face Axel.

"This is life, isn't it, Mr. Hawk, that one should dedicate a lifetime of caring, thoughtfulness, financial responsibility, sacrifices, to a sibling. Fall ever so deeply in love with that possession only to lose her, inevitably lose her, if her name were Lacey Sills Whitehurst. Nothing I could have done would have kept her here. It is the natural course of our species to seek their own destinies. And so she has."

He turned to look out over the lawn again. "What do I have now? Well, I have the yard. I have her portrait. But mostly I am left with fading memories that hurt so deep inside as they fade so fast at my age, compounded by my own inability to retain as much as I used to." Now Axel dared to interject.

"What caused the rift?" The Colonel chose not to answer the question; nor had he answered the previous one.

"She was an ambitious girl. Even in elementary school her teachers warned us about her uncanny ability to be a ring leader. Nothing wrong with ambition, Mr. Hawk." He puffed on his cigar with satisfaction and knocked off some of the ashes.

"Lacey has always been very outgoing and still is. Very important trait. But Hollywood captured her and lured her away from us. Had we lived elsewhere on this planet, it may still have happened; we shall have suffered the same fate. Personally, I applaud her career. She has done well, hasn't she? But in order for her to succeed, we've lost her. That was what life commanded." He sat back. He chose not to look into Axel's eyes. He expelled a deep breath.

"He, Montilladan, only exacerbated the situation. A little bit for me, but especially for Kathleen. Kathleen spent more time with him than I ever did. She informed me that she lectured him on the subjects of protocol, manners, ethics, and routinely exchanged abusive debates that shuddered the peaceful prisms of our hallowed halls." The Colonel shook his head.

"From the very first time that Lacey brought him here, there was an open friction between Kathleen and Montilladan. In retrospect, I realize that this made Lacey sad. I feel that I pushed Lacey to choose between us. This was a very tragic and regretful mistake on my behalf. I miscalculated the situation."

The Colonel stayed on course with other thoughts about the falling out for ten more minutes, rambled on about Lacey at ten to Lacey the starlet. But it wasn't in chronological order. It was an irregular disjointed dialogue where time verged on the obtuse as Axel failed to understand which episode he was referring to. There was no anger to the references of Montilladan as in Mrs. Whitehurst, but there was a continual bleeding of disappointment. Axel thought to himself that this could not possibly be the person whom had arranged for his beating at Fosse's Tavern.

"Kathleen wants me to die happy, pass away in peace, reach a total reconciliation with Lacey before I expire, create a return to past glories in this house with harmony abounding. What she really wanted was Montilladan out of our lives with Lacey home again. Regrettably she has half of that wish, although neither she nor I wished it to happen this way. We could not wish death upon him." Axel recalled Mrs. Whitehurst's bitter words about Montilladan at the cemetery.

"Are you terminally ill?"

The response was immediate. "Hell, no!" Colonel Whitehurst waved his cigar around. "I didn't mean to plant that idea. I smoke four cigars a day, and have a nip of aged scotch each afternoon; there is nothing awry about my old ticker. I just have a permeable sadness in my heart."

"Was Lacey a rebellious youth?"

"No more than any other teenager. She discovered boys at an early age, nine, and they discovered her, too. She was beautiful, even then." He pointed his finger at Axel. "You already knew all that!"

He drew Axel's attention to the backyard again. "This place, Mr. Hawk, was always abuzz with friends when Lacey was growing up. I remember the night that she came home crying from a high school dance, fourteen years old, this was when we were posted overseas. Ian Maxwell had jilted her for Linda something or other, in front of the whole class. Why Lacey insisted that he had broken her heart." Axel listened intently to the entire story as the Colonel volunteered the details of that night. The Colonel's choice of words to characterize Lacey, to describe her, to embellish her, all fortified his great admiration and love of her. He had lived through the emotive turbulences of her teenage years by her side. That was his place.

"Of course, there were more Ian Maxwell's who broke her heart. Of course, that's not why you've come here, is it? To hear me recite these tales?"

Axel decided to go fishing. "Sir, I am quite enjoying your remembrances about Lacey. Can I respectfully ask? Do you approve of her current lifestyle?"

"I know very little of her current private life. She chooses not to share any of those experiences when she returns. She's an adult now, and it is not for me to say or pass judgment anymore on what she can or can't do. She chooses her own fates, bonds with her own selection of friends, crafts her own future. Lacey is free to place her own fingerprints on the course of her life. One should not be disrespectful with a daughter's choices in life. She has to live with them. Sometimes it is mistakes which provide us all with the greatest opportunity to learn, to grow and to mature."

He leaned over to Axel, "Let me ask you a question, Mr. Hawk. Why should I be concerned with Montilladan's death?" The leer on his face was demanding an answer. When Mrs. Whitehurst spoke the word Montilladan, she spit it out with hatred. The Colonel did not even accent the word.

"Because your daughter has a concern surrounding his death and until I finish the investigation, I reserve to conclude what the facts are and whether her concern is genuine."

"You think that there was foul play? I mean, Mr. Hawk, does Lacey believe that there might have been foul play?"

"Again, I can't say Colonel. My partner and I have just commenced our investigation yesterday."

For no apparent reason, the Colonel suddenly launched into a tale of Christmas past. Axel was unclear of what year he spoke of. The tale possessed another five minutes of his time. "There was great joy in this house! A Christmas tale to remember forever," was how he concluded the tale as he sighed heartily. His mood shifted ominously.

"I can't survive without her. You asked me earlier, if I was dying. Well, hell no. But you see how I pine for her, to engage in lengthy joyous conversations once more. I wish that she would pay her respects to us more frequently. I wish that she would develop the same loneliness for me that I feel for her, even if it had meant dragging him around here, but it is kind of late for that now."

"Do you know of anyone whom would want to harm or injure Montilladan?"

"You must mean other than a couple of hundred journalists and thirty-some odd directors? No, I can't say that I do."

"Did Lacey or Montilladan ever mention Roy Spiller?"

"N-no."

"How about a company called MUREX?"

"Not familiar to me. Whatever are you searching for, Mr. Hawk, that you should so unexpectedly show up at our residence with this insistence to converse with me and hurl foreign names in my direction for a reaction?"

"I am just trying to gather more information about Montilladan's life, perhaps, clues and information out of place that can progress our efforts."

"I can't deliver anymore aspects of Montilladan's life to you. I have told you how Montilladan affected our lives, and expressed my remorse on my relationship with Lacey. I believe that the singular person who can help you understand Montilladan is my daughter Lacey."

"I realize that now."

"Was this assault on you last night in any way connected to this investigation? You certainly bear the scars of a battle. Is that why you are here?"

"The affair of last night is under the jurisdiction of our police. Enough said." Axel added, "Thank you ever so much for bearing with my intrusion. I meant no disrespect by it."

On cue, Kathleen Whitehurst burst into the room, moving directly to the bay window. Her timing was impeccable as the cigar that the Colonel smoked had relinquished its last embers to ashes and the Colonel seemed prone to tiring.

"The home aide is here darling." The Colonel delivered a smile to Axel.

"Slipped and fell. My hip is fragile and I can't get around as well as I used to. I take whirlpool baths with a regimented physical routine to provide some fleeting relief." The Colonel gazed into the yard one last time. What was he remembering as he flashed such a look of content? He arose and as Axel shook his hand, he placed his other hand on top of Axel's. "I had so pleasant a time with you, Mr. Hawk, and it was a pleasure to meet you. Please help my Lacey find her peace of mind."

Behind him, Axel recognized the heavy breathing. The Colonel meandered to the desk first, across the study, and then out of the den. Furiously, she turned on him.

"How dare you! How dare you pester us! It is bad enough that you act a fool to follow Lacey's ill-guided instincts. Now you drag my poor husband into this devilish charade. You had no right to come here!"

She screamed, "Leave now!" She pointed the way to the front door with one arm while the other looked as if to swat him. She was speaking so loudly that surely the Colonel must hear this disrespectful outburst. After a brief pause for air, she continued.

"Don't you ever come back here! He does not need to be provoked. What you have done is return him to bouts of deep depression over the loss of his beloved Lacey by this, this totally useless reminiscing."

"Mrs. Whitehurst, there is something terribly wrong about Montilladan's death. If you have information that you withhold from me, I urge you and I to become allies."

"Allies? Have you not heard a word that I have said?" The contortions on her forehead danced, occupying alternating positions as she ranted.

Axel felt compelled to state his position. "But I will continue to probe into this case. Rest assured that we will continue to investigate. If you chose not to be an ally, you must not suppress critical evidence that will thwart our efforts."

"You threaten me?"

"No, Mrs. Whitehurst. I am saying that a swift end to this probe could bring Lacey home again. That is one of the possible outcomes. The Colonel would like that, wouldn't he?"

"Get out and don't you ever come back here. I spit on you and Montilladan. You and your partner have discovered nothing! You are groping in the dark, trying to...to get the Colonel all worked up over these matters, and look at your bruises, you appear to have already found trouble."

The circular arguments were waning. She paced ahead of him to open the door. As he stepped out, he turned to face her, and through a narrow slit that exposed only half of her slim malevolent face, he boldly confronted her.

"Was it his sexual preferences that shattered you? Was that what tore you and the Colonel apart from Lacey?"

The corners of her exposed mouth pulled tight. She quivered. She slammed the door shut. A gush of air rushed out like a prophetic last dying exhale of life fleeing from the house itself. Axel retracted slowly down the stairs, wheeling to stare eye-to-eye with each gargoyle.

"Such a rough-looking lot." He caught her silhouette behind the curtains in the room to his left. She stood at attention, arms folded, bidding him a not-so-fond farewell. Time stood still as they each continued to stare, her grimacing look impaling his confidence again. Axel, as loud as he could, addressed her.

"It is excellent to have a giant's strength; but it is tyrannous to use it like a giant."

Her face displayed disfigurement until, at last, she retreated from his sight. Axel meanwhile strolled across the front yard, all the time knowing that there were cold eyes following him. He took his time, examining the myriad of statues at the wood's edge. They were all in triads- deer, rabbits, turtles, ducks, all expressing the undying hope that she might yet return to complete the trios.

Eventually, he reached his vehicle, realizing that the day had other duties to tend to, realizing that he had lost track of time. Axel hastily drove down the roadway, retracing his steps, all the time making sure that there was no tail on him. He found a broad convenient shoulder in front of a cement windowless mansion to dial Zoe.

He swapped his story of the encounter with the Colonel for her story of how she obtained the dental records. "I'll call Tinker soonest to try and access the dental records from the autopsy."

"Great work gal. I'll phone Thumper and it looks like I got two calls to return when I was in the Whitehurst's house. Catch up to you later." Two calls to return. He didn't recognize the first number, John Beeton but Dr. Montoya had called. Excellent!

He peeled out and headed down from the hills into the city singing to the tune on the radio,

"Joy to the world, all the boys and girls,

Joy to the fishes in the deep blue sea,

Joy to Zee and me. Joy to Zee and me!"

On and on he sang in supposed harmony. His heart was uplifted. There were no breakthroughs in this complex undertaking. But the confrontations with Mrs. Whitehurst, Lacey's confession, his physical beating, his letdown of security were all behind him.

TUESDAY AFTERNOON

D r. Jim Gieske's extensive instructions describing how to bandage his wounds were sent in pure intended intimidation on his voice mail, emphasizing a peaceful afternoon's rest, probably recognizing that Axel would be his same bustling self and infected with energy to burn. It wasn't entirely a relaxing experience. For the past two hours he had resided in geekdom while Thumper surfed on the internet, delving into an intricate weave of sites while Axel's mind was clobbered with an incessant background of pulsating heavy metal music.

He sat attentively observing Thumper, admiring how fast he navigated the keys, gliding in syncopation to the bass tones of multiple clanging accompaniments. Indeed, he remembered that it was he whom had first given Thumper his nickname years ago when Thumper had applied for this job. The nickname had occurred to Axel as Thumper positioned himself in front of the keyboard to pound out a script. It just seemed more appropriate to address him as Thumper rather than Bradley Stohl.

Thumper's fingers were permanently swollen with broad circumferences. As he sat back, he marveled at Thumper's motor skills. Today was no exception as he hit the center of each key with a thud, so swiftly, so rapidly, so proficiently without even glancing at the keyboard.

"No luck, boss. If the coroner captured the dental records during Spiller's autopsy, it is either not recorded or more likely, we don't have clearance. It is just not in any file Clarissa transferred to us. The records could be confidential. Do you want me to call Clarissa back?"

"No! At least we have a set of M's real dental records. We just don't have anything yet to compare them to. Our best bet is to have Zoe confide in Tinker and request them. I was just hoping we could use another route without getting Tinker involved. What about the phone numbers I discovered in Spiller's hideout?"

"Ah, Jenna works at the First Capital Bank, San Pedro branch. I talked to her at length. Nice lady. She turns out to be no more than Roy's contact at the branch for his accounts. Her employment dates back eight years and she has known Roy for two; she is not a friend of Roy's but rather just a business contact at the bank. She did tell me, after I naturally turned on the cyber-charm, that Roy has thousands of dollars in his personal accounts."

"You extracted that from her?"

"Yeah, not a bad stash for a beach bum; thousands of bucks. She didn't want to discuss Roy over the phone, but said she'd be glad to talk to you in person, for any further info about Roy that is, and with proper credentials. I strongly suggest I set up an appointment for you. I also dragged out of her that he has safety deposit boxes, plural."

"Man, I always miss your interrogation techniques Thump. How did you extract that? Safety deposit boxes?"

"I'm tenacious yet courteous, relentless yet tender, inquisitive yet compromising."

"I think it is time to engage Tinker. I'll have to visit Capital Bank with him. Transmit the branch location and number to Tinker, so we can inspect the boxes when we visit. He'll need the box numbers."

Thumper waved a piece of paper. "I'm two steps ahead of you. Remember? Relentless but tender. I know you have a tight schedule, but I'll confirm an appointment at the bank tomorrow with Jenna for you two."

Thumper paused and added, "Zoe called to remind us of our rendezvous at Montilladan's residence at seven o'clock tonight with Tinker. I transmitted the map to get there." Axel removed the folded piece of paper from his shirt, eyed the Bel Air address, and tucked it back in place as Thumper added, "I'm excited. Investigating Montilladan's crib." He turned to face Axel. "No luck on this number. It is not a listed phone number in the L.A. greater area."

"Cellular?"

"Perhaps, except that it doesn't ring when you call. I also tried different area codes. I'll burn more calories on it later. Too many digits for a bank safety deposit box. Maybe a bond account." Thumper shifted from disappointment to animated.

"Now, this phone number is interesting- coastal Los Angeles, warehouse district, not far from LAX, a public number. Look here on this map." Thumper directed Axel's attention to the key map neighborhood displayed on his computer screen. Axel noted from Thumper's finger the locale but his mind, like Thumper's, was anticipating the thrill of inspecting M's residence tonight.

"I am still working on the plastic card key, trying to tie it into an address through the manufacturer. Hope to have an address for you in four hours!"

"Inspection of the warehouse area, visiting the bank, tracking any other leads that these mysterious digits lead me to, that's my morning's work for tomorrow. You have to come through Thumper." Exiting Thumper's hideout, ears ringing, returning to the solace of his inner office, Axel returned Dr. Montoya's phone call. No answer. No Lillian. Voice mail confronted him. He wished not to play this game of phone tag, so he aborted the call rather than leave a message with her message machine. Ten minutes later, the same frustration surfaced again as he tried to contact Nikki. No answer.

No human. It was John Beeton's turn. Success, although Axel drew a blank on the name.

"Hello, Mr. Beeton, this is Axel Hawk returning your call."

"Mr. Hawk, thank you very much for getting back to me so quickly. I really hadn't expected you to call so soon." The voice was not recognizable.

"We know that you are very busy. Let me introduce myself. I am the director of Ace Flying and Parachuting School." Suddenly Axel had a sinking feeling. "You can imagine how disappointed I was when I read of your latest jump. You are, Mr. Hawk, one of our best pupils in the art of parachuting. Most of your jumps are more proficient than my instructors and you understand the elements of navigation, safety and harnessing the air, at least until last Saturday. I do believe that there may have been a previous incident before my tenure here."

Axel recalled the first time that he had jumped early, navigated a similar path to Zoe's house only to find her absent. That time on a prayer, he landed in the field behind her place and dragged the parachute to the back patio of Zoe's to tap loudly on her window. A neighbor was aroused and threatened to summon the police unless he "removed himself from the premises". With dashed hopes, he retreated to his car, just as where he had parked it last weekend. That incident was forgiven by his instructors.

"Mr. Hawk, I want a written apology since we do need to keep records on our jumps. Regrettably, I am forced to suspend you. As I said earlier you are one of our best pupils. Your safety record on completed missions is impeccable. But I can't use your past safety record and the corresponding tracks as an excuse to absolve you of your current misdeed."

The lack of confrontation surprised Beeton. Axel drenched in guilt responded. "Mr. Beeton, I am sorry, and I apologize. Take what steps you require to rectify the situation. I shall have a letter posted to you within twenty-four hours. I love jumping, so I want to jump again with Ace. Mr. Dufour is also upset I imagine."

Beeton was curious. "Mr. Dufour is furious. A resolution so soon is encouraging. You must realize that we just can have people parachuting wherever and whenever they want over the metropolis. Air space over L.A. must be rigidly controlled and monitored. May I inquire as to what prompted this action, which seems out of character?" Axel wasted no time to reply.

"Love."

"Ah, love, a very worthy cause, Mr. Hawk, but a lousy excuse. There is no sympathy from me I'm afraid. I hope that this escapade of love was worth it, Mr. Hawk."

"Even with your disciplinary actions, even with my absence of future jumps, er, yes, it was."

"As a condition of suspension, I must have your locker key returned."

"I will mail it with the apology. Mr. Beeton I will do everything you ask to get reinstated."

"You realize my actions are mandatory. I hope that you will continue to jump with us. There are no hard feelings here at Ace's with the exception of

Dufour, but we must post our trajectories, adhere to them, and your deviation from the posted path must be mitigated."

"I plan to jump again after my suspension is served Mr. Beeton. I am sorry for any inconvenience or embarrassment that I may have caused you or your business."

"The inconvenience is all yours Mr. Hawk and the embarrassment is all yours. You are suspended for four months pending evaluation of your sincerity in your apology and an appearance before our instructors." The line went dead.

He paused to reflect on his actions. Although not proud of breaking the rules, he had not harmed anyone, found Zoe at home, created a new tale of adventure, and had materialized a fantasy by acting out a dream that had possessed him for six months. The locker key? In the top drawer of his desk. He moved immediately to deposit it in a large brown envelope on which he scribbled the Ace address. The letter of apology he would craft later, so he threw the envelope on his desk.

Entering their private washroom off the entry way, he dabbed the left side of his nose with white sticky disinfectant cream just as Dr. Gieske had instructed. After replacing the flesh-colored bandage, he noticed that the scabs on the bottom of his cheek were drying out, but the nose wounds were stubborn. Lifting his shirt to spy deep purple colors on his swollen stomach, a familiar voice interrupted his examination, so he stepped back into his office to greet Speed. They each brimmed with the excitement of the moment.

"Speed! Hey, great surprise." Speed provided a gingerly hug after noticing his physical state.

"Axel my buddy, it's always my pleasure to talk to you."

"Hey, guy, you didn't need to come by. I just wanted to speak to you on the phone."

"No bother, Hawk. Jeannie's working in a clinic today fifteen blocks from here. Speaking of clinics, you should drop by and see my lovely physician wife. She can subscribe at least ten prescriptions to heal you." Axel pulled up his shirt.

"Whoa, Axel! Yikes! What happened?" Speed continued to stare until Axel covered the blossom up. Speed chided him again. "What an ugly montage. Gives me a brainstorm for my next canvas though and I'd get to use all my colors. Tell me what happened pal."

"I had a run-in with two thugs in the washroom at Fosse's Tavern. It is highly possible that they were hired to beat me up and scare Zoe and I away from the present case that we are working on."

"And you want me to take care of them?"

"No, Speed, that's not it at all. Zoe and I turned that incident over to Tinker. However, I had an impetuous desire to contact you because we've hit a roadblock in a current case that Zee and I are tackling and I need your assistance."

Speed was as thin as a rake, and dressed in short sleeve shirt and khaki shorts, which displayed his enormous boney protrusions at the elbows, knees, cheeks and shoulders. Axel reminisced to himself when he and Nikki and Speed were ever so tight in high school, but Nikki dropped Speed from her list of friends when she discovered his drug dependency; now she had dropped Axel, too. The triumvirate was dissolved as Axel rarely saw Speed anymore. Maybe with this untimely reunion, Speed would be back in his routine. They sat at Axel's desk.

"I hear that Jeannie has been an elixir in your life."

"You heard right." Speed sat upright, bursting with pride, all the curly brown whiskers and sideburns trimmed as neat as Axel had ever witnessed them and his hair combed straight back, tied in a knot behind.

"Jeannie is first class. She is the greatest love of my life, Axel. She loves me passionately. I met her in drug rehab after I was released. She was the officer assigned to my case and she saw in me the desire to end this dependency on drugs. She recognized in me my desire to win my life back again, so she has helped me do it. Since my release, we have been inseparable. I never knew that life could be this intoxicating. I swear I'm finally off the stuff."

"I am so gratified to hear that. It lifts my heart to hear that you are back in the real world. You and I both know how perilously close we came to losing you." Speed's raspy voice was bubbling with appreciation.

"Thanks, Hawk. Jeannie took the important first step, just as you did, by forgiving me for past sins unlike some other people we know." Axel wanted to avert a crisis.

"Don't go there Speed." Speed heeded his advice.

"What can I do for my buddy Axel?"

"Well, Zoe and I have undertaken a rather complex case. I'm telling you this in absolute confidence because as long as I've known you, you can keep a secret."

"Damn right I can."

"It appears that the missing person that we are searching for may have two identities- I'm talking about two identities as recognized by legal and government authorities."

Speed unexpectedly caught Axel by surprise by changing topics. "I hear you and Nikki broke up."

Axel took a deep breath. How he desired to put this topic to rest. "You heard correctly."

"Excuse me Axel. I know we're supposed to avoid the topic, but I am compelled to say something to you."

"Okay, Speed, let's visit the matter and put it to rest. My case can wait with friendship first." Axel was nervous about the oncoming critique.

"Axel, I was a bad person once. It took me time in rehab clinics to discover how messed up I was. I let my friends down. My whole life revolved around the cycle of drugs- obtaining them, using them, allowing them to control my actions and deteriorate my existence. They almost killed me as you just referred to." He bowed his head. "When you are alone in a tiny cell in rehab you have a lot of time to recollect about all your misgivings. You have a lot of free time to plan your success when you are free again. Before you now exists a penitent man."

Speed's voice overflowed with enthusiasm. "I thought about you, Axel. I have never had the right opportunity since my release to express properly to you how much your faith in me kept me going. Your routine visits, our man to man talks. In my greatest moments of despair, I reached for you and you were there. She wasn't."

"The pleasure was all mine Speed. I wanted to be there. I remembered you as a decent caring altruistic human being. I wanted to see the real Speed materialize again. We don't have to talk about this if it pains you."

"But we do have to talk, Axel. She knew that I was in pain. She knew I'd done wrong. I asked for her forgiveness on her sole visit but, blatantly, she rejected me when I needed her the most. After that, I wrote her soul-searching notes and she returned them unopened to sender. She exorcised me from her life."

Axel detected Speed's bereavement. *Speed missed Nikki just as he did. How ironic it was that Speed captured his nickname at a local high school meet when he dashed to six track medals; in time his nickname would take on a crueler meaning as his drug dependency grew.*

"So, Axel, I have become a better person. I have cleansed myself. I came here today because I don't want to talk on your cell. I wanted to come by and say thanks for sticking with me and inform you personally about my new life. I found Jeannie. I still have your vote of confidence. I have found faith in God, so Jeannie and I attend church every Sunday. I have new constructive extracurricular interests, including a personal renaissance in painting, one of my favorites as you recall." Speed orated confidently.

"I know that you don't want to hear this Axel, but you shouldn't take any time to miss her." Axel sat arms folded, finding it difficult to heed this advice. Oh, how he wanted not to debate this issue with Speed.

"You're a dear friend, Speed. I have taken note of your words, which define your position. I have my position, too, whereby I still remain in contact with her. Let's return to the problem at hand now that you have had your say. Do I have your concurrence?"

"Sure, return to…as in the cat with two lives?"

Axel elaborated. "Yes, as in this cat living more than one life, maybe even more than two. So, I am wondering where and how this person obtains pertinent official legal documents to support a two count or more in the census?"

"Ah, as in two drivers' licenses, two social numbers, two tax paying ID's, two passports, et cetera, et cetera?"

"Right on. One acquired years ago. The other I think acquired recently which will allow her to fly through an escape hatch to a new life somewhere else by abandoning her previous identity! I'm talking about a whole new life of credentials that cannot be questioned." Speed nodded, conveying his understanding of the situation.

"Well, it all starts with a birth certificate and a social security number. With those two documents, you could get about anything. You just said, maybe more. How many lives are we talking about?"

"Two for sure but, beyond that, Zoe and I don't know. There could be additional identities. We are dealing with a cunning deceitful devil, so I wouldn't put it past this fox to create three or more new lives."

"Okay, so let's figure you got to have both the birth certificate and the social security number. With those documents, you walk into any institution to legally obtain a driver's license, file an income tax return, receive a passport, get credit cards, open bank accounts, everything you need to exist and travel." Speed and Axel shared eye contact as Speed meditated.

"Considering that we can't scour the world to find who could do this, and given that this person has been based in Southern California for her recent life, where does a person go to get these documents? In SoCal, let's say?" Speed shook his head with a tight-lipped smile.

"Axel, I been disconnected from those criminal types for years now, purposefully, so as you know but, if I had to take a guess, used to be a couple of guys down on Whitman Street, but the cops closed them down when I was in absentia. Lots of demand for impeccable forged documents in the California area as you can imagine. However, if you take the risk to obtain quality papers, engage someone good, like real good, a master forger, someone you pay big bucks to, say to compensate the forger for his risk, and then, hmm." Speed gazed up at the ceiling to collect his thoughts as Axel waited patiently.

"Feds closed Shorty Feldman down and Righteous Richard, too; Don Albertelli is in prison last I heard and his business liquidated by the feds; old Grandy passed away last year from cancer. There was a purge a few years ago when illegal immigrants burst onto the scene. That leaves a very short list of suspects."

"Take your best guess."

Speed smiled. "You are crafty, Axel. I know what you want me to say. It is so bloody obvious, so I'll confirm it. Maybe Briss, if he's still around because there's just nobody better."

"That was my only instinctive guess, too. Gorgeous George Brissand. The handsome schmoozer himself."

"Ah, yeah. You remember when I helped you corner him in the alley? And I pulled his pants down while he was having a piss?"

"I recall that we stole his pants Speed!"

"Oh, yeah, I'd forgotten that Hawk." Speed and Axel shared that moment of bonding that Speed was searching for as Axel treasured the return of Speed's spirit. Axel observed the renewed sincerity of fulfillment in Speed's life. The return of his confidant nature was a blessing as Speed rambled on.

"Those sure were the good old days when you were starting your practice and I had not yet fully succumbed to the nefarious side. Axel, I don't hang with any of that seedy crowd anymore, so it will be tough for those people to confide in me if I go poking around for information on master forgers, especially Brissand. You understand that, don't you?"

Axel jumped to his feet and moved to sit on the same side of his desk as Speed. "Speed! I would never ever impose upon you to jeopardize your new found love, and your new found treasured freedom. I would not ask you to risk all you have gained. All that we are doing Speed is brainstorming."

"Who are you searching for, Axel?"

"Someone who has disappeared with a totally new identity. Female, mid-thirties, thin, in great shape. She has been both male and female personas at different times in her life. That is, she has dressed and acted as a male. Just to clarify, her real sex has always been female, no transgender or sex change involved here but a passion to play a male, yes. Spring to the current times. Zoe and I are positive that she has purchased and built a new female identity while recently abandoning her past successful male persona behind forever. That's what she is using for her new life."

"Wow! What a story! Sounds freaky. I'll go poking around to see who's designing new forged papers. It won't be easy as I have said. I'm clean, and… the old stomping' grounds on Hassard Street have changed, too. New crowd of criminals down there, but I will discreetly give it a try."

"I only wanted to brainstorm, Speed."

"It's okay. Your reputation precedes you, Axel, so you can't go there without being noticed. No one will open up to you. I'm best suited to snoop around this crowd."

"I don't want…" Speed stood, lifted his arms and motioned to Axel to halt.

"I don't intend to place myself in jeopardy. For you Axel, I will do this. Make a few personal calls, person to person contacts, walk the streets very cautiously. I know where to poke my nose in."

"I'll pay you for any expenses incurred."

"You most certainly will and I'll keep inflated receipts!"

Axel grinned. "Speed, don't take any chances. Just remember, I don't want you to end up looking like me," and he lifted his shirt once again. "If you see or hear anything, please come sprinting back here. Call Zoe or me or Tinker if our assistance is necessitated." He handed him his card with all three cell numbers on the back.

"I will, Axel. Hell, the thought of looking like you is enough motivation to run away from the slightest indication of trouble." Speed pointed at him as he spoke. "You stayed with me in the bad times, Axel. I owe you at least this small favor."

Speed postulated, "This lady kidnapped maybe?"

"Um, not likely. Zoe and I figure she left on her own accord."

"Maybe, if she really does have multiple legal identities, she's CIA or FBI or…have you and Zoe thought about the witness protection program? That's a sure fire way of getting multiple legal identities."

"Hardly. Take my word for it. She's knows what she's doing and she knows how to execute a crime of misadventure. Although I hadn't considered the witness protection program angle, that's a good one."

Speed moved to the outer office as Axel followed. "You have to keep this assignment a secret. Not even Jeannie must know! Promise?"

"I promise." Axel presented him with a few more details on the caper while being careful as to not expose Montilladan.

"Summation. This person disappeared recently. The metamorphosis has just transpired. Handsome macho male into a beautiful butterfly. I need to know who is cutting papers to create the new persona."

"This sounds like something you could read about in the gossip rags, Axel ole buddy. I will do my best, but how about letting Jeannie take a look at those bruises in return?"

"I am alright, Speed." With their briefing closed, Axel felt compelled to set the record straight. "I know that you and Nikki have differences, Speed, but we do have to respect her rights to make her own decisions. Our breakup is as much my fault as hers. That is a fact. I want you to consider this- that Nikki Louden has matured, she has grown up. She is not the person that we once knew years ago and she has moved on to a new life that doesn't include us. She doesn't have to depend on us anymore and we have to respect that. Give her some respect and space. Please."

Speed tried to interrupt but Axel caught him. "You were wrong before. Nikki and I were drifting apart, she into her world of journalism; me into my world of crime. You and Nikki weren't meant to be, nor Nikki and I. Leave it at that Speed. You and I still have each other's friendship. I intend to connect with you more frequently. I promise. Not just show up when I need a favor."

"Are you sure that I can't drive you to see Jeannie?" As he spoke, he handed a card with his contact numbers to Axel.

"Thank you, but no thanks. Heed my advice Speed. Keep your head up and check your back frequently and if the name of Roy Spiller should appear in any conversation, I want you to call Zoe or me immediately."

"I'm so sorry I missed Burnsie. Give her my regards."

"I'll tell Zee how good you look, too."

As quickly as Speed had arrived, with a sturdy handshake he had now departed. Always in motion, just as in the good old days when he was streaking down crushed red brick paths to the finish line ahead off the pack.

Axel spied his watch. He returned to his desk side to write his letter of apology to John Beeton in an elaborate brush of sincerity. He was putting the finishing forgiveness plea together when interrupted. Thumper entered for a serious interlude by positioning his massif in the chair across from his desk. Axel quickly signed the dissertation and sealed the envelope. "How's Speed doing, boss?"

"He's discovered true love."

"No shit! Lucky guy! Anyone we know?"

"No, she's a General Practitioner who has instilled peace therapy into him. He met her during his rehabilitation. Paraphrasing his own words, his body is cleansed of pollutants." Thumper expressed his glee and turned his chubby cheeks to a glum side. Axel was astonished at the dour look on his face.

"Now that's a look I don't see often. What's wrong?"

"Axel, every time we talk, it's always at the office. It's always business, like, we never get to sit like this, the two of us, alone face to face. Zoe is always close by, or clients are pounding at the door, or the phone is ringing and you have to take a call and rush off." Thumper positioned himself closer by leaning across toward Axel.

"And the point of this discussion is?"

"Well, way I figure it is that we've never had a case where you and Zoe have been exposed to this much danger. I mean, Hawkman, this entire case is weird. You've never been beaten up like this before. Look at you! We never had such a famous client before, and we are searching for a person of notoriety. We got no clues to motive, no idea where to search. We're not even sure what sex the missing person is portraying. Totally weird. Weird. Weird."

"And the point of this discussion is?"

"When I heard that you had been savagely attacked, I couldn't help but think that this person that we are looking for is onto us. I mean, what if Montilladan is responsible for your beating, look at the financial resources at her disposal. With her money, she could hire any thugs she wants. Think of what she could engage to defeat us, and hell, we have hardly started our job."

Axel egged him on. "And the point of this discussion is?"

"The point is that I like you and Zoe, and I love my job as chief, sole researcher at A to Z with flex hours, great resources, high-tech computer toys, and interesting assignments not to forget the outstanding human beings I work with. I've never told you this before, but I think the world of you and Zee. I'm concerned about you two. If and when our cover on this case gets blown, you and Zee could be targets for this maniac. Montilladan could stalk and injure you." Axel used his hand to motion him to continue.

"So, I want to say that I want you two, Zoe and you, to be extra careful on this one. I got a bad feeling about where this case could take us. Boss, I really have come to like you two as I just stated. You two occupy a very special place in my life; you're like family."

Axel felt touched. "Thank you for your advice, your comments and for your concern. Zoe and I appreciate the work you do, and me, I have learned my lesson. I am on high alert." Thumper wasn't finished.

"Thanks for taking a chance on me boss. I never really say it enough. I like my work. But this case sucks. I mean, look at you."

Axel replied. "I did in the mirror this morning and it wasn't pretty." Thumper beamed while Axel added, "I was the entertainment down at Constance and Lieber." Now they both chuckled. Axel leaned back in his chair.

"I remember when we first met. I asked you how you got to be three hundred and twenty pounds."

Thumper slapped his hands, stomped his feet, and shook his full head of disheveled fiery hair. "Yeah, I replied to you by saying that I had been on a diet and lost sixty pounds."

They conversed in sincerity for another ten minutes, Thumper in great appreciation of Axel's window to talk, Axel bestowing Thumper with praise and support. That is, until they were infringed by Nikki Louden in person, boldly rapping on the inner office door, dressed to stun any male. Disappointed that the conversation was severed, Thumper allowed her privacy by excusing himself to retreat into his geek kingdom, closing the door to Axel's office behind him.

"Excuse me, Axel," she politely expressed, "I saw your car parked at the back and took a chance you'd be in." Axel couldn't help himself as his heart was pounding. The sight of her sexiness had evaporated any resistance.

She spoke seriously. "Considering Thumper's shabby appearance, I hope that he produces spectacular results!"

"He most certainly does Nikki. Thumper lives in his own world, but I don't know anyone who can access and discover some of the facts he finds us. Effectively researches all our cases. He is an expert navigator. I tried to call you earlier but, obviously, something brings you here. Lucky me."

She dropped her briefcase beside the chair, continued to take off white gloves while huffing at him. "I wanted to see you in person to tell you how sorry I was when I heard that you had been in a fight and got the worst. I really am sorry, Axel. I didn't know it would lead to this! Honest. You look terribly wounded and much worse than I imagined." Axel stood, just as he did for Speed and gave Nikki the full effect by showing off his purple and blue stomach muscles.

Nikki responded with, "Oh, my. I never dreamed I would place you in this much danger."

Axel was elated at her sincerity. "Who informed you about the incident?"

"Thumper, when I phoned in earlier. I told him not to tell you that I had called since I planned to visit you in person to surprise you. Give you moral support. Axel I truly am concerned for your future safety."

Nikki discarded her glasses on the desk, strutted beside him, and leaned over to hug him tight, forcing her breasts against his shoulder. She squatted to plunk a short peck on his lips. Axel responded. "Gee, I'll have to get clobbered more often."

"Don't get any ideas. I am just glad that you are alive. This is nothing to scoff at."

Axel placed his arm around her waist from his sitting position, and whispered, "I am very appreciative of your thoughtfulness to come by and express it personally. It means a great deal to me."

They broke contact, Nikki, with head bowed, moving to her seat saying, "I had an awkward moment in the parking lot. I bumped into Speed, literally."

"Is that what Speed has been reduced to, an awkward moment?"

"We just don't have anything in common anymore Axel. I wished him well in his new life. He says that he has a new partner in life, a physician. So, that's great news, someone new and responsible to care of him. How he needs it. I hope he doesn't hurt her the way he hurt us."

"I have a hunch it will work out."

"I hope so."

Axel prayed that he had done the prudent thing by asking Speed to risk himself and reputation in the search for M. If he and Zoe were going to locate Brissand, the master forger, Speed would have to locate him. He wasn't going to reveal any of that important information to Nikki and knew that Speed had not volunteered it. Speed's assistance on this case would not sit well with her.

"How is Lacey holding up?"

"Better, now that she knows that you are active on the case. This is all so bizarre."

"Agreed. Can I get you some ice tea?"

"No, I can't stay, Axel. This really was on my route to my next appointment and I just had to insure myself that you were in the world of the living. I had to witness you in person. I just feel better visiting you to express my genuine sympathy and concern since I pushed you into this. You must promise me to be vigilant from here on in."

"I promise. I made a serious mistake to cause this. It was entirely my fault as my ego got the best of me and I won't make fatal errors in judgment again. Three questions before you depart."

She obliged. "Only three, it is all I have time for."

"Did Montilladan or Lacey or her friends ever mention a Dr. Renee Montoya? She is a psychiatrist." Axel was desperately trying to avoid her omnipresent beauty today. Her pant suit was a striking blue, which fit her physique perfectly.

"No, but I know who she is. I have seen her recently once or twice at social gatherings when someone pointed her out to me in a crowd, and surprisingly informed me that Montilladan was a patient of hers. I don't know anything of what Montilladan was being treated for if that is your angle. Honest, Axel, I have never been formally introduced to her."

"Okay. Accepted. Who was Montilladan's best friend, or at least the most frequent acquaintance from your vantage point? I'm looking for a single answer from you."

"I hate to disappoint you, but I didn't track M's social life carefully. If I have one guess, I would state Lacey Sills."

"Okay. Second place?"

"I didn't know Montilladan that well. I can't possibly think of anyone else given the intimacy of those two."

"One last query. Lacey informed me that this affair with Montilladan was a one-time affair for Lacey with a female. That she loves men, too. What about Montilladan? Tell me the truth. A one-time affair with a woman or were there others? And what about boyfriends? And how did you feel about Lacey's involvement with Montilladan?"

"I will share with you some innermost thoughts, just like the good old days of high school when our pledges were solemn. I still trust you."

"You have my word."

"Female affairs are a social behavior that is here to stay. Lacey and Montilladan are not the only bisexual female friends I have, or the only ones in the entertainment industry. I don't personally practice this kind of behavioral relationship because I love men, but I conduct respect for this tendency in my journalism. I don't expose these affairs for profit. I don't expose these affairs to gain the eye of the public. The public and press sometimes turn these relationships into victims. What I am really trying to express is, that I don't use these relationships to sell my column. That is a credo which I have made and have never violated." She drew circles with her index finger on Axel's desk as she spoke.

"I like Lacey no less and no more for what she has told me and I don't know of the details behind Montilladan's private life, so I cannot direct you to anyone else in M's life. I'm sorry, but I never had any urge to investigate the love life of Montilladan, nor Lacey's involvement, until the event I informed you of Sunday evening, which I now place in your hands."

Very unpredictably, she collected her things, passed by Axel to initiate a brief contact and confidently strode to the door. "Sorry to cut this conversation short Axel. I am on my way to an important interview. Just had to see you, to make sure you were recovering. I am utterly sincere Axel when I tell you that I don't want to hear of another occurrence of this sort." She hustled out as he leaned out of his chair to register the final glimpses of her.

"Take care, Nikki," he called after her. Nikki was gone.

Axel sat silently to collect his thoughts. He didn't want to tell Nikki about the Andorran accounts nor the dental records nor Speed's involvement nor of the Whitehurst's. The Whitehursts! He thumbed through a dossier that Thumper had prepared which was now placed conspicuously on his desk. After ten minutes of digesting their lives, the Colonel in the military, Kathleen in her charity work, he decided that the personal encounter with them had left him with more in-depth insight than the profile. He did note where the Colonel had been awarded numerous medals for bravery and was wounded in combat.

Next, his mind absorbed the file on Montilladan and the police report on M's death. Thumper was gleeful on his return. "Dr. Larry Bartlett will see you in one hour. I just confirmed with his executive assistant."

"Terrific work big guy. I knew I could count on you. Now, how do I get there?"

"You can just make it. Head east on Interstate Ten toward Ontario. Take exit thirty-five B and you are four miles from the business. Here's a key map page."

Axel rushed to the washroom to stick on fresh flesh-colored bandages, lathered himself with stomach cream that stank of a hospital ward. Appearances aside, he knew the urgency to confront Bartlett confidently.

He telephoned Dr. Montoya's office once more only to receive again the disappointment of a continuous ring followed by a metallic voice asking to leave name and number. No way. He disconnected.

From her vantage point, she easily identified Nikki Louden exiting the building. "I curse you, you snoop. I always disliked you. What the Hell is the PI telling you?" She pounded the dashboard vehemently. Her blood pressure rose as she witnessed him leave shortly thereafter. Convinced that he had not noticed her as he drove right by her in the opposite direction, she changed wigs, extracted sunglasses from the glove compartment, made a U-turn and accelerated to tail him.

Following Thumper's directions, forty minutes later he found himself encircled by business establishments with low rise discount malls running perpendicular to the streets. At a stop sign, he quickly noticed that the real estate took a mark up in price. Now he drove down a shrub lined boulevard, which housed individual businesses with exaggerated immaculate boards advertising the occupants. He was five minutes early as he spied his target ahead, so he pulled to the side of the roadway to dial the BeachComber Motel.

"Is the manager in?"

"Speaking. Mr. Parnham at your service."

"Mr. Parnham, my name is Axel Hawk. I am a local private investigator. I am trying to locate a Mr. Roy Spiller. Do you know him or recognize the name?"

"Yes, he is a regular inhabitant."

"When was the last time that you saw him?"

"Oh, a month ago or maybe even two."

"I understand that he patronizes the motel?"

"Frequently with his friends, and I would add that they are always welcome here both the gentlemen and the ladies. They exemplify good conduct. My rates are economy scale, but that group treats the lodgings like a high-class home."

"Does he pay with a credit card?"

"Never. Roy always settles in cash and always up front." Axel wanted to hear a different answer. "Sometimes, he pays for his friends to stay here in advance but always again in cash. Roy is a real honest likeable human being. I don't have many inhabitants like Mr. Spiller…and his friends are very polite and clean. You say you're looking for Roy. He's not in trouble, is he?"

"No, Mr. Parnham, not at all. Please don't speculate about any scenarios." Axel didn't want Parnham to start a rumor mill.

"I like Mr. Spiller. He represents good business."

"Has anyone else come inquiring about Roy Spiller?"

"No?"

"I need to locate him urgently. If you see him, please tell him to call this number immediately. Deal?" Axel delivered his phone numbers to Parnham who was more than agreeable to cooperate. He completed the last yards to four-three-three-one, where both the signs for deMox and MUREX, sat majestically twenty feet high over a lily pond rimmed with flowers.

The driveway was circular and took him up a small hill in front of two six story buildings, the first of which indicated executive offices. A valet in blue uniform intercepted him with a cheerful greeting. Before a minute had passed, his Mustang drove out of sight with the valet and the radio blaring.

Upon his identification, a receptionist from the mammoth four story arboretum entry, guided him to the far reaches at the back of the building, where he soon found himself on the sixth floor in Bartlett's outer office, overlooking a broad rich green forest, dotted with long rectangular research compounds and jogging trails.

Once again he bore the brunt of jokes, this time from Bartlett's assistant as he patiently waited for twenty minutes. She probed into the origins of his wounds as he resisted dispensing information. Suddenly an expletive beep signaled his entry. He had great anticipation ever since Hartwig had mentioned Bartlett's name this morning. Was this to be Romeo?

After introductions, and Axel's tiresome explanations about his physical appearance, he exposed to Bartlett that he was a private investigator probing into Montilladan's accidental death, gathering more details on the death and Montilladan's life for interested parties. Dr. Bartlett was poised, ready to assist if he could.

All the while of this initial encounter, Axel felt crushed. Bartlett was early fifties, clearly had an overly paunchy tummy, not particularly good looking with a large protruding beak nose, a hanging double chin, a receding hairline and dark circles around his eyes. This was not Romeo unless Montilladan's eyesight was definitely failing.

"Dr. Bartlett, I visited Constance and Lieber this morning. From the information I received, I understand that your two businesses, deMOX and MUREX, both of which you are President and Chief Executive Officer, will be the recipients of generous monetary donations from the proceeds of Montilladan's estate."

"Yes." Now that Axel had listened to him, he had a familiarity of the south in his voice with a heavy, southern drawl. He even spoke out of one side of his mouth.

"Did these gratuities come as a surprise to you?"

"Yes and no. I will take the time to explain if you will permit me?"

"I would appreciate that."

"Care for a beverage?"

"No, thank you." Bartlett helped himself to a bottle of water and led them to a comfortable seating area situated away from his desk with a panoramic view of the back lots. There, they positioned themselves across from each other at a conference table.

He articulated. "We have nothing to hide, Mr. Hawk."

Now, why did he interject that? Axel was wondering.

"We conduct classical clinical research in the preparation of new products. There is quite a distinction between deMOX and MUREX. deMOX is a company which contracts with MUREX, and other pharmacy research labs, and executes the necessary preparations to enter new drug products into the marketplace."

"deMox is a business which ground truths new products, establishes the characterization and credibility of the product, tests the market for need and suitability, even recommends the price at which the product be introduced for sales. In short deMox commercializes new products. It generates a profit and has shareholders who expect to be paid dividends from the sales of drugs into the market place to appropriate businesses. All of this is determined by a market analysis in which deMOX designs a strategic business plan and identifies the quick hit markets. Only ten percent of Montilladan's generous gifts went to deMOX and they will be used to upgrade our software and our marketing teams with more experienced salespersons."

Bartlett sipped on his bottled water and remained composed. "MUREX, Mr. Hawk, was named after my dear departed wife, Muriel."

"I am very sorry."

"It took two years of my life to mend my broken heart. Thank you for your concern. God took her from me prematurely. She died from advanced osteoporosis, which accelerated after she commenced menopause. Our laboratory, MUREX, specializes in researching women's problems. We research, design, test, manufacture, patent and distribute drugs through deMox to aid in the special problems that women contract as they age. MUREX is a nonprofit organization, a medical research center. Ninety percent of Montilladan's gift will go toward focused research efforts for which I and the board are extremely thankful."

He continued to recite his pride in his companies. "We didn't start out this way. We were a general research laboratory under contract to larger pharmaceutical conglomerates, but after I lost a sister to breast cancer and my wife to osteoporosis, MUREX retooled with a new vision of the future. I should add that from the very beginning, our other strong business line has been in developing drugs to help children combat learning disabilities, that is drugs which can allow the mind to become clearer, become more focused, less foggy, operate at a pace to run proficiently with analytical functions. It was that aspect that attracted Montilladan as an investor and not our emphasis on the other female specific products I spoke of."

Larry Bartlett spoke with conviction. Axel was a willing listener. "Since our initial focus, we have diversified as I said, into the myriad of problems that accompany the aging of women, so now we have a two-fold mission and two business units within MUREX. Most of Montilladan's generous gift will go to the business unit directed at our research in children's learning disabilities."

"Do you ever sell directly into the marketplace, say bypass deMOX, sell your products to the pharmaceutical giants?"

"Good question. After FDA approval, we sell to the large corporations whom have greater penetration to the consumer than us with their brand names. Their big budgets for advertising are a plus. However, I did create deMOX for the purposes of market analyses and sales there are three products to date that we have not sold to the large corporations, for the reason that the marketing study demonstrated to us that we did not need their clout, and that we could sell into quick hit markets of demonstrable needs. These products filled a niche. We gambled correctly as deMOX has delivered."

Bartlett went on to explain product lines, elaborate on the revenues of the deMOX business, arm Axel with annual reports and led him to another bay window to boast of the laboratories on the property. "Our staff level is modest, as we initiate only a few new development projects each year. The interest level from outside investors, who are familiar with the drug industry, is very high."

He pointed to the adjacent structure. "deMOX is located entirely in the building next door, which you saw as you entered the property and the buildings whose rooftops you spy in the woods are MUREX research labs." Axel had tired of the hard sell.

"I'd like to pose more questions about Montilladan."

"Yes," Bartlett responded, "He had a keen interest in our business and sat on the Board of Directors."

"But tell me what prompted the initial interest and the connection here?" Bartlett signaled to be seated again.

"Why, his agent, Paula Piper." Axel perked up. Bartlett had his attention immediately upon the sound of her name. "Paula recruited Montilladan to a Charity Fund Grand Ball which we hold annually. His agent thought it an excellent opportunity to boost his image, as it came at a time when Montilladan's image required repair. Montilladan, luckily for us, sincerely took to the mission we have to address learning disabilities of children, and in particular the disabled children. That night he learned more about their progress from current investors than any pamphlets or lecture that I could have delivered."

"Thus, the following week, Montilladan made a few pledges, exceeding any expectations that I had. Later, Montilladan saw the benefit of our work in bone strengthening and bone integrity as he toured our facilities for women's causes. This resulted in another round of donations toward osteoporosis. I was elated, so I asked him to become one of our Board members. It wasn't just his generosity that sparked my offer, but rather his sustained sincere interests toward our research." Bartlett praised Montilladan's exploits in the realm of charity further. Axel pondered whether the conniving Montilladan had asked Roy Spiller to attend these functions on occasion or M was the sincere individual.

"Montilladan became very active in our affairs and attended many functions. He was an open supporter of our research and I would be lying to you if I told you that I expected to receive as much as we did from the will. These are quite extraordinary magnificent grants that will help us fund the testing of new drugs, which we believe are revolutionary in nature to help children overcome learning disabilities. Montilladan was a very fit male specimen. Usually our highest contributors to osteoporosis have female connections." Axel was a step ahead of Bartlett in understanding M's interests.

"So, Constance and Lieber have informed you of the gifts before the official reading of the will?"

"I knew ahead of time because Montilladan changed his will months ago and informed me of such. The donations are known to me and will thrust our research forward. The reading of the will only confirms it"

"Thrust forward? Such as?"

Bartlett was startled. "Secrecy is the key to survival in our business, Mr. Hawk. It is an extremely competitive environment. Many drug firms are researching the same problems as us; many in a race with us to hit the marketplace first. I regret that I cannot answer your question except to say that money builds a competitive edge in my business, especially in the non-profit arena of MUREX."

"Just to clarify, you were informed by Montilladan himself before his untimely death, not through any attorney, that you might be the recipient of these kinds of generosities?"

"Correct. The first official notice that I actually received of the exact amounts was when Constance and Lieber summoned me to their offices months ago. However, Montilladan was present and did most of the talking, Constance and Lieber just serving as witness to the event." Bartlett seemed to answer that question with some degree of nervousness. Was that truly the answer? He was suddenly tapping his pencil in front of him. Axel feigned an interest as Bartlett once again restated Montilladan's gratuitous interests to the companies. The conversation became circular until Axel begged apology to depart. Bartlett surprised him.

"Is there something unusual about Montilladan's accident Mr. Hawk?"

"No, I am just tidying up some loose ends for a client. Is Lacey Sills an investor here?" Bartlett was silent. Was this question causing him consternation? Bartlett was staring at him.

"Not that I know of. Of course, I don't know all of our investors though for I have a corporate secretary to liaise and manage them. I knew of Montilladan only because of his Director status."

Axel shivered. He stared across Bartlett's office to a bookcase with a multitude of photographs and drew a fright. But why? "Excuse me, do you mind if I take a closer inspection at that montage of photos?"

"Not at all. Ah, why the interest?"

Axel bolted around behind him, his interest mushrooming. He picked up a specific 8X10 framed photo to examine the six individuals in the photograph, each clad in gala attire, standing poised for the photographer. Turning to Bartlett, he expressed surprise.

"Isn't this Dr. Renee Montoya?"

"Why, why, yes. Do you know her?"

"I know she was an acquaintance of Montilladan's. I know her to see her, that's all; I know her to say hello. What is the connection of Dr. Montoya to you and the organizations?"

"An investor."

"Did Montilladan introduce you to her?"

"As a matter of fact, it was quite the opposite. I met Dr. Montoya first, and she introduced me to Montilladan. I don't recall when or where. Later, Paula entered the picture to officially secure a position on the board for Montilladan."

Axel needed to clarify facts. "I'm confused. Dr. Montoya introduced you to Montilladan before his agent, Paula Piper, sent him to the charity? Before Paula recruited Montilladan for your investments and board position?"

"Why, yes. Paula Piper just solidified a commitment that was brewing through Dr. Montoya," he responded as he swallowed hard. "That photograph was taken during a charity dinner to raise funds for my companies. Small world, isn't it? That you should know Paula Piper and Dr. Montoya." Bartlett suddenly seemed nervous as he spoke.

"Yes, small world, indeed." Axel replaced the photograph and frame back onto the desk top and, as he did so, he continued to stare at the six people and their garb. There was something very odd about that photo. Very odd indeed. A nagging, obtuse thought. But what was it that was nagging at him? He couldn't stand here all day, but there was definitely something wrong in the photo! Something out of place! He inspected their dressy attires and examined each face in turn. What was it? Axel committed the photograph to memory. Oh, no, he had lost the thought of concern. Scouring the rest of Bartlett's collection of photos, the faces were unfamiliar to him except for appearances by Bartlett, Montilladan, two recognizable movie stars and of course, Dr. Renee Montoya.

He faced Bartlett. Under the bright pot light he materialized as a very tired looking individual, a very haggard man, sagging face, red eyed. "I know that this sounds crazy, but was Montilladan suffering from any diseases that you know of?"

"No, Montilladan was a very fit male specimen."

"You're sure?"

"I repeat: Montilladan was a very fit male specimen." Axel was astonished. The same answer as if...programmed to respond? Twice now and earlier. Bartlett was still talking. "Absolutely! He took a physical before he joined our Board." Axel took note of that comment. Where did he take that physical? If only he could interview the physician; or maybe Roy Spiller substituted.

"Did Montilladan have learning disabilities, either as a child or later in life?"

"Not that he ever divulged to me. I told you, he was very fit male specimen. He sympathized with our causes immensely. He fell in love with our kids whom we sponsor in the greater city area. He visited with some of the children who are on our medication and experienced their progress first hand. If he actually had learning disabilities in his life, they were never mentioned to me or to our organization and he hides them very well." Bartlett was sweating.

It was time to exchange courtesies. Dr. Bartlett wished him luck and hoped for a speedy recovery from his obvious physical beating. Axel was trying to remember if he had told Dr. Bartlett if he had used the word beaten. Yes, he had. He glanced over Bartlett's shoulder one last time to the photo of interest, but it was now too distant to rekindle any remnants of his previous epiphany. It would be too outrageous to ask for a copy.

Patiently he waited for his vehicle to be returned to the portal by the valet. If only he could remember what had bothered him so much about that photo? He tipped him three dollars, buckled himself in, and then, to his surprise, caught an unsuspecting glance from Dr. Bartlett peaking from behind a transparent drape on the fifth floor level, corner office, staring with a flinty glare, right down to the spot he occupied in the front seat.

Bartlett had obviously walked from the very back of the compound to the front end of the building, to position himself behind that curtain after they had shaken hands. And for what purpose? Their eye contact was fleeting and only as Axel pulled out from under the canopy and gazed skyward, but he recognized Bartlett, and Bartlett clearly made eye contact with him. Axel thought that Bartlett's actions begged for a second meeting.

He noticed not the black Ford parked curbside and to the right of him as he exited the premises. Coming out of the circular driveway, he concentrated on the sharp left turn into the roadway. Inside the Ford, her blood pressure rose and her cheeks tingled as she repeated, "Get hold of yourself!" She growled in anger and spite as she ducked when he moved past her. What was happening? *How could Axel Hawk have connected the dots from Roy's beach hangout to Larry Bartlett? Or had he? Maybe it was just a lucky guess.* She heaved a sigh, shut her eyes. The plan was on course. She was in complete control of the outcome. No one really knew her ultimate goal. It was her secret. It was known only to her. It was too late in the game for it to unravel. So, what if these two busybodies figured out that Roy's accident was no accident. They would never deduce "the why". However, she wrestled with a tough decision. How close were they? Grasping straws? It would be over soon. Discipline. Patience. Confidence. Or a quick strike?

She fondled the revolver in her lap as she pulled up beside him at a traffic light. She stole a glance. He was in his own world, grinning, humming, and lost in his environment. Good.

TUESDAY EVENING

"I'll have a large Cobb salad with Thousand Island dressing, an extra sliced egg, and two, large glasses of cold water with tons of ice." The Green Thumb was sparsely populated at this early dinner hour. This was Axel's habitual standard menu request. He inquired of both the waitress and hostess about Montilladan's tour of duty at the Green Thumb, but it was before either had joined the staff. In all the times he had eaten here, he never heard Montilladan's name spoken nor realized the employment tenure here. He had even overlooked the photo now displayed prominently at the entry upon M's return here for an evening after he became famous.

"I don't think anyone remains here from when Montilladan worked here," Louise said. "There is even a new owner for the franchise. It seems to change every two years. Over there, is his photograph in a black suit." She pointed to an enlarged glossy residing behind the front teller.

"Yes, I noticed it on the way in. Thanks for sharing that. I'm going for a quick stroll on the beach and will return in a few minutes." On his way out he stopped once again to re-examine the photograph of a cheeky Montilladan, clowning around, showing off the menu of the Green Thumb. Descending the creaky wooden stairs at the back exit, he walked one block and bounded onto the sandy beach expanse, extracting his cellular to dial Thumper.

"Hey Thumper, can you do a quick search on our dear friend and Montilladan's agent, Ms. Carol Paula Piper. I noticed that she wasn't in the prepared bios you drafted earlier. How did we miss that Paula was Montilladan's agent?"

"She's tied to Montilladan now Axman. I added a section on her this afternoon, so I'm way ahead a ya. Her name definitely turned up as Montilladan's only current agent. I already called her office to confirm the facts. Wait a sec." Axel breathed heavily. The ocean air was thick as a sauna. Down the coastline, he saw a soupy orange Martian cloud hanging over Los Angeles proper.

"You still there, Axman?"

"I need Paula's phone number."

"Sure thing. Here it is."

Axel punched the number into his frequent contacts list and reminded Thumper to move up his tempo to M's residence soon and "bring the digital camera. I want every room, every wall photographed." After Thump replied, "Geez, you act like I've never done this before," he dialed Paula's office and with luck, she was in and quite surprised Axel by answering her own phone.

"Paula?"

"Yes, who is this?"

"It's Axel Hawk." Axel had met Paula as one of Nikki's dear confidants. On a number of occurrences they had double dated with various beaus of Paula's.

"Axel, how sweet of you to call. You're not calling me to double date again? Like the days gone down?"

"No, not a chance."

"So, what's the occasion?"

"I need your assistance on a business matter."

"As an agent? You are full of surprises."

"No, Paula, I mean I am calling about information on one of your clients."

"Ah, I hate to change the subject on you, but did you know that I am leaving the business?"

"No! Vacation? Hiatus? Sabbatical?"

"No, I am getting married to Ramon Guisti and I owe it all to you! You introduced us. Remember?"

"Sure do. Christmas party two years ago. He's a great guy. Honest. Tremendous sense of humor. Job security."

"Hey, Axel, stop it, I'm marrying him. Remember? You don't have to sell me on my beau Ramon, and it was three years ago, not two."

"Congratulations. When was this decided?"

"About three months ago. You should be receiving an invite in the mail for a reception with friends when we return after our honeymoon."

"Congratulations, Paula. I am so happy for you and give my kindest regards to Ramon. Lucky guy." Axel recalled how he always found it easy to converse with Paula in free-flowing respectful dialogue.

She hit a somber note. "I hear that you and Nikki parted."

"We were both to blame. It is just one of those events in life, so we have both moved on. There are those moments when I honestly miss her, but I will get over it. Sorry, but I have to steer you back to business. I am working on an assignment and need to swing by to converse with you in person. Pick your brain, sort of speak."

"I am so sorry, Axel, I am busy this evening with a very tight schedule as I wind down my affairs. Ramon and I are departing for Italy in two days."

"What about early tomorrow? Any chance?"

"Ah, let me see, check my calendar; ah, well, nine-thirty. I have fifteen minutes only for you, Axel."

"Great! If it helps you out, I'll visit your office?" She replied affirmatively as he confirmed the address. "Once again, congratulations to you and Ramon. Are you retiring, returning or dismantling the business?"

"I am selling it to a larger agency for a handsome sum with no regrets. My name disappears, but that's a condition of the transaction and well, that's business. I had my fun Axel and you can say that I'm definitely retired."

"See you tomorrow, Paula."

"I'm looking forward to it." Paula left him dangling; however, this was an enormous break. Axel knew Paula well enough that she would answer his questions about Montilladan with integrity. When Larry Bartlett blurted out Paula's name this afternoon, he was pleasantly surprised. He had never heard Paula's name referenced in connection as M's agent. Axel checked his watch: five-ten.

Returning to his table, his salad awaited him. He anxiously counted the minutes like a little kid ticking off the minutes before the start of the big game. He found distractions by eating, reading the local paper, digesting the world's events, guessing what they might discover tonight, occasionally looking at the news screen. With paranoia, he cast suspicious glances around the restaurant, eyeing and inspecting every face. He even made excuses for certain stares. Eventually, he found himself navigating south, down the coast road and swinging east toward Bel Air.

It seemed like an eternity from Malibu to Bel Air, as a minor vehicular accident slowed traffic. Escaping on the radio to a talk show of mayoral candidates, the station was showcasing self-centered representatives who could only encapsulate the frailties of their mayoral opponents. Stalled in the middle of the paralyzed freeway with another fender bender directly ahead, he risked exiting to the feeder road at the next exit ramp and navigated through side streets. The strategy paid dividends as Axel found himself in advance of the problem.

His excitement peaked as he finally arrived on Montilladan's street. Parking his Mustang out of sight, one block distant from the estate, on a naturally broad shoulder, his curiosity wanted to absorb the environment of the neighborhood as he entered it, so he walked the last five hundred feet. The ambiance of the rustling sounds of the trees caught in a slight breeze commenced a soft percussion symphony.

Finally, a red brick wall materialized in front of him on his left, demarcating the property line of Montilladan's estate. Axel halted. Looking directly down the property line, as it penetrated the woods, he was unable to inspect no more than one hundred feet before the denseness of the trees blocked the brick column. Poised strategically on the corner of the wall, and again on high pillars at the driveway's entrance, were security cameras recording his every move. The gate was open.

The driveway was broad, furnished in red crushed brick, lined by flowering shrubs, the property closing up behind the left row of shrubs to a densely forested area, and to the right, a rolling green manicured lawn. Across the lea, he spied the other side of the property, also hemmed by the fortified red brick wall, twice the height of the barrier at the front of the estate. He recalled from Thumper's map that the property line on the far side was bounded by a major boulevard. He stopped. Although the road lay directly behind the column, he heard no traffic. Cameras were attached to the tops of the wall on the far side, too. Each arriving individual was screened by abundant angles as they gained admittance to the grounds.

Positioned in front of the main dwelling, lay a triple garage where Tinker's blue police sedan was parked; Zoe's Jaguar beside it. A sidewalk twisted from the side of the garage to the main house. From here it looked like a stark white fortress, a modern day bleached Alamo. As he turned back toward the roadway, it was impossible to see beyond the lot. No sign of neighbors; only tall power poles with sagging lines. Privacy was insured.

There were a few front windows present as vertical slots on each side of the main entry, conveying the appearance of sentries to spy on visitors. The front door was slightly ajar. Once inside, he was stunned by the stark white interior with scantily decorated walls and awkward modern looking furniture, positioned asymmetrically in the middle of each room. Because of this, there was an abundance of play around the clusters of furniture making each room appear infinitely more spacious. There was nothing lavish about the quarters. The wall decorations were distasteful; the furniture offensive. Zoe stood beside him.

She knew herself to sweat very little, but this event, witnessing the snoop Axel Hawk penetrating into her domain was giving her cause for great consternation. Over and over in her mind she sifted through the possibilities of why she was the focus of attention to this twosome and who was paying the meddlesome duo to investigate her life. What possible clue had she laid naked to be uncovered by them? She convinced herself that no one could possibly know of her scheme, her plans, her new drama, and her evil plot. She was getting paranoid as she closed her eyes and walked through each of the rooms in her house, cogitating about any evidence left behind. "Surely, I removed it all." She relaxed.

She smiled and devilishly laughed out loud for the climax was near and they were too far behind her to catch up and arrest her. She fondled the newly purchased hand gun, her new toy, no registration or identifying serial numbers on it. Should she dare walk on the property, in the back lot, and spy on them?

"Not to my taste, either. In fact, is rather disturbing."

"And confusing. You know, Zee, I find it rather puzzling for someone who was very decisive in life to have this repugnant, disoriented taste. What kind of statement does all this make?"

"Maybe it's all part of the big ruse, Axel?"

"Zoe, look at that light fixture on the table! A square black boot base with a foreign green vegetable matter sprouting out of it, proliferating into an array of green tops, each with an orange light at the end. No, thank you."

Tinker entered the living area. "Cool. Even in death, M's getting under our skin, annoying us, probably up there laughing at us. What a joint! Did I hear the word ruse?"

Zoe recovered quickly. "Amuse. I said amuse. I am amused by this dreadful display of décor or lack thereof. Regard that painting!" She vigorously directed their attention to the opposite wall of the living area where a canvas of eight feet by four feet hung, displaying a single red foot in a sea of off-white.

"If you inspect that painting close, like I did guys," Tinker boasted, "it's a mutant foot. There is a tiny sixth toe growing at the end." With his outburst, Tinker strutted across the room around lawn-green chesterfields to the canvas to prove his point with his fingerpost. "Observe."

Axel roared, "What the hell is it?"

Tinker laughed, doubled over as his jocular howling resounded and rebounded off the stark walls to fill the room, and then stood upright, walking to the right side of the painting. His notes of cackling were delivered with satire. "It is a red foot, man, with six toes, you idiot. That's the title. It says so right here," and he pointed out a small bronze plate on the wall and restated. "A small, red foot with six toes, by Jay Lauberkind." All three shared in the humor.

Zoe knocked him in the side with her elbow. "Damn it Axel, what is wrong with you? No appreciation for modern art. Anyone can see that it is a red foot on canvas." Thumper arrived, draped in clunky photographic equipment. Upon his entry he was heard to shout, "Wow! Cool! Alright! I saw this funky furniture on stage at a heavy metal rock concert!" He was pointing to the sofas, chairs, and tables with his body language.

"Hey, people!" Tinker was trying to intercede, drawing their attention to him by waving both arms over his head back and forth vigorously as an umpire. He bellowed. "I have got other cases to solve, other reports to finish tonight. Real live criminals are at large. I gotta Felix, mister congeniality, breathing down my neck for reports. Now, I agreed to this rendezvous. So, go ahead and quickly inspect the premises. Take only photos. Wear these gloves! I will remain here to intercept anyone else upon arrival. You folks have one hour. Starting from now! Let's go people!" He clapped his black elephantine hands for encouragement. "Go. Go. Go." He handed each of them a pair of new yellow latex gloves.

Axel instructed Thumper. "Keep your eyes peeled for any photographs that Montilladan had, look like attendance at gala affairs, charity balls, any dress in formal attire. Capture close up shots of any awards' ceremonies." Thumper cut Axel off.

"Yeah, yeah, yeah, man I know the drill, Axeman. Done it fifty times before. Let me do my job, boss."

"Hey people, fifty-nine minutes and counting."

Zoe peered at Axel. "The kitchen is wild. I have completed my inspection there and found nothing of interest. However, come and take a peek."

To Axel's amazement, it looked like a merry old English obstacle course with an agglomeration of copper pots and pans hanging everywhere down to five and six feet above the floor level. To make one's way to the other side of the room, one would set off a metallic chain reaction. The countertops were cluttered with pasta bins and herb gardens. A bookcase, resembling the leaning tower of Pisa, stood in one corner with an assemblage of cookbooks. In addition, there was a rack of brilliantly colored towels tacked to the side of the bookcase. The stove top, refrigerator, freezer and sinks were all completed in a putrid green finish, with yellow marble streaks accenting the counter top.

Zoe whispered to Axel, "I looked in every drawer, the freezer, fridge, shelves, even under the two sinks and found nothing of interest. I inspected the bar, too. Let's move on out of here. I also thoroughly searched the patio and patio furniture outside," and she directed Axel to an expansive set of outdoor dining ware, "and I looked in the dining room, and bathrooms downstairs. All drawers and shelves have sparse contents. Axel, it's a bit unbelievable but almost as if she didn't live here, or spent very little time here. Nothing of interest. No stains, no wear and tear in this living area."

"I also inspected this living area off the kitchen, turned the furniture over, inspected the pillows, the bookcases, the television, and with no wall hangings, looked for secret hiding places and found none. Peered up the fireplace, too."

"Zoe, I've only seen the outside of the house, the living area and the kitchen and I've got tell you that I feel very uncomfortable in this setting. I mean, the living room furniture is uncomfortable, the art extremely disagreeable, this kitchen is anything but charming and certainly not cozy. I find it agonizing and incommodious to just be standing here."

"I totally agree with you. This is a house of complete disharmony. The house itself seems to be engaged in a struggle." She whispered to him, "A human being in conflict and a house in conflict. Does that make sense? In that small bathroom over there is a painting of a man being skewered. Yes, really!" She looked around Axel to insure that the kitchen door was closed and Tinker not present.

"Axel, she thinks differently than us. Who would ever decorate their abode like this? But I'll tell you what's scary." She whispered again, "We are not inside her head yet. Know what I'm saying? We just don't know what and how she thinks and that's scary. We have to get inside her head Axel. Soon. As you walk around the premises, think about what I just said. This place represents her home; she's comfortable in this ultra-gothic ugly spooky setting."

"Yeah, you make an excellent point, Zee. We're not connected to her line of reasoning and what's driving her." He folded his arms as he stopped leaning against the counter.

Axel returned her stare with his accentuated goofy look. "To the bedroom." After she giggled, she led the way through the metallic inverted steeplechase, to the upstairs just as Thumper entered to capture the kitchen's iron incongruence.

"Whoa! Neat." Thumper was entertained.

As they ascended a broad circular staircase, which covered a steep story and a half, they heard the sounds of Thumper in the kitchen as he set off a chain reaction of metallic chimes. Upstairs, there were only four gigantic rooms. They entered a modern gymnasium, fully equipped with walkers, weights, rowing equipment, belly trimmers, a full track closing the perimeter of the room. Aerobics' equipment and multi-colored mats cluttered the floor; mirrors graced all the walls, which had no windows. A large stereo system with floor to wall speakers overpowered one wall. There were shower stalls, Jacuzzis, cupboards of towels neatly arranged, a linen closet but, as Axel and Zoe rapidly concluded, nowhere to conceal any secrets of Montilladan, although they inspected carefully by tapping the walls for any hidden closets or vaults.

The guest bedroom had only one extra set of bed linens in all the drawers; the closets were bare; dressers contained shirts and socks only. The waterbed mattress top corners were impossible to lift, so they were left to inspect only under the bed. Axel inspected the underside of all the drawers to insure that no documents were taped beneath and descended underneath the bed to extract only high fashion magazines. The hardwood floor was devoid of any rugs.

Zoe moved to the multi-media room where hundreds of video tapes, DVDs and CDs were all neatly labeled, none of the amateur homemade variety. A wall television screen, the largest that Axel had ever seen, dominated the room. This room, too, was distastefully decorated with disfigured nudies, alien-looking plants, and a host of multi-colored rusty horseshoes tacked asymmetrically on the walls. Shriveled human figures sat upon the shelving units. Zee checked behind each of five paintings for hidden safes with no luck and inspected each figurine in the shelving unit. Six clothed mannequins stood in a corner eerily staring back; four others were positioned in the theatre seating.

Finally they both entered the bedroom by way of exorbitant mirrored French double doors. "What a spectacle!" Axel remarked. They stood in the doorway absorbing the panorama. "It must be almost one thousand square feet!"

An enormous four poster bed with an eighteen foot high canopy was the showpiece with its hand crafted ornaments on posts, headboards, and rails. Mirrors presided at the headboard and overhead while the cloth canopy was finished in a silky purple sheen. Zoe observed, "This bed is large enough to sleep twelve people."

There were six, cavernous dressers, two dining tables, one in each of the two large bay windows, which overlooked the back of the estate, and two clothes, hampers of immense volumes. While Zoe rifled through the dressers, Axel inspected under the mattress, between box and foundation, and removed the ornate pineapple poster knobs. He stripped the bedding off and tipped the hampers for any items at the bottom. All this proved fruitless.

Zoe inspected every item in the drawers, including turning the socks inside out.

They moved to the master closets, as Axel was heard to say a decisive, "Oh, damn."

She responded. "Axel, what are you looking for?"

"I thought that we might find some women's clothing here, some article of a female that would present a hint of what she might resemble now. Would any female you know, Zee, select the art we've witnessed and furniture?"

"Axel, get with it! Montilladan played a male, remember? Look around you! Shoes, ties, suits, pants, underwear, socks, razors, male accoutrements: the distasteful decorum. These are all indicative of a man. M portrayed a man! Twenty-four hours a day, she played a man, convinced everyone that she was a man. So, why in hell do you expect to find anything different here in her home to incriminate her?"

"Zee, not so loud. Tink might hear. Hush, hush."

Zoe situated herself on the side of a vast white marble Jacuzzi. "Let us suppose that she really has disappeared to find her true female self. Number one, Roy's death was arranged. Number two, she vacates this spot. Number three, she would have made extra sure she removed all her female toiletries, her bras, her shoes, jewelry since she has to lay low and can't afford to go shopping and take a risk to be recognized. Don't you understand that? She requires all her female accessories now. Plus Montilladan wouldn't leave a shred of any signs of her female life for the police to discover. I vote that she completely house cleaned her female belongings long before the incident. As I said, she can't be seen shopping. There is definitely no evidence of her female persona left here for us to find."

Axel was despondent at her commentary. Zoe finished strongly, "I didn't expect to find any female belongings here and we haven't."

"I was just hoping."

"Hoping? Axel, you are the one that told me that you think that Roy Spiller is buried in that grave. I think we are now talking about premeditated murder by M. If it was M, she cleaned out her evidence ahead of the crime. In addition, if she senses her life to be endangered by someone else who knocked off poor Roy, you know darn well she erased all the clues to track her down. Why leave anything behind as a hint of where to look for her? Or of her new female identity?"

"But criminals make mistakes, Zoe."

"And that's what scares me, Axel; she hasn't so far. Don't you understand? We are drowning in new facts but sadly lacking in concrete evidence. I'm scared. I keep telling you, we're not inside her head yet. We don't know what's going on." They looked at each other in a stare of insecurity. "We are wasting precious time in debate! Let's move it."

"I will search the closets."

"You do that, Axel, while I search the medicine chest; and then I'll tackle these bathroom cupboards."

Axel took his time, digging into each shirt pocket, each jacket, and every pocket in the hanging pants. After completing two walls of clothing, he had only two scraps of paper. One was a dry cleaning ticket; the other he presumed had two phone numbers on it, seven digits, no area codes. He completed the last of the shirts to discover a gray magnetic card key. There were no markings except for faintly etched markings along the side. On a hunch, he checked into a dozen shoe boxes, some pairs never even worn.

Frustrated, he joined Zoe in meditation, positioning himself on a black foot stool. The bathroom had two baths, the larger one with Jacuzzi enough to accommodate six people at one time with over twenty jets all in the shape of protruding busty nudes; the smaller one a very intimate yellow stone finish for a one person bath.

Axel rose to inspect the shower stall. The tiles were custom painted with scenes from the Wizard of Oz. He was admiring the art when the eyes of the Wicked Witch gave him a fright. She had an uncanny resemblance to Mrs. Whitehurst. Uneasily, he closed the door.

There was a small atrium at one end of the Jacuzzi with flowers wilting, or dead in heaps of strewn fallen petals. "Find anything of interest?"

"Yes," and she waved the stub of an airline ticket. "Our girl has recently been to Paris, France."

"Perhaps, onto Andorra?"

"I will wire this info to Jean-marc overseas. See if there is a match between the time of this trip and any withdrawals."

Zoe caught his attention. "Here is something interesting that I discovered behind a fortress of make-up creams," and she waved a small plastic pouch of purple crystals. Axel scratched his head and said, "Voila, I have seen those crystals before." He returned into the closet that he had just searched, lifted the lid of a shoe box, and greeted Zoe with similar pouches. "Drugs?" she inquired.

"I don't know. I have never seen illegal substances of this extraordinary purple color and crystalline nature. Observe the strange grainy constitution, too. I thought they might be absorption salts you find in shoe boxes sometime so overlooked their presence."

"Curiously, Axel, they have no markings on them. No chemical name, no manufacturer, no expiry date, no warnings, just a plain transparent pouch with crystals."

Axel opened one by breaking the seal and carefully stuck his nose in and sniffed. "Ew, what an obnoxious odor with a peculiar, almost metallic, stink."

"Don't you dare put your finger in there and taste it, Axel Hawk!" He passed the open pack to her.

Axel rooted around on the closet floor and emerged with more packets. "Hey there's lots of this stuff in this closet in shoe boxes, so Tinker won't miss a couple of sacks." Axel stuffed four pouches in his pants. "Also, I found a card key." Axel waved it in front of her.

"Hey look, Axel, I have one, too." They examined them to determine matching identities. "Carbon copies, Zee."

"But to what?"

"A Hollywood studio, a parking lot, parking garage. Maybe a locker or something on the grounds. We should check the front door, the garage, the gate to see if the key fits."

"No. The gate and garage are run by remotes. Tinker and I discovered those devices. The garage has two cars, keys in the custody of the attorneys. Tinker and I already checked any outdoor sheds, two of them, and they were padlocked. The police opened them and have the locks."

"A new task for the Thumper. Decipher any information about these cards." Zoe took both cards and deposited them in her satchel. Axel decided to capture additional pouches of the purple chemical.

Ten minutes later they united. Zoe expressed their frustration. "How laborious, no other clues. No hidden documents taped to the underside of drawers; no wall safes or false panels. Axel, don't you think it curious that there are no photos on the bureau." Thumper was heard to give homage to the decor one last time with an outpouring of "Wowser" and "Holy Cow" and "Awesome," while Zee took him aside and impressed upon him the need to extract information from the card keys they had just discovered. Axel decided not to tell Tinker of the purple substance, at least not yet. They stood, all four side by side, at the main entrance for one last look.

After expelling them, Tinker locked up the front door, accompanying them around the grounds as they inspected other the small dwellings and garden sheds. They were empty as Tinker warned. The pool had cabanas with open portals and was devoid of any objects except benches. As they exited the cabanas, Axel drew a fright.

"What's wrong?" Zoe noticed his stare.

"I thought I saw something move in the kitchen."

"Mind playing tricks?" She stared across the pool into the darkened room. "With all that hanging cookware, I am sure reflections play tricks."

"What's this? Mind playing tricks?" Tinker inquired.

"Axel thought he saw something move in the kitchen. Ooh, perhaps the ghost of Montilladan peering out at us."

Tinker wanted to act quickly. "You two run around to the front to see if anyone exits through the front door, I'll stay here with Thumper and we'll gaze inside. I also have this." And he turned on a powerful flashlight, which dowsed the yard. "Quickly."

Axel and Zee sprinted around to the front entry where Zoe looked through the front door while Axel looked behind and under each vehicle. "There!"

Zoe turned and looked as he did across the wide front expanse.

"Someone move into the bushes about fifty yards down the skirt of the woods." He continued to focus his stare at the spot while pointing for her.

"Do you really want us to walk across that darkened front lawn to examine the woods? Besides, look at the high wall behind. No one's going to scale that wall without us seeing them." She was firm in her answer. "Whoever it is, I say let them go. No harm done!"

"That's it, you two," Tinker screamed. "One hour is up. Sorry, it didn't provide any breakthroughs. Thumper and I didn't see any waving pots or signs of intrusion. I'll alert Felix and lock up. Let's vacate the grounds immediately."

As she looked at him, he decided not to send Tinker on a wild chase into the thicket.

Tinker departed, waving to them. Axel, Thumper, and Zoe congregated at the entrance to the property beside her Jag and Thumper's SUV. "Not as productive as I had thought," Axel lamented. "No hidden safes, no female remnants, just the two card keys, two phone numbers, a dry cleaning slip, and these." He held up the purple crystals.

Zoe snapped her finger. "I know a lab technician who can help us. Tinker and I worked closely with her on the police force. I will arrange to have Thumper deliver these to her in the morning." Zoe grabbed the plastic sleeves from his hand, motioned for him to deliver the remaining pouches and explained to Thumper the location where he could drop the samples as Axel continued to peer deeper into the bushes.

He said to Thumper, "When I first saw this substance in the shoe box, I thought that it was that material that they put in shoe boxes, so the shoes don't spoil. It was a stroke of luck that you found a second pouch elsewhere in the medicine chests."

"I'd say, Axel, that the pouch that I discovered was carefully hidden, that it shouldn't be found. How about a nightcap at Charlie's?"

"You go ahead, Zee, I'm bushed. I am feeling the ill effects of my thrashing last night and sore all over, my tummy is throbbing." He massaged it as he spoke. "Only my ego has recovered. Did you say that Jim left me sleeping pills?"

"Yes."

"Well, then, that's it for me. A gratifying hot shower, hot toddy with my sleeping pills, and an early bed. I can't bear another minute vertically."

"In that case, I'll accompany you to your home. I want to insure that you take your medicine, and I will tuck you into bed. No macho-man acts tonight."

"I'll be okay, Zee, if you want to run to Charlie's."

"No way, I want to witness you take that medication. I recall former bouts of macho-man when you thwarted prescribed medicines. Let's rendezvous at your house."

She jumped into her Jaguar, started the engine, and rolled beside him. "I'll race you to your place." She darted out of sight in a burst of acceleration. He conceded defeat. He sauntered the last few hundred feet down the roadway as Thumper passed and honked good night. The key was in his hand bleeping an entry when he heard twigs snap to his right in the woods. He stood galvanized staring hard into the opaqueness as shivers raced up to his nape. He was at an extreme disadvantage. "Who's there?" What a stupid thing to say.

That's it, you stupid bastard. You are looking right at me, me in the depth and dark recess of the woods, and you can't see a thing in this blackout. I know because I passed it earlier and checked its opaqueness. That's it you idiot. Stand there petrified, staring at me. Can you see me laughing at you? Discover all the tidbits of evidence your heart desires, for the time draws close for tragedy to strike. Oh, do I have a delicious surprise in store for you!

Slowly turning the key in the lock, he elected retreat since his thrashing of last night would leave him helpless in any physical combat. Axel entered the safety of his Mustang. He sat and convinced himself that his mind was playing tricks as he envisioned ogre-like forms in the shadows. He slouched into the driver's seat, and never looked back as he tore down the hill.

She emerged from her hiding spot and stood on the deserted roadway, and darted down to her vehicle, and whirled about.

Soon both Zoe and Axel's cars were parked outside Axel's wooden frame home, where, after his shower she treated his wounds, forced doses of medicine into him, as she suspected she would have to, prepared small appetizer servings of cheese and crackers, and finally presented him with a night cap of sleeping serum and hot chocolate.

One hour later, Zoe covered him, pulled down the shades, planted a kiss on his forehead, and left Axel Hawk comfortably in the sanctity of his abode in the second floor bedroom. Axel's nose ached in a dull throb. His stomach muscles were so sore that he found relief only in the perfectly prone stiff position on his back.

In his current drugged state, he thought only of her, listening to her clean up downstairs in a clatter of dishes, and yelling a comforting "good night" as she left. The last sound that he heard was the roar of her engine, which as Doppler predicted, faded gradually.

Los Angeles was soaked in a rare hot humid night for this time of year as the onslaught of humidity suffocating the city in an early fall vengeance. His bedroom was shrouded in total darkness as was his custom to sleep with the faint glow of a nearby streetlight peeking through the edges of the drapes.

The pain killers, combined with the sleeping pills, had made him dopey, his eyelids swollen with the weight of a thousand bloated cells, as if thumbs pressed against each eye and were trying to force their way through the flesh, to invade the skull. In dreams, his face was swollen to ten times its size, and upon his morning awakening, he became weak, was unable to balance himself as his head lobbed back and forth until eventually he collapsed at the side of the bed and dragged himself back to sleep. This dream repeated itself.

He fell into a profound trance until he was awakened by a sole, loud, distinct creak of a floorboard, which disturbed his tranquility. Through the fog, he read the blurry red numbers on the digital clock as twelve hours and four minutes. Was the sound real or just an accompaniment to his illusionary mental images?

Straining to listen, his body demanded more suffocating sleep; a paralyzing silence prevailed, knocking him into dream world once more. The house often creaked and heaved at night, swelling and receding to the response of nature's temperature cycles.

But his skin crept with an accompanying bubbling in the tops of his knees, as he was awakened by an unmistakable second creak of a floorboard just outside his open bedroom door; the sound of a slightly loose board as if it should be shoved back into place by the burden of the full weight of a human body landing on it. There was insufficient evidence to strike these terrifying thoughts from his mind.

His best guess was frightening. His mind wanted him to frantically believe that someone had ascended the stairs to the hallowed second floor of his sanctuary and was standing, sight unseen, in the blackness of the shadows in his open doorway. Axel struggled to see through the darkness. He was too weak to call out. Who would hear? No one but the visitor.

His eyes were consumed with sleep, but there was someone standing there. Or was there? It was a frightening moment as he opened his mouth, but the effects of the drugs would not let him mutter a single sound. He had not experienced dreams of helplessness similar to this before, helpless before an evil, a helplessness of an inability to even mutter.

But this was just another dream. It was acceptable for an intruder to materialize. Zoe had left him tucked in an unconscious state. Let the dream happen. Awake in the morning. It is harmless. His head collapsed into the white billowy pillow.

Suddenly, he heard a third sound, much closer to him. With a slight of strength, he turned to read the clock as twelve hours and nineteen minutes. He had entered a twilight zone; his arms, heavy and stiff, lay outside the covers. Nikki said, "Get your mind straight." It took only Nikki's reminder for him to lay comatose again.

Outside it was a silent sullen night. No breeze. Leaves opened their pores to allow the rich drops into their veins as the air cooled rapidly to dump the humidity as dew. Inside, Axel was tense, totally engulfed in a wicked chase of serpents who had invaded his house. He was passing in and out of consciousness. But which state was which?

Was the performance onstage real? Or the disastrous surfing episode? Or the chase of snakes under the covers of his bed? It was so difficult to tell. Only Zoe would know. He must call her. Did Zee drug him on purpose? He had not an ounce of strength to climb out of bed to contact her.

His whole body froze as one, rigid, solid, frigid piece when he heard a footstep close to him, so close that he was sure that if he were just to move his left arm to the edge of the bed it would intersect with the corporal flesh of the intruder. He screamed for voluntary actions, for his muscles to obey him, but they failed to flee from this haunted house.

The hairs on his legs and arms, all rooted in deep pits, were all brittle, standing upright, brushing against his sticky pajamas, trying to raise the cloth vertically.

Now in this trance, he felt hot humid pulsating air upon his face, torrent upon torrent bathing his tingling cheek cells, forehead, and chin in a suffocating exhaling. Like clockwork, his heart pounded, his body was in spasm. Every five seconds there was a new round of air washing his cheeks. He felt the presence of the demon.

Zoe returned? Nikki to come visit her wounded warrior? A wolf man come to rip out the ripe flesh of his tender throat to shreds? A witch, sent by Madame Whitehurst to put an end to this tomfoolery? Or her? Was she here?

He resisted opening his eyes. Whomever, or whatever it was, was perched directly inches over him. A heat emanated from the being. His mind felt the gravitational pull between his head and the object as the laws of physics predicted. Had Kathleen cooked up a supernatural apparition to bleed him of all life? Or maybe the reincarnation of a witch from *Macbeth*? A vampire come to feast on the delicate exposed veins in his neck of which he was helpless to defend? Was he the subject of Haitian voodoo? All this he thought as the creature came closer and closer yet!

Courage! He must summon courage! He thought, *I am a strong male specimen. Out damn malignancy. I am Axel Hawk. I have the courage to live.* He was swallowing bucket after bucket of saliva, which was drowning his stomach. Was there no way to stop these secretions? But if it had wanted to kill him, it could have done so by now. What did this hellion want?

With no answer to this question, he felt truly terrified by its presence. Desperately, he tried to move his arms. They were numb. The creature had severed them both at the shoulders! He was bleeding profusely to his certain death! Now, he must find the strength to scream for help or perish!

Perhaps, if for no other reason than to startle him, the creature now forced a breath of hot stinking torrid air on him, so distinct that he tasted its fetid cherry blood. Axel needed an exorcist. He thought, *Why this torture?* just as a new bout of breath intersected his dry lips, finding its way into a tiny open wound above his lip. The stench forced its way up his nose, so that it pushed back his breaths.

"If I should open my eyes, may God help slay this creature from Hell. I am not a religious man God, but help me now for all the good I have done in my life! I must command you to help as I lay helpless before the crucifier." Had he whispered these thoughts or just kept them as a prayer to himself? Had the intruder heard his desperate plea?

Axel could not discern any of the parts of his body. In the absence of urinating, his bodily pores opened to expel a rush of hot sweat which bathed him, soaked the blankets, wet his night wear, made his bristles limp in liquid. But he decided to witness his executioner, and in that second in which his eyes opened...he did!

For one, terrifying moment, she was inches away from him, her dark diabolical eyes locked on devouring his soul, expelling her foul air on him as his soul arose to escape to leave only the flabby crippled physical muscles, deteriorated bone, and a mind unable to respond.

There was a sinister wild look on her face as she slowly opened her mouth to expose her glittering, long, vampire-like teeth. With a wolfish guttural growl she descended closer. Axel made a decision to save his life, so with all his bodily strength he lurched forward, pushing her away, executing bodily contact in the process. An immediate tightness gripped his chest. Sweat dripped into his eyes. He used the back of his arm to wipe his face dry. Having conquered the use of his muscles, he sat upright, frozen, perusing the dark depths of every corner of his room, seeking to eradicate all the remnants of the past horrific scene and its co-star. His chest heaved abnormally and tightened in spasm. His stomach burned as an inferno in his pit, his ruddy face was flush with terror. He pinched his legs. He was sitting on the edge of his bed.

A nightmare. Yes, a horrible, horrible nightmare. Zoe locked the door on the way out. But it wasn't a dream! His attention was drawn to the sounds of the devil as she quickly descended the stairs, each step reinforcing his reality, and for one clearly last terrifying effect, she slammed the door upon exit.

Now Axel was engulfed by shivers. His body was burning up yet producing frigid shakes. On his knees, he crawled to the cell phone on the bureau. At once, he heard more footsteps. Gremlins. She had left them behind. It was now twelve forty-five.

His fingers fumbled to complete the dial and he heard her voice, "Hello?"

"Zoe!"

"Axel? Is that you Axel?"

"Please Zoe, come back. They're here. My God, Zee, they've come back to kill me. Zee!"

"Axel, Axel, calm down. You're hallucinating."

"Zoe, she's come to kill me. Please Zee!"

"Axel, slap yourself in the face; pinch your arms."

"Zoe, please come."

"Axel, I have a key. I will be right there!" Zoe hustled from the clutches of sleep.

"Please, Zoe," he pleaded. "I love you. You have to save me." He was delirious.

Axel sat trembling on the floor for twenty minutes until the door burst open. She mounted the stairs two at a time, and she shook him vehemently, begged him to awaken to take command of his life again. With Axel sitting upright against his bed, slowly regaining consciousness, gulping cold water, Zoe immediately summoned Thumper and counted the minutes in silence, sitting beside him, an arm around him, not loosening her grip until Thumper's arrival, all the time holding Axel in her arms and watching the bedroom door's opening.

Thumper appeared totally confounded. She instructed him, "I am taking Axel to my place- again! Help me load him into the Jag will you? I know it's late, but I would really appreciate it if you would stay behind, dust for prints, and search the premises for signs of a forced entry. Watch your back at all times Thump. Axel keeps a powerful flashlight under the sink in the kitchen. Search for footprints outside, too, and drop by. I will still be up. Drive Axel's car to my place if you would, deary. I will pay for your cab ride back here."

"I know the routine, boss. I brought my kit and cast set. I'll call you soon. Too late to raise any objection; I know, it's in my paycheck. Say, what happened here tonight?"

"I don't know, Thumper, but I intend to find out." Zoe and Thumper each grabbed him under an armpit and guided him downstairs where Thumper positioned Axel into the front passenger's seat. He was still groggy as he fought the effects of the sleeping potion. She scooted into the house, retrieved his bandages, his medications, a change of clothes for tomorrow, and flew out of the house, hopping into her Jag, departing for her sanctuary while all the time recalling the terror in Axel's earlier plea, the horror in his eyes when she arrived. It was a struggle to get Axel into her home but, once there, she talked him out of his fright. It was soon thereafter that they sat at their customary positions on her living room sofa again for the third night in four. After gulping hot tea, regaining some consciousness, he launched into his nightmare. He recounted for her the confusing events leading to the punch line.

"I swear, Zoe. I'm wide awake. It was her!" Axel had just raised his voice to her. She, arms folded, had not appreciated the emphasis.

"Axel, you were drugged. I personally administered the sleeping medications to you while taking into consideration your body weight and condition. I gave you an extra dose for comfort to help you lapse into slumber. You could not have been fully conscious of what was happening around you. Even before I departed, you were not fully in control of your senses."

This time it was his turn, and the word "no" popped out at her. "No, Zee! I struggled to open my eyes and, when I did so, what I saw was not an apparition, not a vision, not my mind playing tricks, not a nightmare, but her, Montilladan, come to terrorize me!"

"It was a dream, Axel." They were ramping up a great debate with single arguments on each side. The neighbors were soon to complain if they continued to raise their voices.

"Zee, you have to believe in me. It was her. You weren't there. I was. Please believe me. Why won't you believe me? It was Montilladan!"

"Time out. Think about it, Axel. We still do not have concrete proof that Montilladan is alive until the body in that grave at Forest Haven is exhumed. We have not conclusively convinced ourselves of Roy Spiller's fate. So, she discovers and knows we are searching for proof of her existence. She must know that we have not dug up the grave yet. So, why in the hell Axel," and Zee became annoyed and raised her voice, "why would she hand deliver this proof to us? Hand deliver, Axel! Hand deliver the very piece of evidence that we need. Hand deliver personally that she really is alive!" Zoe kept talking, and was distinctly annoyed.

"She revealed her corporal self to you. It doesn't make sense. Think about it Axel! You have not responded yet. Why would she do this? This is not a stupid person, but revealing herself to us is a very stupid move when she knows we don't have conclusive evidence that she is alive. Very, very, very stupid." Zee raised her voice. "Why?"

Axel was adamant. "To scare the shit out of me; she did!"

"And now you are scaring me."

"You're the one that said back at her residence that we haven't gotten inside her head yet."

Silence prevailed. She sat at the other end of the sofa. With her remark, the two were aware of each other's bodily heaves. Zoe refused to believe that this was a real event. In the silence, she bowed her head and was immersed in trying to ascertain the logic of M's actions. Finally, she spoke softly.

"I know I am repeating myself, but we don't have a single shred of concrete evidence of her existence, Axel, and now she foolishly decides to deliver it to you, to substantiate Lacey's claim. No, Axel, this would expose a weakness to us and cement a flaw in her strategy. I know you believe that it happened. Sorry, I don't."

Axel barked back. "Zee, I don't know how she broke into my house and performed it nor why. All I know is that tonight Montilladan visited me. She invaded my home. She towered over my helpless being, positioned herself only inches from my body. She desecrated me with her hot dirty stinking breath. What can I say? I was paralyzed, that I admit. If I had to guess, whether it was a dream or reality, I say reality." He stood and wobbled to make his next points.

"Suddenly as all this happened, I found an inner strength and I bolted upright. I felt myself. I was alive. I was conscious. I convinced myself that it was a dream until I heard her flee down the stairs, hit each step one by one and slam the door shut, and escape out of my house. With those actions, she reminded me just how vulnerable I am."

Zoe rebutted. "Thumper called twenty minutes ago and told me he has dusted for prints—nothing. Only yours and mine on the door handle to the bedroom and the front door and the rails. He has seen our prints enough times to know." She grimaced at him, reluctantly disclosing other news. "No signs of forced entry from outside. No broken windows. No clear footprints in the beds, lawn. This doesn't make sense."

She left him alone to think while she scampered to the kitchen, prepared two tall tumblers of fresh ice tea and returned to engage Axel. This time she pushed him onto the sofa and snuggled up to him, placing one of her arms around his shoulder.

"I want to support you, Axel, but I am skeptical about M's motives. This nocturnal escapade puts her escape plan in jeopardy. It is a very risky move in a game of high stakes. We are at an extreme disadvantage to all the players in this chess match. We are on overload with the collection of facts but are underachieving. We have learned nothing that moves us closer to proving that Montilladan is dead, or guilty of a crime or..." She stuttered and stopped.

"Zee, why can't you give me the benefit of the doubt?"

"Motive, Axel. What possible reason would prompt her to reveal herself to you?"

"She wants us off this case, Zoe. She wants to scare us into surrender. First, my physical beating; now a torment of mental anguish." He threw a further scare into both of them as they huddled closer.

"Okay Zee, look at me. I know why she did it! It must be because we are so close to a solving this case, or maybe we have uncovered a major clue without recognizing it. Montilladan can't risk killing us, especially with our close relationship to Tinker. I hate to say this Zee but…it appears I have become the hunted!"

WEDNESDAY A.M.

Zoe shifted away from Axel, slinked her slender form to the opposite end of the sofa where she glared at him. "Perhaps, Axel, we ought to tell Lacey to consult with someone else. Perhaps we ought to transfer the homicidal ire of Montilladan to some other business firm, or the police. I think this case has become too spooky. You just gave me the creeps when you recited your encounter, and now at the last conclusion, well, Axel, we didn't sign up for this." Zoe paused and upon his hesitation felt compelled to continue to relieve herself of her sudden frustrations.

"I take these attacks on you personally Axel. They have me feeling insecure— downright angry. If you're not going to return her retainer, I would feel so much better if we solicit Tinker's help. I'm briefing him tomorrow."

She bounced forward to him, clasping his right hand tightly, placing it on her chest. She reminisced about when they first met, when he was a skinny, ambitious, somewhat arrogant, investigator.

"I consider myself to be an excellent judge of character, and thought that in private business we could grow together. I confess, since the very moment that I joined forces with you, Axel, you have taught me a great wealth about criminal investigations, more than I could have ever learned at the academy or in the police force. I cherish our partnership. We are an excellent example of teamwork, fostered by a master and mentor relationship. We manage to secure new clients on a regular basis to keep the income flowing. But never in my wildest aspirations did I sign up to be the hunted of a homicidal maniac! Never in my wildest dreams did I ever believe that we would be the targets of some crazed female lunatic. From day one, I thought we were doing the hunting. This turn of events tonight petrifies me."

Zee sat up. She imitated Ms. Platinum by pinching his bicep. "You've matured and grown stronger. You've had your open moments of frailty for which I admire you, such as tonight and like the incident at Fosse's with Ms. Platinum." Axel countered.

"Zee, I don't like being stalked either and I'm the one who is in the firing line, bearing the brunt of her wrath. But Montilladan wants us off this case for a damn good reason. You Zee, give me the strength to continue, and I give my strength to you. Together, we need to accept her challenge and discover what she fears in us. We need to discover what it is that has caused her to panic."

"At the expense of personal injury? Perhaps our deaths?" Her voice died. She turned away from his gaze. "I think not."

"I promise to protect you, Zee." Suddenly, he lunged toward her and grabbed her and pulled her tightly to him. "I would never let anything happen to you. It would break my heart if I lost you."

"Axel, let me share a reality check with you. My utmost fear is that together we are not strong enough, nor smart enough, to defeat her. She knows what her plan is and we don't have a clue."

"Together we will win."

With a heavy sigh, she retorted, "I know that I am going to hate myself for suggesting this but," and she now draped both her arms around his neck, "why don't you move in with me? Into my townhouse until this case is solved? She knows where you live. I just moved into my place. I'm not in the metro phone registry yet and nor is my internet address. We just have to pray that she didn't follow us here tonight, although I checked constantly and there was no tail when we drove here."

Axel was uncharacteristically about to disagree with her when she hugged him tight with her head buried in his chest. She glued her mouth to his left ear as she spoke with a sense of urgency.

"We need each other for protection and we are not spending enough quality time together discussing this case. Axel we need to massage the evidence. I am deeply concerned about what has happened in such a short period of time because we are at such a terrible disadvantage." She expelled a little sigh and picked up the pace again.

"We are eons behind this criminal." She broke the tight lock embrace to go nose to nose with him.

"I am truly frightened Axel. We seem to be on information overload, but where has it gotten us? Where and what has it led to? Dead ends, dangerous alleys behind us, and blind alleys in front!"

He reciprocated the physical intimacy by dropping his arm down around her waist, while taking his other arm to caress her temple with his fingers. She cooperated further by intertwining their legs, thus pushing her small breasts against him. She whispered. "This is strictly a business arrangement. Sleeping together in numbers gives me comfort."

"Right. Great buns. Sexy body. Alluring voice. Enchanting hypnotic eyes. Super intelligence. Curvy waist. Sexy Cleopatra hair cut chop. Turn-on humor. You're right. Strictly business. I'll move in immediately."

"Thank you. Every girl loves to be flattered. I know you meant every word you just said. However, I have to reiterate, Axel…get focused on our work."

Zee couldn't let go of her burning question. "Why would she visit your place and expose herself? It still doesn't make any sense to me. We have to retrace our steps starting tomorrow to find the answer."

Axel was insistent, "You're right. We've uncovered a clue that we have misinterpreted or discarded or not placed enough emphasis on, and she, the daredevil and risk-taker that she is, has panicked to scare us off."

Zoe was amused and seized the moment. "I got it! She pisses us off by attacking the weaker sex." Axel tickled her ribs until she forced herself free and tumbled onto the floor giggling.

"What clue?" she asked as she still laughed in high pitched cute bursts.

"I don't know, Zee, but there is something bothering me about Romeo?"

"Axel, it's nearly two in the morning. Can we discuss something else besides Romeo?"

"I prefer that theory."

"And I don't," she snapped back but reconsidered. "Okay. Open your mind to me. What's bothering you?"

"Zoe, I truly expected to find some traces of a woman's clothing at Montilladan's residence. I can't believe that she expunged everything."

"We've been all through that. So what?"

"So, what is she wearing? She wouldn't be caught dead shopping for woman's clothes as you said and more importantly, think about this. When she met Romeo, she must have met him as a woman. Where did she change into those clothes?"

"That's obvious and I concede that."

"Alright, then, as a woman, she had to change somewhere other than her residence. At her residence, she had guests, cleaning staff, neighbors, and people walking pets, all of which witnessed her only as a male, Montilladan, coming and going from the residence. So Zoe, she left work as a male, and left her residence as a male, and thus, she must go somewhere else to change into her female clothes and then reappear as a female. So eureka! She has a second residence! One where she goes unnoticed, departing as a female."

"It is late, Axel. I'm not quite following you yet."

"A hideout, Zee. M has a hideout where she metamorphoses from male to female, and female back to male. Some place where she comes and goes without suspicion. She couldn't just leave her house as a female, take a risk of being noticed by a neighbor or passerby. She definitely didn't leave the studio as a female. I think she has routinely been performing this transformation for Romeo. She must have met Romeo as a woman and she has a hideout to perform her metamorphosis from obnoxious hunky male to alluring femme fatale."

Zoe provided a rebuttal. "I prefer a different theory."

"Aw, come on. Mine's good."

She waved to silence him. "Although I give you some marks for your idea of a hideout, I now like to think that deep down inside, she's a woman, and urgently wants the rest of her life back, to live it as her true sex, one which took her instincts impetuously to become a woman again. One that was inspired by either the murder of Roy Spiller or, the untimely but convenient death of Roy Spiller, which she planned or didn't plan. I think she may have been assembling a woman's wardrobe for some time. Now she has the strong urge to use it for the first time. I don't believe in the hideout as much as I believe that she has recently rediscovered her reborn feminine person, recently created a new identity, recently crafted and executed new plans to protect her situation of re-surfaced female instincts."

"Would she kill to protect this instinct?"

"You and I both know she already has."

"Ah-ha, my brain is scorching with a puzzle. So why not kill me tonight? See, answer that conundrum."

"I don't know. I'm very tired, Axel."

"Zoe, she reveals herself to me and doesn't kill me. Although, as you stated earlier it would bring the wrath of the L.A. police on her, but I don't think that's it."

Zoe continued. "So, I think you're right. Maybe we are close to resolving her new identity. Maybe a misinterpreted clue as you has suggested; I'm exhausted Axel; I'm wilting."

"What is in the envelope on the coffee table?"

"Axel, we are wound up in gridlock. We both need our beauty sleep. I need my mental rest as Lacey arrives here at nine o'clock in the morning."

"Here? At your place?"

"Yes, and I also have to drive back to San Clemente to return the dental records as I promised since we already made copies to compare to the autopsy. Let's retire."

"Ah, so Dr. Sorbet allures you to return," he said in his Peter Lorre imitation.

"Business."

"Any chance that he is lying to us and he is Romeo?"

"Not a chance."

"The envelope, please." He pointed to it.

Reluctantly, she tossed it to him as she leaned back against the coffee table, exhausted, eyes closed while she spoke. "Lacey sent these over today. They are photos of Montilladan from Lacey's private collection. Not to be shared with anyone."

Axel continued to aggravate Zee. "Montilladan must have been a Juliet when she met Romeo, and Romeo became star struck by her beauty. That's the way Shakespeare wrote it darling. That's the way it happened. There's a hideout."

"Please, Axel, I'm tired. Even if there is a Romeo, Hell, maybe, they just met at her place, she got naked, and she attacked him, assuming him to be your normal weakling male species, who in the presence of female nudity falls in love by way of instant infatuation of the naked female eunuch. That way she didn't need a wardrobe. Maybe, Romeo's the gardener, her physiotherapist, a house cleaner, an insurance agent, an unsuspecting friend, another actor. In an impetuous moment of disrobing, he was turned on as any male would in the face of a naked female. She wouldn't need woman's apparel if they just got naked. Forever nudies. That's my latest theory."

Axel turned the open envelope and a proliferation of photos suddenly splattered onto the coffee table, and spewed onto the floor. He corralled a cluster of them as he moved to her larger kitchen table. Snagging a magnifying glass from the counter, Axel sat at the table to commence the careful inspection of each one.

"Oh, no, not tonight, Axel, I'm tired. We need to be alert tomorrow." She saw that her argument was hopeless. "Pour me a refill, darling," he responded and tinkled the ice cubes as he shook the tumbler.

"And don't drug me with sleeping pills. I know your devious mind." She poured him a tea and squatted on a chair at the other end of the kitchen table, watching him as he became engrossed in detail after detail, fascinated with every photograph. "Zee, there are so many different but subtle looks of M." As he examined them Axel recalled the fearful encounter of the present night, so summoned his courage to continue.

"Man this is great stuff. Montilladan at the studio, at social gatherings, M clad in formal attire with black bow tie, on the bench relaxing, at the gymnasium working up a sweat," and he shook each photo so she could see, too. There were those that he didn't want to view but knew he had to; the affectionate moments with Lacey. One of them illustrated a firm kiss on the lips; another showed them enjoying an intimate patio moment. There was no doubt about it! In these last few photos, Montilladan was demonstratively a female! Zee departed and left him alone to scrutinize details.

Axel mumbled. "From man to woman in the blink of rapidity." After ten minutes, Zoe reappeared in pajamas, hair bonnet, and her face awash in lumpy caramel night cream.

"Ach! Help! Zoe! Help! She's returned! M's gremlins are here!" he screamed as he jumped from his sitting position, posed to attack, karate style, arms hoisted. "Oh, it's only you."

"Ha, ha, ha. Axel, I am retiring. You are sleeping in my bed to get some rest. I changed my mind. I will sleep on the sofa so I can arise early to greet Lacey."

"What is that hideous mucus all over your face?"

"Beauty cream."

"So this is your hideout where you perform metamorphosis; butterfly into whatever it is that you are tonight."

"It is wrinkle control cream, female-approved."

"Man, where are the fashion police when you need them?"

"Axel! I am retiring. Here." She pointed to the sofa.

He was still staring at her face. "Well, Zee. I would sure like you to ask Lacey tomorrow morning an important question. Who snapped these photos of M and her when they are both embracing females? Who pulled the trigger, just so we understand who is in the know? There has to be another witness to M's real sex."

"I am beginning to lose my patience."

"Me, too. I think we are up to eight individuals who now know M played a great deceit. Maybe the Whitehursts know, too. That would make it ten! Painful as it must be especially for the Colonel." She slugged two pillows. "Sleeping alone tonight, are you sure?" he inquired.

"I like you, Axel, I really do, but not enough to sleep with you tonight. We have to be sharp. I am wiped out." She tucked sheets under the oversized cushions of her sofa and turned out the light on the end table. Zee explained. "I am sorry about Saturday night when you jumped for your love, and Monday night, when you crooned at me, serenaded me with your touching beautiful love ballad and I simply ignored you by turning out the lights, deserting you in your hour of hormonal need."

Zoe now cuddled up on the sofa as he sat in the kitchen still examining the collection. "Axel, our lives are in great danger. We have known that since we committed to Lacey to find her lover. Strength in numbers, Axel. Strength in mental awareness. Go to sleep."

"Agreed. I have been a sap. First for Ms. Platinum. I'll take your bed. No expending calories by making a move on you tonight." He sauntered over to kiss her good night on the only bare spot on her cheek as she said, "I am warming up to the idea of a hideout."

He circled around and came to his knees in front of her. "What is changing your mind?"

"The photos. I have to admit I examined them earlier. Some of these date back over a year. M has the distinctive look and mannerisms of a woman. I know how much you hate to hear about Lacey loving M, but there is more than one photo with Lacey where in my humble opinion, they are unquestionably two women- sensitive, sexy, playful, lovers!" As she talked, Axel moved to the table quickly and extracted one that he knew she was referring to, plus others and brought it to her side.

Beside her again, he stated. "This one where they are lovers looks a helluva lot different than this one where Montilladan is at the Oscars, this one where M is snapped at a public restaurant."

"Right." She was turned away from him. With a big yawn, she whispered. "I tend to agree- that she needs a secretive place to conduct her transmogrification."

Axel opened his eyes wide. "Her what? Her transmorgi—what?"

"Her change, Axel. I will strongly consider the idea of a hideout in my dreams. Good night."

Axel moved from her and back to the table. He took a pad of paper to record the jewelry, the clothes, the hair styles, the make-up, and the people in the photos. The front door bell rang and opened abruptly to startle him as Thumper appeared. In his dragging baggy army pants, he shuffled directly to the pitcher of ice tea.

"Man, am I thirsty." He looked around as he gulped. "Hey, cool digs, Zoe. Hey, the digs come with a beat-up version of Axel."

Axel gloated. "They do now."

Zoe emerged to stare at him. Thumper pointed to her. "Hey, Zee. Whoa! I saw that freaky facial disguise you're wearing last Halloween at a heavy rock concert except it looks better on you." He gulped down fluids again and smacked satisfaction. "Ah."

Axel inquired, "Any thoughts about those access cards I gave you?"

"Wait until tomorrow, Axman. I'll analyze them closer. They could open almost anything. I wouldn't want to play with them too much. It might erase their magnetic patterns. Do you have any snacks Zoe? You know, to munch on? I'm starving."

He didn't wait for a reply as he waddled deeper into the kitchen. She felt defeated and sat up. "Open the fridge. Help yourself. Chips in the cupboard to your left. What about your analyses at Axel's home?"

Thumper discharged a heinous belch. "Sorry. An earlier beer creeping up on me." He grabbed two slices of cheese, a slice of bread, was seen to slap a piece of meat on it and sat down in a billowy chair in the living area, the only one large enough to spread his massif over the landscape.

"I dusted the rails," there was distinctive piggy chomp, "and I dusted the front door handle, and the bedroom everywhere. No clear prints except yours and Axel's that I have matched as I reported earlier." He destroyed almost an entire high tumbler of ice tea in one effort.

"Ah, there is more bad news, Axel. I don't know the specifics of what happened tonight at your house, but there are no signs of forced entry and any mud or soil on your carpets. I just couldn't find any evidence of anyone at your place other than you two."

Axel shuddered. "Zoe, did you lock the front door after you aided me into my place? Or did you leave it unlocked? Closed door but unlocked?"

"Absolutely. I threw the dead bolt upon leaving."

"That's not what I asked. Upon arrival Zee. What happened on the initial arrival of us two at my residence?"

She gasped. "Oh, no, wait a minute. Let me think."

"What?" Thumper knew the *oh no* signal.

Zoe pondered before she affirmed her answer. Her voice was despondent. "I didn't throw the lock when we entered. I didn't even close the door. I helped you inside, guided you upstairs for your shower, and proceeded downstairs as you made yourself comfortable in your bed. It was then that I closed the front door, when I went downstairs to fetch a drink, snacks and your prescriptions. I went upstairs again to administer your medications, eat with you, departed, threw the bolts later on the way out."

"How long before we entered, ascended to my bedroom and your first trip downstairs?"

"Too long. Maybe even fifteen minutes!" There prevailed an ugly silence between the three of them. Zoe broke the tension. "Axel, maybe she followed us inside after we entered. The porch light was off. I was totally consumed with attending to your welfare, assisting you upstairs. I now concede that she could have hid until I left you alone." Zoe appeared to be bleeding of fear while striking her new conclusion.

Zee added, "Perhaps, just perhaps, she was at her residence as we conducted our inspection and tailed you home to your place and waited for an opportunity to enter, an opportunity that I provided." Zoe was convincing herself of this scenario.

"I am so sorry that I doubted you Axel. She must have overheard our conversation about the medicine, maybe even slipped an extra dose into your drink downstairs when I was upstairs with you. I came back for your drink later after snacks. It's highly possible. I'm sorry Axel. She may have been in the house all the time with us until I left, hearing every word, plotting her mental torture for you. I am beginning to believe your apparition. It could have happened just the way you experienced it."

"Creepy," Axel murmured. "She intruded into our private conversation and opened the dead bolt from the inside when she fled. Think hard. Was it unlocked when you returned?"

"I don't know because I automatically placed your key in the lock and turned it. I didn't notice if the bolt had not been thrown and I didn't try to see if the door was unlocked."

Thumper put a halt to his chomping to enter the conversation. "Are we talking about who I think we are talking about? Hey, guys. Get real? Montilladan?" He waved his glass back and forth vigorously in one hand as he spoke to catch their attention. "Surely you refer to someone else?"

Axel moved to join them in the living area and addressed Thumper with affirmation. "Yes, Thumper, her, Montilladan. She visited me tonight at my place."

Thumper smirked in disbelief first until he saw the deadpan looks on their faces. "No way Jose. You believe that Montilladan was the intruder at your place tonight? Now why would she do that? If she wanted you dead, excuse me, Boss, why didn't she just have the thugs knife you? Or shoot you? Why take the risk tonight to scare you to death? And betray to us that she is alive? She would have been better to harm you physically tonight than just scare you. This makes no sense to me." Zoe smiled facetiously back at Axel. Axel was not amused.

Silently, each cogitated an answer. Zoe, in confusion since the minute Lacey Sills walked into their lives, had no idea why Montilladan would betray herself tonight. But she was willing to give Axel the benefit of the doubt, now that she realized that the front door had remained unlocked for some period of time after their entrance, allowing Montilladan to enter and hide until her exit.

Axel believed that they were close to exposing her, that they had misinterpreted a key piece of evidence. In his mind he sifted through the facts of the past day desperately searching for clues to her existence and guilt.

Thumper, meanwhile, was bewildered by all these events. All he wished for was a peaceful, swift conclusion to this case. Silently he prayed for the safety of his close friends as he looked at Zee first, and then Axel.

"So, she has delivered a challenge." It was Axel who spoke with conviction in reply to Thumper. "Catch me if you can. Catch me if you dare."

Zoe challenged him. "This is a person who specializes in deceit, excites herself by her abilities to deceive others and get away with it. This is the great beguiler, not a lady who sheds her disguise on a whim or a dare and shows up one night to say, oh, Axel my dear, catch me if you can!"

Axel was determined. "Okay, I'll restate my theory. She is trying to scare us away. Thumper, I have been trying to tell my partner that we are close to the truth. I think that she knows how close we are. Maybe, we have already seen this important case busting clue. Maybe it's the card keys that hold the answer. Maybe she knows of our conversations with George and Katz, Dr. Sorbet, Dr. Montoya, Larry Bartlett, Kathleen Whitehurst, Constance, and Lieber. Somewhere in this maze lies the answer. In reality, we are not even close to solving this mystery! But she doesn't know that! She erroneously believes that we have made a case busting discovery." Thumper stood to leave as he returned his glass to the kitchen and belched again. "Sorry. Enough debate. I will leave you two alone to argue. Here's the list of addresses that match the phone numbers from Ray Spiller's papers as you requested." Thumper extracted a crumpled piece of paper from his massive shirt pocket and delivered it to Axel. Axel scanned it for its clarity.

"Goodnight. Thanks for the food and tea, Zoe. Hope you both feel better in the morning. I'll get to work on the card keys first thing."

"You are welcome, big guy," Zoe gleefully added.

"Your car keys are on the counter Axel. Gotta go. And don't worry, I guarantee I was not tailed. Had a cab follow right behind me and left it six blocks from here."

Thumper departed while Zoe sat beside Axel where they started one hour ago, on the sofa. Axel begged her. "Can you keep Lacey entertained in the kitchen while I sneak out the front door tomorrow? I have an early appointment with Paula Piper."

"Sure."

"What's wrong, Zee?'

"Can't I at least broach the subject of bringing Tinker into our confidence with Lacey tomorrow?"

"Too early. We still require more information."

"But Axel, we could still honor her deal by allowing her to be the first to talk to M whenever we find her. Tinker moves in to interrogate her if there are any criminal implications. Besides, the next piece of vital information we discover may be our last."

"No."

She barked and shouted at him. "I, Axel, am just recovering from Heather's death. I have no desire to witness you in that scene. I'm sorry, Axel, I won't sleep with you. That doesn't stop me from caring deeply about you!" Weepiness filled her voice. Axel reconsidered.

"I will make a deal with you. Let tomorrow morning and afternoon pass. Invite Tinker to our offices say, late tomorrow afternoon, say four or five o'clock.

Tell Lacey we need Tinker to check some aspects of the case for us. We promise not to reveal her identity and we promise not to reveal M's existence until we have concrete proof. Promise her that we will allow her to meet and speak with M first when we discover her whereabouts, just as we agreed. But we require Tinker's assistance to protect us and assist us in locating her."

Zoe grabbed his hand. "Thanks, Axel, I feel so much better in numbers on this case. Three is better than two, and Tinker's the size of two more. Off to bed with you!" Tugging at him to vacate her sofa, pointing in the direction of the stairs, she followed him upstairs, tucked him in, déjà vu as hours ago, and he collapsed into a deep snore at once. Zoe stood over him for a few minutes, realizing how Axel had made her life so much richer.

She made her way downstairs, checked to make sure the front door was bolted and sat uneasily. When she finally retired, she found herself opening her eyes every thirty minutes on a night when she hungered for sleep. At ten after four she sprung out of bed! A sound at the front door had disturbed her. Had she really locked the door? Had M materialized again? On wobbly knees, she raced to the front door on the balls of her feet, preparing for a confrontation. Yes, it was bolted.

She peeked outside by way of a side-slot window into the quiet solitude of her deserted street, almost expecting the ghost of M to be there in the street taunting her. A black cat streaked across the street and disappeared into darkness behind a shrub. Her forehead creased in frown, her mind materialized intruder outlines at every bush she spied. Feeling uneasy, with a bubbling in her stomach, she crept upstairs to slither into bed beside him. With the covers under her back, she turned sideways into him. Strength in numbers. Zoe felt secure. It was only a fleeting three hours of sleep until she had to arise. Her heart was pounding. Her palms were sweaty.

WEDNESDAY MORNING

It was just like one of those scenes in the black and white movies when the unsuspecting hero wakes up to discover the beautiful dame, who he had been wooing since the beginning of the film, is suddenly cuddled up next to him. So it was that he opened his eyes to find her so. Axel was on his back, one arm by his side, the other around her shoulder and onto her thigh. Zoe rested her head on his shoulder with legs bent, her entire body curled inward toward him, with her slender left leg straddling his torso. It was a painless and natural position for both sleepers. Even if he should hug her tight, she couldn't move any closer.

He admired her beauty, examined her facial features; the soft, rich, tanned skin where it showed through the cream, the noble facial features with long slender dark eyelashes and beautifully flowing eyebrows; her ebony hair was so rich, her physique strategically tucked in at the waist to accent her enticing hips.

At that very moment, she opened her eyes, so dazzling, so deep, so dark, and so gorgeous. After she stretched her arms and legs straight, she recreated her clasp around him again.

She excused her presence. "I couldn't sleep last night. My logic was if M returns, I wanted you to protect me, I wanted you to be the first in the line of fire while I got some rest. You protect me was my first priority; safety in numbers was my obvious second conclusion." She yawned.

Axel agreed. "You're so damn cute Zee; it really requires incredible discipline to resist you. Your mental prowess is so alluring. I believe you are right about Tinker. We need to immerse him in our plan. And you know why?"

"Why?"

"So I can position him on the front line of assault ahead of you and me. But...for your previous suggestion of placing me on the front line, take this!"

He took his pillow and began to wack her with it. She covered her head while pleading with him to halt. Finally he muscled against her until she broke loose and her momentum carried her onto the floor. She was now on her knees by the side of the bed. She sprung up. "Got to exercise and shower. Ignore my groans. They're part of my training."

Zoe bounced up and down three times and darted downstairs to commence her daily ritual. Axel sat up in bed, limped across the floor to determine if he could recommence his exercises. After two sit-ups, the pain rocketed throughout his abdomen on the way into his neck muscles. Instead, he perched himself at the top of the stairs which paralleled the hallway, soothed the excruciating pain in his stomach by massaging himself while choosing to observe her darts and lunges in her martial arts practice in the hall below.

As she paused, Axel was curious. "Do you imagine figures in front of you?"

"Yes, they are all faceless. I concentrate only on their limbs and soft spots. I kick, poke, punch, and maintain a mental scorecard. Each series of actions has five imaginary targets. I keep in constant motion and maintain balance at all costs. No one thrusts their stomachs or noses at you as a weapon so I concentrate on the limbs."

"An offensive drill? Right? As opposed to defensive action?"

"I made this drill up to simulate combat. I don't have arm strength nor body muscle so my advantage is to keep in motion and conduct strategic hits into vulnerable parts of the body. Try to get the opponent to move laterally and in that one second that he or she does, strike, just like in Fosse's can that night." She paused to catch her breath. While she did, he added, "Just like basketball, attack the defender who is off balance. Say, I notice you always stay on the balls of your feet."

"Right, I find it the best way to maintain balance, easy to move, plus for me it is a reminder to take small steps. The next drill is not commercial for television. It gets ugly. I pretend to attack a villain down the hall." She peered upward through the rails. "Unless, you'd care to stand in?"

"Come on, Zee, do I look like a bad guy?" She looked gorgeous, soaked in sweat, pants hugging her, outlining her erotic zones. Somehow the beauty cream didn't seem to fit as it commenced to smear and drip from the saturation of her body fluids.

"Stop staring, Axel! I know what you're thinking. Go and take a cold shower! Now! Before I commence my drill step by step up toward you!"

"Yes, ma'am." Zee was right again. This was no time for another ill-timed outburst of affection so he retreated. In the cool of the mist, he jettisoned streams to pulverize his sore spots. He became lost in the laser beads of water as they washed over his face and dripped onto his chest until she rapped hard on the fogged glass to signify that his shift was over. Oh, he was so enticed to lure her into a watery joint venture but wisely declined.

He was proud of his self-discipline. For now, he dried, dressed in loose clothing, and scurried downstairs into the kitchen as she appeared clad only in a beach towel of blue sea and marine inhabitants. "There is dried fruit, black coffee and hard biscuits on the kitchen island."

"That menu will most certainly inspire me to pack real food from my place when I move in," he said as he first nibbled on a cement biscuit. "If it is okay with you, I will retrieve some real cuisine."

"You do remember that Thumper delivered your vehicle?" She tossed him the keys.

"Yes, dear."

"Axel, do you have a box at your place to put all your belongings in?"

"I probably do. Why?"

"Just in case your movements are being watched. If you leave with a suitcase, and M has a spy posted, it will draw more suspicion that you have moved elsewhere. Any spy will want to know your destination. Leave with a box, probably less attention."

He forced the edibles down gingerly while yearning for a cream filled donut or parmesan scrambled eggs or huevos rancheros. She reappeared twenty minutes later dressed in her business attire of black pants with a killer silky cream business top. Axel shared his agenda with her. "I shall begin my pilgrimage today by checking the addresses that correspond to the phone numbers on the lists that Roy Spiller had. But first I have an appointment with Paula Piper—Montilladan's agent—at nine thirty."

"You mentioned it." Zoe paced down the hallway. "Oops, Axel, I see Lacey parking outside."

"Cue for me to disappear." Axel sprinted two agonizing steps at a time up the staircase with dried apple slices, in time to dodge Lacey's entrance. From the top of the staircase, Axel caught a glimpse of Lacey's figure, clad today in loosely fitting aquamarine gym wear. Her ponytail, extruding through the back of a baseball cap, swayed as he watched her parade down the hallway. Lacey and Zee rested ironically on the living room sofa, which seemed to be the center of attention of this entire escapade, while he maintained a quiet vigil from his perch on the top step where he could spy and listen.

From his distance he could hear Zee's voice as she reviewed the investigation of the whereabouts of Roy Spiller, currently unknown. She also conversed about the will of Montilladan and a host of inheritors. Lacey expressed her sincere regrets about the incident at Fosse's and elaborated about her agreement to cover any unpaid medical bills. Zoe responded. "That's acceptable. Axel is healing satisfactorily without any complications." Lacey declined to speculate whom the underwriter of the incident might have been as Zoe pressed her.

"Did you personally attend the reading of the will?"

"No, I am too upset over this whole affair so I had my attorney attend." Her voice seemed devoid of feelings. She attacked Zoe. "I must protest Axel's visit to my parent's house. There is no earthly reason to involve them into your investigation. My mother will only make your investigations more difficult for she is a very determined, bitter lady. They must remain exempt from these matters because there is nothing to be gained but grief. You must convey my concerns to Axel. Please, I plead to you, don't involve my parents any further. Leave my mother out of this."

Zoe promised to convey her comments to Axel on her behalf. However, Zoe also recounted, to Lacey's surprise, the encounter by Axel with her mother at the cemetery. "My fault I'm afraid. I informed my dad and mother that I had engaged your firm to investigate M's death further. She probably had you tailed there. I am so sorry. It now appears as I precipitated their involvement, but I still want no further interactions with them."

Lacey did not want to address the identity of the photographer who captured her and Montilladan in intimate poses, citing, "It is irrelevant to the case." She became confused and re-circled, adding. "I don't know who took them. Maybe Roy took some of them but, truthfully, I can't recall."

"How convenient," Zee thought, "first citing that she would not reveal the photographer, now insisting she knew not the identity but maybe Roy." Zoe abandoned that topic.

"Truthfully, did you ever witness any single romantic moment between Roy and Montilladan?"

"Roy and M and I spent time together as a threesome, but there were no romantic interludes in my presence. We were just close friends."

"No threesomes?"

Lacey was incensed. Axel heard her chastising Zoe from where he stood. "I told you before absolutely not. Zoe! The relationship with Montilladan and Roy and I was platonic." Zoe did not apologize for the inquiry. She stood, opened the patio doors, encouraging Lacey to join her and thus providing Axel with the opportunity to escape. He did so as Zee entered dangerous waters with Lacey on her next topic, involving Tinker's presence in the case.

Lacey, as expected, balked. "I'm paying your salaries and expenses and I won't authorize that. I am not paying for a police investigation that will lead to the public embarrassment of M and potentially me." Her remarks were spiked with irritation.

Zoe selfishly thought of her own safety and Axel's, too. "Lacey, we promise that we will not reveal your identity. There is surmounting evidence for us to believe that M is alive and that Roy Spiller is buried in the grave at Forest Haven Cemetery as you first speculated. From our findings to date, there are a number of possible scenarios that could unfold, one of them that Spiller's death was not accidental, that Roy Spiller was the victim of an attempt on M's life, or that..." and Zee swallowed hard, "that M may be responsible for Roy's death, an act of convenience for her."

Lacey blew up, her eyebrows lifting, her neck veins bulging through her white skin as she held her head high to set Zoe right. With her outburst, Zee directed them inside out of earshot of neighbors, hoping that Axel had escaped. "I told you. M wouldn't do that. She is not a murderer. I'm paying you to find her not waste time on who killed poor Roy. I want her found."

Zoe was pleased that Axel was not witnessing this exchange of dialogue. Lacey seemed so distant from the sweet innocent individual that she portrayed onscreen, or even from the empathetic moments in their office. Her face was without makeup today, so she seemed so ordinary in looks with bare eyebrows, no lipstick, and no facial cream. Even her hair was messy as she removed her cap now and shook her head of blond frowzy hair.

"Lacey, if Roy Spiller is buried in that grave, one of the possibilities unfolding is the pre-meditated murder of Roy and if so, we must alert my friend Tinker at the department to this. Lacey, I assure you that detective Tinker Lawrence can be trusted. He is an extremely close friend. He won't betray you; he won't reveal M's real sex. He'll honor our deal."

Lacey continued her unpredictability. "Okay, we are in gridlock so I'll trust you. I will compromise with you as I don't want you to get into trouble with the police by concealing evidence from them that could damage your integrity and suspend your licenses. If in your judgment, you think that there is evidence of a nature that your friend can assist you with, I concur so go ahead and contact him with my approval. But when you make this contact, inform me of the ensuing discussion. I said before that I am funding this investigation, not the police! I want to be kept abreast of every detail you tell Mr. Lawrence." Lacey rolled on.

She scolded Zoe. "Let me remind you once more, my identity as your client must not be revealed, and if M becomes absolutely implicated in murder, God forbid, I must have a full briefing on these matters before you approach the police. Furthermore, when her whereabouts are identified, I must have the opportunity to talk to her before any police interrogation. Those are my terms. That is our deal."

Zoe elaborated. "We agree. Axel and I will be present, too, when you talk to her."

"Okay." Lacey added in a soft tone. "You mentioned protection on the phone to me. You believe that I need some protection from her, don't you?" Lacey raised her head and stood only inches in front of Zoe, her penetrating eyes conveying her look of disbelief.

Zoe was brave. "Definitely."

Lacey laughed uproariously and unexpectedly to break the tense dialogue. "She is not going to kill me. That is ludicrous. You and Axel are running amuck out of bounds. However, I'll be careful. My friend Lyall has agreed to escort me the next few days. He's a former cop; Tinker Lawrence may know him; Lyall sports quite a husky physique and he is a crack shot if it makes you two feel any better. He has a license for his firearms."

Zee was relieved. "We're just erring on the side of safety Lacey. Axel and I agree to your terms and you agree to ours that we are present when you converse with M and we have an agreement, and you provide security for yourself."

"Okay, okay, I agree." She was acting a bit belligerent with taut lips and a sneer. She now grew impatient, paced about Zoe's living room, demanding additional details of their investigation to date. Zoe was polite, patiently walking her through all the players that they had interrogated and what had been achieved.

Meanwhile, at his home, Axel packed quickly using a box that had recently housed a new microwave. He selected his essentials of food, clothing, and necessities, carefully placing them inside. The real test of trust had been allowing Thumper to drive his treasured vehicle over to Zee's place the last two nights.

He noticed on the way over that the driver's seat settings made been adjusted for Thumper's size- gigantic.

Not that he didn't trust Thumper's investigation but, in the daylight, he now inspected each window at his home, ground and upper floors, to find any clues of a forced entry. Standing at the entrance to his bedroom, he experienced a rush of the creeps bolt up his back, evoking the saga of last night clearly in his mind. He turned sharply to a faint creak downstairs. The trance fled.

Just as he locked up, his cellular rang. "Good morning."

"Good morning, Axel, Speed here."

"Hey, Speed. Have you any developments to report?" He placed the box on the passenger's seat and sat inside, roof up and secure so he could not be overheard.

"Axel, I was able to confirm that Brissand is still in business. His competition's been shut down by local authorities, or rather eliminated, so he's running a lucrative game of forged identities and papers and he's running it solo. No one seems to know where he is hiding out and manufacturing the false identities, but I will meet with a credible lead today to try and establish his hangout."

"Be careful." Axel eagerly decided to pass on to Speed his nightmarish encounter of last night. He spent five minutes briefing him to impress the danger of their positions. He did not want Speed in harm's way.

"I'll touch base with you later today, Axel. I promise to watch my back." The line was dead.

Axel drove as fast as he could to the Golden Parrot Bar. It was closed but, luckily, the proprietor was enjoying a smoke at the rear of the building on the deck. They conversed about Roy with Axel focused on the business at hand. "Nope. Roy Spiller hasn't returned to my establishment and nobody else has been snooping around inquiring about Roy. However, Katz was anxious to speak to ya. He did say that last night. So I'm passing it on. Did he call you?"

With that info, Axel scurried on foot down to the beach. It was low tide. Only a mother and her two children building crumbling sand castles, with no sign of Katz or any of his cronies. But if Katz had wanted to talk to him, why hadn't he left a voice message? That didn't make sense.

One last stab was to check at the overhang to inspect for Katz and George but, twenty minutes later, further up the beach road, he met with the same bad luck. Recognizing that time was precious, knowing the habits of Paula, and that she would expect him to arrive promptly on time, he bolted for his convertible and plotted the most direct course to her office. It was fun for him to sing out of tune with the top down. The oldies station gave him just that moment, so he did so: "Lou-i, Lou-i, yah, yah, yah, yah, yah, yah, me gotta go, yah, yah, yah, yah, yah, yah, yah, Lou-i, Lou-i."

Paula's assistant escorted him to her private office. Patiently he awaited her, inspecting the plethora of photos on the wall, where he found famous directors, household television stars, philanthropists, awards' ceremonies, even himself with Paula at Fosse's Bar. He took particular notice of Paula's recognition by the local charities. Turning, he noticed that this double room was part of a living room area adjacent to her library. Suddenly, her petite angelic frame graced the room. Axel sunk down on one knee, extending his arms open.

"Hey, hey, Paula, I've been waiting here for you." She opened her arms and strolled forward with a barrel of mousy laughter.

"Hey, hey, Axel, I've been waiting for you, too." Paula burst to embrace him and they danced a single loop around the room to complete the first verse of the song. She offered him a seat beside her on a very, very, long plump mauve sofa in the living room sector of her expansive office.

"Paula, your life is saturated with celebrities. It must make you feel important. Do you really want to give this fame up?"

"I'm content, Axel. I set out to build this business ten years ago. Back then I always said to myself that the day would come when I would sell at the right price. Somehow through all my tribulations, I have arrived at my predetermined destination. The business will be run by my able assistants who will move into the new company as part of our term sheet. For myself, I want time off from working fourteen hours a day. I want a husband and I want to have a family. I'm not getting any younger. Love conquers all and I don't mind."

Axel knew the meaning of love conquers all. This case seemed to be rife with that phrase. "You always look so relaxed, Paula."

"I can't complain. And you?"

"Business is booming, surrounded by friends, surviving financially, of course, broke up with Nikki but, as I have said, it was for the betterment of the both of us. In reality, I held her back as we drifted apart."

"Face reality, Nikki's at the pinnacle of her career. I've seen her at so many influential gatherings recently. However, you, Axel, you're a survivor." She glanced down at her wrist watch. "I am sorry to inform you that I am pressed for time. Don't mean to be rude, but how can I assist you?"

"I'm researching Montilladan's death for a client. There are some aspects of the accident, the estate, and the circumstances, that require clarification, shall we say." Paula's big dark brown eyes were set on him and she returned an inquisitive stare. She shifted incommodiously in her seat at the sound of Montilladan's name. As Axel continued his lengthy apology, she shook her head, her brunette long hair swaying off and onto her shoulders.

"Montilladan," she murmured barely decipherable. "How I miss him at times; on other occasions, I am glad to be rid of his arrogance and unpredictable shenanigans. But no one I know ever wished death upon him. He trusted my advice implicitly and allowed me to negotiate some tantalizing monetary contracts for him with three different studios. Oh, I interrupted you." She discontinued her flashback.

"I would like to ask you some intimate, personal, bordering on strange, questions regarding Montilladan. You must not reveal a word to anyone of this conversation, not even to Mr. Right. Not the police. Not anyone. What gets discussed now, stays here. Promise?"

Paula sat closer to say, "You're petrifying me, Axel. What's going on?"

"No need to be scared. Condition two. Only answer that which you feel comfortable to respond to."

"Can I ask you something before we commence?"

"Certainly."

"Was Montilladan's death possibly not accidental?"

Axel was aghast. He tingled all over. Did Paula know something to draw her to this end? He had to respond, but be careful in his choice of words. He also just heard her state that no one would wish him dead.

"Ah, I don't know but...a long shot. That's all I can say at this time. Zoe and I need to investigate deeper." Why did she ask that? He had to pry it out of her.

"Okay, I'll cooperate. Let's see where this takes us." She rose to her desk to instruct her assistant to guarantee their privacy. Paula always looked so trendy. Today, a color coordinated green outfit with red dangling red ear rings and very long burgundy nails. She had the longest slender fingernails that Axel had ever witnessed. Upon return, she positioned herself even closer to Axel, as he ventured into Montilladan's past. "Who were Montilladan's closest friends?"

"Oh, I guess Betty Wilson, the make-up artist, Lacey Sills, myself as guardian of his career, Tony Wells from the studio who also managed most of his business affairs, Stu Givens, and rather than ramble, Axel, well, perhaps I should fill you in."

"Go ahead."

"Axel, believe it or not, Montilladan was not a natural social creature. If there were oodles of people at a party, you would find him in the corner with one or two others, or out on the balcony for air, or strolling in the gardens. Did he love attention? Absolutely. Especially on the movie set and with the press, and on television and in front of the camera, he was a publicity hog. But he tended to make only a couple of close friends in each movie, and focus his relationships on them. He wasn't a recluse. He was a natural party-goer but not a natural blender with people." Paula didn't pause.

"However, Axel, I found him to be charming in one-on-one situations. He lost his arrogance; the rough edges of his rapport with the public were distant. So, events like, ah… having lunch or dinner, a night at the theater, working out at his private gymnasium, a walk in the mall, negotiating a con-tract, why Montilladan was on his best behavior. His altruistic nature shone in these situations." Axel recalled Lacey's similar comments of M's charm in private.

"I should say that once in a while, he actually showed up here at my office with friends, usually male. I never really noticed who they were. He just dropped by; I think he trusted me. I was a rare commodity for him."

Axel probed further. He needed to know of any strong male acquaintances. "Did he like men?"

"No," and she chuckled and roared with laughter. "You have to stop read-ing the gossip rags. That suggestion is unfounded."

He ventured astray. "Were you and he...ever..."

"Heavens, no!"

"Sorry, I had to ask." Paula seemed unaware of M's double life and that was actually a relief to Axel.

"I choose to answer that insinuation by you to set the record straight."

"You were very close to him though?"

"Yes."

"Did he ever mention a Dr. Renee Montoya?"

"N-no, but I know who she is. I have chatted with her briefly at social gatherings."

"Roy Spiller?"

"Never. Don't know any Roy Spiller." Paula was cogitating, placing her thumb and index finger under her chin.

"Did he ever mention any serious enemies? Someone who might want to harm him?"

Paula paused while fidgeting. "Never ventured there, Axel." She jabbed at him. "Where is this going?"

"We share something in common Paula. We both have doubts about his death. You alluded to it earlier. Zoe and I suspect it. We have no concrete facts, just insinuations that have surfaced. Let's confide in one another. Tell me what you were thinking only moments ago when you implied that his death might not be accidental?"

She lost her composure as her voice became suffocated with fraught. "It is only a hunch Axel. I probably spoke impetuously. I shouldn't have spoken at all..." and Axel interrupted.

"But you did so tell me. I promise to keep your secret. What were you thinking? You blurted it out and I heard you say that you have doubts about his death being accidental."

Now her expression lost its charm. After a silent interlude, she nodded her head to agree. "Okay. I agree to tell you in strictest confidence." She exhaled with a sigh. "That same day he died Axel, something very, very peculiar occurred. Montilladan called me to wish me well in my new life and to inform me of a wedding gift which he was sending to my office. He was so alive on the phone, ripe and bursting with optimism about his life, about strong feelings on his fu-ture. It was almost as if he was speaking like there was a new life ahead for him, and I felt from his upbeat delivery that an event had happened in his life to create some sort of transformation. I mean, he was rapturously happy for me that I had found my man of the future, and that he was going to find his mate soon and he...he rambled on and on about some new found happiness, a new Xanadu. I felt that there may be a new partner in his life. But he never really came out and said that...never told me who it was. But Axel, he sounded deliriously happy."

After a noticeable hiatus, she added, "It just seemed to be so eerily strange and ironic that one hour and fifty minutes later, after Montilladan made that phone call to me, that he should tragically die. Axel it gave me the creeps and I have not shared my feelings with anyone."

"Where did he call you from?"

"That also was strange, Axel. He emphasized to me that he didn't want anyone to overhear our call so he said that he was in a phone booth in the back lot of the studio where they were filming. I could hear some commotion in the background. I don't know why he didn't use his cell phone. He always used his cell phone. Always Axel. That call was so out of character and I thought they dismantled all the phone booths on the lot."

Paula took a deep breath, shivered, and set her arms in motion to warm herself by rubbing them over her shoulders. "I have only a hunch, Axel. I mean, a man calls me to share his exuberant future vision of life, calls me to express this new found oracle, and hangs up and goes to meet his maker. And calls me from an old phone booth? Something just didn't seem right Axel. The contents of that phone conversation have haunted me since that day. It has been very bothersome to me ever since. I...I..."

Axel aided her. "How did you find out that he died?"

"The studio called me. So did the producer. As his agent, I gave them a short list of other individuals to notify. It just seemed to be all so incongruent to have an uplifting conversation, and then, you know, fall off the cliff." Paula wiped away a solitary tear with her index finger.

"Thank you for sharing that with me. You've been very helpful. I'll keep it in confidence." Axel was ecstatic. Paula had probably just confirmed that Montilladan was escaping to a new prosperous life with her Romeo.

"Okay, now you tell me the foundation of your suspicions."

"Someone was observed inspecting, or perhaps tampering with the rails of the balcony hours before the shoot. That person may have spelled out the death scene by compromising the integrity of the set. I stress, may have! You must keep these facts to yourself Paula."

"I've been tempted to ask you since you entered, but do the horrible scrapes on your face have anything to do with this investigation?"

"Possibly. I was attacked at Fosse's Tavern the other night. Once again, Zoe came to my rescue."

Paula stood abruptly, retreating to the far end of the room to peer out a window. He had always known her as an optimist, a cheerful lady. This pensiveness was the first time that Axel had ever witnessed her out of that charming jovial character.

Paula wheeled around. "I want you to find the bastard that did this, if murder it is. M is a great loss to our industry, to all of us, arrogant as he was." Axel sprung out of his seat to join her. They faced each other to hold hands.

"I speculated only. We have just commenced our investigation, Paula. Keep all of this confidential. I did stress to you that this incident may not be an accident. That line is being investigated but not proved yet. Did Montilladan ever make any references to bookies?"

"No."

"Debtors? Organized crime? Spats with friends?"

"Axel, I can't help you except to say that I have a hunch, woman's intuition that Montilladan died at a very strange time in his life- a time in which he had appeared to have found a new meaning to life."

"Did you ever witness a mean vicious streak in the man?"

"No, I saw him lose his temper with reporters and directors, but that was Montilladan, and it was mostly show. He never liked journalists ever since they overplayed the incident of him supposedly touching one of his female co-stars on set. That turned out to be false. As I said, he was charming in private settings. I often felt all these public displays of rudeness were put-ons."

"I understand that you convinced Montilladan to play a more definitive role in the organizations of Dr. Larry Bartlett?"

"Yes, Montilladan took a shining to the kids on his very first engagement, and he formed sympathies to their cause. He donated significant time and money to Larry's companies. I don't know the details. I do know that he spent time at the labs where eventually he was appointed to the Board of Directors."

"Anything unusual about that?"

"Not at all."

"Were Montilladan and Bartlett good friends?"

"To my knowledge, they enjoyed an occasional dinner, a friendly drink, attended fund raisers, but nothing out of the ordinary that I am aware of. They made a scene one night- in a restaurant! Capers, I recall. I was there. Tempers flared so I went over to calm them down. It turned out that it was Montilladan who was creating the disturbance. Larry Bartlett just sat there and was being scolded. Maybe they weren't best of friends. I really don't know Axel."

"How long ago was that?"

"I would guess at four months ago. I made a note of it because I had a reservation there that night." She examined her daily calendar to find the date of her appointment at Capers, wrote down the date, and passed it to Axel.

"Ever hear of a dentist residing in San Clemente named Dr. Sorbet?"

"No." She expressed her urgency to leave for an appointment by checking her watch again. Axel was disappointed.

"I am still curious as to how you obtained those scrapes on your face and if you can connect it to your prowling around Montilladan's death?"

"It was an unfortunate casualty of the business. As I said, two ruffians seemed to get the best of me at Fosse's Tavern."

"I'm sorry, Axel, I must go. You take care of yourself. Do us all a favor, if murder it is. Watch out for your invite to my soiree when we return."

"Supposed murderer and yes, I'll RSVP as soon as I receive it. Good luck, Paula. Mums the word and I hope you've found true happiness." They hugged and Axel left her and exited. It was almost ten and he had sleuthing to do by inspecting the addresses that corresponded to Spiller's notes. Thumper had created an itinerary of all the addresses in geographical order, complete with page size maps. Back on the pavement, he thought about Paula's future one last time and roared down the street to start his inspection.

The first phone number corresponded to a hair salon in a low class shopping district not far from the Golden Parrot Bar. Roy, from photos, didn't have much hair. It was always cropped short like Montilladan's. "You certainly wouldn't require an appointment at this establishment," he mumbled. Did a friend work here? He stopped to spy on patrons moving in and out of the shop for ten minutes. He passed on the opportunity for closer contact.

The second address was a low budget film studio in need of external repairs and just two miles south of the downtown core. It would not be wise to attempt entry without a pass as he observed the tight security. Axel noted the name, drew a sketch of the entrance, observed the paucity of parked cars behind the wrought iron fences, and drove onward to the next locale.

The third place was a warehouse on Macey Street, in the middle of a block of dilapidated empty warehouses, in a long line of buildings crying for occupants, jumbled with "For Lease" signs, east of the airport. He parked to scan the area. Quiet. Run down. A bus stop six blocks behind him at a mainstream gasoline station was the last sign of civilized life. Vagrants had staked out their territory across the street in a grassy lot strewn with empty drums and twisted iron. This neighborhood had seen better days. A 747 passed overhead in its descent.

He checked Thumper's notes. The building was owned by Aaron Schuler Productions. Now, where had he heard that name before? Why wasn't his mind functioning? Further down the block, empty lots were dominated by For Sale and For Lease advertisements. He made a U-turn on the deserted street for a last look at the warehouse when he now spied what looked like a card key entry. Could it be?

He was lucky that he had retained one of the mysterious duplicate plastic keys himself. Axel parked in front of the warehouse, looked behind him and in front, rolled down his window, left the engine running, exiting his vehicle with deliberation darted to the box, producing the card key, sliding it across a red electronic eye many times in different positions, only to obtain the same disappointing results. Why would Roy Spiller have a phone number to this warehouse written down in his goods? That was indeed a mystery. This summoned a return after the remainder of his stops.

He sped off to the next locale. What was to be the big break? Frustration to date. What clue had scared Montilladan? The fourth location was a residence along the coast about two miles south of the airport. It was an abode of modern stark architecture and sparse landscaping. Thumper had not been able to determine the owner's identity. Was this Aaron Schuler's residence? M's hideout? A close friend from a past life? Maybe even M herself hiding in there, peering out of a window cursing his presence while staring at him right now. The carport was empty so he could not record a car plate. Axel was brave and exited his vehicle to stare further at the dwelling. No blind blinked; no one emerged. The taunting was useless.

He did take note, however, that the entrance to the driveway and home was on complete view to any neighborhood spies. Not a likely place to perform the necessities of a quick change artist. The next two addresses led him to hostels. Entering each, Roy Spiller's photo was not recognizable by either manager. He called Zoe for some good news. Lacey had left abruptly after agreeing to terms to bring Tinker into the fold. "What an uncomfortable conversation, Axel. I hope it didn't rock her faith in us." Axel reiterated segments of the conversation that he had overheard.

"Lacey has no knowledge of Jenna, the bank accounts in Andorra, the dentist in San Clemente, nor could remember who had photographed Montilladan and herself in intimate settings. How convenient. There is one possible breakthrough." Zoe continued.

"Thumper says these two gray plastic card keys were manufactured and issued by MetraComp Security here in Los Angeles. The batch starting with seven, seven, four, two were sent to Columbia Security. Thumper used his charm to find that Columbia in turn installed systems for RAY-X Productions. A printout of their properties shows they are scattered in the area east and south of the airport. I suggest we check each one out together. There aren't that many. We might get lucky and discover that one of the keys opens a location up."

"I confess. I long for your company, too, after a fruitless morning. I have one of the identical keys and it hasn't proved worthwhile yet." Axel cited his coordinates and parked his Mustang at a corner gas station in anticipation of her arrival. In the interim, he returned Dr. Montoya's call from Tuesday. With luck on his side, Lillian, thoroughly annoyed at him, answered the phone. After placing him on hold for five minutes she patched him through.

"Mr. Hawk?"

"Yes, good morning, Dr. Montoya."

"Good morning. I'll get right to the point Mr. Hawk. I've given your trade proposal some serious consideration. I believe that it would be beneficial both for business and curiosity to arrange a next meeting." Axel was bubbling.

"Excellent." Before he could initiate a conversation, she grabbed the headlines.

"Meet me at seven o'clock Thursday night at my residence, four, four, seventy-five Spruce Lane in Westwood. If you can't locate the area, call Lillian. She will send a map. Let's make a deal. You tell me why you are interested in Montilladan's accidental death, and I in turn will disclose to you, very discretely, the real singular reason as to why I was treating Montilladan." Axel jumped in his seat as he realized a dream come true.

He had not even written the address down, nor flipped to the correct page in his key maps, nor had the chance to formulate further dialogue, nor had the chance to thank her profusely when she ended with, "See you tomorrow evening, Mr. Hawk." Dead air now confronted him.

When Zoe arrived with sandwiches to go, they positioned and abandoned her car in a secure bank parking lot nearby. In Axel's Mustang, they perused the list of properties that RAY-X productions owned, trying to rationalize which one the card key might give access to. It didn't take Axel long to zero in on one address, the exact warehouse on Macey Street he passed earlier. "Aaron Schuler owns RAY-X Productions?"

"Yes, you know who he is, don't you?"

"I feel like I should."

"Axel! Special effects guru extraordinaire."

"Right! I knew I had heard the name before. Of course! Aaron at the movies!"

Immediately, as Zoe touted Schuler's accomplishments and awards, he rang Thumper to leave a message to construct a profile on Aaron Schuler. As they ate, they fled to their first stop, Macey Street, he proposing a hunch to Zee. "How about Aaron Schuler as Romeo?"

Zee gagged on her food, while giggling simultaneously. "Axel you obviously haven't seen Schuler. You can't possibly think that dumpy, stumpy, grumpy, lumpy Aaron Schuler is Romeo?"

"Possibly. He's a great risk-taker. Broke into the business with his brilliant array of original special effects. Creativity and risk are not strange bedmates."

"Axel, take a look at me! I am a real woman. I guarantee you that he is not M's physical type."

"Now how the hell do you know that? Without interrogating Montil-ladan? Instinct again?"

Zoe jabbed at him. "Someone, hmm, someone," and she peered at him, "once gave me some wise advice about our business. Do not expend any energy on zero percent leads. We will visit the warehouses I agree as it is a lead, but Aaron Schuler is not Romeo. I shall give you some of your own advice. Do not expend any energy on Aaron Schuler as Romeo."

"Okay, now I have some good news for you. This warehouse on Macey Street is the object of phone calls by Roy Spiller to a land line inside. Now you tell me in addition, that your gray card key might possibly unlock it? Mine didn't earlier, so let's hope the other key does."

First, they drove down the littered streets around Macey, inspecting the neighborhood, circling blocks and convincing they were not being tailed. Except for an occasional drifter, an hourly security worker on a golf cart driving away from them as they made their final approach, a few stray cats, and a rat walking a tightrope on a wire overhead, it was still. Axel wanted to be absolutely certain so they drove around the vicinity three times more. Even the buildings on adjacent streets appeared empty with large glaring signs tagged to barbed wire fortified iron fences. Broken window panes dominated the vacant fortresses.

They came to rest directly in front of the target, the same warehouse that Axel had passed by one hour ago. Zoe had obtained the second card key from Thumper, so emerged, and walked to the front box to swipe it across the interface that controlled the front entrance to the property. Frustrated, she returned to Axel. "No luck. Not a match. Your card doesn't open it; nor does this one. That fence is too high to climb."

"Too coincidental, Zee. That phone line in there might be a clue. Let's drive to the end of the block and turn right. I think I spied a back alleyway behind the structure. The key won't open the gate to the property, but maybe there's a lock to the building." Abandoning Axel's car curbside, insuring that they had not been followed by waiting a few minutes out of sight of the street, they proceeded to strut down the deserted dusty rutted back alleyway.

The narrow gauntlet abounded with glass, dirty rags and green trash bags stuffed with smelly refuse. Two burned out metal frames of vehicles and one disfigured yellow school bus blocked their path. Cautiously, Axel stepped inside the bus expecting to discover hobo heaven but, instead, was confronted with the pungent odor of urine in rotting seats.

The alley ahead intersected the back of RAY-X's property, so they ambled further, studying the adjacent structures for signs of life. With luck there was conveniently a narrow opening at the base of the wire fence. After both bodies gained entry by slithering under the fence, they found themselves navigating through a back lot of tall grass, inundated with decaying wooden props and gangly rotten facades. "Zee, my curiosity has peaked as to why Roy Spiller had a phone number to this decrepit structure recorded in his annuls."

"I agree."

The warehouse resembled a cannon-battered fort with pockets of stucco tumbled to the ground exposing a putrid-colored undercoating. There were steel barred windows on every level and a network of stairs clung to the side of the building and lead to solid small iron doors at each elevation; the ground level doors were wide and tall enough to drive a truck through. Unluckily, all the doors appeared to be padlocked and not opened with a card key. Two small side doors and a third side drive-in entrance were obviously bolted from the inside. No sign of guard dogs. No sign of security. No sign of cameras or monitors. Axel noted deep tire indentations in dried mud leading to the padlocked double doors at the back.

"Okay, big guy, hoist me up onto your shoulders."

"What? I am still crippled and sore from my thrashing. Remember?"

"And I am a ninety-pound featherweight. Now, Roy Spiller had the phone number to this building. The phone's on the inside. Do you or do you not want to see what's inside this dilapidated mysterious citadel?"

"What are you going to do?"

"See that third floor opening? Up there." She pointed. "I'm going in."

"What? How can you scale up there?"

"Axel, hoist me up!"

"That's breaking and entering."

"It is not. That window has no glass nor bars. It's just entering. Besides, look around you. Why is a warehouse, so bleak, and in this part of town, bolted up so tight? We've already ascertained there is a phone inside. We have discovered that Roy Spiller had the phone number and was calling here. To whom? And why? Let's unlock the truth with our only chance. Now, shut up and hoist me up! Look around you, there's no one watching."

Axel leaned his body tightly against the wall for support, braced his body by placing his arms against the wall, moaned as Zoe mounted his shoulders, and sincerely emitted expletives to absorb the pain surging through his back and chest. After her presence left, he strutted away from the dwelling, looked to the heavens, and saw her grab onto a protruding drainpipe, witnessed her perform the amazing high bar act, first swinging herself wildly back and forth on the protrusion, and then up and onto what was left of a second floor metal balcony which swayed as she landed. She stood upright briefly to brush herself off and without hesitation, advanced again to intersect a third floor protruding metal beam with Axel gasping in awe below.

Before Axel could shout to warn her, she had completed the third phase of her gymnastics routine, pulling herself up onto the ledge of a window by utilizing the merest of undulations in the wall. Axel was left spellbound recalling her past exploits in a mountain climbing expedition.

Having completed the synthesis of her sortie, Axel bemoaned his fate if she should tumble, and he be forced to cushion the blow by catching her. However, she glided through the air one last time, latching onto the ledge of the targeted open window. With great dexterity, she maintained her balance. Before he could call to her, she disappeared inside.

Five minutes elapsed when he heard her distinctive high-shrill raptor-like trademark whistle. She sounded three shrills. Rounding the corner, he spied her halfway down a narrow chute on the blind side of the building, where Zoe had unlocked a side door from the inside. She motioned to him to hurry along. Axel gingerly navigated around broken glass, being careful not to touch the property line fence, which also had glass chards galore encased in the steel.

Entering, he saw that there were enough windows in the building's roof to allow a misty, dusty, orange light to douse and outline the contents. From the doorway, Axel and Zee stood perusing and panning the warehouse cluttered with props, mannequins, parade floats, and a variety of facades.

"Well, Axel, this was your idea to come here, so let's look around for the infamous phone. There doesn't appear to be an internal security alarm so our presence should remain undetected."

Serpentining their way through a crowd of mannequins, all with their backs to them as they passed, Axel took time to look at the menacing faces over his shoulder. Moving down an aisle, she touched his arm as Dorothy did to the Scarecrow, to point to the Tin Man and the Wizard. The rest of the aisle was adorned with twenty foot high statues of dragons, elephants, a plethora of shrubbery, and an assortment of tall rubber palms. Next, an onslaught of African animals in a safari backdrop confronted them.

At a well-lit crossroads, they parted. Axel followed a pathway into the old wild-west days, complete with green cacti, weather-beaten stage coaches, colorful saloon fronts, deep watering troughs, and the climax- Dodge City jail. He took a minute to inspect boxes of six guns, each copy a harmless toy. The western theme carried on to the end of the aisle with more facades of hotels, livery stables and barber shops, ending at the telegraph office. He peeked through to verify each one in depth. All were nothing more than frontal pieces. No hidden offices with phones.

"Axel." The sound startled him just as he had become immersed at staring into a sheriff's office that housed two jail cells, the only non-façade piece. He barely heard her cry but knew enough to vault quickly. Facing into blinding beams of light as the sun pierced directly into the area, he walked briskly on one side of the aisle in case he needed to retreat to shelter. Retracing his steps to the crossroads and in the direction that Zee had followed, he heard her summon him a second time. "Axel."

He tiptoed down a boardwalk, turning, startled at once by a mannequin of a gunslinger staring out of a window at him. Finally, he saw her perched on the top of a fence, peering into the other side. Container upon container was piled up inside a secure compound.

She addressed him. "It may not mean anything, but I am going to record the contents of these buckets." As if in the Olympic high jump, she retraced her steps and ran twenty paces, vaulting over the fence and landing as an acrobat at attention. Judges would have scored her dismount at ten points. Behind her, on the other side, Axel sat for a few minutes and spied what looked like a house trailer, forty feet long, sitting by itself at the end of the next aisle. He jogged to the door and was unable to budge the door with three tugs. The handle refused to turn. Zee sidled in behind him.

"What are you doing?"

"Jostling this door. Trying to get it to open."

"I'll bet a card key might do it."

"How would you know that?"

She smiled. "Because there is a card key lock for this unit right over there," and she directed his attention to an enticing black box at the far end of the trailer somewhat purposely hidden from view.

She took the keys from him, panned them in front of a beckoning red beam. No luck with the first one. They both jumped as a distinct click revealed an unlocked door as Zoe passed the second key in front. Axel turned the door handle. Presto.

Inside the elongated trailer, it was pitch black as the windows were sealed. Zee fumbled around feeling the wall and flicked a switch, which ignited a series of overhead fluorescent lights. They stood together, side by side, in bewilderment.

It was clearly one large wardrobe container. Row upon row of neatly pressed and arranged women's clothes greeted them. Axel moved quickly to inspect the footwear collection on shelving to his left. There were black shiny polished formal wear, suede casual, high heels, low heels, and flip-flops, elevator shoes of immense size, gym shoes, casual leather slip-ons, and scuffed brown cowboy boots.

Zoe meanwhile sat down in front of a grandfather desk, opened it and became engrossed in a jewelry collection of rings, earrings, berets, pearl necklaces, an array of watches, sunglasses, medallions, hair adornments, shiny gaudy pins, all neatly catalogued in the compartmentalized massive desk. Axel opened a voluminous nearby cupboard and was stunned. Before him were laid out hairpieces for men and women in all cuts, shapes, colors, lengths and styles. He noted auburn, blonde, brown, tan, red, streaked, gray, deep charcoal, and an abundance of sideburns and moustaches and even a goatee beard. A further search showed a variety of trimmed beards in black and brunette.

"Axel, look!" Axel moved closer to Zoe who had tugged open a drawer to discover a smorgasbord of contact lenses in multi-tints, each vile distinctively marked with the effective color. "Blue, green, hazel, brown," she recited.

"Let's look in drawer number two, Zee." Now he yanked on the next drawer, which revealed a display of false teeth, from elegant and classy, to an illiterate tobacco stained look. Zee inspected each one as Axel turned his head and quickly drew his attention to a counter halfway down the container. "Here's the phone." He dialed the number from his cell. "I guess we know now why Roy Spiller was calling here."

Zoe summarized. "The card key that opened the lock was the one we discovered at Montilladan's residence and Roy called her here. Success."

As Axel listened to an empty message machine, Zee disrupted him by calling out. "Hey, Axel! A beautician's paradise." She turned on a light overtop a mirror and sat down to inspect all the cubbyholes of a bureau built like a Victorian doll house.

"Lookee here, Axel. Observe, a drawer of eye lashes, eyebrows, plentiful powders, makeup creams and a box of lipsticks," and as he approached her, he evaluated the pullout, which had twenty to thirty capsules.

"There can't be that many shades a single girl can use."

"Now, Mr. Hawk, you know there are."

He picked up a sample. "Best Monday Night? What kind of lipstick shade color is that?"

"Obviously to entice a target on Monday? Sound familiar?" As she laughed and he grimaced, their attention focused to the back of the van.

"Oh, boy, hats!" Axel selected a Bowler hat first, and then a broadbrimmed formal one, and then a baseball cap. Meanwhile, before she had a chance to try on a hat, she made a startling discovery.

"Uh-oh. Axel, these materials in this cabinet are unique. I know of this collection. It is used to alter the color of your skin. Look at all these shades, everything from rich tan to a hospital sickly complexion, to tarnished tin." As she stared at Axel, he motioned her with a serious dead pan face to the next station.

"What is it?"

Axel knew. "Built and designed for hi-tech crime- spying and devious motives included. A kit of techniques to create false fingerprints! I've seen this only once before."

But she was not easily distracted and was engrossed in the stand-up bureau. "I love this clothing. The themes from super-tight to baggy to oversized. Hey, Axel, look, the Hawaiian scene. And here's just what I require for the Crazy Horse Saloon in Paris," as she extracted the tiniest itsy-bitsy yellow bikini that Axel had ever seen.

"Care to retain and model it for me?" She swatted him. As she searched the clothes cabinets, Axel signaled with an enthusiastic wave.

He was astonished. "In this closet Zee, flesh props!"

"What?"

"Flesh props. I used them once before on a case to disguise me in the presence of people that would recognize me. They actually are flesh props. You stick them on, you wear them, whatever, to change your bodily features. You can fit them to your physique. Look, one for a false forehead. Here's a pair of cheeks." He was excited as he continued to plunk items in front of her.

"Observe, full face masks which can change your entire facial appearance and guaranteed to fool anyone. They tuck under your chin and at the scalp line. Wow! Here, my dear, is the granddaddy of them all. A near body suit. Oh, my, complete with size thirty-eight double D breasts," and he proceeded to give her a demonstration by pulling the suit up to the front of his body. "Zee, my favorite," and he withdrew a rather obscene set of flesh. "Butt props."

"Serious?"

"Yeah, sure of it. You fasten them around your butt. Gives you instant pounds on the rotunda for a perfect disguise."

"Really?" She reached around him to expose an even more controversial piece. "Falsies. Paddings. Haven't seen these for years."

"Tempted?" he inquired. She swatted him again across the chest with them before she replaced them. Her attention focused on the next cupboard, open to expose fingernail implants.

Axel shuddered. He moved beside her, forced her to sit down facing him on a small chair while he pulled up a bench across from her in the middle of the trailer. There they sat, sharing a telepathic chill. Zoe spoke first.

"Well, Axel, we found her hideout. We're in the dragon's lair."

"Exactly. Creepy isn't it? But not a dragon's lair, Zee, a chameleon's den. The laboratory of a virtual shape shifter." Her legs tingled at his suggestion.

"We have to be certain, Axel. After all, Aaron Schuler specializes in props and special effects."

"Zoe the evidence is in. The card key we found at Montilladan's opened this trailer. Roy Spiller had the phone number to this joint." Axel rose and went back to retrieve an item from the jewelry counter.

"I will swear on a stack of bibles, Zee, that M is wearing this jade piece in a photo that Lacey left us where they are, girlies. Swear." He displayed two beautiful mother of pearl necklaces. "And these, too."

"I will swear," and this time he moved down the trailer to the entrance and retrieved an unusual pair of jet black and white shoes. "Zoe, look at me.

M wore these shoes to a private ceremony, also captured in Lacey's photos. You know what they say: if the shoe fits!"

"Lastly, I hate to admit it but, with flesh props, padding around the waist, a Cleopatra platinum wig," and he waved it in his one hand "and this incriminating piece of silver clunky jewelry," which he hung in his other hand "guess what!"

"I already figured it out Axel. Ms. Platinum was Montilladan in disguise! How creepy." They sat in silence and absorbed the surroundings.

"Axel, since we first set foot into this trailer, I have had a terrifying thought which has preoccupied me."

"I know what you are thinking. Say it." She looked down at her feet, up at him, and up and down the length of the unit.

"Montilladan is whomever and whatever she wants to be. She can cruise around incognito, in disguise as anyone. Damn. I don't think that we or the police have the slightest clue of the performances that she is capable of giving, nor the appearances that she has conjured up, nor what she looks like. I swear this lady could pass me on the street unrecognizable. She is totally immersed in a fantasy world, and she designs her characters here in this lair."

Axel wanted to build on her thoughts. "I don't even know if we really comprehend which appearance is the dominant one. I mean, look at all this! Wigs, elevator shoes, flesh props, contact lenses, falsies, false fingerprints, men's clothes, women's lipstick and on and on and vampire teeth, just like she wore the night of the intrusion."

"Exactly, Axel. I think that Lacey was only half right when she confirmed that Montilladan was the world's greatest male impersonator. I believe that the other half of that equation should read that she is also the world's greatest female impersonator. It is just like you said earlier, a shape shifter, a chameleon in the true sense."

He snapped his fingers. "Zee, I wonder if confusion is overtaking her. Maybe that's why she requires Dr. Montoya's help? Maybe, she's become unhinged. Maybe she's having an internal struggle for a single identity. Oh, I forgot to tell you that I have an appointment with Dr. Montoya tomorrow night. Maybe that's what Montoya's going to tell me, that Montilladan is confused and is in a struggle between male aggressor and female dominance and Dr. Montoya is mediating the battle."

"Except there goes your Romeo theory if the male persona is winning." She paused and stood up. "This lab is fascinating. Imagine, Axel, she waltzes in here one sex, changes, departs out as a completely different individual and different sex." Zoe was not smiling. She caught his stare. "What are you thinking?"

Axel explained, "Scarier still, what if Montilladan comes in here one person, one personality and departs as another. Don't give me that look. Hear me out. Hear what I'm saying. She enters with one personality, most recently the actor Montilladan, and departs with another totally different personality. Maybe, she's now so talented that she can swing into the personality that fits the garb, create the personality that is necessitated for the situation. Maybe she's many people in her own mind. Maybe, acting has become an obsession with her to the extent that the real Christian, the person born and raised as Christian, doesn't exist anymore, only Montilladan the actor using the world as his and her stage."

"Now that's scary. We ought to be damned afraid of her, Axel. Just like last night when she paid you a visit. I am beginning to believe that she has become cocky, confident, violent, and dare you say now, unhinged and schizophrenic!"

They were both silent. "This place gives me the willies. Let's get out of here now, Axel!"

"Not just yet. Let's continue our inspection- just for a few more minutes, Zee. This case is a tug of war between my confidence and my bouts of insecurity. But now I'm feeling a surge of confidence to take this bitch on and beat the crap out of her!"

"Yes, and count me in. Someone named Axel Hawk always reminds me that there is no such thing as a perfect crime. Every criminal mind makes one fatal mistake. We've found her lair, but what is M's mistake Axel?" Zoe already knew the answer.

In a hostile tone, he stated, "Intruding into my house. Taunting me! Daring us to catch her if we can and so we will." He stared up at the ceiling to recite in a loud voice, "M, wherever you are, we accept this challenge."

Zoe flinched. "Not exactly the words that Lacey would want to hear, but that's the spirit, Axel! I love it." She shook her fist in a victory salute. She clapped hard.

"Axel, I will have to sit Lacey down to inform her of the bad news, that the possibility is now strong that Montilladan is most likely the criminal in our tragedy. M has to be brought to justice, or at the very, very, least, seek proper psychiatric treatment while locked away in an asylum."

"You've convinced me, Zee. Lock her up; throw away the key. I think we should take one last look. I feel uneasy every minute here just like you. As soon as we depart, I'll arrange to post a lookout on this place."

"Repeat. I want to leave here."

"Search, Zoe, quickly."

"We have the card key, the jewelry in my pocket, shoes slung over my shoulder, the confirmation of the phone number as evidence. This is great. Hey, Axel, I brought this photo with me. See if you can locate these clothes. They are unisex." They shared an examination and searched.

Axel moved to the rear of the trailer to examine full facial masks and pants while she scoured the clothing closet. In his exuberance, he picked up a black cane and accidentally knocked over a box on a counter and to his surprise, out fell six more packets of the purple substance and different sizes of syringes. He whistled to her while waving the packets. "Here they are Zee, more evidence. Whatever is in these packets we need to know their chemistry soonest." He pocketed some of the syringes.

"Great. Axel, let's leave." He ignored her to search for more packets. Meanwhile she thrashed through hangers when suddenly her attention was seized by a very distinct metallic clanging sound. Immediately, she doused the lights, which prompted Axel to join her at the open entrance to the trailer. They stared into dusk light.

Just as she whispered in his ear, they heard a vehicle motor rev, die, rev again and an engine shut off. A second clang resounded in the building as an iron door sounded to open. Axel squeezed her hand and signaled for an immediate departure by tugging her out of the trailer, just as voices intruded into the space. Next a loud sloshing sound, like water, a tap turned on, filled their senses. There were voices with indeterminate words.

Slowly, stealthily, they sealed the door behind them. Hunched over, crouching, Axel led a sortie directly down to the other end of the aisle away from the noises and to the side wall where they had entered; she was in close tow. Near the wall they commenced to creep on all fours, taking advantage of the large props to hide themselves, slinking underneath a section of six horses, rolling under antique cars from the gangster-era thirties, slowly making their back to the small door where they entered.

As Axel took cover behind Smokey the Bear, Zoe meanwhile, found her pants stuck on a hook protruding down under a vehicle. He nervously analyzed her situation. With a noisy jerk, and a rip in her lower pants, she was free to join him as they assessed their situation. They were one hundred feet from the side door. They had to depart before their visitors noticed their intrusion.

In their haste to enter the building, they had navigated through a maze of mannequins, depicting different armed themes. Now they faced this collection. Once again, they communicated without saying a word. Zoe stood beside Axel, and one by one, stared into the glassy eyes of each powerful menacing subject. Axel started on the right side where a crusader stood. Beside him, a G.I. Joe was at attention with a tommy gun and an ugly alien adjacent to an armed mobster. Meanwhile, Zee peered into the eyes of two swashbucklers, a demon, and a gunslinger from the old west and to a female oriental fencer.

She blinked!

And as she did, she screamed with a blood-curdling yell, flying through the air swishing her sword to dismember Zoe's head. Zoe ducked, curled and rolled while Axel stood stupefied as it all happened so precipitously. Now there was a new complication. Recognizing the odor, he peered downward to see that his precious antique running shoes were soaked in gasoline! That at least explained the sloshing liquid sounds that they had heard earlier.

Meanwhile, Zoe pivoted and kicked her right leg high over her head to strike her assailant's arm above the elbow, forcing the attacker to re-grip the lance while wincing in pain. But her assailant did so quickly, and swiped in a compact velocity swoop. Zoe retreated, adeptly jumping over the blade as it passed knee high. She landed, turned, embraced an iron bar, turning around just in time to deflect the fencer's third strike, countering by swinging the bar twice at her assailant to gain the position of the attacker, trying to knock her off balance.

Axel was glued to their battle, but a sound of rustling behind him caused him to turn to face a row of menacing bikers. He had just completed the surveillance of the mannequins when a motorcyclist sprung forward wielding a chain. Axel felt the rush of air over his scalp as the blaggard unexpectedly jumped on him, and they tumbled to the concrete outside the limits soaked by gasoline, rolling over and over, each man trying to retain the top advantageous position. However, Axel lost and soon the iron links were on his throat with the grimacing hairy beast roaring in a boast of success, spitting into his eyes. There was absolutely no question about who Axel was engaged with. It was the bearded Appleman.

Zoe deflected four more thrusts of the lance with her tool bar until the momentum of the next lurch carried the fencer to her, at which point she kicked her leg up and under the fencer's chin to momentarily stun her, leaving her vulnerable and gasping for air as she clutched her throat. They were of the same wiry build but fought as two draconian killers, each giving all their strength to swift tight jabs with their weapons, each savoring seconds to inhale precious air.

Zoe saw the perfect time to zero in on her Adam's apple so she strode forward to strike a severe blow with her left tight fist, grabbed her worthy assailant around the neck, tossing her up and over and onto the cement mat. She clutched a mock wooden champagne bottle to smash it hard over the victim's head just as an arm squeezed her throat from behind.

Axel, meanwhile, in his ailing condition, had to make the ultimate use of his next blow or face defeat. He brought his knee up with swift force into the crotch of the brute to take maximum advantage of the age old pressure point. The giant yelped. In a second of weakness, Axel flipped him over, and stood to deliver a second crippling blow with his foot into the loins. He grabbed a wooden club from a caveman mannequin and swung wildly into the stomach of the menace as he tried to stand. The next blow was to his head and the brute collapsed while writhing in pain, loosening the grip on his irons, rolling about to try to re-group.

As he eyed him, Axel was distracted. A golden haze rose behind him. It was coupled with a pungent odor and the unmistakable crackle of orange lick flames. In between the props, Axel saw a wall of black and salmon smoke materialize, behind it slapping flames devouring the contents at record pace, and exponentially rushing toward them. Swiftly, he raced to Zoe's aid, striking her second assailant on the back with a tire iron, causing him to release his partner from a choking grip. As he did so, Axel kicked him forward, and took a short thrust at him from behind, knocking him into a large open casket where he completed the kudos by slamming the lid shut. The female assailant was still lying prone groaning. The Appleman was rising to his feet.

From here, Axel kicked off his gasoline-soaked runners and shed his socks. He grabbed her hand, tugged Zee to her feet, and together they fled, hand-in-hand, racing furiously for the open door, jumping out into fresh air, she behind him, just as the first heated ripples of flames fried the side wall and spat out of the door beside them. They raced down the side of the building. Windows popped overhead. Glass showered. He led her to an old tub, turned on its side, halfway across the back lot where they hid for a minute until the glass shards ceased and they could catch their breath.

They dashed to the fence, into the back alley, streaking to Axel's car in the street where he first removed dirt and small pieces from the bottom of his feet. He buckled himself in, they said nothing and they peeled out and swerved to return the vehicle toward Macey Street. As they turned the corner, they saw a white van departing from the premises hurriedly. At full speed, the Mustang roared down Macey Street just as an explosive shower of debris landed behind them and orange flames surged out of the pores of the structure. Axel commenced their hot pursuit. The white van was speeding away from the crime scene.

"Fasten your seat belt. We're going in!" The van quickly accelerated down the deserted street, hogging both lanes. Axel revved up to seventy, preparing to close the gap.

"Don't kill us, Axel! We've got a ninety-degree turn ahead."

"Binoculars! In the glove compartment! I will get us close enough for you to identify the license plate. I'll stop so we can alert the police. Or use your cell to zoom in and take a photo."

She opted to grab the binoculars, focusing on the van. With the bumps in the road, with the subsequent jostling, it was impossible to zero in on the plate.

"Hold on!" They flew at break neck rapidity out of the gauntlet of the warehouse area into an intersection, skidded and pirouetted, and swung into the street. The Mustang swerved, as the rear end ran out of control, swinging them across a boulevard onto the wrong side of the street, but with luckily no vehicles to interfere with his maneuvers to regain control. The backside of his Mustang hit the curb, and spanked a large red city trash can on the sidewalk before he bolted back onto the street level.

He continued down the wrong side of the roadway, separated now from his target by the thin grassy patch. Three pedestrians were in the road ahead at the next intersection so Axel leaned on his horn frantically as they scattered in fear for their lives. "Sorry!" he offered as he ignored the stop sign and passed the startled bystanders.

Axel was still on the opposite side of a road as a sea of high shrubs now prevented them from eye contact with the van. Now a lorry was heading right for them so he swerved, air born through short stubby foliage over the boulevard, making he and Zoe bump their heads on landing, causing him to momentarily lose control of the vehicle again as they intersected the impact of the pavement with a thud, sideswiping a pole on the opposite side of the street.

As she screamed, he deviated to avoid a light standard just yards ahead. Now a new problem arose. The lights in the intersection in front were yellow, soon to be red. The van would make the caution. They would not. He hit the accelerator, careening to ninety-five, racing at light speed through the intersection, noting out of the corners of his eyes the confused crossing traffic.

"Got it!" Zee yelled.

Axel decelerated just as a line of fire trucks headed past them in the opposite direction. The sirens and activity had brought spectators into the street, some of them focusing their attention at his Mustang, some gawking at the tornado-shaped smoke clouds behind. He decided to relocate.

At the first chance to stop, he did so in a grocery parking lot behind the store. Quickly, he dashed in his bare feet to inspect the damage to the back of his car. Inside the vehicle, she could hear his cries. "Depressing."

Solemnly, Zee joined him to inspect the scratches and knocks, to comfort him by placing her arm around his neck and over his shoulder. She spoke. "She's destroyed her past Axel. Whatever roles she played, whatever occasion she dressed up for, whatever demonic feats she concocted, whatever satanic roles she wrote for herself, they are all gone, Axel. She has vanished to her new life. Now I know why she intruded your house to taunt you. The evidence is gone, all destroyed. Of that, I am now convinced. She's fleeing right now and we're helpless."

Axel was irritated. "How bloody convenient that she chose that moment when we were in the warehouse to eradicate her hideout. Erase it all right in front of us." He kicked the damaged section on the passenger side.

"I am really bothered by something. She is always one step ahead of us. How does she do it Axel?"

"I can't stand it. First she beats me and then she mentally terrorizes me. Now she tries to incinerate us!" He looked at her. "Murder us!"

"Axel, I take this very personally, even more so than an hour ago in the trailer." With that comment, she walked away from him, strolled through the parking lot, phoning Thumper first with details of the incident, then Tinker to leave an urgent message regarding the van's plates, asking him to mount a trace and identify the ownership. She summoned Tinker's help and a meeting later at their office.

When she finished, she joined him. "But why didn't she kill you last night? She had the chance. If she really killed Roy Spiller that was her chance to strike again. We still haven't answered that. What does it matter whether one murder count or two?"

"We discovered the lair today, Zee. Perhaps, she was there. Perhaps, she witnessed the battle from a distance. I firmly believe that she ordered our execution today. Tie up the loose ends of A to Z."

"What are we close to, Axel? What is it that we know that she should kill us? And now she destroys all the props of her deceitful life?"

"I said it before, Zee. We are in error. Today I think it useful for you and I to revisit this entire case, and examine every little single detail, every testimony of witnesses, to determine what that single clue that we have overlooked. She may have destroyed her warehouse of all her personal props, but this bitch, I believe, can't live without the deceit she has spun, so my guess is that she will live to regret this move."

"All the evidence destroyed." She gave Axel a big hug. "Sorry about your car hon."

"Thanks. Not quite all evidence destroyed, Zee. After all, I witnessed her in the flesh and can testify to her existence. And," he delivered a huge grin as he extracted from inside his pants pockets items of jewelry, a false fingerprint set, packets of the mysterious purple substance, and then bits of a full facial masks, and syringes, "all this." Regrettably, Zoe examined her form fitting attire with the absence of pockets or any ability to stash items.

Axel placed three pieces of jewelry in her hands. "I have seen these three pieces, too, in the photos that Lacey left us. I am designing a leisurely afternoon to retrace our steps. How about you?"

"There are two really great pieces of news about this escapade Axel. One, we must be very close to her without knowing it for M to now takes steps to terminate us."

"And two?"

"Two. Thank the Lord Almighty that your antiquated, smelly ugly, unsexy, outlived, disgusting, stained running shoes, veteran of numerous catsup stains, muddy trudges, and caked salsa have gone down in valor for a worthy cause. Those long lasting shoes were not befitting of you. They finally are laid to rest."

"But they were so comfortable," he lamented as he looked at his sockless bare feet.

"Yes. And so will the new pair that I am treating you to. First stop, the mall and the shoe store. I am purchasing you a new pair of running shoes. On the house. My special treat."

"Oh, woman, thou hast madest my day!"

WEDNESDAY AFTERNOON AND EVENING

"Axel, you look mahhhhvellus in those new treads. Now, that's what you should have worn when Lacey came a calling." Zoe had driven to the laboratory in record time, Axel relaxing beside her, mulling over their close call.

He quipped. "A few drips of orange salsa at a Dodger game, a jog on a rainy evening, some misfired knots, a spilled beer at Fosse's, and they'll be broken in!"

Zoe harped. "I know abandoning your Mustang at the dealership repair is upsetting you but, look at it this way, Axel, you drove the vehicle there, so mechanically, it functions. Just think of it as a cosmetic tune-up."

Zoe parked her black Jaguar in an elongated parking strip in front of the three-story, dull brown brick building, in sight of the security booth. Bouncing up a gentle grassy incline toward the main entrance, Zoe realized she had to distract him from the damage to the Mustang, so quizzed him.

"When is your next production?"

"We are taking a hiatus for the next month before we gear up for the holiday season with a Shakespearean production- the Merchant of Venice."

"You actually lobbied for Shylock? That is so, so, so out of character for you."

Axel stooped dead in his tracks halfway up the knoll, forcing her to turn and confront him. She expressed, "What?"

"Exactly. Zoe, I am your stereotype good guy. Oh, Axel, you are such a sweetheart, play this romantic. Oh, Axel, you're such a nice guy. Oh, Axel, take this role of the hero who slays the dragon and saves the damsel and the entire town. Well, I need to prove to myself and you and the acting world just how talented I really am. So, Shylock is the perfect vehicle for me to break the mold of Axel Hawk, hero and good guy."

She motioned him to join her. "I am aware of the local productions where you played in dramas and comedies and adventures but…Shakespeare? What attracts you to go on stage to perform Shakespeare?"

Zoe obviously knew the territory, for as soon as they entered the building, they made an immediate left to descend well-traveled carpeted stairs into the dark depths. "Like anything else in life Zoe, an influencer. My senior school English teacher, Miss Botts, had a passion for Shakespeare. Our English classes were periods of enrichment. She could take that passion and excitement from Willie's plays and transfer our entire class back in time. Like a magnet, she attracted me to her energy, instilled in me the foundations of an appreciation for acting, prose, plays and even old Willy. Besides, I enjoy the comradeship of our acting group; we're a tight clique. Just like your wine tasting clubs."

She kept the pace while he ranted. "Later, I realized what this bard was. He was but a man who could commit to words all that drives life for us. Humor, revenge, loyalty, labors, sex, misfortune, betrayal, greed, you name it, and, of course, deceit."

She stopped and turned and muttered. "Which way?" She paused to get her bearings.

"Love, frailty, sarcasm, war, revenge, lust, sex, defeat, betrayal, victory, tragedy and, my personal, juicy favorite: sex and murder."

Zoe added, "And ghosts and witches and storms and kings and..."

"You got it, except his style of writing sometimes confuses people. You have to look past the style of writing to get hooked. You appreciate the story lines even more. If you look deep enough, you find the riches of life buried in Shakespeare. Speaking of life, do we know where we journey to fair maiden?" They had circumvented a corner to encounter a menacing iron door labeled, KEEP OUT! THAT MEANS YOU!

"I have been here endless times when I retrieved analyses from Cyn for the police department. What terrifying secrets lie behind this portal? This way." She motioned as she heaved the door open to a series of other compartments, which also wielded signs to KEEP OUT. They entered a small laboratory with a female technician clad in white lab garment.

"Cynthia!" Zoe gave her a hug. Cynthia in return responded with pleasantries.

"Zoe Burns. You are so sensationally thin, a sexy trim. How I envy you so. I exercise and exercise and exercise and I burn three hundred calories a month."

"Thanks Cyn. You look like you've lost a few pounds."

"Yes, I have girl. I am glad that you noticed, but I know you, and you're just being nice."

"Meet my partner, Axel Hawk."

"Ooh, definitely my pleasure. Cynthia Dopson, thirty-one, unattached, outgoing, great sense of humor, low overhead, easy to please. I'd state by your scarred looks that you definitely need someone to take care of you."

"Cynthia!"

She heeded Zoe's warning. "What happened?" Axel blushed.

"I lost a recent skirmish and, yes, it hurts. It could have been much worse except Zee stepped in and ran them off with her martial arts' strikes."

Cynthia looked with admiration toward Zee as Zoe warned her, "Cynthia, you never change. Always flirting, always testing guys, however, as you can tell from Axel's appearance, this is serious business. Axel needs no further female distractions."

"Cynthia you play the role of lab technician to perfection, dressed in your long white lab coat spattered with years of showy chemicals, even a chipped button on your coat. Oh, how I remember those geeky safety goggles from chemistry classes. Glad Zee and I don't have to adorn them. Or do we?"

"No, no need to ask you. I just finished up an experiment before you arrived." Her hair was short, dark brown, straight, chopped irregularly at the top of her forehead. Axel noted that she was tall, perhaps even five foot ten with a proud predominant forehead. Zoe and Cynthia recalled past associations through Zoe's previous detective assignments while Axel perused the surroundings. There were ovens, five wash sinks, Bunsen burners, gas jets, cupboards of neatly labeled chemicals, labeled cupboards with an assortment of cutlery and dishes. On one table an elaborate computer system towered.

"Your cohort, Thumper, delivered these purple samples to me earlier. Is he a member of your team?"

"Yes," Axel joined them, "he's our computer guru and brainy nerd. Also performs everything from automobile repairs to investigative surfing on the net, to chess tournaments to the most complete collection of heavy metal T-shirts I've ever encountered. Thumper performs all the dangerous expeditions that are required on the web to gain us intelligence. He also consumes four hamburgers at a sitting. What about our mysterious purple crystals?"

Cynthia replied despondently. "Your famous purple crystals don't seem so mysterious. Rather ordinary I'd say. Let's sit down here at this large table. I constructed some diagrams to illustrate my points."

On rickety aluminum foldout chairs, they sat around a stark white table with Cynthia as the center of attention. She removed her lab coat and confidently declared, "I first want to assure you that I have all the latest analytical equipment to conduct whatever analyses are required. Two doors down, is another lab, which is also at my disposal."

"Just a quick tour. Over there are optical microscopes. Behind us, the fun stuff- burners, ovens, the cooking, the bashing, the analytical scopes, the physical and chemical properties unearthed, no pun intended. I can unravel any chemical formulae and molecular structure with effort."

Axel was anxious to hear about their find. "Is this an illegal substance?"

"Well, my guess is probably not. I am rambling on trying to impress you. Sorry, I need to focus. Axel, let me take charge of this conversation. Firstly, let me set your mind at ease for the crystals are not illegal drugs, and not poisonous and not toxic. The worst thing is the stinky odor, as you probably detected already. These purple crystals are actually an inorganic compound, consisting of two very common chemicals, connected by inorganic radicals. Radical, in simplest term being something that connects the two basic chain lengths, in this case connecting them by electrical charges and weakly by a metal." She reached under the table to produce a poster.

"I took the liberty to sketch in a diagram what each of the two compounds look like. You can see from the structure, and from this depictive formula note that these chemicals are based on oxygen, calcium, chromium, and other common components as the major parts with some metallic connectors."

"What are these compounds used for?"

"Axel, patience, please. Bear with me for that's where I am heading. But, before I do, I want you to understand something. Here I have drawn for you my best guess as to the structural configuration when you link these two together by radicals. Underneath, the possible resultant formula as inferred by my spectrometers and scopes."

"Notice the introduction of three chain links. One of these is a boron compound; the second, a titanium compound replacing a basic part of the structure; lastly, a selenium radical subbing for these two chemical arms. Thus, when I write the combined formula, it shows two compounds, connected by three inorganic substitutions, here, here, and here."

"Now, Axel, you asked about recognition and importance of these substances." Cynthia was enjoying herself. In her bubbly soprano voice, she lectured. "I quickly recognized this compound with the calcium-chromium derivative. If I had to categorize it, I would say that it is used in the treatment of osteoporosis."

Axel perked up. "Bone deterioration. A possible connection to Bartlett's specialty." He was speaking to Zee.

"What?"

"Nothing Cynthia. Continue."

"Please note that I was referring to only part of the crystal. That part is not a new product. It has been tested, non-addictive, non-toxic, FDA approved with slight harmless side effects."

"What happens when you bond with the other chemicals and radicals and compounds?" Axel was anxious for news.

"I am a chemist first. I consider myself a superior analyst. I deduced this formula earlier. After I did, I sat to ask myself the question of why someone would want to manufacture these compounds in totality and link them to the one that contains this FDA approved part. I mean, the single most powerful drug derivative is the one with these radicals of selenium and boron absent. These bonding substances diminish the effect to treat the effects of osteoporosis."

"You mean, Cyn, that to treat osteoporosis leave the substance as the simpler compound with the calcium-chromium derivatives only and not the entire complex mix?"

"Exactly. Actually, with all the derivatives included, I did discover something weird. There is no record of this more complex purple compound anywhere in medical journals or patented indices, or patent pending. Nor in the records of FDA approved drugs nor pending drugs. The only approval and record is of the first chemical link."

Axel jumped to a conclusion. "So Cynthia, someone has manufactured a non-approved drug, and...so, in that sense, it may be considered an illegal substance?"

"Possibly, but that's jumping to a possible erroneous conclusion Axel. There are countless substances in development that are not recorded on the test sites. They only become transparent when they seek approvals. It is not prudent to disclose them to competitors until you have a final product ready for patent with a definitive chemical formula. However, there are also products that have failed and been discontinued and it could be one of those in which case only the manufacturer knows of its existence." Zoe leaned over to Axel to whisper.

"There was no mention of osteoporosis in the autopsy of Montilladan. There is no mention of it in any medical records or treatments of M. If she was the individual consuming these crystals, she didn't take this for osteoporosis."

Cynthia interrupted. "Ahem, I don't know what you are whispering about but, before you two create a mystery out of nothing, my medical opinion is, given my understanding and analysis of this compound, this substance is harmless. Observe."

Cynthia extracted a single crystal with a pair of tweezers and plunked it into a small beaker of warm water that had been sitting on her stove top. Stirring it vigorously, the material dissolved to form a transparent light pink solution with an offensive stench, which she wafted toward Zee and Axel.

"I have just shown you that this drug can be taken orally by dissolving it in warm water, but I haven't the faintest idea what for. It won't kill you. It has no effects on sexual performance. It might make you barf since it has an unpleasant taste and odor. It certainly has no obvious usage to me. The only other thing that I can add is that it has unusually complex metallic bonding patterns to stabilize the entire drug, even in solution where I left it to sit on the counter overnight and returned to find curiously, that it had not decomposed."

Zoe scanned Axel and Cynthia. "Yet someone has gone to the trouble of manufacturing this substance in sufficient quantities, and someone else to the trouble of hiding it in their shoe box and in their bathroom cupboard."

Cynthia piped up. "I told Zoe when she called that I would have to charge you for my analyses. However, given how little I have deciphered, it's on the house. It's the least that I can do to assist an old friend."

"Cynthia, let me pose a completely hypothetical scenario to you. Please don't laugh. Don't get alarmed. Zee and I get paid to let our imaginations run wild."

"Axel," Zee motioned.

Axel did not heed her advice. "So let your imagination run wild. The police appear at your door. They bring to you these purple colored crystals. They say to you that someone has killed on behalf of these chemicals and that they are responsible for heinous crimes. They demand to know why." Cynthia's gaze now expressed consternation.

"Your task, Cynthia Dopson, is to speculate why these crystals have inspired people to criminal actions. As ridiculous as it sounds, speculate."

Axel sat back. Zoe stared at her friend. Cynthia shuffled uncomfortably. After gazing at the ceiling for minutes, she answered. "I have to disappoint you. There is no earthly reason known to me to kill for these crystals. There is nothing in the formula that would cause me to consider this chemical illegal, or ultimately powerful. I can't even make a wild-assed guess. My official answer, sorry coppers, is to take your mystery elsewhere to a chemist brighter than me."

Zoe pressed on. "Can you at least check some files online to determine if this is an experimental drug?"

"I can do that much for you, Zoe, and still at no charge. It is a long shot that I will find anything."

"Confidentially, Cynthia, see if you can find any reference to these two companies." Axel scribbled the names. "And are they associated with its development?"

Axel relayed to her, "deMOX, that's small d-e and capital M-O-X; the other is MUREX, all capitals, sounds M-U-R-E-X." He passed her the note.

"I'll check, but I don't have the same high hopes as you do that this chemical holds high drama. I'll also perform some additional analyses and ask one of my more experienced cohorts for an opinion."

After exchanging courtesies, they departed disappointed with the results. Strolling across the parking lot, Axel lagged behind forcing her to turn.

"What are you pondering?"

"Zee, it is just too much of a coincidence that M knows Bartlett, Bartlett's firms are manufacturing drugs to aid osteoporosis, and we discover this unregistered purple substance at M's residence which is in part used for the treatment of osteoporosis." They arrived at the front of Zoe's Jaguar and stood there to debate.

"Axel, that was unfair to ask Cynthia to speculate like that, to put her professional opinion on the spot and scare her to death."

"I didn't want to overlook a single theory that she might have."

"But you didn't have to petrify her."

"Who me? Axel didn't." The speaker was Cynthia as she surprisingly sauntered forward with a grin. "After you two departed, I got to thinking about Axel's concern and I had what might be an important afterthought for consideration."

"Great." Axel smiled back at her.

"Look at this packet in the light." She held it up so they could get a clear glimpse of the entire package against the bright blue sky. She extracted a nail file from her pocket of the lab coat. She shook the package until it exposed inside a discoloration. With the file, she pointed to a definitively small white discoloration in the middle of the packet. "Curiously, every crystal has exactly one of these tiny white smudges. As smart as I profess to be, I don't know what the purpose of this is. However, it must serve a purpose, probably to stabilize, but this sure is peculiar. I haven't analyzed it yet, because I have been focused on the hard purple stuff."

She removed the crystal from their vantage point and placed it back in her pocket. "I'll determine what the relevance of that singular color is. I have a hunch, given the formula of the pink stuff, that it may also be highly ionic."

Axel showed no hesitation. "Absolutely. Any angle counts. You don't suppose, Cynthia, that the purple hard crystalline material is a housing or disguise for the real purpose —illegal drugs or other?" They conversed briefly; Cynthia left, but not before Zoe advised her to lock the crystals up every night. "And during the day when you are at lunch or on break!" she yelled after her.

Axel watched Cynthia until she was out of sight. "I think that we need to expose our discovery of these crystals to Larry Bartlett. Coax a reaction and get a rise out of him."

Returning to their office down congested freeways, Axel made the best of his time by trying to keep contacts open while Zoe drove. He chatted with Nikki on the phone about Lacey's mental welfare until the conversation turned sour and Nikki hung up. Retrieving his messages from his office voice mail, Speed had left a message on the negative results to date on his efforts to physically locate Brissand; Katz had phoned but only to determine if Axel had located Roy. Katz also conveyed that for the first time, there was some worry on the beach about Roy's prolonged absence. Axel noted the panic in his tone so dialed the Golden Parrot Bar. The bartender confirmed, "Still no sign of Roy Spiller." Axel reluctantly prognosticated his fate to Zoe just as she maneuvered into his parking space. Axel stood to recite a mock prayer for the safe and cheap return of his Mustang while she held his hand.

Upon their arrival at the office, Thumper tossed him some keys. "Must be nice to have friends in the automobile business Axel. They left you a loaner, free of charge. A valet parked it in the back lot. A fully loaded mid-sized baby blue sedan. Makes sixty miles per hour top speed."

Axel groaned while Thumper produced the profile of Aaron Schuler, confirming an appointment with him at his studio for early Thursday morning. Axel excused himself while he placed a call to his friend at the body shop to thank him profusely for the rental and plead with him to provide an estimate of repair costs soonest. He reported the accident to his insurance agent and sat in the inner office loafing.

As Zoe entered, they agreed it was a time for a quiet afternoon to revisit all the events leading up to this moment. So Zee and Axel bantered back and forth, accounting for all the events to date, briefing and re-briefing each other from Lacey's visit, to Axel's confrontation with Mrs. Whitehurst at the cemetery, to the discussion with Felix and Tinker. They reread the police report on M's accidental death. Axel recited his search for Roy Spiller to Zoe; she orated about her trip to the ill-fated movie studio. Zoe typed in every meticulous detail.

"Axel, there was one piece of curious evidence at the studio that I neglected to tell you. While the technicians swear they saw Montilladan inspect the balcony hours before the scene was shot, the gate attendant where the cast pass through and sign-in, showed me, and remembered, that Montilladan did not drive up and sign-in until only one hour before the scene was shot. Conclusion. Roy Spiller signed in one hour ahead of the shoot; conclusion, someone else, most likely the real Montilladan in disguise, entered as another person earlier, changed into M on the set, tampered with the set hours previously and then changed back into someone else and exited."

"Another circumstantial fact in the favor that M killed Roy," Axel muttered, and they moved on to other testimony.

The fight at Fosse's was painful to relive, although Axel sang the song of "Something Stupid" again for her benefit until she purposefully left to refill her cola and Thumper from his den yelled, "Chill out." Axel spoke of Constance and Lieber, and Dr. Montoya and Lillian. Zoe briefed Axel on her full conversation with the Dr. Sorbet. The visitation to the Whitehurst mansion was next, followed by conversations with Speed, Montilladan's bankers, and Dr. Larry Bartlett.

The haunting took over thirty minutes to relive. From obtuse to givens to the ridiculous, they re-examined all the situations. Zoe's only guess as to their imminent danger was their possession of the dental records. Zee postulated, "Without an exhumation to prove that M isn't buried at Forest Haven, no one, including Felix is going to believe this tale." Axel speculated that the discovery and possession of the purple crystals could be an important discovery.

The outer office door slammed shut. Tinker, with veins bulging in his tree stump-like neck, stood in the doorway of the inner office as Zoe and Axel sat surprised. Instead of yelling, Tinker stalked around the room. He had never loomed so large to Axel before. Even with thick soft soled shoes he created a thud with each step.

Zoe broke the tension. "Tinker, did you receive our message?" Tinker was unmoved by his friendship for her. He was a man on a mission. He pounded his left fist into his open right palm. He stuttered three times before finally being able to blurt something coherent.

"I received a call from the fire department a few hours ago. It seems that there was a three alarm blaze down on Macey Street. Seems that an old warehouse went up in smoke and all that's left are smoldering cinders. The fire chief informed me they haven't concluded their investigation yet, but this is a clear case of arson since there are multiple gasoline containers on display at the site and substantial evidence of fuel torching. And guess what? This burned out warehouse comes with a charred male corpse inside. No don't speak."

Hands on hips, he thrust into action. "I was informed of something really, really interesting. Some of the terrified locals got a license plate number from a red Mustang Cobra that was observed fleeing the scene of the alleged crime. Low and behold, old Tink looked up the records to play a hunch, because you know how upset I get when people tell me that a red Mustang is at the scene of any crime in Los Angeles and guess what I found?"

He staggered and turned toward Axel. "You know, Axel, the very red Mustang that fled the scene of that crime, the one that has juicy dents due to bashing city trash cans and running into public utility electric poles..." Tinker was struggling how to vent his frustrations. "Guess what?"

"No. Don't answer. Don't guess. Somebody put your plates on that vehicle, the vehicle for which we have an A.P.B. out, put plates on your car. What a dirty rotten trick. Transferring license plates to a look-alike fire engine red Mustang is a crime in California." Tinker was working himself into frenzy as they sat and diligently listened.

"If I were you, Axel, I'd lodge a complaint. Way I figure it, you need to call the cops Axel, and file a report. You know why? To report this dirty rotten trick or maybe to report the theft of your vehicle and the subsequent use of your vehicle in this crime. I had an afterthought. Maybe they'll even try to return it to you and incriminate you."

He came up for air. "This is your friend, Tinker; soon to be your ex-friend unless I get some answers. I am not leaving this office," and he jumped up, slammed the door, took a chair and sat in front of the door, "until I get some satisfactory replies to my concerns. Now, what the hell is going' on guys? You are investigating a clear cut accident on a movie set. Suddenly Axel gets beat up. Now you are implicated in arson. And we got a charred corpse to deal with. Know what else? We got a witness says that there were two people in the front seat of that fleeing red Mustang, a man at the wheel, sort of answering Axel's description and a female with short jet black hair in the passenger's seat."

Zoe wanted to answer, but Axel signaled her to leave it to him. Tinker did not rest. "This is serious shit guys. The fire inspector told me that even though some individuals will argue a spark could have set off this inferno given the desiccated nature of this old structure, and given all the evidence of flammable materials inside, arson explains the four empty gasoline cans. Now, what were you two doing at this blaze?"

Axel addressed Tinker. "We admit were at the site Tinker. We do not deny that fact."

"Surprise, surprise! Let me register that in my brain! Did you start it? Accidentally? Unintentionally?"

"No. No. No."

"Did you see who started this fire?"

"No." He broke it to him gently. "We were too busy trying to save our own lives. We were inside before the arsonists arrived; we were subsequently attacked, Zee by two assailants and myself by the Appleman. That blaze was intended to charbroil us into well done. Luckily we defeated our attackers and escaped with our lives. I am talking about escaping death Tinker."

"Attacked? You two? In danger? That really is difficult to believe!" Now Tinker's veins on the side of his forehead looked like two purple pipes.

"First, Axel, you get beat up on Monday night, and now you just happen to be at the site of criminal activity this morning. I haven't informed Felix about this. I am giving you the benefit of the doubt until I interrogate you. I cancelled the A.P.B. on the Mustang because I know it's yours. It wasn't out back so I figure it is in tow or at some body shop or abandoned."

"It's at Reggie's Body Shop if you need to view it to complete your report."

"Now for the truth. I'm miffed, but I want to hear what happened. Now! And I want all the details." Tinker's last words echoed around the room like a regurgitated threat. "I'm really pissed and you know what, just consider me a pissed part of your permanent team from this point on."

Axel stood. "Okay. You sit down, Tinker, over here, closer to us, in front of the desk, beside Zoe, across from me. Relax, Tink. We'll share what we know." Tinker made his way, his enormous hulk dwarfing her physique, but he didn't take his glare from Axel. Mentally, Axel rehearsed his speech.

"I'm afraid I have some surprises for you. I would plead with you to remain calm as I spew them out. I'm not going to start with the fire. Rather, we need to go back in time."

Tinker's breathing returned to normal as he sat, arms folded. Axel gathered his composure. "Let's go to the root of our investigation. Number one, there is a strong possibility that Montilladan is not buried in the gravesite at Forest Haven Cemetery."

Tinker grinned. "That's a neat trick since I saw his ruby innards splattered all over the cement floor when I arrived at the movie set, and hundreds of witnesses saw him take his fatal dive, and hundreds more attended the funeral and burial."

Axel opened his desk drawer and passed a photo of Roy Spiller across the desk to Tinker. "The man in the photo is Roy Spiller, a part time Hollywood novice, a Hollywood stuntman, a vagrant beach bum, a Montilladan look-alike. Montilladan met Spiller years ago, they befriended, and in time they became very good friends, and since they were both adventurous, both risk takers, extreme lookalikes, both in the acting business, they started a dangerous foolish game, a game in which Roy Spiller began to substitute on film sets for Montilladan."

Zoe piped up. "Spiller's probably buried in Montilladan's grave, Tink. The circumstantial evidence is mounting."

Tinker confessed. "Okay. Sure coulda fooled me; I thought you passed me a photo of Montilladan. I can see where this might have occurred." Tinker looked back and forth at them and railed. "So let's suppose you two are right. I'll give you credit that you uncovered this fact, for now. Good for you. Kudos. No crime yet. No concern. Spiller died in the accident. He's buried at Forest Haven Cemetery. I'm with you so far but…why doesn't Montilladan come forward to confront a minor Hollywood scandal. No crime has been committed. Sounds like a great story. A few bruised egos. A few confused directors. A bunch of happy journalists. A scandal like this will dissipate over time. It also provides Montilladan a huge publicity stunt, like he's always craving for. Maybe even a boost in popularity. What's the big deal?"

Axel floored him by speeding to the second punch line. "Tinker, Zoe and I firmly believe that we have uncovered some evidence that Montilladan compromised the movie set earlier before the ballroom scene was shot that day, and Montilladan intentionally murdered Roy Spiller. We are talking about pre-meditated murder. Montilladan used the scene in the movie to execute a personal murderous event of Spiller in front of hundreds of witnesses who believed that Montilladan, not Spiller, perished. Just as you believed when you walked through that door a few minutes ago. Just as the final police report and autopsy believes."

"What? Are you two nuts? Felix won't believe that shit. Nor do I! We investigated. What concrete evidence do you have?"

"Tinker, Zoe and I have concrete evidence. Zee discovered that someone bearing Montilladan's description was on the set long before Roy Spiller arrived and signed in at DelMar Studios that same morning. In addition, two technicians saw Montilladan inspecting the balcony set, more likely altering the integrity of the balcony rails. If you check sign-in records as Zoe did, Roy Spiller as Montilladan did not log into the set when the so-called balcony inspection occurred. Are you following us? We believe that the real Montilladan logged in earlier as someone else, changed into and dressed as the real Montilladan, and sabotaged the set. Spiller arrived on the set hours later, signed in as Montilladan, to meet his maker. The two technicians swear that Montilladan inspected the set before Spiller arrived, inspected it in the exact place where the rails lost their integrity."

Tinker glared back at Axel, breathing hard. "Go on."

"Want me to tell him?" Zee asked.

"No, I'll tell him."

Tinker's voice rose to an angry pitch. "Tell me what?"

"Okay, here it goes. Wish me luck Zee." Axel took a deep breath, stared at Tinker for a minute, and blurted it out. "Tinker, please believe what I am about to tell you as truth. Zoe and I have a sole expert witness, of huge credibility, who has personally testified to us that Montilladan is of the female sex, that Montilladan is a male impersonator, probably the best ever in the history of all entertainment. I mean ever! Montilladan is a female who duped a whole populace of movie-makers, movie-goers, friends and police."

"Bullshit! How do you know that?" Tinker was riled as he raised his voice again.

"Our client, who cannot be revealed to you, is a close friend of Montilladan's, and at the funeral home, late after everyone else had departed from the wake, our client lifted the garment cover and discovered the body in the casket was a male, discovered the body in the casket was not Montilladan." The room was silent for minutes so Axel continued. "The body in the casket was a male, Tinker, a male named Roy Spiller; the female, Montilladan, the murderer has disappeared. From the facts we have gathered to date, Montilladan killed Spiller and no one would know any better about this perfect crime except our client, who lifted the blanket and saw the nude body of Roy Spiller in the casket." Tinker just sat as granite, mind reeling. The silence was broken by Zoe.

"Tink, our client is a very, very close friend of Montilladan's and has seen Montilladan nude on numerous occasions, so knows that Montilladan's true sex is feminine, and that she is a male impersonator. Our client also is aware of the history of Montilladan in the entertainment business and knows the events around when this transformation took place."

Tinker shook his head in denial. "Oh, God in heaven, please tell me this isn't true? If you know the word bullshit, God, please give me a sign. Now!"

Zoe moved her chair beside Tinker and placed her arm around him. "God is not here Tink, but I am, and I am going to tell you that Axel and I speak the truth."

"So, you're telling me that this is what your case is all about. Your client hired you to find Montilladan because your client knows that a male is buried at Forest Haven Cemetery in Montilladan's gravesite, and Montilladan is still alive."

Sheepishly they replied simultaneously, "Correct."

"And you strongly believe that Montilladan had Roy, what's his name, killed by destroying the integrity of the balcony set earlier before the phony Montilladan arrived?"

"Correct."

Axel offered an apology. "Tinker, Zoe called your office earlier to inform you that we needed to talk this afternoon about our case. You obviously didn't receive the message. If you call your office right now, they will confirm this. We planned to meet with you and disclose all we know. We have been spending the last hour capturing all the facts. We apologize for not engaging you sooner."

Zee elaborated. "The danger level has risen to red. The fire on Macey Street almost killed us. In addition, I filed a report on your message machine of a fleeing vehicle, a white SUV, and its description. What these witnesses reported to you was the flight of the primary witnesses- Axel and I. We chased a white Ford van fleeing the scene at high speeds. This was after someone tried to snuff us out! I called your office immediately after I was able to read the license plate. Tink, please call your office. Check it out."

Tinker looked as a boiled beet. Yanking his cellular from his holster, he walked away from them into a corner recess of the room, punched numbers to converse gruffly with the person on the other end of the line, barking inquiries until he was satisfied. His associates bore the brunt of his demands. He sat back down. "What were you two doing at that warehouse? You haven't answered that yet."

Zoe assumed the conversation. "We were at the warehouse chasing leads on this investigation. A series of events led us there. Largely, that Roy Spiller had been calling a phone inside that warehouse on numerous occasions and in addition, Axel and I found card keys made by MetraComp in Montilladan's possession, which corresponded to that Macey address. It turned out that they did not open the gate to the grounds nor the building itself but a trailer inside."

"So how did you get inside?"

"Be patient. It's rather complex." Axel intercepted Tinker's anxiety.

Zee directed his attention to her. "Tink, I scaled the wall and entered by an open window. Inside, we found a trailer, which the card key opened. Axel and I established by clothing, jewelry and other items that the contents of the trailer belonged to Montilladan. The deserted neighborhood of Macey Street and this trailer was where Montilladan changed from male to female, and female back to male. It was her cosmetic lair."

Zoe pressed on. "Our inspection was interrupted by the arrival of the arsonists. We did not get a good look at any of them except the Appleman. As Axel previously stated, we were attacked by three assailants. I was attacked by a swordswoman who tried to decapitate me; Axel, by the Appleman, disguised as a chain wielding motorcycle thug. While we were engaged, a third person grabbed me from behind. I swear I did not get a look at my two assailants; another person, or persons, ignited the gasoline while we were in combat. We can testify that gasoline ran into the proximity of our physical encounter. We luckily overpowered the assailants and fled in Axel's Mustang at high speeds down Macey Street, pursuing them, and turning onto Levine, where witnesses saw us travel at high speeds."

Axel expressed concern and remorse. "Tinker, we may have knocked out one of our attackers, not the Appleman. I pushed him into an open casket and closed it. I'm sorry. That may be the corpse they found. I'm sorry, but Tinker it was us or them. We acted in self-defense. It could easily have been us in there as charred remains."

"I'll require statements later from both of you."

There was silence as Tinker taunted Axel with his body language. He was silent as he digested their testimony. "I confess that we traveled at speeds beyond safe limits. I also confess to obliterating a city trash can at the corner of Macey and Levine as I lost control of my vehicle, but we had to travel at high unsafe speeds to get close enough to identify the license plate."

Zoe revealed a crumpled piece of paper. "This is the number that I called into your office. Axel's right. What the pedestrians witnessed was the flight of the witnesses, not the criminals."

Tinker decided to phone his assistant again so departed to the outer office to do so. Axel led Zoe into the far corner of the room distant from Tinker to whisper.

"We have to inform Tinker of what's happened. Follow my lead. Do not reveal Lacey's identity. I also don't want him to know about my meeting with Dr. Montoya on Thursday. She won't talk to me if Tinker escorts me to her residence. Any and all other information should be disclosed to him."

Axel received two thumbs up of approval from Zoe just as Tinker returned, closing the door slowly behind him. "Someone is gonna get killed. Probability, one of you two. That would surely make me even more incensed, so talk to me. What else is there?"

"Make a deal with us Tinker."

"Axel this is now really official police business. I put up with your beating and filed it. However, I know of your stubbornness. It's famous. What deal?"

"We will divulge to you the results of our investigation to date on this missing persons' case. In return, we will not disclose the identity of our client. In return, you must not disclose what we tell you to Felix yet. I think he will over-react."

"Over-react? Over-react? If I tell Felix what you just told me, he will arrest you two and formally charge you with spreading extraordinary illegal bullshit! He will have you two committed. Man, this is unbelievable stuff."

Axel finished with a smile. "Sorry, we will take you into our confidence under those terms so that the police are aware of our results to date. You are part of our team going forward, but the three of us have got more immediate investigative work to do." Tinker sat down in his own fumes.

"Why not, Felix?"

"In time, Tinker, but not now. It is as you said, we don't think he'll believe our tale, just as you so eloquently put it. Tinker, more importantly, Zoe and I feel strongly that Montilladan may have plans to disappear soon, like next few days. We have to keep going uninterrupted by Felix. The three of us."

"Oh, God, I hate this. What are you two doing to me? However…okay, talk to me. I want the truth! I want you to fill in all the blanks. I know you skipped over some vital pieces and if I think that Felix will buy it, I'll recite this tale with gusto and confidence. If not we work for forty-eight hours on it, and I present him this whopper."

"Fasten your seat belt," Zoe urged him. Tinker pretended to do so to break the tension. He ordered Axel and Zoe to silence as he spoke.

"Let me get this straight so far. One. Montilladan befriends a look alike named Roy Spiller, a Hollywood stuntman, and they start playing switchies, whereby Spiller substitutes for Montilladan in certain scenes of Montilladan's movies."

"Right".

"Two. You think Montilladan planned and executed the pre-meditated murder of Roy Spiller by deliberate destruction of the integrity of the film set of Sweet Sherry South, and thus Spiller falls to his death."

"Right again."

"Three. Montilladan is a female and is the greatest male impersonator of all time and has played all of Hollywood and her directors for patsies. Why? Because she discovered she could pull it off and get more roles…and obviously more money."

Zee interrupted Tinker's summation. "Sort of correct. She auditioned for the role of a male years ago in a play, won the lead part, got discovered and became accepted as a male from that point on. Little did she know that she would rocket to stardom and fame as a male actor. That probably wasn't part of her master plan, but it happened."

"Four. Your client and you two are the only people that know Montilladan is not dead, because your client disrobed the body at the funeral parlor and noticed that the body was a male."

Axel hesitated him this time. "Partially correct. We know, now you know, but…who else knows? Could be more than us four."

"Well, if your client knows that an au natural clue is the only way to identify Montilladan, it makes sense to me that your client is a boyfriend and he noticed this physical feature while they were engaged in extracurricular activities."

"Nice try for entrapment, Tink but, at this time, no comment. We will not divulge any information at this time about our client. Let me continue from here. Zoe and I are close to solving this murder. We believe that the beating I took was to slow us down. We now believe that the Macey warehouse was torched intentionally to destroy the evidence of Montilladan's double life as she plans to escape and no longer requires the lair to change back and forth into her male and female disguises. She had the opportunity of finding us there. A path of clues led us to that warehouse as we previously stated."

"Man, they don't know Axel Hawk and Zoe Burns! Do they? You can't be slowed down." The tension in the room was slowly evaporating.

"What?" Zoe captured the conversation. "We previously referenced the trailer. The warehouse is owned and operated by Aaron Schuler Productions. We don't know whether Schuler met Montilladan or knows Montilladan. What we do know is that the card key found in M's residence opened the trailer lock and we found it was being used by Montilladan to change from male to female and back to male. There were wigs, clothing, make-up, shoes, eyebrows, even false body parts and plenty more!"

"Butt props, falsies, all there, Tink. Every known prop to create false identities was in that trailer." Axel continued. "So someone attempted to kill us as they torched M's past. The blaze destroyed all the evidence that could have been used to implicate her in this crime and perhaps others. We rescued a few items from the incineration."

"Tinker, Axel and I need your help. Axel and I believe that we are ever so close to an important clue. It is now obvious that Montilladan has no regrets about eliminating us. However, other than the discovery of the trailer and our client's testimony about Montilladan's double life, we are at a loss as to what other piece of concrete evidence give Montilladan and her accomplices away. I will spend some time briefing you on the clues to date."

Axel reinforced his request of earlier. "That's why we called your office earlier. You have to believe us Tinker. We need your involvement." Zoe moved to in front of him.

"We have a client who hired us to investigate if Montilladan is still alive. If M is alive, we are obligated to inform our client first. If there are criminal implications, we promise to turn Montilladan over to you so the police can step in. We have not done anything to jeopardize our client's trust and we won't. Our client knows that we intend to bring you into our confidence today. I received this consent earlier."

Axel was adamant. "Reality check. Zoe and I firmly believe that Montilladan is destroying the remnants of her past. We have three possible theories we're working on. One, she is escaping as a female to a new life. Two, there might be a Romeo, a male lover, that even has possibly influenced her, or abetted her in her crimes and they plan to escape together. We have no idea who Romeo is at this time. Three, after seeing the contents of that trailer, she could be disguised as anyone Tink. It is scary to think of all the possibilities of disguise."

Zoe drew Tinker's attention. "Sitting in that trailer was creepy when Axel and I came to the realization that Montilladan is an expert at playing male and female roles in real life. In addition, she has killed once, tried again today, and we hope that she doesn't know of our client's discovery at the funeral home or else our client is in the same danger as Roy Spiller."

Zee held up her hands. "Just for the record, I want to state that there exists the possibility that Montilladan wants to return to live life as a female again, female instincts overriding every part of her life, Romeo or not. Axel thinks a Romeo drives her; I think she drives herself and wants to live life as a lady because she has missed that lifestyle and been in abstinence too long." Tinker was interested in this line of thought.

"Female intuition?"

"Tink, take it from a woman. This lady has reverted to her natural born instincts. It must have been a buzz being a male impersonator and duping everyone, earning big bucks for it, but the game is over and, unfortunately, murder is the means to her escape. The murder of Roy Spiller causes the main piece of evidence to evaporate."

Axel added. "There is another scary idea we have, that the possibility exists that she has more than one personality, that she fits into her disguise with the personality, too."

"So, we are taking you into our confidence, and you have to delay informing Felix until we apprehend Montilladan, but travel with us on our adventure. Also allow our client the opportunity to speak to M first even if there are criminal charges. Agreed?"

Tinker wasted no time. "You know what you are saying. This lady has killed, has no qualms about a charge of assault and battery, now arson and attempted murder. I'd say she's more dangerous than ninety-five percent of the criminals I deal with." He hung his head and shook it. "This criminal has no conscience."

Tink bit his bottom lip. "If we don't tell Felix and he finds out some of this from another source, I'll be joining the ranks of the unemployed. This is serious shit goin' down. The longer it drags on, the worse Felix will be."

Tinker pointed his long index finger at Axel for effect. "I earlier said forty-eight hours. I'll tell Felix that you need my assistance on this case and I'll inform him that you witnessed the fire on Macey Street and I'll promise to him that I'll drag the truth out of you as we go sleuthing together. And as I said before, you have to trust me, too, to make the call of when to summon police reinforcements."

A traditional lock of hands signified their pact as Tinker initiated the ritual. Zoe was relieved. "I have another condition. Tinker, now that you are on the A team, it is your responsibility to step out front when danger strikes and protect Axel and I."

"Yeah, now I get it!" he shouted. "Ole Tink's ass is always the first to get kicked and it still doesn't get any smaller. Look." They all shared a moment of bonding and silliness as he turned and shook his booty while Zee expressed a silly "Tee-hee." Axel chortled.

Tinker sighed with a heaving of his chest. "Reluctantly, in the end, he'll chew me out and take that piece of my ass but, like I said, I got lots of ass to give. Hell, I got an exquisite idea. I got a better idea. If Felix fires me, then I'll just join this agency. The cars you drive, nice cushy office, sleep in late, eat donuts, drinkin' at Fosse's Tavern while I'm at work, flirting with platinum blondes, seems like the pay is better, too. I'll stop using Tinker and go back to my real name, Aldred Lawrence, so we can name it AA to Z or A-squared to Z."

Axel retorted. "Now that thought inspires me to co-operate fully with you, keep Felix informed, and keep you in the force."

"Hey, Axel, I want to talk to the foxy lady alone. I got some more questions. Do you mind?" His head thrust toward the door to signal Axel's departure.

"I'll leave you two alone. I'll be in Thumper's kingdom if you require my input. Zoe had planned in sharing our files with you." Axel was left standing in the middle of the entry as she closed the door behind her to seal their privacy. Axel extracted his cell phone and dialed Speed first. He was eager to talk.

"No luck, Hawkman. I have only scratched the surface but forged papers of the nature we talked about are not common business. As I said earlier, probably only Gorgeous George Brissand can do it and is doing it. No leads on his whereabouts. Rumors about a new place in town that he runs, but people are reluctant to talk about it with me or they honestly don't know his lab. I visited a few previous hangouts of his, but no one's seen him lately. I'll check a couple of other places out shortly. Brissand's covering his tracks thoroughly."

"I have some bad news for you. Someone tried to barbeque Zoe and me earlier. We narrowly escaped with our lives. Look over your shoulder. I don't want you to take any unnecessary risks. I think you should shut it down if you don't have any success by end of today." Axel hesitated to inform him of the exact details of the action as Speed probed.

"I'll call you first thing tomorrow morning, Axel. I have one reliable tip about a neighborhood that Brissand's supposed to be in. I've got a few allies there. It won't be too dangerous for me and I'll heed your warning."

"Speed, I owe you." Axel heard Jeannie's voice in the background as Speed excused himself. He sat in the entry to examine their email. What luck! Jeanmarc replied that he had located the bank and identified the accounts in Andorra, and had made arrangements to visit the bank managers tomorrow. Zoe and he would receive a report of his findings soon. He would call on a secure phone line or transmit an email depending on the results.

Just as Axel sat back to relax, Thumper summoned him to his hideout. Entering the dimly lit cave, he wondered how a body could exist in this total darkness, except for the luminescent glow of eerie poster art and the faint light of the two large computer screens. "Don't you have eye problems? How can you stand this dreary cell?"

"Boss, twenty-twenty eye sight and dreary to you is another man's paradise. Just look at Metallica jumping out of that poster and into this room. How about Janis? Cool eh? She's sprayed with fluorescent tinsel and the fluorescent guitar is behind you."

"Well, it does beat Montilladan's taste. That much I can say. What have you found?"

"No other phone number of Spiller's matched any of Aaron Schuler's connections, only the burned out warehouse." Axel felt like he was wallowing in information overload. Thumper continued to talk, but his mind was dreaming.

Where was she now? Where was she fleeing to? One of the characters of this drama had to know more of her whereabouts.

"Axel, look at this," and they shared some screen browsing examining profiles of the characters in their play. It was twenty minutes before Tinker opened the door, appeared in Thumper's domain, and demanded, "Do you have any hard liquor on site?"

Tinker motioned for Axel to join them with by swooshing his enormous hands. Before Axel did, he instructed Thumper to obtain an appointment with Jenna at the bank soonest. As Axel entered, Tinker wasted no time. "Amazing! Either this is the biggest pile of crap that I have ever heard in my entire life and we can rest easy, or we have one of the greatest cons of all time to solve and we truly are in mortal danger. Since we're all getting paid, let us assume the later. Personally, I don't think that anyone would believe this crap so I think we are perfectly safe to interrogate anyone on the planet."

Tinker addressed Axel. "Zoe recited the exact events at the warehouse, and Montilladan's haunting of you at your place and the search by Speed to find Brissand and other stink that's happening. She also informed me that Montilladan is walking away from a huge payday by starring in Sweet Sherry South, part two." Tinker shook his head in disbelief. "Now, why would she do that?"

Axel responded. "The press will have a field day on us, Tink, if they find out! We'll have more sightings of Montilladan by fans than Elvis. Not to think of the paparazzi's involvement."

Zoe inquired of Axel. "Do you still have your blackboard on rollers in the closet?"

"Sure." At Axel's confirmation, she lugged it out of the cubbyhole into the center of the room. She summoned Thumper to join them. As a teacher to her pupils, she asked them to sit around the table, and she addressed them.

"When I worked down at the police station, Tinker and I used to brainstorm motives and list all the characters in the crimes. Let's have a go at it! We will take turns until we exhaust the list. What we are searching for is motive for Montilladan's desperate actions, assuming that she was responsible for Roy Spiller's death. We are trying to determine why she has decided to affect change into her life, decided to abandon a fortune in future income, leave her safety net. No challenging each other's fantasies. No elimination of ideas. Let our minds wander. Let our minds run amuck! What do you say? For fun, if for nothing else. How about it guys? I'll scribe all runaway notions."

The four nodded in concurrence. Tinker sat down in front of the board; Thumper positioned himself next to Tinker; Axel sat comfortably at the other end of the table. Zoe, marker in hand, stood and was anxious to commence. She glared at Axel.

"What?"

"I will write it at the top of the board."

"What?"

"Axel, say it so we can move on."

"Okay. Love slash Romeo. The love of Romeo is driving this woman." Tinker looked at him and added, "Slash real sex. That's what she's possibly been missing! Sex with a man."

Zoe accused them. "You men." Thumper rose, bellowing, "Glad that's over with. Now I can get back to work." In parody he began to leave, when he wheeled and shouted, "Drugs, and or, drug deals. Lotsa money if you don't get caught. Common motive for murder and greed and she acts demonic, like the haunting. Maybe she's on drugs or heavily involved. Maybe we're going to find out the purple crystals play a bigger role and are illegal and worth millions. Maybe she has to escape her drug connections and deals. Maybe she is unhinged because she's a big time user."

Zoe scribbled Thumper's idea and motioned to Tinker to encourage a response, but Tinker instead inquired, "Thank you Thumper for that motive, cause now I get to ask: What purple crystals? You're holding out on me already!"

"Don't get excited. Axel and I discovered purple bagged crystals at M's residence and again in the trailer that was destroyed in the fire. However, a chemist friend of mine, you must remember Cynthia Dopson, is analyzing them. If they're illegal or dangerous, we'll inform you."

Tinker was not happy. "Cyn Dopson. There is a new player in this chaos every time someone opens their mouth. You know, for a very wealthy movie star, I couldn't help notice how sparsely her home was furnished so maybe there are zealous creditors. Her money may be tied up elsewhere, say due to gambling, bad investments, illegal investments, debt we don't know about. You know it's a common occurrence for people with wealth to suddenly and frequently overspend."

Zoe recorded, "Could have suffocating debts that we have not uncovered yet. Need to check her bank accounts further tomorrow."

"I won't discredit that Zee. Did you inform Tinker about the foreign bank accounts?" She nodded a yes. "If she's alive, she's set the plans in motion to collect."

"Yeah, Zee informed me," and Tinker added, "and maybe that stash is protecting her from her creditors. Maybe that's the deal. Escape with her Andorran stash to a new life and away from creditors."

Zee scribbled, "Axel's friend Speed suggested that possibly she is in the witness protection program. How else can you pull this kind of caper off? And how about her mysterious background, plus the fact that she has multiple identifications that we know of. Maybe more than we know of. You need help big time from authorities for what she plans!"

Axel retorted, "Shame on those who hide her. I personally don't give that thought credence, but put it on the scoreboard." Axel further replied, "She is her own master of disguise. She does not require any assistance from the government." Tinker agreed with a beaming smile.

Tinker reminded him, "Rules, please. Do not dismiss anyone else's theory. Very good Zee," complimented Tinker. Axel piped up. "Psychologically unstable. She has snapped! That's my next guess. She's become an uncontrollable psycho of multiple unpredictable personalities. She's gone crazy. She is a killing machine. Perhaps as Thump mentioned, driven by drug dependence."

As Zoe recorded Axel's thoughts, Thumper jumped up and down and shouted, "I got it! I got it! Leave it to my twisted and perverted mind."

"Okay, Thumper, your turn."

As they stared at him, he moved in front of them, waited until a dead silence overtook the atmosphere and filled the room with suspense and stunned them by softly whispering. "Montilladan is trying to escape from someone, someone who wants to find Montilladan and exterminate her. So she devises the perfect murder and escape hatch. However, that someone looking for Montilladan gets smart, and hires us to find her!" An eerie silence stabbed at them. Suddenly, the room seemed darker as the sun disappeared. Tinker was impressed but challenged him.

"Whatever made you think of that bizarre sick twisted plot?"

Thumper was quick to reply. "I watch too many film noir movies. I mean, whatever motivated Lacey Sills to lift the robe? Unless, she wanted to confirm that Montilladan was really dead and really in that casket. Maybe, she was the one in disguise that set up Montilladan to be killed and killed poor Roy by mistake. She's an actor. She could have entered the set in disguise earlier. Now she's desperate. So she engages us to do her dirty work, find Montilladan on her behalf and allow her time first to interrogate her, before police, when we find her. Don't you see? We are the ones risking our safety and our health while Lacey sits quietly and safely in the background, waiting for results."

It was too late to retract Thumper's theory. Tinker clued in. "Ah-ha, thank you very much Thumper. So, Axel and Zee, the Lacey Sills is your client? I don't believe it." Tinker was shocked and the expression on his face conveyed it.

Thumper covered his face "Oh, no, sorry, guys. Oh, what have I done?"

Axel lamented. "It's okay, Thumper. I guess we should have told Tinker earlier. I guess we also forgot to inform you, Thump, that we withheld the identity of our client from Tinker. Now the cat's outta the bag."

Zee elaborated. "Tinker, you must promise to be sworn to secrecy about this. Lacey is paying us for results and part of that is keeping her identity unknown as our client. Can you promise?"

"Given the rest of the bull shit you've shared, sure, I promise."

Zee continued, "Lacey lifted the garment at the funeral parlor after everyone had departed and was astonished that the genitals were of a male, and that it was Roy Spiller in the casket. So now you know what Axel and I are assigned to do- find Montilladan for Lacey Sills."

Tinker stood up beside Zoe, walked to the board, pointed and banged his hand on it. "How do you two know that Thumper isn't onto something here? What a theory. This case is bizarre and his suggestion no more ridiculous than the yarns you've spun to me. I'm serious." Zee felt shivers. A bout of concern surfaced in the foursome as each weighed the implications. "I think there is a possibility that she lifted that robe to confirm M's death, just as Thumper outlined to us, and was shocked to find Roy there in M's place. Man! This is a Hollywood thriller. The hell with credit for solving this crime, I want the book and movie rights." It was Tinker who spoke softly and followed on.

"Very good, Thumper. It's a long shot. What a twist though, Axel Hawk and Zoe Burns set up by a client, just like in the old black and white film noir classics, and just like in the mysteries of the best sellers. If it is true, we are disposable pawns in this game. Lacey Sills is your client, I never would have guessed. This is getting freakier by the minute given Lacey and Montilladan are both females. Lacey is a female, right?"

Axel punched Tinker as he stared at Zoe. "It's your game, Zee. You haven't written it completely down yet. Are you going to record Thumper's twisted creepy motive?" She captured it as "A to Z set up by LS to find M."

"I don't want to play anymore," they softly heard her say.

Tinker replied quickly. "I got another completely different angle. You two said that that warehouse contained all the essentials of a quick change artist, a chameleon. You also stated that Montilladan and Spiller were risk takers. Well, supposing, just supposing, that Spiller discovered that Montilladan may have murdered before. I know you don't want to play anymore Zee, but my next suggestion is that this murder was not a one timer for Montilladan. Roy discovered something evil about Montilladan's past, was blackmailing her into these Hollywood gigs and roles, and she iced him. After all they were close. He blackmailed her for past deeds; she did him in. Rack it Zee, Spiller was blackmailing M over her past crimes."

Axel saw a crack open to use Shakespeare to express Tinker's motive. He stood, menacingly, suggested, "Ah, there's one did laugh in one's sleep, and one that cried out, 'Murther!'"

"Columbo said that?" Thump jawed excitedly as he pointed at Hawk.

Zoe was animated. "Guys, these are all credible ideas. Any other thoughts?" She also wrote down M=Montilladan=Murder. She was still reeling over Thumper's bizarre idea.

"A variation on Tinker's," Axel said, "maybe blackmail by someone else because her grand deception had been found out. Thus she had to create her death and disappear. Roy was an innocent sacrificial lamb."

"Very, very good, I like that, too, Axel," chirped Tink, "because it makes sense. She conveniently kills Spiller to put the blackmailer off her scent. Lacey is innocent unless she's the blackmailer. Another nice one."

Axel and Thumper shook their heads in agreement as Zoe recorded blackmail. As Zoe scribbled it, she reinforced her idea from two days ago. "I think guys, ahem, I have the floor, that she just wanted to become a real woman again, to follow her natural tendencies so had to escape this chapter of her life. No blackmailer. No Romeo. No other reason to murder than she just wanted to forfeit her career and follow her natural instincts. To once again be a woman."

Tinker grinned. "Man, I was just thinkin', if this caper about Montilladan is true and word gets out, the auditors are going to be checking everyone's pants come Oscar time before they go up there to receive a statue." Tinker's whooping smile ignited a joyous outburst. He added, "Also the auditors be lining up for the job of checking inside the pants of the stars. Furthermore, I say, do the check on the red carpet walk and let the entire worldly viewing audience have some inclusion in the fun and surprise, too." Thumper was bent over. "Oh, yeah, Tinker, you're a real hoot."

"Ole Joan Rivers can add pant and panty inspection as part of the red carpet show and pass judgment on that fashion." They all bellowed until Zee turned serious. "Okay, point taken. I think her time as a man is expired. She just wants to be a woman. Romeo does not enter into the equation I propose, nor do any of these other factors. I pray that your theory Thumper, about us being set up, is erroneous, but your idea just reinforces the need for security first."

All four studied the board. Zoe reminded them, "Axel is also correct though that she might be engaged in a new life that offers her something that she does not have now, a boy friend."

"Freedom," stated Axel. After two minutes, Axel took the marker from Zee to address the gathering. "Sorry, I keep analyzing this list and seeing the same thought leap out at me!" He tapped on the top of the board. "Freedom most naturally couples with Romeo. This gets my singular vote." He passed the marker to Thumper.

Thumper arose and checked another theory. "The bitch has snapped, gone insane, too many gigs as someone else, coupled with the fact that she impetuously desires to be a woman! I vote that she's mentally confused, dangerous, snapped, on drugs and most importantly is more than one person." Thumper put tick marks beside the captions of mentally unstable and desires to be a real woman.

Zoe did not surprise them. "I have given this some thought. I believe that she has had powerful help to pull this off. Even with that help, what drives her is what God gave her when she was born- female instincts. She hasn't snapped. She has no Romeo. She's perfectly sane and knows exactly what she is doing. She just wants to live her real female instincts out, and killed poor Roy to escape. Montilladan murdered Roy Spiller in pre-calculated and pre-meditated cold-hearted, cold-blooded murder."

Tinker was the last to vote. "This tale is surreal. I know we are trying to zero in on the most compelling motive, but I vote for two ideas. You know, Thumper scared the hell out of me with his insinuation that we are being set up. I thought about this. We had better be at least a bit suspicious of Lacey Sills, hard as it might be to refute that idea, difficult as it is for Axel, Thump and I to see the evil behind her pretty little face. After all, Axel, one of the conditions of my entry into this group, is that we agreed to leave Lacey Sills alone with Montilladan when you found her, and I stress alone, before I have the opportunity to interrogate her. Alone to do what Axel? Kill her? So I give one half of my vote to Thumper's creative suggestion even if it is just to put us four on red alert. Let us exercise caution, please, around Lacey Sills. As I just said, she wants to see M first to possibly bump M off before the police get a chance to question him, excuse me, question *her*."

"But I also favor Axel's idea that she has found Romeo. So I give the other half to that. No offense Zee. If Axel's correct, we better find Romeo and determine how dangerous he is, too."

Zoe bolted up from her seat. She was ecstatic. "No offense taken because we have witnessed a first! It deserves a huge round of applause for Tinker finally agrees with Axel Hawk on something. Now that's the most dangerous event in this entire case!" Tinker's cellular buzzed just as he was the victim of her humor.

"Talk to me, Conan. Yeah. Yeah, yeah, damn! Damn it! Okay. Thanks. Thanks, Conan." He sighed.

"The white van was stolen earlier today from a car wash in Anaheim. Police found it abandoned at a shopping mall parking lot one hour ago. We found the rightful owner. The owner's clean and is a reputable family man. He filed a theft report earlier. The vehicle has been wiped clean. No trace of gasoline containers; no blood residue and no fingerprints."

Thumper excused himself. "Not a bad list of motives. I need to finish my profile on Aaron Schuler for you, and get appointments confirmed. I have also got to finish the analysis of clues from your place, Axel."

"Fingerprints?" Tinker was inquisitive. Axel elaborated.

"From my nightmare last night, in which M materialized and came to haunt me."

"Yeah, Zoe told me." Tinker confronted them. "Now why would she do that?"

Zoe agreed. "That is what I hound him about, too. Axel's evidence that he heard her bound down the stairs and slam the front door is overwhelming, as long as he wasn't still under the heavy influence of the sleeping potion."

"I keep telling you. I don't know why she did it except to scare us off this assignment; we are so close to an important clue I guess, or inker, she is daring us."

"And she didn't attack you?"

"Only mentally."

"Then she just departed? Immediately?"

"Correct."

"How much did you have to drink last night before beddy?"

"It was her Tink. There is also the possibility that maybe she was searching for files on this case at my house. I was drugged from my pain killer prescriptions. Zee and I think she followed Zee and I back to my place from her residence, and it could have been her lurking there in the bushes. She may have entered when Zoe was upstairs tending to my health and the door was left unguarded and unlocked."

"Jesus, Axel, you sure lead an exciting life. We gonna tie up an entire police unit to follow you around if you keep this pace up."

Tinker snapped his fingers. "I want that list recorded, Zoe, and sent to my cell. Now let's construct a list of all the characters in this zany plot. As Shakespeare would want us to do and as Ole Tink wants us to do. I want to know everyone who has stepped into this pile of crap." Tinker expressed his disbelief of the whole affair by shaking his head as Zoe took her cell phone and captured the blackboard in a photo. She sent it immediately to Tinker and Axel. She offered, "Axel, you start."

Tinker warned them, "Do not omit a single individual."

Axel recited, giving a hesitation between each offering, allowing Tinker to digest or interrupt. "Nikki Louden, Lacey Sills, Montilladan, Roy Spiller, The Colonel and Mrs. Whitehurst, and Katz and George."

"Whoa, whoa, whoa, not so fast buddy. Hold it! Who are those two dudes? Katz and George? And remind me again who the Whitehursts are? Come on Zee." Axel placed Katz and George into context, including their admiration for Spiller, Spiller's presence on the beach, and Zoe picked up the pace to identify the Whitehursts for Tinker once more. Axel elaborated on his encounter with Mrs. Whitehurst at the cemetery and concluded by stating, "Mrs. Whitehurst knows more about Montilladan than she lets on."

Tinker looked back inquisitively. "How do you know?"

Axel smiled. "Man's intuition. Okay Zee, you take it."

"Dr. Sorbet, the dentist from San Clemente, the Appleman and his partner, identity still unknown. By the way Tinker, now that you are on the team, can we have permission to match the dental prints of Montilladan I retrieved form Dr. Sorbet, to the victim's? See if there is a mismatch? Or match? I'd like to hear the opinion from the examiner who performed the autopsy. We have a clean copy." Tink affirmed by strongly agreeing. She glanced at Axel and focused her stare at him and gave him the goofy look. He took the hint.

"Dr. Renee Montoya and her assistant, Lillian, Aaron Schuler, Dr. Larry Bartlett, and Jenna."

Tinker interrupted again. "Halt. Halt! Halt! Halt! Lillian? Jenna? Zoe, you left those out of the epic. Also what does Dr. Montoya have to offer that I already didn't get from her interrogation?"

Axel took up the cause. "Jenna is Roy Spiller's personal banker and just an acquaintance. I have not met with her yet. Thumper is arranging a time for us to meet her tomorrow. Larry Bartlett manages two medical research firms where Montilladan sat on the Board of Directors. Montilladan also made huge donations out of the proceeds of her estate to Bartlett's businesses."

Tinker was curious. "How did you find him?"

"Through the settling of Montilladan's estate."

"Any chance he is Romeo?"

Axel was quick to respond. "No, not a chance."

Axel elaborated on both Schuler and Bartlett.

"Put Mr. Hartwig on the list, too, Zee, from Constance and Lieber, he administers M's affairs, and Paula Piper, M's agent. Retracing to your previous inquiry Tinker, Bartlett owns and directs two medical businesses, one engaged in pure research, the second in marketing of new drugs into the public market."

"Ahem," Zoe slyly blurted.

"What?"

"Tink and I noticed that you conveniently omitted your buddy, Ms. Platinum from the list."

"Not intentionally. A minor character."

Zoe reminded him, "The mind operates strangely when under stress, Mr. Hawk. By the way, Charlie phoned earlier to say that Ms. Platinum did not make an encore performance at his bar last night and of course, we know why."

"And Montoya?" Tinker inquired, "I noticed you skipped the doctor."

Axel complied with Tinker. "As you know, Dr. Renee Montoya is Montilladan's psychiatrist. Zee and I think we should at the very least consider the possibility that she may be aiding and abetting M to escape into her new female life. Lillian, her assistant, may or may not be privy to the Montoya-Montilladan conversations."

A contorted charcoal face stared back at him. "Well there is definitely one fact I believe, that Montilladan needs help from a shrink. The way these facts are unfolding, we all are going to need help from Dr. Montoya before this is finished."

Axel emphasized to them. "Romeo. Put his name down. He's a major character, his name is not on that list! And place a big question mark beside his name?"

"Yeah, I tend to agree with you Axel. Okay, enough of this madness for now. Felix just sent me a text and I have to rendezvous with him in another locale, pronto. You know, Axel, I'd prefer to hang around with Zee and you on this case but, so far, you have been beaten, had your ego bruised, smashed your car, been visited by a ghost, destroyed a pair of vintage shoes and almost been skewered and charred. I pass to meet with Felix instead. However, tomorrow all day, Tinker hangs out with you! You where the action is." He placed his arm around Zoe.

"Thank you for taking me into your confidence, although, right now, I haven't got a clue how we are going to solve this mystery and find Romeo. Maybe we'll dig out clues from the investigation at the warehouse fire. Mail me our agenda for tomorrow later, will you Axel? It's you and me Axel tomorrow buddy. Ole Tink is at your side all day. See you honey." They hugged, Tinker departing, leaving Zoe and Axel to stare at their notes on the blackboard.

"What's bothering you? I recognize that look and it is not the goofy look. Your tone betrays you."

"Every criminal makes one mistake, Zee. We retraced all our steps before Tink arrived. Somewhere in this suffocating mess is her downfall. Somewhere on that board is a misguided clue."

"Axel, she has already been sloppy. She left the card keys in her residence for us to find; the purple crystals may yet be important; her lair is destroyed, but we found it, witnessed it, and extracted evidence. She will err again. This crime is not perfect Axel. We already know that!"

Thumper entered and delivered good news. "Aaron Schuler tomorrow at nine-thirty am and for you Zee, Jenna at the bank at ten. You'll require a policeman present so I arranged for one. Tink will sign off later." Axel rose to thank Thumper with a pat on the back, instructed him to send the itinerary to Tinker, and looked astonishingly into the outer office at the figures of Colonel Whitehurst with an austere looking Kathleen Whitehurst in tow. He motioned Zoe to turn the board around quickly, and instructed Thumper to leave. The Whitehursts entered.

"Mr. Hawk, please excuse us for an unannounced intrusion. However, we are fortunate to find you present." The Colonel was his polite self.

Axel introduced Zoe and they exchanged courtesies for over five minutes, sitting around the oval table. The Colonel carried the conversation with pleasantries and expressed additional sincere regrets over Axel's beating. Axel couldn't even begin to guess their agenda. After further chatter between the Colonel and Axel and Zoe on local weather and traffic, the Colonel spoke up.

"Kathleen and I had a long talk. As a result, we have decided to share a private matter with you. You may find that it has nothing to do at all with your investigation, but we will allow you to be the judges. We have decided to confide in you. Therefore, we are here to deliver testimony and evidence."

Axel shuffled in excitement. "Zoe and I appreciate your trust in us." Mrs. Whitehurst remained silent with her head bowed. The Colonel was attired in white gym clothes as if he had just finished tennis matches; Kathleen was dressed in her usual gloomy black dress.

"Well, here we are so permit me to begin. Unknown to me until recently, Kathleen had Montilladan trailed by a private investigator. As you know, Montilladan and my wife did not get along and Kathleen wanted to obtain damaging information from Montilladan's private life to force a breakup between Lacey and Montilladan. In short, Kathleen hired this investigator to discover something to turn Lacey against Montilladan." Axel made eye contact with Zee. She, as he did, had the glint of anticipation in her eyes.

"My wife was hoping that there would be evidence of betrayal through another lover; perhaps, documented evidence of a crime or misdemeanor by Montilladan such as illegal drug use; or maybe even a close association with undesirable elements." Zee thought that it was as if the Colonel had overheard their recent past analysis. "The trailing proved futile except for three curious events. We are here to convey to you these events and for you to be the judge of what conclusions might be reached from these three episodes." The Colonel gave a cue to Kathleen.

At this point, Mrs. Whitehurst opened a large black bag and extracted some items. She finally acknowledged Axel and Zoe by presenting them a series of photographs, laying them in view on the table, where they could all inspect them. Mrs. Whitehurst reluctantly commenced her dialogue at the Colonel's hand signal and verbal prompts.

"These photographs were taken by the investigator in the parking lot of an upscale Sunset restaurant called Capers. Montilladan had dinner with this man," and she pointed to a cozy corner where the twosome sat side by side in a booth under dim gold lighting, apparently dining. At this glance, it seemed business rather than pleasure. Axel couldn't quite make out the identity but assumed it to be Larry Bartlett. "Kathleen, continue."

"On this night when these photos were snapped, they had words, as evidenced by this later photo which illustrates some irate gestures." She uncovered two from beneath the pile. "Our source informed me they did not speak kindly to one another as he walked by unnoticed, and later overheard them from an advantageous position at the bar."

"Then," Mrs. Whitehurst sounded off meanly, "they met in the parking lot, and the investigator snapped these five photos," and she laid them in sequence from holding hands, to embracing to strong salivating kisses. "You can very clearly see under the light in these that Montilladan is passionately kissing another man. How disgusting! Men kissing men and in public!"

Axel was thrilled. Now there was no question that it was Larry Bartlett! Mrs. Whitehurst was oblivious to the photo's possible true meanings. She rifled into the pile and produced a mystery to her and her husband, but not to Zee and Axel. "Now, this mystery man is handing numerous small pouches to Montilladan from the trunk of his car," Mrs. Whitehurst elaborated, "and then she kissed him again on the cheek, endlessly. Look. What a public spectacle. We don't know what is in the packages, but the investigator clearly stated to me that before the transfer of these packets took place both scoured the parking lot and made sure there were no witnesses. Our man was hidden behind bushes."

"He blew the pouch up in this one frame," the Colonel spoke, "but the packet turns out to be a violet discoloration and quite blurry in the street light, that is, if this is the true color."

Axel and Zee made eye contact to mutually and silently express, "Another concrete absolute connection between Bartlett, Montilladan, and the purple substance. Ammunition for a next meeting with Bartlett tomorrow and with Tinker present!"

Kathleen needed further prompting so the Colonel expelled an "Ahem, Kathleen."

While she rummaged in her purse, The Colonel explained. "We caught the news today and witnessed the fire of the warehouse down on Macey Street. This may not have a connection, but it certainly prompted our visit. Kathleen?"

"Montilladan visited repeatedly this exact warehouse in a slummy district that burned down today." Zoe and Axel gleefully winked at each other. "Why? We don't know. The detective could not gain entry. It appeared to be deserted. Every time that Montilladan went there, our man had to stay blocks away for risk of being uncovered for there was nowhere to hide. Here at least is the address.

You can have the photos he took, but they are indistinct because he shot them from a distance." Axel noted that it indeed was the destroyed sight on Macey Street. The evidence confirmed their conclusions of earlier and destroyed any hopes of an additional hideout.

"Finally, Montilladan dated this girl. I thought I could use this to break Lacey's heart, to turn her against him, but he died only days after I received these prints. I shut down the investigation upon his death. Here are photographs of Montilladan with the mystery girl. They seem to be rather close friends from the mushy kisses they exchanged through a window and in this club."

Axel signaled by body language his supreme surprise to Zoe. "Thank you very much Mrs. Whitehurst. These photos are extremely helpful. We are so grateful for your trust in us. Our investigation is proceeding on course and this information may be vital to our case." The Colonel nodded; Kathleen looked away. To the surprise of Zee and Axel, the Whitehursts departed almost as swiftly as they had arrived without even anecdotal good-byes. The Colonel smiled and waved; Mrs Whitehurst, the reluctant informer, was acrid to the end but clung to the Colonel as they left. Axel turned to Zoe who couldn't contain herself. "The lady in the photo? Dr. Renee Montoya?"

Axel smiled. "No. The mystery girl is none other than Lillian, Dr. Montoya's office assistant. It is definitely her. I'd hazard a guess that Lillian is definitely one of Montilladan's lovers from this affectionate display! If we hurry, we might just catch Lillian at closing time and show this to her for a rise. What do you say? Up for it? It's now a strong possibility that Lillian may know where M is."

"She will dodge a confrontation. Axel, get real, Lillian is going to blurt out M's location?"

"She won't admit it to me, but you could bait her and try and open the door for us."

"Me? What are you thinking, Axel? That Lillian knew Montilladan and introduced M to Dr. Montoya to seek professional help about M's multiple personalities? Ew! Every time I hear that I get shivers because it points to a very disturbed woman."

Zoe warned him. "You're racing too far out in front Axel. Consider this. Maybe Lillian met M through M's visits to the office, and this is a harmless date. Remember, innocent until proven guilty. Lillian could just be another jilted lover of M's."

Axel raised his eyebrows. "As long as she has seen M nude, I am interested in talking to her. You drive, please. I'll leave my rental car here. God this is depressing. First my face, now my car. I hope nothing else gets punched today."

They cruised back north along Sunset Strip West just before the rush hour traffic, weaving through lanes as only Zee could, squeezing into spaces between cars when Axel thought there is no room. Precious time was lost in the commotion of two busy intersections as Axel counted the minutes on his watch. Finally, with many scenarios between Bartlett and Montilladan mapped out in his mind during the drive, they arrived and parked one block away from Dr. Montoya's office, just at the eve of closing time as shoppers escaped and businesses hibernated.

Hustling, and now in front of Dr. Montoya's office door, Zoe tapped succinctly on the glass pane. It was slightly after the posted closing time. Luck was on their side as an unsuspecting Lillian opened the door to chat with Zee just as Axel slid through the crack. Lillian was appalled that she had been duped. "The office is closed and Dr. Montoya has departed. I can also say that I didn't approve of your devious strategy to gain access to Dr. Montoya's office on Tuesday. Your friend should be ashamed at deceiving me again for access."

Axel solemnly informed her, "Meet my associate, Zoe Burns. It isn't the doctor that we want to converse with. It is you." Lillian was taken aback. She closed the door and leaned back against it.

"Me?" He produced a striking photo of Lillian and Montilladan exiting a nightclub, arm in arm, dressed royally, she looking at Montilladan with apparently lustful eyes. He handed her a further one in the club where they snuggled and kissed against a dark backdrop. Upon recognizing the scene, she exhaled, fidgeted with her fingers and passed the photos back to Axel. Lillian gesticulated to have a seat.

"So I dated Montilladan. What about it? That is neither a crime nor a curio. Better still, let's do a reality check. Reality one, he's dead. Reality two, I didn't kill him. Reality three, I don't miss him in the least. I didn't even enjoy that particular date. What do you want from me?" This striking side of Lillian jolted Axel as she was coldly manipulative.

Zoe attacked. "How many times did you date him? Over what period of time? And excuse me, but the kissing bout appears pretty chummy."

She snapped back with a voice lowered by two octaves. "That is my personal life, and I don't have to answer any of these stark questions and I have nothing to conceal. I don't like you, Mr. Hawk; I don't care for your associate either. However, the answer to your question is three or four dates. That's all. Question two, we dated over two months and it wasn't serious. For me it was a lark to date a huge celebrity like Montilladan, be made a fuss of over everywhere we went, ogled by onlookers and in front of other people, and I loved being photographed by the press. It gave me a rush. I never did that before. People treated us like royalty. If anyone had made an ugly issue out of us, I would have dumped him at once."

"Did it get serious?" Zee inquired. Lillian seemed to shudder.

She expressed irritation. "None of your damn business."

Zoe played the tough guy. "Sex?"

"None of your damn business!"

"Sex?" Zoe was tenacious. They had to know. They both stared back.

"Absolutely not!" She was emphatic.

"Are you lying to us?" It was Zee challenging her again.

"Strictly platonic and how dare you, you witch. Get out!" She was on her feet waving her arms but, very curiously, started to volunteer information. "I'm very attractive, very sexy, I have a great body and I know it and use it. I date lots of men because I am sexy and I'm sought after. I pick my spots to initiate and have sex. I am not that easy. Get it?! We had a few memorable passionate kisses. Montilladan never made any serious sexual advances toward me nor me toward him. We were trying to find chemistry on our dates and it was… so-so. Are you finished snooping around? You are both disgusting."

Axel opened up a new line. "So that's why you had passionate kissing? The affair was so-so?"

"Leave."

"Did you discover anything quirky about Montilladan?"

"What kind of stupid question is that? Whatever do you want me to say? Talk about quirk, look in the mirror."

"Ever visit him at his home?"

"Yes, twice at parties that he invited me to. I attended those with someone else as a date and for the record, I never visited Montilladan alone at his home when we dated for sex or dinner or exercise or whatever."

"What was the relationship between Montilladan and Dr. Montoya?"

"You will have to ask the doctor. I don't speak for her. And if there was anything, would you expect me to betray my employer with juicy tidbits of gossip? I'm loyal to Dr. Montoya. Look, get it straight. I dated Montilladan three or four times. It is not a crime in California for an attractive single girl like me to date an unmarried movie star. I discovered that I never really got turned on by him, only by the thrill of being his companion in public. He's dead. Dating him is dead. Conversation over." She stood and opened the door.

"Did he ever mention any other homes, like beach houses or skiing lodges, foreign properties that he owned?"

"No, never. Montilladan and I never really hit it off." Axel pondered why she continued to talk after ordering them out. "I liked him though. He was a regular charmer. He was sexy, outgoing and outrageous at times. He died shortly after we initiated seeing each other, soon after our fourth date. I mourned for him briefly, but I wasn't that close to him. I got over him. I don't wish to answer any more questions. Montilladan is dead. I think that we should exhibit some respect for the dead. What happened between Montilladan and me was simple. It was innocent and definitely not serious. Let it be. I can't imagine why you ended up here?"

She was fidgeting. "Why in the Hell do you two want to interrogate my affairs with Montilladan? I would think that anyone had better things to do in life."

Zoe stood inches in front of her. She, too, recognized the upwelling of anxiety in Lillian. "Did Dr. Montoya know of your dating?"

"Why don't you ask her? She doesn't care!" She had reached an irritable status as she bit her bottom lip.

"How did you meet her?" Zoe planted the word "her" intentionally with finesse. Axel didn't flinch.

Lillian's cold eyes narrowed. With lips now pursed she stood inches from Zee to reply. "Her? Who the Hell is her? Dr. Montoya? I interviewed for this position and she hired me."

"Oh, excuse me," Zee re-cast, "I goofed. I'm sorry. I meant to say him. Montilladan. Sorry. Him."

Lillian stared Zoe down. "I met him here at the office. I must go. I have a date tonight. Excuse me."

Lillian strenuously motioned to them to depart the premises by waving her arm. Slowly they exited each casting a look toward her until she disengaged contact. At street level, Axel was eager to quiz Zoe. "Woman's intuition?"

"Hard to tell. She could be telling the truth, Axel but, if you must know, if I had one guess, my intuition tells me that there is more to her story. I think she's lying big time. Her body language, her nervousness, she was incredibly fidgety. This all points to lies."

"Now how could you possibly deduce that?"

"You asked me about my intuition."

"Okay. Lying about what?"

"Most of what she said." Axel chided her.

"Man Zoe, if only I had that woman's intuition I would be so much more dangerous."

"Well you don't have it and men don't. It sets us apart. Besides, didn't you catch that slip? Lillian specifically said goodbye, insisted we leave, and rambled on for another five minutes defending her position."

"I'm happy to break off this conversation today, but I reserve our rights to cross-examination Lillian after I interrogate Dr. Montoya tomorrow evening at Montoya's abode."

Two hours later, after pouring over the profiles of Aaron Schuler, rehashing the events of the last three days, they were sitting on Zoe's infamous sofa eating gelato desert after an Italian dinner and sampling one of Zoe's favorite Californian Cabernets. The doorbell rang and Zoe returned with Cynthia Dopson in tow.

"Hi Axel," she waved as her bubbly personality continued.

"Cynthia, how good to see you, and it is my pleasure." Axel stood to receive her. "The wine and gelato are a great combination, believe it or nor. Would you like some?"

"I'll take just a taste of the wine. I have a possible dinner date later."

She slung her heavy tote bag on the floor and leaned over to extract a folder. She sat down beside Axel and pretended to size him up. "Nuts! I wasn't expecting you to be home Zoe. I wanted Axel all to myself."

From the depths of the kitchen, Zee was heard to order, "Cynthia, behave!" Cynthia sat moved closer to Axel while sipping a half glass of red wine.

"Mm mm, what a great taste Zoe. Okay, let us launch into business. When we last visited, I had completed a rush analysis to help you two out. I gave you my results. Tonight" and Zoe joined them, "I have a very startling discovery to reveal."

Axel perked up. "You have our undivided attention."

"I am the chemist, Axel, so give me my award winning moments please without interruptions." She extracted some diagrams and spread them out on the sofa in front of her.

"I have been so focused on the chemistry and purpose of the purple crystalline material that it was only later today I made a huge discovery. This whitish discoloration in each crystal is a liquid. I missed that initially because I thought it to be a solid, too. I extracted a few samples and presto, it jumped out of the analyses at me. It is a derivative of compounds used to tighten the skin and provide cell rigidity. After pouring over the formulas for hours of both compounds, and using my knowledge of chemical reactions, both biochemistry mixed with inorganic chemistry and organic chemistry, I have reached a preliminary daring conclusion. The purple material not only retards bone deterioration but, in combo with the liquid material, might miraculously enhance muscle cell structure at the same time. What I am saying in layman's terms is that, the ionic presence reacting with the liquid derivative creates bulging, sturdy cell growth, using mineral elements to strengthen cell walls. Just a theory but a good one."

Axel sat back to absorb what she stated. Zee was filled with inquisitiveness and inquired. "Cyn, this substance can cause muscle development? You mean give you…. ah… extra strength?"

"No, I mean could provide super strength by first accelerating and then maintaining rapid, healthy muscle tone and strong cell walls as long as, and here's the key, injections are continued."

"And for guys, all this without sweaty sessions at the gym?" Axel asked.

"Yes."

"No more steroids for bulk up if approved?"

"Correct, except I don't know the side effects of this drug. It provides great muscular body that doesn't necessarily sag over time and retains cell wall structure as long as you inject."

"What is the probability that your guess is correct?"

"Hold on. There's more. There is no evidence of this compound on the net, nor in any medical journal or drug test sites, as either a submitted or pending patented drug. Furthermore, and this is important, only the manufacturer knows for sure what the side effects of the drug are. My initial guess is that this drug is potent, very potent, to build strong cell walls like no other drug and possibly in conjunction retard the aging process with continual injections. Risks unknown."

Zoe and Axel sat quietly absorbing her dialogue so Cynthia continued. "I'd say further that those syringes that Axel discovered are evidence that you don't take this substance orally, you dissolve it in warm water, stir vigorously and inject right into the areas of the body you want to stimulate cell strength and growth in, recognizing it reaches other areas in lesser concentrations. If you want to make your entire body strong, you are looking at a lot of body sites to inject."

They were still in thoughts. "So I can conclusively tell you that whoever is manufacturing this product is doing this without regulatory oversight or regulatory approvals and obviously since you found it outside controls, they are distributing it illegally."

She further defended her position with talk of biochemistry, referencing the interaction of the materials using some page size diagrams.

"I have been around the drug business and drug analysis a fair amount. If I had to guess, the side effects are retarding its entry into the marketplace. It has to be or I would have heard of this potentially miracle compound."

"There's one other potential conclusion I reached. I discovered that the crystals are of differing strength when dissolved in water, that is you can mix a dose from dilute to strong. I think you inject smaller diluted doses over time to build up your cell strength, but the more concentrated solutions could, on a one time injection, or infrequent injection, cause the muscles in the area of injection to take a different shape."

Zoe spoke up. "The person could change appearances for a short time!"

Cyn affirmatively shouted. "Yes, like a shapeshifter, and when you discontinue from a one-time injection, the muscles relax and go back to form with only temporary short bruising since the materials in the cell wall just move out of the body and the cell relaxes again. Please," and she raised her hands with palms out toward them, "this is only conjecture."

Zoe summated. "So, in summary this drug is powerful. It reinforces cell membranes and walls, could retard aging along prolonged exposure, may cause short term shape shifting with one time or infrequent usage."

"Yes, I am almost certain given the chemistry that it could cause high blood pressure, but who cares."

She finished her wine and looked at her watch, informing them, "I'm so sorry. I have to run. I really do. Here is my unscientific report, a simple explanation to what I have said. You should be able to follow my logic in this brief I wrote for you. No charge." They chatted for only a few minutes, and Axel thanked her profusely as she excused herself to what she would only describe as a potential new hot date. Zee followed her down the hall.

"Cynthia, how many copies are there of this report?"

"Only this paper copy I just gave you and the original on my laptop back at the office."

"Do us all a favor. Discuss these results with no one, put the original document on a stick and hide it; send me a note or call me where you have hidden it and delete the original soonest from your laptop." They hugged. "Thanks, I owe you Cyn."

"It's okay. We're even. I'll tell you why some other time."

Zoe watched her drive away and looked for any activity on the street. It was quiet and she recognized all the vehicles in her proximity. She remained in the darkened entry, posing as a spy until she was satisfied that Cynthia was not followed.

Finishing their desserts, Axel reinforced how important a meeting with Bartlett was becoming. "Mrs. Whitehurst's photos suggest that Bartlett, for all his physical and personal shortcomings, might be Romeo. A most unlikely candidate, but the serious smooching suggests otherwise, unless Montilladan is thanking him profusely for the drugs."

Axel proposed a theory. "I have no idea Zee what Montilladan is up to, what scheme she has hatched, but I have made my mind up. She walked away from lucrative riches by killing her opportunity to star in the sequel to Sweet Sherry South. I think she did that because this scheme, whatever it is, however risky, generates a bigger payoff."

Zoe did not want to enter into debate so just acknowledged his idea by nodding.

Tiredation soon outran both of them. Zoe startled him with a radical suggestion. "I propose that strength in numbers should be our adopted motto tonight. I'm beat, too. We have a busy day tomorrow and I certainly would feel more secure...so...so I suggest the idea of sleeping together upstairs in my bed with the proviso of 'no hanky-panky'". He was elated.

"Can we at least cuddle up?"

"Yes, as long as you promise to be a good boy and keep your hands in non-sexual locales."

"Well Zee, we know that M is using the mysterious drug and it makes sense that Bartlett is the supplier. If Cynthia is right, there are multiple selfish purposes for its use. It makes me feel insecure to know that Montilladan is a real shapeshifter, not only in disguise with lenses and clothes and make-up but, now with injections, to make one's self loom bigger." She simple agreed and left to go upstairs.

Later, she changed into her zebra pajamas, which wowed him with the skin tight bottoms until the monster cream made its appearance again. Over a hot chocolate, laced with his pain killers, Axel lamented, "We are spinning our wheels, girl."

"I know. She has destroyed her lair. At least, the Whitehursts confirmed the location of her lair plus helped confirm the connection to Bartlett, and made a definitive connection to Lillian. When do you see Bartlett?"

"Earliest possible appointment is Friday morning. I'll take Tinker with me. That'll intimidate him."

"What are you doing?"

"I am staring intently at these photos Lacey gave us. You are positive that Aaron Schuler is not Romeo?"

"I am positive, but you and Tinker pass judgment tomorrow. I've seen Mr. Schuler on the talk shows so he is not the one. He's a genius, unpolished and certainly not handsome."

"Well, it certainly wasn't Roy Spiller because he's dead, and Larry Bartlett doesn't seem her type. We are missing her mate. I have a suspicion that we haven't met him yet."

Zoe insured that the front door was bolted; the patio doors too. She tugged at his hand to guide him upstairs. Not a word was spoken between them until she snuggled up to him. He decided on the last appropriate words before the consumption of sleep.

"Friends, Los Angeles, countrymen, lend me your ears; I come not to bury M, not to praise her, the evil that men do lives after them, the good if oft interred with their bones, and so let it be with Montilladan."

Zee's snoring signaled that she was asleep. "A good speech wasted," he thought.

Axel placed his arm tighter around her and in dreams on this night they each found peace.

THURSDAY MORNING and AFTERNOON

A walk down the halls of Ray-X productions was a mind twisting experience for Tinker and Axel. There was a kaleidoscopic door every six feet, each door bedecking Axel and Tinker to pause and absorb some notable special effects worthy of Aaron Schuler. But these were more than placeholders. Axel admired the depth of the three dimensional scenes, the darting characters, the shivering electronic bolts of lightning, and in two instances a menacing hologram which seemed to protrude into the hallway as they approached the gremlin.

"Cool, huh?" Directly in front of them, his gum-chewing secretary with an exaggerated sway directed them to a large room at the end of the long tunnel. "Aaron will arrive shortly. Enjoy the show guys."

Tinker was puzzled. "What did she mean by that, show?" Tinker peered over his shoulder. She smiled back with an evil leer and opened her brown eyes wide, and left.

They were in a large oval office. Or was it oval? It was suddenly difficult to espy into the murky corners to their left and right. Schuler's desk was separated from them by a white picket fence. The windows were covered in heavy cloth material depicting fight scenes of Aaron's fantasy flicks. Standing upright and staring at them, were a series of mannequins- a grim reminder to Axel of his torturous ordeal in the warehouse on Wednesday morning. As he glanced over his shoulder, he saw that the back wall was a series of black doors. He was not sure through which one they had just entered. Which one would lead to their hasty retreat if needed?

Axel now fixed his stony glare on a pirate. The more he examined it, the more alive it seemed. Tinker leaned over to him to whisper, "Creepy. Look at his impish eyes."

"No thanks."

Aaron Schuler burst into the room with a bolt of infectious energy. Zoe was correct. This couldn't be Romeo. He resembled someone from the fraternity of the Pastry Chefs College, and was a prime candidate for an early heart attack if his weight was not exponentially arrested. Schuler was in his mid-forties with receding hairline, roly-poly sagging belly, a large derriere, and enormous but magnificent, Dumbo-like ears. Definitely not M's type. Tinker leaned over to Axel in amazement as Schuler made his way behind his desk to whisper, "This is the brains behind one of Hollywood's greatest special effects empires?"

"Yes, keep quiet. Let him talk."

After introductions, Schuler was exuberant. "Hey, sit down and relax. I always support the finest men of the Los Angeles Police Department. Mae and I have not missed their charity ball in seven years." Axel was now relieved that Thumper had booked the appointment under Tinker's name. They were here officially on police business.

With courtesies behind them, Tinker spoke to him. "Mr. Schuler, we have three items of police business to discuss with you today. May I express my appreciation to making yourself available on such short notice." Schuler was about to expose another bad habit by lighting a thick badly rolled cigar, but the reference to three pieces of business jolted him. Aborting the cigar, he picked up his phone to summon Terry. He leaned back in his tilted chair and explained.

"If there are three business issues that the police are interested in, I require my right hand man, Terry Martinez, my operations manager. Do we need an attorney present?"

Tinker replied immediately. "No, sir, not unless you sense you do." Terry Martinez entered and in contrast was a trim, tanned, well groomed, mid-forties muscular specimen, with a deeply furrowed face, contorted in the forehead and chin. Martinez asked for identification. Tinker allowed him to inspect his badge at will and presented him with a card. Axel presented his business card. Martinez kindly returned the badge and retained both their business cards as Tinker launched into the purpose of their appointment.

"Gentlemen, I would first ask you about the fire at the warehouse on Macey Street." Martinez and Schuler sat together across from them, Schuler's double chin appearing and disappearing as he nodded. Martinez sat still, his neatly pressed mauve shirt without a wrinkle.

"The Fire Marshall will be in contact with you soon. It looks like arson from first examination of evidence."

"Arson? Mischievous kids?"

"Yes to arson, Mr. Schuler, and no to kids. Did you have the contents insured?"

Martinez answered. "Yes, sir, we did. We actually have owned that property outright for many years and bought it when the street was a thriving locus of desirable warehouses. The structure and contents were insured for very little now because the building was old, dilapidated, in need of gross repairs, and deemed to be uneconomic given its usage and our inability to sell the property. The contents were mostly worthless props whose values had depreciated to near zero over time, and had seen better days in parades and movies. It mainly served as a storage facility. I might add that we do have safety inspections annually and the structure was never viewed as a fire hazard."

"Were there any anomalous valuable items?"

Martinez was convincing with bouts of politeness. "No sir. The props in there were outdated, strictly low income generators. They were in much greater demand years ago. As I previously stated, the warehouse mainly served as an off-site storage."

Martinez articulated further. "However, there were infrequent occasions when we leased or loaned some of the contents to local parades and sometimes, to other film studios on short term consignments, and on occasions to charity functions. I can produce the list of contents for your examination if necessary."

Axel confirmed their interest by jabbing Tinker softly in the side. "Yes, would be helpful, Mr. Martinez."

Martinez politely excused himself to retrieve the document. Schuler interjected, "Hey, you don't think that we torched our own place to collect insurance on depreciated items? Do you?"

Tinker calmly assured him. "No, we are here to collect the facts, Mr. Schuler."

Martinez returned. As he passed the document to Axel, he addressed Tinker. "We will co-operate sir. You'll notice when you examine the list, that all the contents were insured for a minimum. We don't stand to gain much. We probably won't re-build but rather spend the money to demolish what's left standing and clear the lot in order to place it up for sale."

Axel challenged Martinez. "Do you know of anyone who would want the warehouse burned?"

"No sir. I am surprised that arson enters into the equation." He was ever so polished. "That street is often the residence of midnight drunken hooligans. They tend to use the windows as arcade targets, or light fires out back to keep warm on winter nights. We've had some problem with drug usage in the back alleyway behind our lot but never had any problems in the daylight hours before. We share in employing a local security guard with five other property owners. The security reports back to us on unusual events and altercations."

Axel struck at the key issue. "I see from the list you provided that there was a large container inside."

"Container?" Schuler inquired.

"Oh, yes, there was," Martinez elaborated "that trailer was positioned in there over three years ago and belongs to a third party."

"A third party?" Tinker inquired.

"Yes, the warehouse was not an income generator so to cover a portion of our property taxes, we rented out extra space inside the warehouse to third parties. We even rented some space to another studio to store their props. That trailer you're referencing belongs to a nice lady."

"She?"

"Yes, would you like her name?"

"Absolutely." Axel replied without hesitation. Martinez left them for a second time, and as he did so Schuler stood, leaned over his desk, and as a great Hollywood director, startled both of them as he cried out, "Lights!

Camera! Action!" The lights were doused. Axel and Tinker sat stunned in a pitch black setting.

Two gangster-like mannequins on opposite sides of the room engaged in a shouting match and with no warning they buzzed laser beams in front of Axel and Tinker, who jumped in their seats. The streaks of incandescent blue pops were frightening; aqua reflections pulsed from Tinker's glazed head. The scene culminated with one of the mannequins suffering an open chest wound with profuse bleeding. The lights returned. All was quiet. No damage was noticeable in the props by neither Tinker nor Axel. They looked at each other in amazement.

Schuler roared with laughter as his belly bobbed up and down. "Great, eh? Fooled ya!"

"Did I read that you are also an illusionist, Mr. Schuler?"

"Yes," he boasted. "That was my original trade. I began as a master magician when I came to Hollywood years ago. I was employed as an illusionist in a carnival act, but the special effects of the glittering lights of Hollywood beckoned me. The rest is history."

Thumper had overlooked the fact that Schuler was a former illusionist in building his profile. Martinez joined them and handed Axel the document, which further itemized the destroyed contents in the warehouse. In addition, he volunteered the identity of the renter. "You wanted the lady's name that rented out space from us. Ah, her name is Karen Soetchling. We have a post office box number as a contact for her. She pays us twice a year faithfully."

"Does she ever come into the office?"

"She mails a cashier's check every time."

"How did she first find the space?"

"She answered an advertisement."

"Did you ever see her?" Axel kept plowing ahead.

"Yes, I met her when she moved the trailer into the warehouse, when she signed the contract. I gave her access keys to get into the property and the warehouse and she installed her own security system on the container itself."

"She volunteered to do that? Or you insisted?"

"That was none of our business how she secured the trailer and contents, Mr. Hawk."

"Did she install the phone line?"

"No, we allowed her to use the line which was already installed, and not used by us anymore. We added the phone line into her trailer, and the overhead to her billings. That was part of the deal- use our existing line." Axel was disappointed, but realized how convenient and crafty the move was.

Tinker probed. "What did she look like?"

"She had a Scandinavian look with blonde hair, tanned skin, very tall, and an attractive fit figure. She was pleasant enough and dressed respectable in a business suit. She spoke in a foreign accent. Honestly, I only conversed with her long enough to conduct our business."

"What did she need the space for?"

Martinez answered him specifically. "Not any of our business, Mr. Hawk. In the terms of the contract, it specifically states no drugs, no alcohol, no weapons to be stored on the premises; no certain flammable materials, no transfer of the lease to another party without our approval. I took the time to cover all these conditions with her, so other than that, it is none of our business. She understood and agreed and signed. She has been of no trouble to us."

Tinker spoke up to demand a copy of the lease. "No problem sir." Martinez departed again for the third time as Axel and Tinker braced themselves with white knuckles for another virtual onslaught, looking left and right and behind them. Schuler instead, asked, "Surely you don't think this Karen Soetchling burned the premises to collect on her insurance policy from the contents in her container?"

Tinker definitely wanted to divert any suspicion away from Karen Soetchling. "No sir." Martinez returned promptly to say, "She was a good tenant." Martinez presented a copy of the executed lease agreement to Tinker.

Tinker opened to the first page and informed Axel. "There is no address, no phone number, and no contact information other than a P.O. box number with a postal code."

"That's the way she wanted it sir. No problem with us as long as she paid her rent, which she did." It would be a chore for Thumper to locate the owner of this box number now, as Axel already deduced that another phony identification was used to obtain it. Tinker asked Martinez, "How many times did Ray-X visit the warehouse?"

"Only a few times a year, just to extract a few props and floats for parades on July fourth, Martin Luther King Day, Memorial Day, ah... Easter, Christmas festivities. Those were our only requests for props and facades. We always had a representative onsite if a third party was the borrower."

Schuler proudly piped up to add, "Rose Bowl parade on instances."

Martinez nodded to agree. "The materials inside were outdated for movies, even in today's cheesy genres."

"Can you ask your staff if they ever saw anyone else enter the trailer when they were there? Or see Ms Soetchling again?"

"Sure, I have your cards so I'll get back to you." Martinez was very cooperative.

Aaron Schuler grew impatient. "You said that you had three issues with us. What is the third one?"

"We have addressed two- the case of arson, and the contents of the warehouse, including the trailer. The third I think we have also covered, and that is the owner of the trailer. Mr. Schuler, did you ever see this lady at any social gatherings perhaps?"

Martinez replied for both of them. "Mr. Schuler never met her, only myself."

Axel had one last stab. "Mr. Schuler, did you ever hear her name at social gatherings or parties around town?" His head shook with a decisive negative.

Tinker issued instructions. "If this Ms Soetchling or her representative contacts you because of this incident, I want to be informed immediately. Please obtain a phone number and personal contact information."

"You have our word, sir."

"One more favor. If anyone else comes calling and asking questions about that trailer or about Ms Soetchling, call me at my office and speak to one of my people if I'm not there." Tinker was prepared to shake hands when Aaron Schuler seized his attention.

"There is one last issue," Schuler urgently replied. Tinker was curious. The room immediately was bathed in gold hues. Suddenly Schuler's desk was being tossed about as on stormy seas and was moving to the right out of view, in dark recesses as he waved at them in a sneer.

Axel and Tinker were left stumped as they watched Schuler retreat to the very edge of the room. Suddenly, the lights blinked, the room was fully lit and Schuler had disappeared. His desk, on the other hand, was back in front of them behind the picket fence as if it had never been removed.

Martinez assured them. "Aaron left at the beginning of the illusion. What you observed was a laser image of him. He can't resist teasing his adoring public. Integrate his knowledge of an illusionist with his expertise in special effects and you have a very, very mad but talented Aaron Schuler."

Martinez courteously escorted them outside and into the parking lot. On the way out, Martinez reinforced his future cooperation. After his departure, Tinker was left puzzled. "What did we learn from that rousing episode, Axel?"

"Well, Tink, they are telling us the truth, and if that is the case nothing much. The lair is permanently destroyed. Any evidence of M's double or multiple lives vanished. Karen Soetchling, ala Montilladan, would be a fool to contact them again and you and I both know that!"

Tinker was unfashionably quiet as they departed, so Axel called Speed to make efficient use of their time. Speed was direct. "Axel, no one else is cutting the papers that you are talking about except him. George Brissand's your suspect. I finally got an address for him. You want to check him out today?" Axel didn't hesitate. After conversing with Tinker, he barked instructions.

"We'll meet you in thirty minutes. Just case the location. Wait! On second thought, don't go near it until we arrive, but rather conceal yourself in some spot where you can spy on the entrance. Mentally record any traffic of people coming and going. Execute one walk to record license plates of any parked cars in the vicinity. I'm bringing the police with me." Tinker turned to glare at him.

"Excuse me," Axel apologized so Tinker could hear him, "let me rephrase that. I am accompanying the police." Tink gave him a thumbs up.

Speed confirmed. "Okay. Brissand's at 1019 Stewart Street. It is two blocks off of Route 49. If you exit on Mandy West, make a left, go under the freeway and turn right on Stewart, four blocks ahead." Axel noted the turns as Tinker poked him for information.

Speed concluded. "It's a rough neighborhood, but your baby's safe from any theft down here as long as Tinker rides with you." Axel's despondently replied with a sarcastic, "Ha, ha, but I'm driving a low-class rental while my beauty is in the body shop."

The experience at the bank was fruitless. "I'm so sorry", Jenna stated to Zoe as if it were her fault, "but I seldom saw Roy Spiller. He came into the bank on an irregular basis to withdraw large amounts of cash at one time. He rarely wrote checks even though I set up a checking account for him. I also set up three other accounts to purchase bonds because he wanted some of his cash converted into municipal bonds. There's also a safety deposit box."

Zee noticed the absence of any rings on Jenna's fingers so took a chance. "Don't take this the wrong way but...you are kinda cute. Did Roy ever hit on you? You two ever date?"

"I do take offense. Roy Spiller is the consummate gentleman. Always treats everyone, including me, with a cheerful greeting and respect. Roy always took the time to thank me profusely for any assistance. I hate to disappoint you, but I know nothing of his personal life." With Zoe's insistence, and without a search warrant, but a strong reference to the LAPD, Jenna finally agreed to an inspection of the contents of the safety deposit box. "As long as we conduct the inspection together, and in a closed booth."

In addition to some foreign bonds, Zoe discovered a birth certificate issued by the state of California under the name Roy Spillerman, cancelled checks of small amounts of no interest, some coins, and photographs of the suds gang with George sitting beside him, his arm draped around him. She asked for a photocopy of the birth certificate. Jenna obliged and left. As she did, Zee had even less luck with other documents. It was thirty minutes wasted, except for a further eulogy to Roy by Jenna, confirming further the outstanding qualities of the man and a confirmation of Roy's serious sources of income, probably from his acting gigs. She left hastily to drop the dental records by the police station and team up with Thumper back at the office. Thumper needed to focus now on Roy Spillerman and not Roy Spiller.

"Well, Axel, we are uneventful so far this morning."

"Not entirely. We eliminated Schuler as Romeo."

"Some consolation prize. I guess we just keep digging; we gotta make our own break on this case."

"It makes me feel heavyhearted Tinker, every time I hear Roy Spiller referenced. That man was held in the spirit of earnest, deepest respect. If only you heard what I did about his command of the troops on the beach. Reality show material." Tinker expressed some anxiety. "You shoulda confided in me sooner Axel. This case deepens with every turn."

"I am particularly uneasy about our conversation to the studio, for you informed me that Montilladan is using these drugs for a prolonged life, change shapes and fight bone and cell deterioration."

Eventually they navigated into a low-rent business district. As they reached the address, the street was dominated by three-story buildings, shops at ground level with apartments overhead, the apartments accessed directly through narrow neglected openings between the shops. Axel spied Speed standing at the nearest corner to the address, pacing back and forth, motioning toward a reserved parking spot for them.

"Any visitors?" Axel closed the vehicle's driver door and approached Speed directly; Tinker surveyed both sides of the street.

"No, it has been very quiet since I arrived. I can't confirm that Brissand's in there, Axel."

Tinker put his arm around Speed. "Axel informed me of your risks to find this gent's establishment. The city of Los Angeles thanks you kindly, Speed, if you are correct. Tinker's the name." They had met through Axel before but rekindled as they shook hands and Speed returned the salutation. "Thanks. There's his establishment, the one across the street with the battered looking bluish door. Apartment number five, third floor."

"Do you have your cell phone with you Speed?"

"Yes." He waved it.

Axel gave him instructions. "Remain here at street level and alert us of any incoming characters on my cell, especially if Brissand shows. I'll leave my mobile turned on."

Speed nodded an affirmative. Meanwhile, Axel and Tinker fastidiously ascended to the third floor, Tinker grimacing on each step. The stairs were littered with debris of aluminum soda cans, half eaten bags of chips, wads of gum and stained pieces of clothing. The smell of grunge suffocated them. Their arrival was frequently announced by the multitude of squeaky creaks, which were accentuated by Tinker's weight.

Arriving, there were three flats on the third level. Brissand's door could have easily been smashed open by a swift kick from Tinker, but Tinker rapped, instead. With no answer after five raps, Tinker yelled.

"Brissand, if you are in there, open up! This is the Los Angeles Police. Open up sir at once!" No stirring inside. The only sound was made by flies hovering at an open window at the end of the hall. A couple from the neighboring apartment sheepishly peeked out and Tinker menacingly waved them to disappear. Tinker pounded harder, once more summoning Brissand. A squeaky hinge alerted them to another intrusion into the hallway by a thin blonde man decked in underwear briefs.

He addressed them in a low voice. "I haven't seen him today and I usually do, sir. I don't believe that he's around today. Is he in trouble?"

Tinker was annoyed. "Thank you very much for the tip. Now please retire inside your unit until we have completed our official police business here."

Surprisingly, Tinker turned the handle and the door revealed itself to be unlocked. Before they entered, he withdrew his Glock22 from his holster, ordering Axel to stay a distance behind him at all times. Axel concurred. "Good idea."

The apartment was in a shambles. Brissand obviously was not an ardent subscriber to good housekeeping. Clothes were strewn around the living room over moth-eaten furniture. Axel looked to the left and was disgusted at the dirty dishes piled in the sink in a galley kitchen, the odor of ten day old garbage attracting a crowd of multi-legged crawlers. They ventured deeper into the flat where an antiquated television was on low volume setting. The furniture in the dwarfed living area was second-hand junk. Suddenly, Tinker surprised Axel by holding his revolver high over his shoulder on alert.

Tinker's tensed hulk suddenly surged and blocked Axel's way, his legs spread. As he turned back to Axel, his face now brimmed with intense ferocity. A warning sign of an approaching struggle? Tinker motioned to Axel to remain on the spot in the middle of the living area by pointing to the spot while he tip-toed to an adjacent room. Axel intersected Tinker's concern as a pungent sweet offensive odor swept up into his nostrils and almost induced vomiting. Axel was frozen on the spot for ten seconds when he heard Tinker distinctly utter, "Jesus."

Tinker exited the bedroom, his arms limp by his side. "You got enough nerve to try and see if the body in here is Brissand? I gotta warn you. It ain't pretty. He's been dead a day I reckon."

Axel proceeded sheepishly to the entry, needing only a glance to recognize George's curly blonde locks, his already rotund nude figure bloated to bursting with death. Blood from his body had seeped out of his being, soaking the mattress and floor rugs with a bowel-of-the-earth musty odor. There was a bullet hole to the side of his head, two more through the heart. Mercifully it was administered as he slept in peace, Axel hoped.

Tinker immediately summoned assistance from his office and instructed Axel, "I'll remain behind. I want to be here when the experts examine this sight for fingerprints, hair, and other evidence. I don't know how I parachuted into this nightmare of mixed-up sexes and senseless murders, but I now know that this escapade officially has two dead bodies, one at the warehouse and one here and possibly a third in Spiller. Couple that with arson and I gotta tell Felix the whole story pronto. I'm sorry, Axel, but Felix has to know. This really is an official police nightmare."

They were interrupted by a callback from his unit. Tinker filed instructions while Axel patiently waited for Tinker's call to end. "Keep a sharp eye, Hawk. Tell Zoe what has happened here. I'll also stay behind to interview any witnesses. I'll talk to other tenants. I'll catch up to you and Zee later and brief you. Keep Thumper posted of your whereabouts and keep your cell phones on so I can find you. I suggest that you leave before Felix arrives." Axel covered his nostrils and quickly turned away.

"And Axel! Please try and stay out of any more trouble."

Axel turned, white-faced. "Tinker, I have a bad feeling about all this." He moved closer and whispered to him. "She's cleaning up loose ends. She's disappearing soon- forever. I know she is. She's leaving no traces behind. Arson in the warehouse, murdering poor Roy, now Brissand. She's bolting Tinker. We've got to find her."

Tinker surmised solemnly. "You and Zoe and Thumper, you're loose ends. If anything happens to my lady, I'll never forgive us."

"I'll call Zee and warn her right now."

"And what about Lacey Sills? Loose end or antagonist?" Axel was silent. "I'll warn her, too, even though she's on our list of suspects. Tink, Zoe briefed you on what we discovered, that is all the contents in the trailer in the burned-out warehouse?"

"Yes."

"A virtual factory of a shape-shifter, a chameleon; she can look like anyone she wants, and play the role to perfection. So it is my turn to warn you. Never let your guard down. She could be anyone, even the hooker at the corner down the block, a businessman in full attire, even one of L.A.'s traffic policemen, even the arriving coroner. Anyone Tink. She's the ultimate deadly masquerader. Be damn careful. Look everyone in the eye for the truth."

"You just gave Ole Tink the chills, but I will be careful. I'll tell Felix to keep the press at bay because we don't want to alert or scare her. Man whatever her true motives are she's using murder as a means to achieve them. She's number one on our wanted list."

Axel descended the stairs rapidly and punched in contacts. "Zee, Brissand's been murdered. Shot three times. Listen to me. She's tidying up loose ends and that could mean you and Thumper and me. Close up shop for the afternoon and disappear until we meet later. Call Lacey and speak directly to her body guard. And get the body guard's credentials while you have him on the line." Zee was rattled but heard every word.

Speed anxiously overheard as Axel barked out orders on the cell and deduced that he should execute a hasty departure after Axel informed him of the murder in a number of graphically chosen words.

"Brissand's dead as you heard me tell Zoe." Axel watched Speed's face change to long and pale.

"You think the person you're searching for did it, don't you?"

"Definitely." Axel tugged at Speed's arm as they stood in a recessed entry to a local store. Whispering, he said, "Speed, take a circuitous route home. Stop for gas, maybe a soda, but keep a lookout for any tails. If you suspect one, call me and I'll alert Tinker and we'll have the police intercept."

So, you've discovered George? Who cares? Who gives a shit? And who is your dorky looking friend. Doesn't look like any cop to me. That's it; put your arm around him. Assure him he's safe. Brief him on what you know, which is nothing. Whisper, psst, psst. Spin, spin, spin. You haven't clued in yet, have you? And the hour is late. You only have a few hours left stupid. I'm safe. I'm in a hurry to leave or I'd take the opportunity to stroll down the street and walk right by you two, maybe clumsily stumble into you. Maybe fire a shot through your heart and conduct a hasty retreat.

Now, what the hell? Your friend's leaving? So soon? And there you are, looking around, that's it, keep panning, oh, I love how you're trying to be so inconspicuous and I know that it is you. A little more. Come on, Axel. Keep going. Ew, I love it. You're almost here. Come on, a little more, that's it. Yes! A buzz! Eye contact. You see me. You're looking right at me and me at you and you haven't got a clue. What do ya think? Am I hot stuff? Or maybe just a cold-hearted murderess? I got better things to do.

"So long sucker."

He swore to Axel to be vigilant in his activities, keeping a stern lookout for unusual characters, keeping his cell handy. Axel thanked him for his assistance, encouraged him to submit his expenses. "Let's make plans for a sporting event in two weeks." As Speed disappeared from sight, Axel stood at the street corner with snakes crawling in his stomach.

Was she here now? Cloaked? Watching him? Targeting Speed? Stalking Tinker? Laughing at him as her climax unfolded? And Tinker and he helpless? Was murder becoming a routine event for her? Was she here to enjoy the discovery of Brissand's dead body? He was skeptical about the sincerity of every face he spied. There was the butcher sweeping the street, the badly attired loafer with baggy jeans sauntering away from him, but pausing to look over his shoulder at him! A fixed stare. Now but broken as he turned the corner. The well-tanned lady with two bags of groceries. Where did she materialize from? There was a solitary person behind the wheel of a black Mercury across the street. Stoid. Staring at him from inside the recess of the vehicle as he finally made his gaze in that direction. He calmly stepped off the curb toward it just as the engine sounded and the vehicle sped away. Those eyes were blue. Was it her? And now as he turned and looked in the opposite direction up the street, there was a tall slender woman crossing in the intersection, turning her head, staring right at him. He shivered. Why? It didn't look like her. Paranoia?

Racing to the comfort of Zee consumed his thoughts as he peered far up the street at the Mercury turning out of sight. He moved to his rental, strapped himself in, lobbed his head back, adjusted the rear view mirrors every other second to study the scene outside. What was out of place? He pulled out and departed the scene.

Zoe was on the phone when he arrived, taking copious notes, signaling Axel to remain calm until she finished her call. Axel deduced from her polite dialogue and bubbly nature that Jean-marc was the recipient of her flattery. At length, they finished. Before she had a chance to brief him, Axel informed Zee about the discovery of Gorgeous George.

"I never much liked George, but he deserved a jail sentence for his worst crime, not death. Tinker kicked me out. Official police business now he said. Gotta inform Felix. But Tink knows what to look for- signs of Montilladan! Either M found what she was looking for and killed Briss, or Briss gave her the copies of her documents and she wasted him."

Expressing further sympathy, Axel lamented. "Zee, you never met Brissand. He was a jolly character, great sense of humor, likeable sort. I'll bet when she shot him, she never gave it a second thought. I wonder if he begged for his life but, more likely, he died in his sleep." He raised his voice to her. "And why are you still here? I want you lying low. She could be out there in our parking lot now, planning to rush us!"

"Chances are, Axel, if Briss' place was ransacked as badly as you described, she found what she was looking for in Briss' apartment, pocketed the evidence, and killed him." Facetiously she razzed him. "The day's not a total waste. At least you discovered Romeo in Aaron Schuler. Right?"

"Okay, okay," Axel threw his arms up, "I admit that you were correct about Aaron Schuler. He's not Romeo, not even close." Axel conveyed the rest of the meeting to Zoe, including the not so mysterious Karen Soetchling and Schuler's attempt to scare Tink and him with a shoot-out."

Zoe was eager to tell of her news. "First, my trip to the bank to see Jenna turned up only Roy's birth certificate and confirmed his cash assets. His real name was Roy Spillerman. Here's the big break. Jean-marc visited and confirmed that Montilladan has two bank accounts in Andorra. Montilladan either withdraws or transfers large sums of money in cash and bonds every time she is on the continent. Over the past year and even as late as two weeks ago, however, she was remotely transferring funds. As Constance and Lieber told you, there still are significant amounts in the bank. Brace yourself for this next piece of info." Axel slumped behind his desk.

"I am sitting down, Zee. Spill it. Hurry. We have to vacate the premises."

"There is a co-signee on both accounts." She was rifling through her copious notes. "Montilladan and Adam Bartlett!"

Axel was excited, but then it sunk in. "What? Bartlett, as in two tees at the end Bartlett? As in the same spelling as our Dr. Larry Bartlett?"

"Exactly."

"Adam? Not Larry Bartlett? Adam Bartlett?"

"Yes." Zoe was searching for a specific file on the desk. "Here's Thumper's profile of Larry Bartlett. By the way Axel, Larry Bartlett's middle name is Jason, not Adam, just in case you are wondering. In addition, he has no brothers by that name, no sons by his marriage to Muriel, never been married before and his father's name was John Wade Barlett."

"But Zee, rather coincidental to be a different Bartlett, considering our confirmation that Montilladan and Larry Bartlett know each other, and they were linked by the purple crystals, by dates, by the board. How about a name change? An alias? Papers crafted for his future?"

"Axel, you're the one who ruled out Bartlett as Romeo. And me, too, I vote he's not Romeo. Having any second thoughts?"

"Oh, this is so damn perplexing. Damn it. Bartlett's such an unlikely candidate to be Romeo. He just doesn't fit the bill even though he was caught in the act by Mrs. Whitehurst's spy of smooching Montilladan in the parking lot at Capers. We keep uncovering more clues. Where is the linkage Zee?"

"Axel we need a meeting with Bartlett."

"Tinker and I will have to wait until tomorrow. Thumper's trying to arrange it soonest unless I can convince Tinker to barge in on Bartlett tonight. Official police business. Damn, I don't get it. Who is Adam Bartlett? Where did the Hell did he materialize out of? Did Jean-marc get a description of Adam Bartlett? From the bank employees?"

"Jean-marc says that no one has ever seen Adam Bartlett. Montilladan has performed all the banking transactions to date. The bank employees that Jean-marc interviewed did confirm the identity of Montilladan as the person who physically visited the bank numerous times. The address on the bank accounts is Montilladan's California address."

"This is perplexing. I better call Tinker within the hour. We need to interrogate Bartlett sooner rather than later. I think we should make our move tonight. If I ask Tinker to barge in on police business, we are sure to secure an appointment."

"Axel, there's always the possibility that Montilladan is playing mind games with us, like having Brissand manufacture papers to create the false existence of Adam Bartlett."

"I'm so confused by this development."

"There's more bad news. Jean-marc informed me that even though there are significant funds in the account now, the manager informed him that more funds of the two Andorran bank accounts are being transferred during the next five days as both accounts are pillaged, per instructions of Montilladan, before the accident. The bank is legally obligated to perform the tasks and there is not a thing that we can do about it. Unless we can obtain an International court order in twenty-four hours, applicable in Andorran courts, Jean-marc has exhausted his honest efforts and most of the monies will fly away Axel."

"Doesn't Montilladan need Adam Bartlett's consent for the transfer?"

"No, Montilladan has sole transfer rights; Adam has personal withdrawal rights."

"What? Do we know where the funds are being transferred to?"

"No, that's confidential so Jean-marc was unable to find out, but it goes without saying they will be transferred to her permanent residence, or find their way there circuitously."

"If only we could get that information, by any means. This is just a part of her criminal act."

"Jean-marc discussed this issue with his peers and he apologizes because he can't get a court order to discover the destination. There isn't enough evidence to warrant it. Since the transfer papers were signed previously, she's been planning this for some time. The bank is just following the executed orders of Montilladan." Axel's spirit sunk.

"Obviously, premeditated murder; obviously, pre-meditated transfers. She just continues to stay three steps ahead of us. That's our problem, Zee, and we're still not thinking like her. It's amazing. She was ahead of us at the warehouse, at Fosse's, at Brissand's, at the Andorran banks. What's her next move?

Think Zee. Where would she go next? It's the only chance we have, to beat her there."

Zee sighed. "More bad news. The report from the fire chief arrived by way of Barry in Tink's office. There's nothing left of the trailer. It was completely disintegrated. Our assailants fled, and the one charred remains of a human at the scene left nothing to identify the corpse. You always said that we have to make our own breaks, Axel, well, we are on information overload. If ever we needed a break on a case, let it be now or she flees from us forever. This whole case stinks." She slammed her wad of papers onto the table in disgust.

Zoe sighed. "Sounds like you're right, too; she vanishes in the next few days. By the news from Andorra, Brissand's death, and your haunting, we may already be too late."

Axel couldn't stop thinking about it. "Who is this Adam Bartlett? Zoe, it has to be a new forged identity, just like hers. Presto! Eureka! Zoe, Montilladan is Adam Bartlett! She forged a new male identity to divert suspicion from her new female persona. That's why she murdered Brissand. Only he knew of Adam Bartlett."

"Pasta for dinner, anyone?" Thumper entered with a tub of pasta take-out and commenced to place three settings of plastic knives and forks and napkins around the conference table.

"Pasta? At a time like this? I'm glad you two are taking my previous warning so seriously."

Thumper was rational. "We have to eat Axel so we may as well eat and discuss the case. You can eat and pace the room at the same time, while Zee and I eat. Hey, Axel, that is what I ordered for you- pace and pasta. In addition, I believe you require sustenance for your meeting with Dr. Montoya."

Axel recognized the tiny packets of seasoning that Thumper was pulling out of the bag. "I don't want to offend Dr. Montoya so light on the garlic."

Zee jabbed Axel in the ribs. "Ooh, want to have good breath for Dr. Montoya, do we? I am the one who ordered the early dinner into the office. Now I have to retrieve the wine." Zoe departed momentarily and he slumped further into his chair to rest. With eyes closed, he examined all the characters in this play while the sweet odor of the fettuccini wafted up his nostrils.

Tinker called to interrupt his thoughts. "Axel, Brissand's been dead for nearly thirty hours. The fingerprint lab is working overtime in his apartment, in the hall, in the stairwell, at the ground entry. There are no visible signs of Montilladan's presence at the crime scene, but we'll keep poking around. I did discover a huge stash of forged papers, some copies, some originals, and some dating back five years, hidden under some floorboards under the bed. This will keep our immigration people occupied for months. However, the boards were out of place under the carpet so I figure she found what she was looking for."

Tinker was heard conversing and returned. "Brissand was most likely shot with a Smith and Wesson, nine millimeter which can be easily concealed in a handbag. No one heard anything; no one witnessed any visitors to Briss in the past three days. It was a clean murder and clean escape."

Axel in return asked Tinker to clear his schedule tomorrow. "Thumper will send you tomorrow's venue. We have to visit Dr. Larry Bartlett's offices early in the morning, although I prefer to visit him tonight. Can you make yourself available later this evening? I know he'll respond to police business."

"Why?"

"Zoe found out that Montilladan has foreign accounts with a co-signor named Bartlett. I figure it is worth a talk with Larry. Plus you and I agreed that the purple crystals are implicating him."

He passed Bartlett's address and contact info on the phone to Tinker and briefed him further on the status of the Andorran accounts capped by the bad news of the imminent transfer of funds.

"Axel! There is no way you are visiting this dude without me. I'll get back to you soonest on my availability tonight." Tinker was loud and expressive but thoughtful enough to inquire how Axel's stamina was holding up in the face of his wounds.

"The scrapes are healing and the soreness subsiding. Considering all the recent close calls, I calculate that our luck has run out. The next close call could spell disaster."

"We'll talk later bud."

Axel turned his attention to Zee and, they agreed that Lacey be briefed on the full events of the day, so Zoe grabbed her dinner and relocated to outer office to contact Lacey. While Axel ate he overheard her ten minute conversation and by Zoe's dialogue, assumed Lacey was not happy about the sudden twist of events, which forced the police into the middle of their space.

As with Tinker, she did not inform her of the visitation to Dr. Montoya's residence tonight. She did, however, tell Lacey that a key witness to this case, Brissand, was dead, and unfortunately, the evidence seemed to indicate that Montilladan was the prime suspect given the papers that Montilladan now probably possessed. She received a re-confirmation of Lacey's intent to have a bodyguard present— always. Lacey promised to send the credentials of her guard.

Within twenty minutes of the termination of that phone call to Lacey, Axel's dinner conversation with Thumper was rudely terminated as Nikki appeared in a tight strapping yellow pant suit. With a gloomy sullen entrance and stare-down glare, her body language told Axel to excuse Thumper. Axel used his head motion to Thumper, but Zee sat down beside him.

"I come here to represent Lacey's interests. She called me to say that she suddenly is not happy that you brought the police into this case so early. Granted, she did agree with Zoe to make a deal and Tinker's name was mentioned."

"Sorry, Nikki, but today's news brings the death of a George Brissand, the same Brissand that probably forged a passport and other alternate identifications for Montilladan. Brissand's murder is a police investigation Nikki. Whether Lacey approves of it or not, this is now official police business with the murder of George Brissand. Zoe just briefed her within the hour. Seems you arrived here hastily."

"Lacey called me. Luckily, I was in the neighborhood."

"You have to go back to her and emphasize that this new development has thrust Tinker into the middle of our dealings. Please, Nikki, take our side for our safety."

Nikki interrupted him to back off and switch topics. "Okay, however, Lacey wants me to affirm the deal personally with you, Axel, that you will honor her, that you agree to allow her to speak first to Montilladan when you find her." Thumper's eerie implications floated in both their minds as Nikki continued. "She needs to hear truths from Montilladan and about all that has occurred. Confirm it right now!"

"We'll try our best. Tink may get to M first but, if we do, we'll keep the bargain. You can confirm that much to Lacey." Zoe glared at Nikki and added, "Reluctantly."

Nikki slung her oversized purse over the arm of a chair at the table and rested. Axel found an excuse to rise, sit beside her, clutch her arm in arm.

"The word complex does not do this affair justice Nikki. Someone tried to kill Zoe and me yesterday by frying us in a warehouse fire; now a key witness in this case has been murdered. You know darn well that I had previously been beaten and also had my house broken into. In a twist of why we were hired, the evidence indicates that Montilladan is either the murderer, or an accomplice. In reality, Montilladan is deeply implicated in all these crimes and if Tinker has his way, she'll be in cuffs and isolation and interrogation with he and Felix long before we intercept her. Even worse, he's probably briefing Felix right now. There could be an APB out for her, a detention for questioning, maybe even a leap to murder charge, I don't know. It's up to Felix. It's up to the evidence."

He had her attention. "I'm sorry Nikki. Tomorrow, after a critical visit with a Dr. Larry Bartlett, I think we should meet with Lacey. For her, it won't be pleasant- the murder, the arson, the attempt on our lives. Zee keeps reminding me that we didn't sign up for this. Tell Lacey this was not of our choosing and it will not be of our choosing if we locate Montilladan first and a police order prevents us from keeping our deal. You realize we can't promise?"

Nikki didn't offer a protest. "Lacey didn't tell me all of this."

"She doesn't know all these facts yet. Lacey hired us for truths. She stood in this office and summarized our future efforts as the search for Montilladan. We will conclude this search. We will locate her but, when we do, you need to prepare her for the worst. I feel like you are the best option to do this."

"I'm sorry to hear about this attempt on your life yesterday, I mean lives plural, you and Zoe. I never dreamed it would lead to this. What a mess. You've never been so close to a murder case before, Axel." Nikki bowed her head. "Be careful. I still like you Axel. I am mortified at how dangerous this case has become but, through all the complexities, you must try to remain loyal to she who pays your bills."

"Zee, Tinker and I will find M. I'm sure of it. You just have to understand that the evidence is mounting against M, that she is possibly guilty of two murders, arson and two attempted murders."

Zoe interrupted. "And a beating of Axel. Reality check, Lacey's paying us to hunt down a very dangerous criminal. In the final scene, we won't misplace our loyalties, but I guarantee you that there will have to be a balance between our goals and justice. I obviously briefed Lacey one hour ago, but it would be a great favor if you could do so again."

Nikki's heart still raced from Axel's earlier remarks about Montilladan's motives. "I'll talk to Lacey and pave the way for your briefing tomorrow. Two o'clock work?"

"As long as we're alive."

Nikki appeared to be lost in thought. "Okay." She nodded an affirmation and continued, "I'll break the news gently to her about Montilladan's deep involvement and be careful. Any other contacts or favors you need from me, don't hesitate to call." She stood as Axel did and gave Axel a tight hug, and waved an extended goodbye to Zee on her way out, and as her visit Tuesday, departed suddenly without fanfare.

Axel pounded out a phone number as Zoe stared caringly at him. He made eye contact with her and picked up her vibes. "Mrs. Whitehurst. This is Axel Hawk. I know this may be a sudden and perhaps inconvenient time, but Zoe Burns and I are coming over to your house. No, no, no, no. Please don't interrupt. Please don't leave. We have to talk Mrs. Whitehurst. We'll be there in about an hour and a half. Please confirm you'll be home. The Colonel, too? Good. Thank you. I appreciate it. Goodbye."

Zee was astounded. "What prompted that?"

"The photos aren't enough. We need that original physical written report generated by the private detective now! Time's running out."

Thumper returned, "Got a hankering to be with you guys." As they ate in silence, each confounded by all the turns of the case, Axel found solace by staring at her, a truly beautiful person. She caught him making serious eye contact, noticed his inspections so she kicked gently him from under the table.

"So what are we drinking tonight?"

"It is a Louis M Martini Cabernet Sauvignon from Napa Valley, 2007. Is has deep rich odors and tastes of blackberry and currents with a spicy tinge. Notice the elegant strong finish that persists." As she spoke, she gazed into her glass and swirled the contents softly.

"Ooh, what do you think Hawkman?"

"I'd rather have my amber beer, sparkling, golden colors and big, bold taste with a faint buzz finish but, not bad this Cab…not bad Zee. Good choice."

She smiled at him. "Don't give me any crap. I know you like this one." He guzzled it down to her grunt of disgust. After the snack, Axel changed into a clean set of casual clothes, tan slacks and Dodger blue shirt, which he had brought to the office, and shaved for Dr. Montoya while Zee just sat and watched, and worried.

Soon they were winding their way to the Whitehurst estate in separate vehicles, soon to be on route to his critical rendezvous with Dr. Montoya. Axel listened to the radio. The tune was "You are so beautiful to me." His mind was definitely not straight.

THURSDAY NIGHT

The performance of two days ago was recreated by ambling across the grassy expanse to announce his arrival, except this time he was accompanied by Zee. Once again the door seemed to be slightly ajar, and as they drew nearer, déjà vu, Mrs. Whitehurst thrust it open, traipsing outside to intercept them successfully. She was seen to lock the door behind her and purposefully pocket the key in one of the oversized pockets. Her displeasure was quick to surface as they spied her taut grey pencil lips. For a person of petite stature, she possessed a very dominating presence.

"The Colonel is preoccupied with a nap and does not deserve to be disturbed. He is very tired from the recent events and as usual, you are impertinent Mr. Hawk. We did you a favor yesterday and still you are still imposing on us. I agreed on the phone to see you because I have already learned of your tenacity. You are so ungrateful by placing these further demands on us. What do you two snoops want now?" Axel and Zoe stood as stone, patiently awaiting the tirade to conclude.

Axel graciously motioned to Kathleen to situate herself on a wooden crafted bench to the left of the front entry with he and Zoe positioned at each end, leaving her room in the middle. Mrs. Whitehurst finally sat down when Axel motioned a second time. Kathleen Whitehurst was impatient. "I have errands to perform and I must tend to the Colonel's needs when he awakens, so be quick and be gone. What is so important that begs my attention?"

Axel leaned forward, hands on knees, positioning himself to view her face. "We have two topics to discuss with you, Mrs. Whitehurst. We do sincerely apologize for the intrusion. Firstly, we demand the truth from you. A witness to possible crimes that Montilladan has committed has been murdered. Yesterday, someone tried to kill Zoe and I because we are ever so close to discovering some evil truths about Montilladan's life."

For the first time in their brief relationship, Kathleen Whitehurst was staring at Axel with a degree of concern and perhaps a hint of interest. Did Axel even detect a miniscule swipe of respect?

268

"Zoe and I want an answer, Mrs. Whitehurst. What caused you to hate him so? Or should I dare say, what event caused you to develop extreme disappointment in your Lacey? Cause you inner embarrassment? We absolutely have to know if we are to achieve justice and swiftly conclude this case. You can share your burden with us Mrs. Whitehurst, and trust us to keep it secret for we only want to help Lacey, the Colonel and you. Please, Zee and I are your allies."

Zoe reinforced the message. "We are all on the same team, I promise. We will protect your words sanctimoniously Mrs. Whitehurst." As she turned to Zee, Zoe softly pleaded. "Mrs. Whitehurst, please find it within you to help us."

There was no sniffling, no sobbing, no remorse, only an extreme bitterness swelling in her as her teeth clenched her bottom lip. After a precursory glance at both of them, she snapped back. "You know." There was an extended pause, a complete silence in the air. "Don't you?" Axel did not hesitate.

"Yes, of Montilladan's double life and yes, we know." As Axel stared, he was mesmerized by her obsidian eyes, appearing to have souls with hues of lost hopes dancing about in them as the breeze lifted shadows in and out of the bench.

Zoe offered her hope. "We can help each other. We promise. We must hear your thoughts first. Please, Axel and I are so concerned that Montilladan is planning to vanish forever; possibly eliminate us before she departs." For an instant, she meditated.

Gazing fixedly onto the vast front expanse, she was as if one of her granite statues, and she commenced. "He...came... here... one night rather intoxicated, stoned perhaps, I couldn't tell. Lacey wasn't ready to depart. She was upstairs showering. He came to drive Lacey back to her loft. The Colonel had driven Lacey to our place earlier that afternoon. We never did get along, this Montilladan and I. I knew in my heart that our Lacey could have done better than him, but Lacey was always so stubborn you know. Once her mind was made up, it was impossible for the Colonel and me to change it. Having said that, our Lacey has always been an impressionable child."

Now her voice trembled. "The Colonel departed right after dinner for a meeting at his lodge, was away at a social gathering with some of his retired military colleagues. Montilladan and I sat alone in discomfort of our kitchen. I told him that I had discovered some information damaging to him by having a private detective tail him. I threatened to reveal it to Lacey unless he agreed to stop seeing our Lacey."

Mrs. Whitehurst struggled with the next words. Zoe and Axel both captured her continued references to our Lacey. "I showed him a sample of the photos where he was carousing with other women at parties, departing with them, kissing them, one photo even fondling them. I withheld these photos from you yesterday. It was my most damning evidence and I didn't want you to have them." She spoke with a slow burn. "I have not shared these with the Colonel either."

"I showed the photos of him in dress as a woman. The hired PI took these as Montilladan left a residence in the middle of the night and followed Montilladan to a nightclub. I struggled to understand what was happening. Why would a male want to dress up as a woman? Montilladan was a very complex character."

Kathleen perked up. Her voice was strong. "All hell broke loose in my kitchen. First, M was angry, cussed at me for being a meddler. I feared for my life, as Montilladan quietly leaned over and called me unspeakable debasing names, words I had not heard before, addressing me in the voice of a demon, and threatening me. Suddenly in the maelstrom, a disquieting calm came over this creature. He salivated as a jackal, resting both elbows on the table, waiting to devour me, and then whispered to me, 'So do you know what I am? Male or female? Or maybe both?' Montilladan stated that if I decided to ever breathe a word to anyone of his private affairs, or to Lacey, he would ruin Lacey's reputation as a goddess and an actress. Forever! He reminded me how powerful he was." Kathleen swallowed hard.

"It was then that Montilladan informed me that he was a male impersonator, that he was a female, as he, she, he, she, and Lacey and she, she... he spoke to me that she...that is they were conducting a romance as females. I almost had a stroke at those words. My heart raced, my chest ached in pulses, a tightness tugging at my heart. I had no idea that this would be the secret I would uncover that Montilladan was a male impersonator. It was the last thing I would have ever guessed."

Her body shakes came in an onslaught. Zoe and Axel allowed her to recompose herself as she brushed aside Zoe's motion for help. "When did this encounter occur?" Axel inquired.

"About one month before Montilladan died." She tossed her head back and forth to look at both of them.

"I felt ice water in my veins, an anger burn in the pit of my body as he, I mean she continued to fix her glare on me. It was astonishing as Montilladan, the male, changed her voice, and opened her shirt again to reveal small breasts, smooth, very feminine, devoid of bodily hair. She commanded me to shut my mouth about the joke she had played on Hollywood or else, because Lacey was now part of this plan of deceit. Lacey would suffer as an accomplice."

Kathleen paused for effect. "She commanded me to not ever, ever interfere in Lacey's life again, or else."

Kathleen Whitehurst had told all with a brave face, but now she placed her hands to her mouth, bowed her head, and in an assault of cement tears, she commenced a squealing. Zoe hugged her tight while Axel, on his knees in front of her, clasped his hands in hers. "Why would our dear, dear Lacey ever want to take part in such a deliberate ruse? Or be intimate with such a vile creature?"

The sobbing ended when she grunted, inhaled with a loud sniffle. "The Colonel doesn't know anything about this. You must never let him discover this. I love that man until my last breath of life and Lacey's involvement in such deceit and practices would kill him. Lacey is his proudest possession. It is more than just the idea of being female lovers you understand, it is this terrible plot that this person played out with fellow actors, the accolades as the fans, you know, peers, well, you know. I must live out my life to protect the Colonel from these secrets. I believe that Montilladan was wrong to do this and my private investigator is sworn to secrecy, too."

Axel felt compelled to add. "The Colonel has two, lovely possessions."

Kathleen stumbled through gravelly words. "The Colonel and I are too old, too set in our ways, too conservative, too stubborn, to understand some of today's changes in social behavior. Perhaps, if Lacey had disclosed this open unusual, romantic interlude up front to us, things would have been different. But the grand deception, this is all too difficult for me to accept, and I know for the Colonel to accept. I know society is accepting these relationships, but this practice goes beyond that acceptance with the deceits of all those people by Lacey and M in their profession. I know that Montilladan was primarily responsible for this. I know it! But my..." She just stopped talking.

Zoe assured her, "You have our word that we will protect the interests of you and the Colonel. However, in the end, it may be in the hands of others to decide what truths will be revealed. Investigative journalism runs deep these days."

Axel sat beside her to place his arm around her, too. "You were afraid that if we dug too deep into Montilladan's past, we would discover and reveal these facts? That's why you tried to buy us off?"

Kathleen nodded. "Reveal them through your former girlfriend, Nikki Louden, the social reporter. Oh, yes, I know about Ms. Louden. Lacey mentions Nikki often, and of her connections to major news through her syndicated column online. She told me of your strong friendship with Nikki. It made me nervous. I panicked. I was afraid if you discovered too much all would be lost before I could drive Montilladan away."

Zoe took her hand. "So you were not aware that Lacey had revealed these factors of Montilladan's double life to us from the beginning?"

"No, I assumed that she hadn't and I was terrified to ask. I calculated that a healthy bonus might deter you. I miscalculated your ethics. I am sorry for the disrespect that I showed you in our first meeting, Mr. Hawk. Will you please accept my honest apology?" She turned her head and in her sad eyes Axel was compelled to nod a yes. Axel wanted conclusion so he exposed the second purpose.

"Could we borrow the complete investigative report? The original report of the investigator? We need it and all the photos. Could you please trust us with it just for a day or two until this affair is concluded?"

Mrs. Whitehurst stood, asked to be excused, marched as in regiment to unlock the door just as a ceremony of tears rode down the outline of her cheeks dispensing themselves in her facial wrinkles. Axel and Zoe waited impatiently on the bench, lost in their thoughts for her return. "Axel, I can't believe we're in the middle of this mess." She had no more time to speak as Mrs. Whitehurst strode forward, holding a large brown envelope. With conviction, she encountered Axel.

"Even before you spoke, I figured that this is one of the two reasons that you referenced. There are few pages, but it is insightful." She voluntarily thrust the package toward Axel.

"So here it is, the report from the detective and you have my permission to use the contents as you wish. I didn't volunteer this earlier for obvious reasons as the detective trespassed onto Montilladan's property and caught Lacey and Montilladan in some awkward moments. That infraction seems minor now that you have informed me of the attempt on your lives. Colonel doesn't know of this trespass either."

Axel unfortunately had to stab her but had to know. "You confronted Lacey with all these facts, didn't you? Your sadness runs too deep." Kathleen Whitehurst froze. Her sorrowful eyes darted back and forth.

"Foolishly, yes. It drove a stake into my heart to hear her talk of her love and admiration of Montilladan, her awareness of Montilladan's games, but especially as she described herself in love and as respecting Montilladan's secret from Hollywood. This is all so darn confusing to an old woman like me set in her ways. You will have to excuse me. Heartbreaking might be a more accurate description. It is the lifestyle that she has chosen. I haven't convinced myself to respect her decision yet. Most of all, selfishly, I prefer not to read about it in any public journals as I said earlier."

Axel took her hand. "We will guard this information with our highest discretion."

Mrs. Whitehurst moved closer and placed her hand on top of his, which held her other. He thought how it didn't seem as cold as the first time they met. "Mr. Hawk, can you find it in your heart to forgive an old foolish woman who lives in past values and who treasures only what is important to her husband, and dedicates to protect him from?" She never concluded her request as phlegm choked her passageway. Axel appreciated her position to protect the Colonel.

"We are friends, Kathleen." Moving forward he spread his arms wide and hugged her tightly, as he felt her boney hands dig into his back for dear life, her tiny head bury itself in his chest, felt the help she was summoning from them. When she released, she startled them with an inquiry, "You stated earlier that Montilladan is alive. She was responsible for the murder of her stand-in? Wasn't she?" Axel did not want to create more consternation for her. He chose his words carefully.

"There are some irregularities of the accident which need to be explained away. There exists that possibility. That is all that we can say at this time."

Zoe was curious. "What would ever make you think that?"

She held her head high, her thin facial features proud and chiseled. "I shall help you by telling you that she is not dead. I felt it before you told me. Call it woman's intuition, call it a silly guess, a hunch, but there is too much interest in this so-called accident by you two and Lacey for finality. I sensed it that day that I encountered you in the cemetery poking around the tombstone, talking to yourself." Axel admired her, smiled back.

"We must leave now Kathleen. Tonight, we have pressing engagements."

"I am so sorry that I did not trust you earlier, Mr. Hawk. I don't want that report back. I don't want it in our house. Do with it as you may until justice is served."

"Please, Mr. Hawk is gone, Axel has arrived. I want you to address me as Axel so say it."

"Axel," she reiterated and broke her first smile, a thin parting of her lips, the grin pulled up at one side. "Axel and Zoe, I have now at last found the trust in both of you to wish you to succeed to find this beast."

"Thank you, Mrs. Whitehurst." Zee and Axel stood at attention as she scurried into her house at the sound of a ringing phone.

Hastening back to their vehicles and departing, Axel stopped only to purchase a single red blood blooming rose at a florist's shop before situating themselves only blocks from Dr. Montoya's house, adjacent to an expansive park green and picnic area. They were alone as they rifled through the investigative report together by sitting at a picnic table, under an oak tree and in a far deserted corner beside the parking area.

There were multiple references to Larry Bartlett, once again reaffirming the link to Montilladan and emphasizing the importance of a summit with Bartlett. The additional photos of M and Lillian looked harmless enough. Lillian appeared distant, disinterested at best in some of them. Records of the visits to the Macey Street were vague and inconclusive but documented, concrete evidence of Montilladan's visits there. Only once did she arrive with an occupant, male, description unknown from the investigator's position.

The female interests in the intimate positions at the night club were unknown to Axel and Zoe, but they displayed M's feminine side. Glancing at his watch, Axel suddenly informed Zee of the hour. "It's show time."

"This report only seems to confirm what we already know." She stood, and they sauntered beck to their vehicles. It was time for a vital confrontation.

It was an upscale Westwood district, expansive lots, expensive dwellings retreated from the roadside by exorbitant landscapes adorned with mazes of flower beds and trimmed manicured hedges, which discouraged solicitations. Curiously, this was not the case with Dr. Montoya's residence.

Hers was a stately southern plantation home with four ivory imposing pillars presenting a majestic entryway. The garages to the home were at back with private access, perhaps he thought, through the dense wooded lot he had just passed. The front lawn was graded into five tiers leading up to the house. If one followed the pathway and steps from the street, one would be on broad view in the middle of the lawn. The lack of hedges and obstructions provided a full panoramic view to the grand mansion from the roadway forcing you to turn and admire the setting.

The acreage was well lit, streetlights directly in front, ground lighting amid the low foliage, and a floodlight in a tree beside the house bathing the front grass and beds in dazzling brightness. In addition, Axel perceived the subtle ground lighting that outlined the sidewalk from curb to mansion.

Zoe inched by him in her Jaguar, made a slow U-turn and positioned herself two houses distant from the Montoya residence in a location with clear view of four-four-seventy-five Spruce Street just as she and Axel had planned. Axel abandoned his rental vehicle across the street from Dr. Montoya's house just as Zee blinked her lights to signify the commencement of her vigil.

Axel strolled across the street, up the sidewalk admiring the impeccable landscape with a small model lighthouse in view to his left. Camera imbedded? He was suddenly spooked as the beacon turned on, casting a divergent ray that circled the yard. Shaven, showered, long slacks, he resembled a college junior on first date trying to impress a sexy freshman. A single rose was touted as a token of friendship. Arriving, there was no need to search for a doorbell as she opened the door to greet him, smiling vivaciously back at him.

Dr. Renee Montoya was dressed in a long black clingy satin dress, tight over her mid-body with exposure of her olive skin on her shoulders, arms, and half her supple breasts exposed. Her physique seemed so unlike that of the business attire two days ago. Her jet black hair was pulled tightly back into a bun, crowned by a tiny silver tiara, resembling a tender Spanish senorita. She displayed sexy curves with enticing buttons pushing in all the right places.

"Good evening, Axel Hawk." Her cheeks were incredibly rosy. As Axel adsorbed the flattering smile, she extended her arm to receive the rose, and thanked him as he followed her into the foyer after greetings. She led him down a redwood floored hall into a dimly lit back living area furnished in opulent antiques. The house was much greater in depth than Axel guessed from the roadway. A mellow fire kindled in the fireplace for effect given the temperature of the day. It worked for Axel. The environment was totally relaxing as yellow and tan shadows pranced around the soft stained wood paneling. A bottle of chilled white wine resided in an ice bucket with an incense aroma of pears emanating throughout.

As she excused herself to the adjacent palatial kitchen to complete a telephone conversation, Axel watched as she opened a cupboard, extracted a thin clear glass vase, turned on a tap for water and deposited the rose. He gazed down and spun the wine bottle around to make a mental note of the vineyard. It was French, a white Grand Cru Chablis. The tap of her high heels signaled her movement into his area. She stood beside him and touched his shoulder as she offered an apology.

"Regrettably, Mr. Hawk, I must inform you that the wine is not for us. I am expecting guests later so thus my formal attire. However, I do have two other bottles in the kitchen cooler so we could sample a single glass each from this one, if you wish so. Yes?"

Was this all part of a master plan? Anticipation destroyed, only to be rekindled or the beginning of a sincere relationship? "If it does not inconvenience you, I'll accept one glass."

A modern effortless twister was used to extract the cork. She proceeded to pour two glasses of wine while motioning to Axel to sit in a high back chair, which provided the best views of the fireplace, the decor, and naturally, Dr. Montoya.

He realized that the room was decorated in extravagant taste with antique copies, he thought, of Dutch Masters, offset by uniquely crafted dried floral arrangements. They toasted mutual success. She did it again, by inaugurating her ceremonial rocking motion. Resting across from him on a fashionable brown-clothed love seat, her annoying, distracting, rocking ritual commenced on cue. Montoya sat cross-legged, just as she had posed at her office on Tuesday, and waved her crossed leg- up and down, up and down.

"So, Mr. Hawk, thank you for the rose. In return, I offer you a glass of vintage white French wine. Trade number one accomplished. Both parties satisfied I presume?"

She certainly had a soothing effect on him, enunciating each syllable succinctly, establishing eye contact and not breaking it. Quickly, he cast his thoughts back to Tuesday when he recognized the danger of being hypnotized, so immediately sat up attentively.

"Please dispel with formalities. You can address me as Axel. I insist, just as you did at the door when you greeted me." Her face incurred a stern, menacing transposition as her eyes narrowed with an accompanying tightening of the lips.

"Not during business hours I can't. I made it clear that this meeting was to be strictly a business discussion. Did I really call you Axel, accidentally, upon your arrival?" She smiled and chuckled as she shifted and tugged her dress down.

"Yes. You sure this is all business?"

"Yes."

"With imbibing?"

"Most certainly."

"Do I read an insinuation from you that we should make a sincere attempt to communicate during non-business hours?"

Her voice was smooth as velvet. "Not from where I sit," and she paused before finishing and emphasizing, "Mr. Hawk."

"It is time to initiate trade number two."

"Exactly, Mr. Hawk. You first."

"First let us establish the rules."

"Rules?" The room was instantaneously filled with her contagious silly amusing giggle. She placed her right hand on her Adam's apple to calm her choking, and leaned into him. "You can't be serious?"

"Yes, the understanding of the next trade."

"No." She became irritated. "You've witnessed too many macho movies with knife fights. There are no rules. We agreed. This is simply a business arrangement."

Axel blurted out. "Oh, yes, there are rules." He took charge, sitting his glass down in front of him. "Bear with me and I will tell you why my firm is interested in Montilladan, and why we are conducting an investigation into his death."

He sought an affirmation but received none, so he continued. "You will divulge to me exactly what Montilladan was being treated for. Additionally, how the treatments were being received."

A woman of few words, she looked at the shadows of the dancing flames on the ceiling, pausing for effect. "Agreed, so you go first."

"Oh, no, that's not in the rules." Encore, another silly outburst of giggles.

"But Mr. Hawk, I insist. You are my guest so I am being courteous. You first."

"Do you have a deck of playing cards?" Now her succinct pulses transcended into an aria of cackling.

"You must be kidding?"

"No, please retrieve them."

"Really, if we both tell the truth as we have promised to do then it matters little who goes first. In the medical profession, a trade of information must be built on mutual respect."

"Exactly. But, as your guest, I insist that you go first or it is card time."

The smile evaporated. Abruptly, and clearly irritated, Dr. Montoya strutted out of the room to return with a deck of playing cards. "Your touch of immaturity is certainly disappointing, Mr. Hawk. It is not amusement that earns respect in my book."

She shuffled four times and she whispered, head down, "Rule number three Mr. Hawk, no strip poker." In a sexy, almost porno additive, she sexily announced, "Well, not tonight." And continued to finger the outside of the deck by rubbing her fingers of her left hand over and over it, up and down for his amusement. Axel wondered what game she really had in mind for him.

Another subliminal message? Why should she tease him? Finally, the cards were shuffled for the fiftieth time. She passed them to him, but he returned them to say, "Your honor."

"This is absurd. I think you are so childish." She lost patience cutting a seven of clubs.

Axel wasted no time and turned a queen. "How prophetic- a black queen, the queen of spades." He turned the card to face her. "You perhaps?" Now he paused for effect. "But...nuts!"

"Nuts? But you won."

"I was thinking that I should have saved the queen of spades for strip poker night. It is always advantageous to open strip poker with a winning first move." He could tease her, too.

Dr. Montoya sipped her wine. Her lips parted, her tongue proceeding as a wave to wipe a solitary droplet from her bottom lip in a movement that swept her entire lower lip. She leaned back against the back of the love seat while staring at a painting of Paris on the wall behind Axel. She commenced her erotic rocking. Axel sat back to relax, but not before he checked his rear.

"Montilladan was a very unusual person. He was an irregular patient in my office. Sometimes, he would call in desperation to be seen by me, insisting that he require urgent appointments on consecutive days. That I drop whatever I was doing to tend to his every need. There would be a hiatus, weeks on end without hearing from him, where he would even blatantly not keep his scheduled treatments."

A log disintegrated into ashes and splinters, crashing to interrupt her monologue as it showered the room in ghostly embers. The space overflowed with the scent of burnt almond. She left Axel dangling as she filled her wine glass and consumed a double sip. Axel noted that she had violated the one glass rule imposed by her as he watched her Adam's apple bounce up and down. Now, she turned to glare at him directly.

"Confidentially?" Her eyes impaled him.

"Absolutely!" he assured her. She exhaled with a rush.

"Montilladan's stability in life was not to be found. He struggled with what the future would hold for him. Eventually, he sought my professional advice for severe psychological reasons. He wanted more than his present life had to offer but, in his way, were certain obstacles." In a loud, distinguished statement, she confessed. "You see, he suffered from multiple personalities."

He interrupted. "Excuse me, Dr. Montoya, for my interruption, but was Montilladan completely cognizant of this malady? He confessed openly and freely? Or did you have to convince him that he suffered from this ailment?"

"Montilladan knew absolutely and exactly the nature of the dilemma he was living."

Axel would have been disappointed if she had said anything different. He and Zoe had suspected as much as they had inspected the lair in the warehouse on Wednesday. The many looks of M, potentially transformed into the many personalities of M. It had to be. It all made sense. Dr. Montoya had just confirmed it for them. Although he felt relief at this confession, he felt anxiety in parallel.

"How did you meet Montilladan?"

"At a Hollywood party. He rather swept me away with his charm, his boasting and his big talk of future roles. He could be ever so charming when he wanted to be. That was indeed most of the time. We weren't romantically linked. Rather, it was a natural magnetism that evolved between patient and doctor once we got to know each other." Renee Montoya stopped to take another sip from her glass, now peering over the top of the glass, as a pitcher to home plate, to glue her eye contact on Axel. Stunned as he was by her, he suddenly felt uneasy as her two magnetic eyes appeared bulbous and penetrating now from behind the wine glass. And how many sips?

"The very first meeting, that is the very first therapy session, was extremely uncomfortable. The second, he brought out his charm as on the night we first met; the third, we never looked behind us. We had syncopation which established mutual trust."

"When was this?"

"Mm, a year and a half ago."

"How severe was Montilladan's illness? Is that the correct medical term, illness?" She seemed uncomfortable as she shifted before answering by propping herself up and plunking down.

"Yes, I believe that in Montilladan's case we can refer to this as an illness, since in Montilladan's case...it clearly led to confusion in his life. It was a mental depression, and it was a state of physical being that I felt could be cured. This state accounted for his bouts of irascibility." She paused to take another healthy sip, which emptied the contents. He still had still one half of his glass left.

"How severe? Well, I concluded that it certainly was not beyond correction, although, without my assistance it quickly would have reached hopeless proportions."

"How many personalities do you think Montilladan had?"

Dr. Montoya commenced an examination of him just as in her office. By the time she reached eye level a minute later, Axel was ready to intersect her examination, and she was ready to respond. Barely audible, she said, accenting the 'two', "At least two dominant strong-willed ones. The recent emergence of other personalities grossly complicated matters."

Axel was prepared for her response. "Can you describe these personalities to me?"

"No. Not part of our agreement. To quote Axel Hawk, it would break the rules. However, I can tell you that Montilladan was a much maligned and misunderstood person. His life reached epic achievements in the performing arts. He was rarely acknowledged as he should have been for his magnanimous acting abilities. This was a talent extraordinaire, which constantly came under unnecessary criticism from the press and public. People should have taken the time to understand this person better. In the end, I helped him achieve a focus on one distinct personality going forward." Axel felt uneasy as Montoya spat these last lines at him, and perhaps the world. She suddenly seemed drugged, as if addressing an audience. She leaned forward. "Re-watch some of his films and you'll see a genius at work. You will concur."

Dr. Montoya's last words gave Axel another shudder, for Montoya talked in a tone of respectful penetrating bonds between her and M, presenting a strong defense of his actions as if she sensed wrong-doings but was defiantly defending Montilladan's actions, yet she had gone out of her way to disconnect any romantic link.

"Did you ever meet Lacey Sills?" She stopped rocking. "Ah, the ever present Lacey Sills. The beautiful Lacey Sills. The mind-possessing Lacey Sills. A man's pinnacle for fantasies, yes?" She placed him off-guard by her references as they were replete in affection for Lacey. "This is the second time, Mr. Hawk, that you have injected her name in our conversations. Distrust of my original reply? You remember, at my office, you already asked me that question? I said…"

Axel regretted that entree. He had to alter the topic quickly so interrupted her rudely. "Is it possible that one personality of Montilladan was good and another dominant one, in polarization, say evil?"

Dr. Montoya displayed a capricious tendency. Now her rocking was rapid. "I will not answer you. I said already that he was misunderstood. It is your turn, Mr. Hawk. I believe that I have fulfilled my part of the bargain. I am not obliged to disclose to you anything else regarding my treatments of Montilladan. Even in the death of his character, I have violated the privileged bonds of patient and doctor. I did this for you out of respect for our agreement. I didn't even broach these subjects with the police." As her sexy tone turned sour, her index finger was fully extended, and with a malevolent tone she said, "It is your turn. I have completed my part of the bargain."

Axel suddenly felt vulnerable, for after all, he and Zee had suspected the problem of multiple personalities from the visit to the lair. Now he had to complete the bargain. There had to be carefully selected phrases.

"Perhaps, Dr. Montoya, and I must emphasize the word perhaps, with greatest sincerity, perhaps based on only circumstantial evidence to date. Montilladan...is...er...um...not dead?"

The incessant annoying rocking halted abruptly at the sound of the word "dead". The room suddenly felt cold as Axel spoke that word. As if a beautiful porcelain figurine, she sat stoically, not the slightest movement. Neither spoke. The fire seemed to dim. Time passed. The room was eerily comatose. Axel sat his glass on the table in front of him in an attempt to shatter the silence. Without blinking, without a heave in her bosom, without a twitch of eyebrows, Renee Montoya sat frozen, her stare fixated on him.

Axel felt a degree of uneasiness encompass his body. Was he imagining it or had he just heard a sole footstep behind him? He perused over his shoulder in a moment of sensing someone standing in the dark recesses down the hallway. His mind was playing tricks. He convinced himself that there was no one there. What thoughts was she preoccupied with? The next move was hers. Axel pledged that he would guarantee it by his silence. Would she play the game forward as pawn or bishop? Or more likely the black queen? He fixed his glare on her face. Finally, it came.

She raised her voice to send shudders in the room. "How utterly, absurdly, ridiculous. Montilladan is most certainly...dead. You have tricked me. Foul! Foul! I cry foul on you! I gave you the truth about Montilladan and you repay me with this ridiculous myth! I trusted you and you failed me. Hundreds of witnesses watched him fall to his death. Hundreds shed real tears and bereavement at the site. The coroner's office examined the body. I attended the funeral. He's buried at Forest Haven Cemetery. I even went to the wake. How dare you!"

She placed her glass down, opened her arms in disbelief and scolded him. "An audience of cast and crew witnessed this actor die in front of them, plummet to his death ingloriously, and now you sacrilegiously pose this irresponsible gossip? This is your half of the bargain? You are a fraud."

"Foul? Fraud? Why do you believe that?"

Renee Montoya elevated her voice in anxiety. "I just told you how he died in front of many witnesses. These same witnesses testified to this fact to police, some of them profited by appearing on television talk shows and news casts to inform the world that he bled to death in front of them, bled before medic teams could arrive. Bled right there, on the cold hard cement of a film studio. He died in his own backyard, in his own ocean of blood in a much undignified manner I might add. Don't you think so? Shouldn't you show some respect, Mr. Hawk? I am utterly disappointed in you."

She turned. Her posture shifted upright, her choleric eyes focusing on him. He noticed the lack of inquisitiveness in her response; rather the presence of spite, anger, defense! Yes, a super defensive position.

"I can't believe I fell for this. This is preposterous. Friends paid respects to him at the funeral parlor as I said. Your ill-placed shock treatment is not appreciated. Had I known that you thought him not to be dead, I would never have agreed to this meeting! You haven't traded me anything of value. Fraud!" She was irate as she sat up.

She swallowed hard and shook her head. "I shared with you a sanctimonious piece of his life, and for what? You owe me."

For the very first time, Axel perceived a crack in her classy static composure. Why was she trembling slightly? Her hands fidgeted. Here was Dr. Montoya displaying her first blemish. Should he attack? Or allow her to complete her challenge? She shifted again to rearrange her whole body, even uncrossing her legs, only to re-cross them.

And then it happened! A light-headed sensation crept from the pit of his bowels, moved through his body cavity, firmly into his head, like an anode and cathode connecting by electric spark, rendering everything in between as tingling, resulting in a fuzziness, which pervaded in his head, accented on his forehead. It now possessed his eyesight. *Was it the wine? Had it turned? Had she drugged him? No. What was happening?* He couldn't quite understand.

It was the last shifting of her body, that particular rearrangement that had triggered a long lost thought, flashed from the photo in Dr. Bartlett's office, of the six people, the garb, that night, their postures at the gala event, in that photo. What was it? He had lost that fleeting thought in Dr. Larry Bartlett's office most likely because of his weakened physical state. Now, her movements had recreated the moment in Bartlett's office, had caused the lost thought to resurface as she posed. He was recalling the photo she was in. But why? And what was the connection? *Concentrate Axel,* he mentally screamed.

Suddenly, he was sweating profusely, feeling his heart pounding in agitation, causing saliva to fill his mouth cavity. Was he experiencing a heart attack? Not likely from symptoms that he had read. He connected! Back to the photo! The six of them. It was in front of him now. It came back to him. The six people in that photo. He froze!

In the background, Renee Montoya continued to talk, to explain away his preposterous stupid theory. Every fifth word registered to Axel; the other four were faint bleeps as he struggled to regain control of the vital systems of his body. Axel strived to demonstrate a false sense of calmness and awareness before her, exhibiting a false cool demeanor as she circled the evidence once more. He connected again!

Something was terribly wrong! His confidence was devastated, causing his head to spin, preventing him from speaking. Yellow flames pranced on the walls as a log smashed, momentarily bathing the room in incandescent light, as if trapped in one of his favorite Shakespearean death scenes in the cold drizzling nights of England. Thoughts of escape permeated his brain. But why? What was direly wrong in this death scene? What had just happened? Was she a threat?

It struck him anew! He wasn't feeling well, that was it. He had to escape! Now! Methodically, she emphasized "royally absurd", "disrespect for the dead", and "foolishness", in her gallant summation. Finally, she turned to face him.

She stopped rocking. "Are you feeling okay, Mr. Hawk? You suddenly appear flush, and your cheeks are red. You are perspiring freely; I see the beads on your face, and my goodness your cheeks are now beet red. It wouldn't be the giant holes that I have punched in your arguments, would it? Feeling embarrassed?" She stood and moved closer to him.

Axel felt a need to distance himself so he stood up and put distance between them. "I have a touch of indigestion. I acquired it earlier today. It serves me right for eating at the greasy junk food road stops. I need to take some anti-acids so I best depart. We've completed our trade in utmost confidentiality. I am very app...app...appreciative of your time." He retained enough awareness to emphasize *utmost*. She sighed in disappointment.

"Just as well, as I am expecting visitors any minute. However, I feel that I have been severely taken advantage of by you. And you call yourself a professional." As she spoke, Axel stood, stumbled to re-gain his composure, walked deliberately toward the front door with no distractions, counting the steps, feeling every step forward was a step out of the clutches of one of the witches of *Macbeth*, hearing every slap as his shoes hit the solid hardwood. Would she really let him depart? Would Montilladan appear as he reached the door? Would M come out of hiding? Did he really see someone standing in the shadows of the foyer ahead?

What game was this? He summoned courage to turn. His eyes were out of focus. The light-headed feeling possessed him. Had she hypnotized him during those earlier moments when he felt lost in this world? How long had he been vulnerable?

Feebly, he stated, "Thank you for your time." It was all that he could muster. They shook hands; his were greasy.

"You are now sweating profusely, Mr. Hawk. Perhaps, it is the flu, not indigestion. Do you want to wash down quickly? There is a small bathroom behind that door."

No, say no! Say no quickly. He blurted out, "No thanks. My stomach needs help. I'm suffering from an embarrassing attack of gastritis. Thank you for your time Dr. Montoya. You have been most tolerant of me."

"I am so disappointed at our trade, Mr. Hawk, disappointed at your..."

He descended down the walkway not turning to see her as she continued to address him, struggling to see Zoe, praying that she was watching out for his life, praying that she had his naked rear covered. After ten steps he quickened the pace. Would he die before he reached his beloved Zoe? A scene to torment her life forever!

Apparently not, for entering into his vehicle he checked the back seat for trespassers and goblins, took a sideways glance back to her house where she was not in sight, and glided back down the boulevard to the municipal park where he and Zoe had examined the detective's report thirty minutes earlier. Once there, Axel rolled down the windows to inhale cool air fervently. Zee joined him immediately, hopping in, recognizing his distressed state. In his malaise, she shook him.

"Axel. Axel! You don't look well. You are panting for air. Axel, are you okay? Answer me. Are you okay? Speak to me! Axel, you don't look well." Zoe was now elevated to sincere concern as she observed his ruddy red face, soaked shirt, glazed over eyes. Axel's mouth was now arid after a bout with endless liquid generation.

"Axel! Answer me! Do I need to summon 9-1-1? Have you been poisoned? Are you having a stroke? Did she drug you? You're scaring me, Axel! Did she hypnotize you? Dammit say something!"

Zee grabbed his wrist to take his pulse. It was strong. Perhaps too strong, pounding. Finally, he uttered, "I'm not well, Zee. I am not hypnotized. I am not dying. Worse than all of those, I am in a state of shock. The ghosts of Shakespearean tragedies are ill at ease tonight."

Unpredictably, he opened his car door, scrambled out of his vehicle and darted across the clearing to a picnic table by the stream's edge where he stood bending over, inhaling deeply, motioning her to join him. Zee hustled in a state of panic with her cell phone, lost as to what might have transpired at Dr. Montoya's, depositing herself beside him on the bench, constantly peering over her shoulders for any uninvited guests. Zoe locked her arm in his and held it tight.

Axel orated. "Every criminal mastermind makes one fatal mistake Zee. There is no perfect crime. I've told you this time and time again." She was glued to him as he stared back across the grounds to their vehicles, locked on the traverse that they had just cut.

Zoe provided encouragement. "I'm listening."

Axel turned to face her. He exhaled. "I've recovered from my initial shock. I was sitting there conversing with Dr. Montoya, composed, relaxed, and attentive. We were sipping wine and my mind was so wrapped up in this case and in her testimony. She confirmed what you and I had guessed when she informed me that Montilladan was suffering from multiple personalities, a regular schizophrenic." He faced her. "Curiously she defended him to great extremes, excusing that most everyone did not understand him, and that he was so charming, so honorable, with his motives and actions largely misunderstood by the whole world. She lambasted the press and public."

"Continue."

"At great risk, I dropped the bomb and informed her that Montilladan might not be deceased. I took great care to emphasize the words, might not be dead. She defended the position that Montilladan was most certainly dead. Bolts of shivers launched up my back." Axel grabbed Zee's hands.

She was anxious. "What happened? Tell me. Cut the suspense will ya?"

"It hit me. When I was in Dr. Larry Bartlett's office, he had a photograph on his credenza of six people at a galarama function, dressed to the nines in formal attire. They were sitting around a table. Two of those people were Bartlett and Montoya, the other four not instantly recognizable. As I stared at that photo Zee, I recognized something very peculiar about that photo, but I lost the thought in my beat up weakened condition. Zee, tonight, as I sat across from Montoya she shifted her position and for a fleeting moment she posed as if in that photo, assumed the pose in that photo, and I suddenly had that same flash as in Bartlett's office, recollecting that photo of the six people, and I drew a fright, as I recalled Bartlett's photo. Out of the blue tonight, came a startling revelation from that photograph. An impossibility! But a reality Zee triggered by my remembrance of that photo."

"Axel, cut the drama or I'll punch you in your sore tummy! Spit it out!"

"I looked at her Zee. Montoya. She sat there. I saw her speaking, defending Montilladan first, and proclaiming his death. She shifted in her seat, and it came to me. Larry Bartlett's photo, the one that has possessed me, suddenly materialized right in front of me, and the photo of Montilladan by the pool that's in our records, the photos that Mrs. Whitehurst just gave to us of Montilladan materialized, too. The truth could not hide anymore."

Axel held her tight. "I know that this sounds crazy Zee but, incredible as it seems, I have overlooked the simplest detail in this wild ride."

"Stop the dramatics, Axel. On the count of three, I want the truth. Whatever you've discovered in those photos is my property, too. Remember A to Z! We're a team. I want to know what happened back there! You're still shaking and sweating."

"Zoe, I am determined to nail her. She has issued an ultimatum. We accepted. I know that you are not going to believe this, but Dr. Renee Montoya and Montilladan are the same person!"

Zoe broke the lock of hands, stood up, and paced quickly away from him, turning, returning, now ready to confront him. Sternly, she criticized him. "I am sorry, Axel, but I will challenge you on this idea. I'll even strike a wager on it. I'll even go back right now and ask her myself personally."

"I wouldn't do that. It would be ill-advised and you will lose the bet Zee." His voice brimmed with confidence.

"No, not even with all the makeup, all the props that we examined this afternoon, will I believe that pretty Dr. Montoya is the Montilladan."

"You have seen Montilladan only in photographs and I have witnessed Dr. Montoya in person."

"No! Weird! Not believable! She couldn't pull this off. Please claim brain damage from your beating, will you?"

"She is a mastermind, Zee, a shapeshifter, a killer, cool, a chameleon, but I finally found the singular, fatal mistake! The one singular fatal mistake, which exposes her. Before I tell you what it is, that mistake was confirmed further by her insistence that Montilladan is dead. Of course, he is to her. M's dead. Dr. Montoya has emerged victoriously from the struggle."

"What is this so-called invincible clue?"

"Zoe, she left a profile for us in the warehouse. It was all there. As Dr. Montoya was interacting with me tonight, Montilladan was playing her perfectly. Montilladan can change her clothes, her accent, her voice tone, her hair color, her fingernails, her personality, the color of her eyes, the shape of her nose, her gait, her sexiness, her attitude, her skin color, her skin complexion, the adornments, all down to the last detail, even use props to change the shape of her cheeks, even add to her bust as she has done with Montoya, even take injections to alter her muscle tone. But she overlooked one detail!"

"You recognized a piece of jewelry that Montilladan wore in the photo at Bartlett's?"

"No."

"A facial mask that we saw previously at the warehouse?"

"Not even close." The cockiness overwhelmed his answer. "You are going to hate me for this." Zee put her hands over her ears.

"Oh, no, don't say it, Axel. Oh, God no!" She dropped to her knees. "Please not that! Don't do this to us."

"I will say it, Zee, because criminals have been laid naked before me on other occasions by my same observation."

She continued to position her hands over her ears and shook her head. "Oh, no Axel, don't say it!"

He spoke. "Sherlock Holmes can keep his expertise in tobaccos and deductions; Axel Hawk lays criminals bare by their ears."

"Axel, don't say that."

"Zoe, listen to me. She can change any feature that she wants to, her voice, use muscle expanding injections, use different color eye lenses but that lady Dr. Renee Montoya, is Montilladan. She has the identical ears that I saw in the photograph of her that Lacey gave us and I witnessed at your townhome. When I saw them in the picture on Larry Bartlett's shelf in his office, I knew that I had seen them before, but I lost the connection in my state. But tonight, when she shifted in her seat and turned sideways, and for the first time I got a clear unobstructed view of that entire right ear of Dr. Renee Montoya, I became woozy because I realized that I was sitting only five feet away from the famous shapeshifter herself, Montilladan."

Axel was on a roll. "The shape of the lobe, the interior geometry of the ridges, the curls at the top of the ear, the size, the ratios, she even has a tiny distinctive black discoloration on one ridge. They are a match. It is one of my specialties. I admit it. I'm an ear freak. I can identify people by their ears. Zoe, it is the last element of disguise that con artists think about as they change their appearances, but ears, if you study them like I do, are as distinctive and revealing as any other element of the human body, if you take the time to examine them and commit them to memory, as only I can!"

Zoe shook her head in disbelief. "This is so difficult to believe, Axel. Can't you make the connection by her teeth, by the smile in one of the photos for it is so much easier to buy."

"Zee, I didn't examine her teeth."

"Oh, Axel, I don't know."

"Come back to the car. I want to show you a photo," and he bolted across the park without her, leaving her shaking her head as she sauntered behind. By the time she arrived, Axel had extracted the exhibit from the console and as prosecutor stood waiting for her. "M in conversation with Lacey Sills and in her marine haircut. I give you the point that she looks different than Dr. Montoya, but that ear in the photo is the ear I examined and witnessed minutes ago on Dr. Montoya. It is the identical ear. This babe really knows how to change appearances. But she has screwed up with one mistake."

"Oh, Axel, it would be so much easier to believe if you had just seen a tangible piece of evidence. Nobody, not even Tinker, or Felix, goes around inspecting people's ears and committing them to memory."

"It's her. I swear it! The evidence betrays her."

"Okay, okay," and Zoe nodded her head, "I believe you."

"We have to return."

"What? No way!"

"Absolutely."

"Axel, Lacey Sills paid us to find Montilladan. We are obligated to report back to her when we found her. We are getting compensated to do so. If you are so bloody confident that we have just found Montilladan, then I say we call Lacey to authenticate our discovery and turn this whole friggin' case over to Tinker for further actions right now. We will simply return to guard the residence so she doesn't leave unnoticed. And by the way, we are definitely not confronting that gal up the hill at that house without Tinker. We are unarmed and she is a murderer."

"I need to verify it."

She was irritated. "Time out! What? You just did! You just convincingly belabored the bloody points with me! You confirmed it! Now you are having doubts? You want to go back and re-confirm. Listen, Axel, if anybody can positively identify Montilladan, Lacey can! Get it? Lacey Sills will know before anyone else whether that person," and she angrily pointed in the vicinity that they had vacated earlier, "in Dr. Montoya's house is Montilladan. She will know. They were lovers; they were intimate. Ears or not, Lacey will know without observing her goddam ears." Zoe was increasingly upset.

Axel was determined. "We are going back, with you acting as my sentry and bodyguard."

"But why?"

"I have to get another clean look at her ears to be sure. I was so foggy earlier as I realized that I was in the spider's web. When I first noticed those ears and I made the connection why, I got nervous, so much that I had to excuse myself as I started drowning in my own sweat bath. Now my courage has returned to the forefront. I've regained my composure. I need to return to the front line of battle."

"You left, Axel."

"I'll return with an apology. I told her that I had to leave abruptly because of indigestion, to retrieve some anti-acids for my upset stomach. I'll return to apologize for my rude exit. I will return to apologize that I disappointed her in the trade, and that I feel badly about disappointing her and I would like to make it up to her. I won't go into the house. I promise Zee. I'll just hang around the front door and convince her that I did not own up to my end of the bargain and will make another appointment soon. We'll call Lacey and Tinker and wait for them to arrive."

"Don't do this Axel. I'm your partner. I vote to confront her tonight but with Lacey and Tinker present. Let's call them now. I can't take the risk of physical contact with M."

"Meaning?"

"Meaning that I am not as financially secure as you are. I have bills to pay, a mortgage on my townhouse, and monthly payments on the Jaguar. We deserve to be paid our fee for finding Montilladan. I'll phone Lacey right now. Let's not take any chances, this bitch is dangerous and I add, unpredictable. I will summon Tinker. If you and I have assembled the clues correctly then she is a murderer, Axel! We need protection."

Axel grabbed her by both shoulders. "I want to return to confirm my suspicions."

"Axel, she had you beaten, broke into your house, tried to barbeque us, bewitched you with a near heart attack. You just can't waltz up there, Axel, to a killer and say, oh, can you please turn your head, pretty please madam, so I can get a better look at your goddamn magnificent, goddam incriminating ears."

Axel pleaded. "I will stand at the front door. Let me return for less than two minutes. If I go inside, it is because the plan has gone astray, or she has me at gun point. Call Tinker immediately if I enter, then race to my rescue. I need the proof. I'm going back. Are you with me?"

She moved to touch their noses. There was weepiness in her voice. "I...I...I like you Axel Hawk. Please don't take that the wrong way. This is a calculated unnecessary risk that we take. Please don't do this." A magnetism drew them together until their foreheads leaned against one another, their noses rubbed.

"I will be okay. Trust me."

"Oh, I hate to agree to this. There is the potential for so much to go wrong. You are sure that it is her?"

"Words tell lies; ears don't."

"I hate myself for doing this but...okay. But deviate from the plan one iota, and I will have police and Tinker's swat team here. And, furthermore, deviate and I will come in legs blazing."

Now they had their arms around each other followed by a serious wet smooch, which she initiated. Her confession of feelings for him had magnified his confidence. They broke the lock and reluctantly, she followed him back into the neighborhood, where she repositioned herself as before with an excellent view of the front of Montoya's house, this time a house closer, with Tinker's number punched into her cellular, to stroke in case she had to execute.

However, Zee noticed, as Axel did, that Dr. Montoya obviously had company as a black Cadillac was parked curbside directly in front of her residence at the end of the walkway, and a small light blue foreign car behind it under the street light. Axel parked in the shadows, two estates distant, doused his lights, and crouched down. A waiting game commenced; or should he intrude upon her company of possible co-conspirators?

It was nearly twenty minutes later when a very tall, muscular man emerged from the house, wearing a long trench coat, hunched over and sauntering toward the Cadillac. Even at this distance, the broad shoulders, gait, and bodily square features betrayed him as the elusive Appleman. With the absence of his cellular, Axel prayed that Zoe spied the criminal, photographed him, and immediately relayed Tinker of his presence.

A neighbor was conducting an evening's stroll with the companionship of a mature German Shepherd. They intersected LaForge just as he reached his automobile. The stroller acknowledged LaForge and he waved in return. Two joggers were now making their way toward Axel, and the Cadillac.

The Appleman started his engine, the headlights blazing into Axel's vehicle and eyes, so he slouched down on the seat as LaForge passed, impossible to retrieve the license plate. Impatiently, shifting uneasily in his car, his bowels swelling with a squishy sensation, he let five minutes elapse and hustled up the center walkway toward the house bounding two steps at a time. His confidence was flush; his curiosity peaked as to Montoya's other guest.

The evidence of the conspiracy was abounding as the cast of characters had solidified their relationships. He rang the doorbell, took three steps back, found courage to address her, but there came no immediate acknowledgement. He announced himself a second time and could hear the doorbell ring resounding inside. Through the narrow slats in the side windows, he peered down the hallway expecting her any minute. With no Renee in sight, he turned the door handle to find the door unlocked. With this motion complete, he waved to Zoe who bolted from her Jag to the front door in a personal best hundred yard dash.

She wasn't afraid to give advice to Axel who was still looking around the door when she arrived. "You are not trespassing into this house Axel Hawk. Do not trespass into this house."

"Right! Let's both be stupid! We'll both trespass. Follow me." The hallway lights were dimmer than his previous visit. There was a distinct sound of running water upstairs, a faint chorus of music straight ahead.

"Dr. Montoya? Hello? It's Axel Hawk!" His loud page of hello rebounded off the marble stairs, reverberating first, and followed by an eerie silence as the music stopped. "Hello, Dr. Montoya? Are you home?"

"Axel, my guess is that she's upstairs running the bath water. We should wait outside. Let's not be idiots."

"With an unlocked front door at this hour? And the Appleman so recently departed? And who is her guest? You think they're taking a mutual bath? Stay right here, Zoe. Do not move from this spot. I'll walk down the hallway to the kitchen and living room to look around. First sign of her descending down the stairwell, yell and alert me."

Zee grabbed his arm. She whispered, "You will do no such thing. I don't like this, Axel."

"I promise that I will stay in your sight at all times. Look how straight that hallway runs. I'm just going to walk to the end of the hallway very, very, very... slowly. Keep your eyes peeled alternately on me and up there for her."

He thrust his arm from her grasp. Stealthily, Axel tip-toed down the gauntlet. As he neared the living room and kitchen, he could hear an infrequent crackle from the dying pyre of logs, which blazed earlier. Reaching the backroom, a dimmer in the kitchen and glowing embers from the fire provided the only light.

In the shadows, he recognized two inverted wine bottles in the ice bucket. Three glasses were set on the table. As he approached the kitchen, his foot slipped on a glossy spot. Peering down, his skin became pimply. His brand new running shoes were ensconced in a pool of deep red liquid; a stream that smelled and looked of blood! He dared to follow the varnished path around the kitchen island where he came to a petrifying halt.

The body was in sitting position and propped up against the refrigerator door. Her eyes were wide open in terror and her mouth cast agape in horror. There was a single bullet hole administered to the right temple with blood still gushing down her cheek, onto her neck and breasts, sluicing down her arm and onto the floor, creating the pond he had just intersected.

Axel jumped as the head rotated with a twitch to face him, and with her last dying breath, in an ominous voice, barely decipherable, Lillian whispered, "Mureeeeel." Her head collapsed downward.

Axel motioned for Zoe to join him as he flicked the kitchen lights on. She dashed in six, giant steps, arriving, preparing to attack; but, in reaching him, gasped at Lillian's dead body and sighed in sympathy. "Oh, my heavens, poor Lillian. Another loose end tidied up."

Axel crept closer, positioned himself on his haunches to feel her pulse. "She's dead. She said the word Muriel before she died. Obviously we now know why the Appleman was summoned here. An assassination. But where's Montoya?"

Zee shouted, "Axel, let's get the hell out of here. She's still upstairs and may have heard us." Now she saw the damage. "Oh, no. You've soiled your new shoes. Remove them. Now!"

As Axel stared back at Zoe, he noticed that her eyes were fixed not on him or his shoes anymore but on a recessed light fixture in the ceiling. She continued to stare up until Axel realized her concern. A second stream of pink liquids was dripping from an overhead light fixture and seeping toward their vicinity.

Immediately, he abandoned his shoes and ran beside her as they leapt up the stairs two at a time to the second floor source, to the room over the kitchen.

The sound of running water grew stronger. The hallway was dark. Zoe led the way, feeling the wall to the sound of water. Carefully, she opened a bathroom door and stood in shock at the entrance as Axel joined her to witness the Appleman, drowned in a pool of overflowing pinkish water, in a very large ornate bathtub. A single bullet hole had shattered his forehead like Lillian. Zee reached for a bath cloth and used it to turn off the water. She summated.

"Damn almighty, Axel. She did this. It was her dressed up as the Appleman! She walked calmly down the path, into the Caddy right in front of us." Now she was irate and yelling. "She's escaped again!" She kicked the side of a bureau in frustration.

"Did you get the license plate of that vehicle, Zee?"

"No, it was too distant."

"Me neither, I had to hide from the headlights. Did you call Tinker?"

"No, I was about to when you signaled me."

"Nor did I. Don't have my phone." They both felt deflated. "Can you call Tinker right now?"

"Yeah." Zoe was breathing hard.

"Tell him to put an A.P.B. out for a black Cadillac with an Appleman imposter. He's not going to be happy when we inform him of what we discovered."

"I know, Axel. Stop telling me what to do."

Axel ranted on. "But hold it all for two minutes. Let's search the premises before we scram. Quick. I'll take the bedroom and baths upstairs. You cruise downstairs."

"What are we looking for?"

"Damned if I know. I haven't the faintest idea. But look for any other incriminating evidence in drawers, closets, shoes. You know."

In his haste, he headed directly for shoe boxes and shoes and discovered an abundance of the purple crystals. He slipped all of the packages into his pockets. He brushed aside clothes, tore apart dresser drawers and noted nothing of interest. Faint sounds resounded in his head, a scream of arriving officials. Scampering downstairs in his bare feet, crying out for his partner, he waited impatiently.

Zoe couldn't believe her discovery. She opened the pantry door, combed through shelves and between two boxes of dried pasta, when it jumped out at her. She stood there stunned. Axel summoned her but this time with a "Quickly, the police are nearby!" They raced across the lawn and, as they did, Axel spat, "I told you to wait dialing Tinker."

They were sprinting, but he heard her as she replied. "I didn't. Someone else must have called the cops. Meet you at the park, but this time I'll meet you on the far side, away from arriving authorities." They split, each scampering into their vehicles, departing just ahead of the first police car, Zee hoping that no nosy neighbors would finger them as the culprits."

Once again Axel led the way and swerved into the nearby public park for the third time that evening, finding a spot in the shelter of a cluster of trees. Zoe joined him to map their next course of action while she desperately tried to reach Tinker again, and again, until finally he answered.

Tinker was furious. "What? Two more murders! How do you find these victims? Damn! I ain't conclusively solved Brissand's yet and now you got two more. Do not move. Stay put! I got the address, I'll be right there!" Zoe informed him of the evening's excitement and of Axel's discovery of Montoya's impersonation. Tinker was on his way replete in expletives.

"Axel, Montoya murdered Lillian and the Appleman and conveniently departed the premises as the Appleman. She's not only tidying up loose ends as Montilladan, but I think that tonight's the night, the night to escape!" Zoe admitted to Axel's theory that Dr. Montoya was really Montilladan.

However, Axel was deep in thought. "She has no lair Zee. She can't go to her former residence, the trailer's gone. Where would she go?" Tinker phoned back to confirm that he was on his way. Zee failed to mention that they had left the residence. After Zoe disconnected, Axel blurted out, "Romeo. I just realized how stupid I've been. Bartlett should be a higher priority and Lillian in her last dying breath blurted out Muriel to me."

"Zee, we need both cars. Follow me to Larry Bartlett's house. He may not be Romeo, but I suddenly have a hunch of how he fits into this plot and how stupid we've been. Let's go!" She stood there not responding. "Zoe, time is precious. Why the look?"

"There is something that I need to tell you Axel before we go."

"Now? We need to run, Zoe."

"No, Axel, now!"

"What's wrong Zee?"

Zoe clutched his hands and broke gridlock to extract something from her purse. She was blunt in her remarks.

"I've made an important discovery in Dr. Montoya's kitchen pantry, for I found a photograph of Adam Bartlett." Dramatically, she passed him, without any explanation, a square polaroid photo developed in black and white. Axel was thoroughly confused, unable to make any sense of the abstract images as he examined it from every angle before returning it to her.

"I surrender for I have no idea of what or who I am supposed to recognize in this frame. Was it taken at night? The theme of the image totally escapes me. What is it?"

Her deep dark peepers penetrated him. "It is an ultrasound photograph of a fetus and on the back of the image, look," and she turned it over, "it clearly states a recent date and Dr. Renee Montoya's name. You see Axel, you were right. There really is a Romeo. It's not Larry Bartlett, nor Roy Spiller, nor any male lover, nor any adult male. Montilladan is in love alright, with her child."

"Montilladan is pregnant!" Axel felt cold waves flutter over the skin on his arms. "No wonder Montilladan had to escape from the life of Hollywood, give up starring in a sequel, tidy up loose ends, and depart the life of a successful actor. She doesn't show as pregnant yet but soon will."

Zoe finished what each was thinking. "And when she does show, Montilladan would have a great deal of explaining to do."

Axel was still soaking the implications. "Bartlett's deceased wife's name was Muriel. Are you ready for ascent and assault at Bartlett's? We have to intrude his place now. We can't wait for Tinker."

"But I promised Tinker that we would wait here until his arrival and we are unarmed."

"Call Tinker back. Give him the address of Larry Bartlett. Tell him to meet us at Bartlett's as soon as he completes his preliminaries at the Montoya house." Zoe split to her Jaguar; Axel to his rental until she hailed him.

"Time is of the essence, Axel, so I'm driving. Get over her. No rebuttal." Axel was easily persuaded, so they buckled in and she peeled out of the lot, Axel already bracing himself for the carnival ride. Hurriedly, they left to confront Larry Bartlett. Axel sat and tried to rationalize what the climax might resemble. Zoe, in her wisdom, smiled and reiterated.

"Hey, Axel, Montilladan's son, Adam Bartlett ties all this together."

THURSDAY NIGHT, LATE

"Here it is, Alamitos Bay."
Loose gravel crunched under her tires as they carefully inspected each home. "Over there," and Axel pointed to a white stucco Spanish style house, red roof tiles, set back from the road by two hundred feet. She turned the vehicle into a straight narrow lane lined with short stubby Junipers and was rolling stealthily toward the car porch when an oriental strongman in a black frock, stereotype of a Sumo wrestler, appeared out of the darkness, precipitating an interruption to their path. The lights from Zoe's Jaguar lit up his muscular form. While they were pondering their next move, the guard tapped on the hood and motioned them to stand beside him.

"Well, if it isn't Tiny Chin." Axel had bad memories of his last encounter. They emerged and stood at attention.

"Do you have an appointment at this late hour?"

"We will after you inform Dr. Larry Bartlett that Axel Hawk and Zoe Burns are here with news of three murders by his femme fatale friend."

Tiny stood as a human fortress, legs apart, mumbling into a walkie-talkie, his back turned to them. In silence, arms dangling, he awaited his instructions. A breeze jostling branches provided the only background noise on the street. Axel recalled five years ago when Chin, a muscleman for a strong-arm drug group, bounced him twenty feet into a deep culvert. He felt like every bone in his back was shattered.

"I can't believe you know him?" she whispered.

"Five years ago at a criminal trial, it was my testimony that implicated Tiny. The eyes of the Chinese dragon lay on me as I sat naked in the witness box spewing condemning evidence of Chin's role in crime. The defense proved, however, that Tiny was divorced from the drug deals and that he purely played the role of a protector, not enforcer, for the mobsters, and knew nothing of their drug dealings. For this he received three years prison with probation. I haven't seen him since."

A buzzing fragmented their conversation. Chin mumbled. "You can go. Park your vehicle right her," and he motioned Zoe to a soft shoulder on the right. "Stay in the middle of the driveway where I can see you. Move directly onto the walk that goes to the front door when you reach the carport. First I must frisk you." Tiny moved forward. "Okay. Do as I instruct." He witnessed Axel's bare feet. "New look Hawk?"

"Huh?"

Chin actually chuckled. "Shoeless and sockless. Business must be bad."

Axel realized his situation. His new shoes had been abandoned in the pool of blood at Montoya's residence; his soggy socks discarded. Zoe pleaded to Chin and Axel to remain as she sprinted, popping the back trunk, and extracting a second new pair of gym shoes before Chin could object to her actions. "I purchased two pairs of shoes for you today Axel. The second's for a special occasion, like right now."

Chin went about his assignment of searching them. Axel was grateful as he laced them up, still sockless. Out of earshot of Chin, he whispered, "Luv ya Zee." Chin barked at them as they approached the residence. Zoe prompted Axel. "You mingle with the strangest people Axel."

"I can't help it. Life happens."

"Well that's just great news that I'd like to hear for this very moment, that Chin isn't on our side."

Axel moved in front, motioned her to watch their backs while he inspected the front entryway, a very cavernous alcove with multiple iron doors. One door creaked and groaned and Dr. Larry Bartlett was heard to mutter, "Come in please."

They were startled upon entry as the door was slammed shut by a remote control, which Bartlett held while standing fifty feet deep in the structure. "Good evening, Axel Hawk. I had a strong suspicion that we might reconnoiter before tomorrow's scheduled appointment."

Axel strode toward him while introducing Zoe. Bartlett was in blue pajamas with a matching housecoat, and in an obvious state of agitation. "Zoe, such an unusual name. Your name is almost a statement in itself- bold, unique. Please join me here, in this bay window which oversees the back lot."

They moved to a sunken alcove adjacent to the kitchen. As they sat around an oval glass table, Bartlett and Axel flanked Zoe, who had the best view of the spectacular well-lit area. She vowed to herself to keep sentry every second for any darting figures or disfigurement of the shrubbery. Bartlett's hand oscillated as he poured sherry into three goblets, returning the decanter to the middle of the table. After two generous gulps, he timidly asked, "What brings you here?"

Axel was firm. "No time for circular bullshit Dr. Bartlett. Time is of the essence. Three murders connected to a bizarre plot have led us to your door tonight." Bartlett seemed startled and puzzled.

"Earlier this evening, I had an appointment with Dr. Renee Montoya at her private residence. Zoe and I returned later to discover two dead bodies, one in the kitchen and one upstairs. Earlier in the day, the dead body of a small time conman and forger named George Brissand was discovered. His death can also be linked to Dr. Renee Montoya, alias Montilladan."

Axel's pointed remarks shook him further. As Axel examined him in the light of the chandelier, Larry Bartlett appeared so much older than their first meeting. In an excited tone, he now demanded, "Who has died tonight?"

Zoe answered. "Dr. Montoya's secretary, Lillian, and a tough man criminal by the name of Appleman LaForge."

Bartlett bristled at the sound of Lillian's name. He could barely be heard to whimper, head bowed, "Lillian. Lillian. When will this insanity stop?"

"It will stop when you confess Dr. Bartlett. There is strong evidence to connect you to Dr. Montoya, dare I say Montilladan. Zoe and I need to know your exact relationship to her. In addition, I demand to know why you have engaged the services of a known dirty henchman, Tiny Chin. You can't deceive me for I know his history and reputation from a former crime. It's your lead Larry."

He continued to hang his head and gave a solo sniffle as he again recited Lillian's name. As he looked up, redness rimmed his eyes; baggy pouches were prominent underneath; deep furrows scared his forehead, his cheeks sagged. Circling his thumbs, while loosely clasping his hands, the fidgeting continued on end. Zoe commenced the interrogation, sensing that a further prompting was required.

"When did you first meet Dr. Montoya? Or Montilladan?" Bartlett tipped some additional sherry into his goblet, took a deep breath, opened his eyes, and sat back lifeless, staring out the window into the bathed yard.

"Three years ago I lost my Muriel. We were married for twenty-two years. I never loved anyone so deeply. After her death, I was in a dark depression and everything I did, everywhere I went, and everyone I met just magnified my lack of strength to recover and to face life again. My mood was melancholy."

Bartlett extracted a tissue from a box on the table to toot his nose vigorously. A quiver haunted the raspiness in his voice during his dialogue. "We met one night at a social function just down the street at a party held by my neighbor. She, being Dr. Renee Montoya, was there. How did I first meet her? I remember well. I was moping around the dessert cart planning a sugar high to invigorate myself. She approached; immediately, we engaged in a free flowing conversation, the first one that I had with a member of the opposite sex since Muriel's untimely passing."

"She had a great sense of humor and a soothing voice. She made me smile. She provided reflective uplifting moments. She was so polished. I invited her to a trendy new coffee house in downtown Long Beach, so we departed prematurely together to indulge in pastries and coffee until after midnight." Gathering his thoughts, there was a faint glimmer of hope in his voice.

"She discovered that I needed psychiatric help to get over my loss, and I discovered that she, as a professional, could help me. I saw this as an opportunity to get to see her often. I wanted so much to get to know her better. So I visited her regularly and she probed my mind. She was a tonic to my acrid misery."

His eyes filled with moisture and overflowed, falling to moisten his night wear. Bartlett rose with a jerk, proceeded to move to the kitchen sink where he sprayed his face with cold water, returning to sit with a crumpled towel, which he flung over his shoulder. "Crying towel," he said.

"Dr. Montoya was wonderful food for my soul. I found a new courage to ask her out on dates. She was my renaissance. We became close friends. We dated regularly as much as her busy schedule would permit and, yes, we had sex. I fell in love within three months only to fall off a precipice again." Axel and Zoe let him recite the saga in his own time, realizing that every minute lost was a minute to allow M to escape.

"She was hysterical one night when I called at her home. She clasped onto me the moment that I entered her residence, tugging me upstairs into a bathroom. It was unbelievable. There we were, just the two of us in a tiny locked bathroom. I couldn't imagine what was to follow. I sat on a lowered toilet seat; she climbed into her bath tub and spread her body out, draped her legs over the side. For the next hour, she poured out her heart to me about her double life as Montilladan. She talked about how she had come from Miami to Los Angeles to find her fortune in acting, how she was rejected time and time for parts in plays and film, how she got her big break while auditioning for a male lead role, and how she rose to stardom and solidified her deception. She produced overwhelming evidence about this caper as my stomach churned and my bowels grumbled. She never looked at me once during her entire testimony." His voice reached a raspy crescendo.

"When she confessed to me whom she really was, I was at first disappointed. But then she revealed a scheme to me to bury her life as Montilladan and she convincingly stated that all she ever wanted to become was Dr. Renee Montoya, a female, my lover, and forever my wife. She would end Montilladan's reign, she promised, and escape with me into reality."

"She pleaded with me for my support. She begged me to forgive her of past duplicities. She explained how she was trapped in a man's body after that successful audition that changed her life for all those years. She also told me how she obtained false papers and degrees to manufacture her life as Dr. Montoya and produced a phony birth certificate from New York. She was most persuasive as I was still in a fragile state. I loved her; I wanted her to succeed; I wanted her; what else could I say?"

"Her plan to escape, she explained, was to disappear from the Hollywood scene by faking her death. She needed my help, my love, my affection, my understanding, and my patience while she gradually destroyed all the pieces of the life of Montilladan." He sadly looked at each of them.

"I wanted to help her. I loved her. This could be my new project, to construct an eternal love, to give a new meaning to my existence, to fill the void left by my Muriel. Foolishly, I gave her all that she asked for. I never dreamed that she would sink to illegal acts. I swear I never knew she would murder anyone to achieve her new freedom." He dabbed each eye with the towel, sitting upright to speak affirmatively.

"Love conquered me. At that moment, I loved her as Renee Montoya. I had seen Montilladan interviewed, and in the movies, and wanted nothing to do with him. I prayed that the person I witnessed was an act. She told me that she was in a battle for her life with this alter-ego stuff. I had to help my Renee. I had to help her outlive this alter-ego. We made love all night, she discussing her plans to exonerate herself from Hollywood the actor Montilladan; me, wanting myself inside of her again and again. The excitement within us reached a climax. I left her house that following morning with a new vision of my future life- the renaissance of Dr. Larry Bartlett; the new Mrs. Renee Montoya-Bartlett."

He refused to stop babbling. "Then...Paula Piper called unexpectedly and told me of Montilladan's interest in my institutions and what a character builder this would be for Montilladan's image and possibly an outlet for donations. I can't possibly tell you how creepy it was to have Montilladan visit our facilities and...interface with me. It was as if looking at another totally different human being, perhaps from another planet. I looked deep into him for any signs of my tender affectionate Renee. I didn't find her. I did not find any affection. As Montilladan, she played a repulsive, cold, icy reptile to perfection. It scared the Hell out of me!"

Zoe noticed that his shivers showed up as goose bumps on his arms; Axel was glad that Lacey be not here to witness this outpouring. Zoe checked her watch. The uneasy silence was smashed when Bartlett slammed his fists down on the table full force, screaming an outburst from his tormented soul. Zee stood up, placing her arm around his shoulders. He collapsed to tabletop while burying his limp head in his folded arms. Axel retreated to the sink to soak the towel in cold water and returned to offer it to Bartlett.

"Are you taking a sedative?"

"Yes, but I have much more to tell you that you can't possibly know about Montilladan. I'll take my medicine later because you must know her secrets."

"Dr. Bartlett," Zee pleaded, "time grows short. The police may uncover your relationship with her from evidence at Dr. Montoya's house. In addition, Axel and I feel that she plans to exercise her escape tonight."

"And I know that she most certainly does. Tonight she plays in the final act of the play she wrote." He was wild-eyed.

Zoe struck into the matter. "Do you know that Dr. Renee Montoya, I mean Montilladan is pregnant?"

He was quick to respond. "Yes, of course I do."

"Your child?"

His Adam's apple bobbed as he swallowed hard; he closed his eyes, bit on his lower lip, and barely audible replied, "Yes."

Zoe inquired. "Planned?"

"No."

"Are you secretly married to her?"

"No, although we planned to marry until recently."

Zoe continued this line of questioning. "What transpired to upset the plans?"

"The nightly news. The report of the death of Montilladan. I had no idea that she was going to sacrifice a human being to orchestrate her escape. She informed me of how Roy Spiller died so conveniently so she could live, so that we could both live new lives. She informed me that you two were snooping around, asking questions about Roy and Montilladan and...she confessed to me that she had planned a beating for you, Axel, and further actions if you persisted."

He became delirious. "Then it happened." He shook his head. "Slowly, her personality changed, she lost the golden soft touches and warmth of Renee. You must understand that those events- the beating, the death of Roy Spiller- these were the evils of Montilladan. You can't imagine as I sat alone one night to try and make sense of this madness and ask myself. I asked, where has my beloved Renee gone?"

Zoe checked her theory. "It's to be boy, Adam, isn't it?" A short swift nod confirmed it.

"Yes, we had planned to name him Adam. But time is short and you must know of the greatest deception of all. You had better come with me upstairs for there is a deadly deed that I need to expose to you." Axel aided Bartlett to his feet. In haste, he led them upstairs down a long hall and through a bolted door and into a spacious modern clean laboratory at the back of the house. Axel thought that this lab was enough to make Cynthia Dopson quite jealous. Zee was amazed at the size and the awesome diversity of the equipment. Piles of paper surrounded a computer system with a humongous screen hiding the entire wall. There were no windows.

Bartlett closed the door behind them. He intercepted their gait and planted himself in front of them as he garnered up enough courage. "I have a confession to make. You must listen carefully. I have broken the law. I have broken my code to perform with responsibility and integrity. I have let my peers and my profession down. Most importantly, the charade must end and I must face the consequences whatever they may be." He bowed his head.

"Don't interrupt. You must keep this confession in secrecy until the time is appropriate. This is very, very important." Axel and Zoe nodded in strong affirmation.

"After Muriel's death, our lab placed an emphasis on the cure for early osteoporosis just as I informed you at the office Mr. Hawk. Time after time, we failed to get our drug approved by government agencies because the side effects were too much of a health risk. They said our work was sloppy. I became frustrated, so I ordered a whole new approach to the specifications of the problem."

"By a fluke, one night here, I believe that I may have discovered a wonder drug, a drug that could go further than curing osteoporosis." He preferred the melodramatic, so I waited for complete silence.

"I think I have developed a drug that could retard the aging process! In fact, with a guinea pig, I believed that this drug could prolong the life of a human being significantly by providing early catalysis for strong bones, firm muscle development, competent cell structure, and enduring body and organ structure!"

Zoe interrupted him. "Thus, you conceived a child out of wed-lock, out of scientific necessity, the first new wonder-child, Adam. Adam Bartlett! The first superman based on your new miracle super drug!"

"Yes, Miss Burns. She was very persuasive, this Renee Montoya of mine. When I recited to her in this very room of my accomplishment, she convinced me to allow her to be that first human guinea pig, she convinced me to impregnate her, and she is going to give birth to a child whose fetus has been injected daily with a solution of the wonder drug."

At this cue, Axel reached into his pockets and relieved his pockets of packets and packets of the mysterious purple substance, tossing them one by one onto an elongated table next to Bartlett. "Zoe and I discovered these at Dr. Montoya's house, a trailer hideout Montilladan used to change in, and at Montilladan's residence."

"What you have there, Mr. Hawk, is about four hundred thousand dollars' worth of the drug, if my research and market analysis is correct. I would prefer if you would allow me to keep these under lock. The patent of this drug will be famous one day. I reserve that notoriety for MUREX and myself."

Zee was curious. "How does she inject it?"

"Simple. What one does is just boil bottled water, dissolve the contents of one packet into one eighth of a cup of the boiled water and inject doses directly into the fetus each day. The remainder is stored in the fridge. One batch keeps for two weeks." He grabbed the packets and cobbled them into a desk drawer.

"Does she also inject this drug into her own body for her purposes?"

"Yes, and with side effects still unknown is playing a dangerous game with the lethal amounts she administers."

Now Larry Bartlett slumped in the executive's chair. "When I heard that George Brissand had been murdered, I suspected my sweetheart. I knew, for she had told me that fateful night in her locked bathroom that it was this very same Brissand who had forged the papers for the education and degrees and total fabrication of Dr. Renee Montoya. The degrees were from a small medical establishment out east that no one would ever check. He even designed government certificates and a license to practice. My heart lost its glow for her. Something now was terribly wrong."

"When we heard about Spiller's death, she wanted to celebrate. She talked about completing the details here in Los Angeles before we split. She exposed her plan for me to sell my interests in my companies and to escape with her with my funds. Brissand had created false passports for both of us, and a future false paper on Adam. It was then that I finally faced the reality and convinced myself of her foul play in the so-called accident of Roy Spiller. Up until then, I had buried my head in the sand."

"What are the side effects of the new drug?" Axel wanted Bartlett to state all the facts.

"Only time will tell, and I doubt if any side effects will be noticeable until the child grows into his twenties or thirties. The only calculations I have point to an increased synapsis of the brain and longevity of life through retardation of aging processes, like retarding bone deterioration, like retarding any shrinkage or deterioration of the muscles. Above all, this drug provides muscle cell structure retention. On the negative side, there could be mild paralysis of minor organs such as the liver and brain damage and high blood pressure, but who is to say without a history. It is this potential paralysis of the liver and an indication of possible head tumors, which defer the drug's sanctioning by government authorities. The authorities are fools who don't weigh benefit versus gains." Zoe diagnosed these last words to be uttered with blind ambition. Axel sat paralyzed by the unveilings.

"Possible disorientation of personalities, they say. Psychosis, they say." He was bitter as he spoke those last words.

"My studies show conclusively that the drug must be taken at an early age. All the injections are made directly into little Adam. The doses are being self-administered by her although Renee recently complained of her tummy feeling tender and of stomach muscle spasms."

Zoe challenged him. "Renee Montoya and you have played a dangerous game, Dr. Bartlett, by manufacturing and administering a non-sanctioned drug. You were correct earlier. It will be considered a crime."

"In our defense, we were consenting adults. Plus, Muriel, God bless her soul, was incapable of bearing children. I saw Renee as the means to achieve an important mission for me, which is a possible continuation of my Bartlett heritage, a continuance of the name; my own son to grow to be the first superman, to run my businesses after I die." His head wavered and he was barely heard to say, "Foolishness. That's what it is I'm afraid." His voice cried out for sympathy; Zoe felt none.

"The nest eggs in Andorra. Your money?"

"Ours. We planned to transfer it to our retirement home in Central America. I also have a separate account in France. That is, until I made up my mind to bail out. A personality change has come over her." He was angry. "Dr. Renee Montoya occupies the body less frequently every day while the evil Montilladan possesses her frequently."

"Now you fear for your life, so you hired Tiny Chin to protect you from the woman that you once loved."

"From the creature that once loved me! It breaks my heart to admit it, but yes, you are correct. It was me who broke off the affair. It was when I heard of Brissand's death that I informed her that I wished not to be a part of her scheme. And for that, and the information that I possess I feel that now she may try to exterminate me. In escape, she will not be my beloved Renee Montoya. The only existence in her natural habitat will be the devious and ruthless Montilladan, a transformation I wish to witness no more." Bartlett seemed distant.

"With this conclusion, I informed her that I will not accompany her into her new life. She has at last revealed her true colors. Not much of an existence for me if I agree to go with her, but just as torturous as I stay here separated from my little Adam."

Bartlett's composure deteriorated and he commenced to sob while the shakes accelerated. His eyes glassed over; his last words had reached a slurring status.

Axel inquired. "Curiously to me, Lillian spoke your wife's name as she expelled her last breaths of life. Why?"

Bartlett remembered Lillian. "Poor Lillian, so innocent to be drawn into this web of lies and murder." Bartlett opened a desk drawer to extract a map.

"Lillian was trying to give you the clue to the escape hatch. I gave Renee my boat, The Muriel, docked here," and he circled the desk, opened a map, and summoned them to see as he circled the Long Beach Marina and placed an X. "Here at Pier Seven is where you will find her. Giving her this escape hatch seemed the best way to assure her estrangement from my life forever and provide safety for little Adam. She is very seaworthy. She had a good mentor, me."

"She departs at midnight tonight. If I am not there, as you can see I will not be, she leaves alone for Mexico. She's already bribed Mexican officials for her entry. You must understand that it was the least that I could do to protect the innocent little child. Except now, I realize too late that I am abetting a murderous criminal and may face serious consequences. I swear to both of you that I knew nothing of her murderous plans until recently." His eyes searched for sympathy again.

"The bloody tale is complete. As you can see, now I have second thoughts." Bartlett checked his watch. "You have just enough time to prevent her from departing in the Muriel if you hurry, if that is your goal. My grieving heart will somehow find inner strength to testify against her in this convoluted mess if you wish me to do so." Now tears streamed openly with associated histrionics.

"I realize now, that…ah…to administer the drug to poor little Adam was wrong. It was Montilladan who inspired me, motivated me, convinced me to take this giant step, and not Renee. I was so infatuated with Renee that I lost my sense of morals when Montilladan encouraged me; I was too weak to recognize her motives. I have jeopardized my entire career, my company, my reputation. Ooh, I have to clean up this mess. She was just so persuasive. Go back east across the bridge you passed over to get to this community and turn south on the coast road. You'll come to the marina within five minutes."

Axel sensed an emotional onslaught as his breathing patterns suddenly became distended. He shattered into tears and buried his head on the desk. Axel leaned toward him to express their thanks for the truths. "We must leave you Dr. Bartlett to intercept her. Thank you. You need help. After we leave, please promise Zoe and me that you will check yourself into a medical facility right away, or call some friends to stay with you tonight. Please."

Zoe added to Axel's request. "You cannot possibly endure this mental anguish of lost love, once again. First Muriel, and then Renee, and now Adam. I believe that you might be headed for a nervous breakdown."

Bartlett reached into a drawer and extracted an object, tossing Axel a card key. Axel immediately recognized it by the markings as a duplicate of the second card key that he and Zoe had discovered at Montilladan's residence. "You'll need this to gain access to the pier. It is permanently secured. You must be very careful as I believe her to be totally irrational and unhinged. You know firsthand of her murderous instincts. She might be armed."

Axel stepped forward, thanked him on their behalf, and immediately apologized for their precipitous departure. Zoe did likewise. After they clamored down the stairs, they hailed Tiny Chin outside. Zoe, realizing Axel's discomfort, paused to instruct Chin.

"Please do us all a favor, Chin, help your employer. Believe in me. He requires medical assistance immediately, or the presence of some trustworthy friends. He is in a mentally unbalanced and drained state. Promise to take action?" After he affirmed, they raced for her vehicle.

Zoe shouted. "No time for your cautious, lollygag driving. Prepare yourself for the race!" Axel reluctantly did so and proceeded to try to contact Tinker who was still at the murder scene. No luck. The signal on Zee's cellular was weak. Within minutes they were on bridge, turning south toward the marina with little time to intercept her departure.

Zoe, to break the tension, asked, "What would Shakespeare say now?" Axel wasted no time to respond.

"Driveth like hell, woman!"

THURSDAY, MIDNIGHT

"Rats! It's not a signal problem Zee. Your mobile phone doesn't work." Axel looked up, alarmed, and panicked. "What speed are we at?"

She snapped back. "Never mind, just you sit back and relax. I've played enough video games to adeptly execute these maneuvers. All you have to do is close your eyes, or keep them open, but keep quiet, and savor the thrill."

"Thrill? Scream? My pants will be wet soon if you keep this up. Watch out he's changing lanes!"

Zoe was weaving in and out of traffic as Axel, eyes agape, one hand clutched to the dashboard, the other hugging the undercarriage, was scanning for police vehicles while frequently playing back seat driver to no avail.

"Slow down, Zee! Holy..."

"Axel, I need to concentrate. Leave me be!"

"That green van!" No problem as she passed and cut in front. Overhead a plane was descending into LAX as Axel calculated their ground speed as dwarfing the airplane's speed.

"No problem, relax." After what Axel believed to be the longest twelve minutes of his life, heart pounding, shirt soaked in perspiration, minutes counted off his life, they were cruising down the seaside road, decelerating, anxiously searching for an access to Pier Seven.

"Park here." Axel identified the lot for the marina. He wasted no time. "I'll break for the pier while you get to a landline to alert Tinker."

"Deja vu, Axel! Just like the previous cases when we were ahead of Felix and Tinker on the trail of the villains and didn't have a single solitary respectful second to inform them of our position and of breaking developments. I hate what they will do this time."

"Wrong. We do have one single solitary second. Now call Tink!" Axel slammed the door shut, pranced out of her sight onto the main boardwalk, which provided the artery from which all the piers spawned, noting the card key entries. Suddenly, there it was in front of him, Pier Seven.

"Card key. Card key." He felt the outline of it in his pants. Passing it over the red eye, the beam was broken. The box on the high wire door clicked and signaled his safe entry. He left it slightly ajar if he should require an instant retreat, or if Zoe should require access.

Once on Pier Seven, he hunched over, tried to creep in the shadows, and scrutinized each boat for the name Muriel. This collection of monstrous cabin cruisers was each customized in extravagant finishings. Traversing the dock, with some twenty boats examined, he was disheartened. He had reached the end of the pier and there was no Muriel.

He stood up to examine the route he had just taken and noticed that there were three empty slots. He checked his watch. Ten minutes to twelve. Had Montilladan not kept her part of the bargain? Had she departed earlier? Had he himself in his excitement misread a boat's identity? Was she refueling elsewhere in the harbor? To return here later for Bartlett? Was he in his haste on the wrong pier? Or too sloppy as he checked the namesakes?

"Think, Axel, think," he encouraged himself aloud. He decided to carefully retrace his steps, quietly sneaking along, hugging one side of the pier, backtracking, and bent over and observant. With his same attire of earlier this evening, he would be recognized if she spied him first.

Meanwhile, Zoe contacted Tinker, explaining in detail the depressing news about their visit to Larry Bartlett's and Montilladan's escape from the country at midnight to Mexico by way of a high speed cruiser, the Muriel. She gave Tinker their location over the outbursts of expletives at his end of the phone, asked him to notify the Coast Guard and then, with arms flailing as in the Olympic hurdles, head high, nostrils wide as a great filly at the finish line, she bolted to pier side. Reaching the master gate, she discovered it open, entered, and reduced her pace to a steady gait. No initial sign of Axel within her scope of view. She scanned the collection and came to the end of the pier puzzled, just as Axel had only moments before. It was still not quite midnight. No Axel. No Muriel. No Montilladan. No luck. No clues. She was puzzled. Intently she listened.

A burst of a chugging sound grabbed her attention. A three deck cabin cruiser was motoring slowly out of the harbor, churning up light waves behind her, navigating between tight pier ends and buoys. Now in a spotlight, impossible to mistake, the name Muriel was in large bold blue letters on the white background on the stern.

She saw it, just as Axel had read earlier. The only chance. A rock breaker, a marine speed bump with a tight pinch, which prevented controlled speeders from accelerating out of the harbor, an impediment that provided the only access aboard the Muriel with the greatest Olympic leap if the boat passed within reach. In full flight, she ran into the second desperate sprint of her life, passing two curious onlookers, searching for the advantage that would allow the jump. Turning toward the obstruction, just in time, she spied the solitary figure of Axel's physique disappear into the blackness of the sea as he leapt from the breaker and into the night. She saw him swim to catch and intercept the craft, yanking himself up into danger.

Zoe came to a halt at the peak of the breakers. Bent, out of breath, she knew she could not swim fast enough to catch the Muriel, so retreated back to the landline phone to inform the Coast Guard immediately, if Tinker hadn't already done so. She dare not call after him and alert the black widow. For a fleeting second, she spied her friend Axel Hawk for the last time, hanging onto the side of the boat for dear life, as the Muriel steamed out to sea, kicking up a lively spray, heading into the somber void of the black Pacific with Axel in her diabolical clutches.

Axel hit his left cheek and right knee on impact with the rear side of the cruiser. He prayed the damage was minimal and not a vulnerability given his looming confrontation. He recognized the necessity to climb onboard as he dangled precariously at the stern, and in close proximity to the propellers. Any fall would suck him under and instantly chop him into pieces.

He swung his left leg over the rail with a quick burst of strength to survive. He grunted, heaved his body up and onto the back deck. The Muriel was a seventy footer he gathered, with three decks, with Montilladan probably on top to guide her out into the caliginous ocean before establishing autopilot.

Axel reckoned that he had only a few precious minutes to restore his breathing patterns, rest his sore cheek, check his bruised knee, and design his next moves. He had to concoct a plan to stall the craft for Coast Guard inter-section but the realization surfaced that he had minimal knowledge of sea crafts of any kind, let alone a sophisticated sea cruiser. Axel cogitated about some logical ideas but struggled to even know where to disconnect the fuel supply, signal for help, or impair the electronics. A thud in front of him caused him to turn. He had guessed wrong. He had mishandled the situation and now lost whatever advantage he had fostered.

She sprang down the steps so quickly, and was upon him with a hand gun positioned at him from twenty feet away. "You are such a fucking nuisance Axel."

Montilladan stood as a marksman on the range with both hands gripping the gun, legs spread comfortably, and aiming perfectly at his midsection. Tonight, she resembled the Montilladan of old with marine crew cut, fiery angry eyes, dressed in army camouflage top, jeans of greens, browns, and black paint blotches. Her wiry unisex physique betrayed her. Axel knew that the real Montilladan had resurfaced by Bartlett's comments, and the fight between Montoya and Montilladan and any other personalities, was over. Montoya was dead; the demon had won. He assessed her strength by observing her sinewy arm muscles. He knew that any physical combat was going to be arduous with his recent beatings and bruises.

"You are such a pest."

"Good evening." He slowly stood erect, hands on hips. "I was hoping to find Dr. Montoya at home, to be able to apologize to her for my rude behavior earlier this evening and to apologize for my seemingly abrupt departure."

"Dr. Montoya is dead, asshole."

Axel tried to exhibit a calmness. "Right. And so is Lillian, Brissand, Roy Spiller, the Appleman. All your works?"

Her whole permeability had changed. Her voice was powerful, disrespectful, angry, and loathsome. But the eyes, they were so replete in triumph. As he examined her, he knew that he would need luck to defeat this enemy; there was absolutely no possibility of Zoe leaping out of the darkness to save him tonight.

"Yes, they all completed their assignments, just as I had planned. If it wasn't for you, that bitch-partner, and that stupid meddling Lacey Sills. Lacey in her utter witless moments hired you to investigate the accident. Why? I want to know!"

For the first time, Axel now realized that she hadn't pieced all the clues together. That's what saved Lacey's life. Initiating a dialogue with her, to distract her, to consume time for help to arrive, he calculated that this was his best chance for survival. "Lacey lifted the robe at the funeral parlor after everyone else had left. She was shocked to see that it wasn't you in the casket, that it was Roy Spiller and Roy's genitals."

She shook her head. "I figured as much but was unable to confirm it. That stupid bitch tried to ruin everything. What's wrong with her? I went to my own funeral, for Christ's sakes in disguise and no one recognized me. It was priceless. I was a middle aged man, bearded, stout, casual black attire. God, and that stupid Lacey looked at me, said a courteous hello and didn't even recognize me." Montilladan laughed uproariously. "I," and she waved the gun at him, "even saw Givens there, stood beside him, and he didn't know who the hell I was."

"I thought you and Lacey were an item."

"No more than any of my other lovers. I loved them all. She smothered me with affection. I liked it."

The boat intersected higher waves, which sprayed onto the floor before the next further intersection lightly sprayed both of them. Through this, Axel remained despondent for Montilladan swayed not an inch, remained glued to her spot, holding her ground as the craft maintained her course, cold drips slipping from the base of her chin, eyes focused on his face, weapon aimed at his belly. Now depressingly, darkness engulfed them as the last remnants of land lights disappeared.

Axel wanted the remaining truths from her. "You are carrying Roy Spiller's child, aren't you?"

"God, you're smart. Or you've talked to that real nitwit Bartlett. What a waste of talent though Hawk. A good meal for the scavengers of the ocean when they chew you up just like chum stews. How did you figure that one out? That Spiller is the father?"

"Easy. It bothered me that Larry Bartlett was overweight, high hairline, a medical geek, boring, not the adventurous physical specimen worthy of planting seeds within your body to create the next generation of, how shall I say it: Wonder-boy."

"Go on."

"When you discovered Bartlett's wonder drug it pushed a megalomania like you to new heights. You just had to have him, didn't you? For one of your trophies. You needed his wonder drug. You needed his money. You needed his boat. But you required a perfect male physical specimen for breeding. That eliminated Larry Bartlett. But you had to convince him that the child was his in order for him to cooperate in your ultimate scheme of consuming his illegal drugs and providing an escape hatch."

Axel gloated to inflame her. "So, tonight when Bartlett revealed the master plan to Zoe and me that you and he had conceived Adam, I figured that he had it all right except for two important details. One, that Roy Spiller was the father of Adam Bartlett, not him. Less genetic flaws that way. Plus the resemblance of Roy to you was uncanny. The child would certainly look like you and Roy to carry on the legend of Montilladan in your own mind. None of the dumpy genes that Bartlett had." She scared him even more than the first encounter with Mrs. Whitehurst as she returned a satanic smirk, pulling her lips taut, crooked, malevolent eyes fixated on him as she cocked her head.

Axel meanwhile was enjoying himself. He had her attention. He was successfully stalling for help. She obliged. "Keep going."

He had to work an attack plan out in his mind. "The way I figure it, Larry Bartlett was damn lucky that he didn't show up tonight. The only purpose he served from this point on was to provide another high for you as you dumped his remains into the bottom of the ocean. One less witness to your murderous rampage."

She laughed hysterically and concurred. Axel spoke again, but this time he paced across the stern. "As Montilladan would say, he had completed his assignment. He had served you well. You gave another encore performance to win his affection as Dr. Renee Montoya, to gain access to the wonder drug, didn't you? Or was there any semblance of true love, or feelings for Larry?"

"Shut up! Goddam you! It was so perfect when Roy died. I appeared on stage to fix the props perfectly for his death scene. I witnessed it from the lower stage as one of the dancers. Idiot Givens ogled at me and never for a second knew who he was drooling over! It was the first step to my freedom. It was the first step on my path to a new life. But it was Roy Spiller who was so goddam fucking stupid. He fell in love with himself, never dreamed I'd cut him down. He never guessed that Montilladan was coming to an end."

Now, she came into his proximity, strutted around him keeping the pistol focused on him, yelling at the top of her lungs. "I told Roy of the cash that I had stashed away in Andorra. Part mine, part Bartlett's from his MUREX profits. I deserved that money from him. Bartlett provided that compensation to me for letting me take all the risks of this birth. All the risks of polluting myself with his illegal, unapproved, purple wonder drug. Bearing all the risks of any side effects."

Axel taunted her. "You won't get away with this scheme."

She screamed at him. "I am the one who has to tote around this child. I am the one who painfully has to inject that solution into my belly every day, and God it hurts for the twenty minutes after ingestion." She pulled up her shirt to reveal rich magenta splotches dotting her stomach. "Look. Look what the wonder drug does. What the hell are these splotches? Bursted blood cells? So, why shouldn't I be compensated?"

"I am the one who risks my body and provides the nourishment to this child. Me! I take these risks of applying an uncertified drug." She now pointed her index finger of her free hand at her chest and thumped her chest with it as she spoke loudly, "Me and me alone!" Above the roar of the motor and the hiss of splashing water she screamed.

"I told Roy of the child that I carried, his child, and of the enhancing drugs that little Adam was taking, to make us famous years from now as the world recognized that our child would not age normally. Montilladan and Roy Spiller would be the famous parents of the first superhuman. It was a chance for immortality."

She shook her head wildly in disbelief, but only for a second so that Axel could not respond to the slight break of concentration. *Too late, I must initiate another second dialogue to distract her,* he thought to himself.

"But the stupid bastard Roy couldn't believe it. He didn't want a part of this experiment. He said to me that he felt that I had unfairly trapped him. Trapped him? He wanted to take over permanently as Montilladan and let me escape. He proposed that I just disappear and he continue the role of Montilladan. Right then and there, I knew that he had become a liability. The stunt he performed on that fateful day was really to be his last for me because he had turned against me, abandoned me, fallen in love with the ruse. I made sure that he paid for his betrayal. Just like that blackmailing shit Brissand! He tried to suck more money from me for the passports and the forged medical degree and my new driver's license. What a leach. He chose poorly. I was there when you and your associates discovered him."

"I sensed it."

Montilladan smiled and shouted to the heavens. "I mean Spiller and I were two of a kind. How could I have been so wrong? In the end he was a gutless phony. This is his child." She patted her belly with the gun. "Ungrateful Roy suddenly didn't want it. He even cursed me for that night when I didn't use my birth control methods."

"He had a heart. I don't think you do."

Montilladan screamed only feet in front of him. "Shut up! Put your hands out from your body where I can see them or I'll blow your fuckin' eyes out." Axel did not hear any signs of rescue yet, even as he searched the skies for the lights of a chopper.

"The whole goddam world believed that I was deceased until that stupid Lacey Sills ruined it. Yeah. I had other lovers, some male and female. Somehow, she thought that she was to be my one and only. She is so naive. I hung around with her only because she got off on me and my fame."

"Why did you kill Lillian?"

"She was expendable. She always was. I paid her handsomely to keep my secret. Four or five times what any secretary would earn on any paycheck. I found her at a bar one night. She was just out of reformatory, unemployed, desperate for a job, good looking, on the lam and I calculated that this was a great gig for her and she was an easy convert. I replenished her well to keep our secrets." Montilladan sighed.

"She had to come with me or suffer the consequences. Needless to say, she also chose poorly. I had the Appleman blow her out just after you left. Lillian was there when we talked earlier and heard every word you said. Her car was at the back. Left behind, she could become a huge liability." Montilladan boasted of her further accomplishments.

"Just to complete the affair, I invited the poor, gullible Appleman upstairs to make love to me in return for eliminating Lillian. The last words I heard Lillian say were that she had changed her mind, that she would come with me after all. She screamed for mercy. Hah! She was so insincere."

Axel interrupted her. "You should return to Hollywood. Your crowning performance should be that of the Tin Man."

She moved to feet in front of him now to wave the pistol in his face while maintaining that menacing smirk. "In the bathroom, I used this gun. The Appleman was too greedy. Before we made love, he demanded more money for Lillian's murder, wanted to be re-compensated more for past deeds. Taking all the risky chances, he said like beating you at Fosse's, setting fire to the warehouse. His usefulness to me was apparently over, so the way I figure it, in the end I did society and the police a huge favor by taking him out."

"Cops can take their pick as to what killed him. Drowning, or a bullet to the head. Either way, it is one less wanted poster the cops have to issue and one less fugitive they expend time on. They should be grateful."

The boat suddenly accelerated and turned. "Yeah! I love it! Autopilot. I had to learn the systems of this craft and Larry was an excellent teacher once I turned him on. When I used to parade naked around this deck as Dr. Montoya, he would show me everything about this boat that I needed to know."

She laughed. She looked at the heavens for a second to shout, "Thank you, Larry, wherever you are. I locked in the coordinates and away we go Mr. Hawk. Plenty of fuel to make Mexico. Ooh-la-la. The paid-up authorities are my friends at the isolated port where I land in Mexico. They won't give a shit about any murders or crimes back in La-La land. By the time the system notifies them, I'll be long gone to my next destination and they'll be drunk on tequila."

"What lies, telling me all about your treatments of Montilladan."

"I only did that to get off on playing games with you and you fell for it because I am so perfect."

"You won't get away with it." Montilladan ignored him. The wind kicked up and the wave base grew a second time. Now she moved to expose the visible vertical bulging veins on both sides of her neck. Her soaked tight cut top accentuated her small breasts as she drew closer again. Axel commenced his plan.

"You will be a tormented woman for the rest of your life Montilladan. If you kill me, Zoe Burns will hunt you down wherever you are, where ever you go, she'll find you, even if it takes the rest of her life. I know Zoe. She won't let you get away with this and she will extract her revenge. And here's the best part. Revenge on you and your sweetie pie, little Adam. Yes, on you and on little Adam. She'll find you both before the birth. She was the one that discovered the ultrasound image at your residence. Think about this you bitch, little Adam will die, too. Just think about her mission. Seriously, I'll surrender now. I know my dear Zoe. Fantasize about your death, because I am!"

At the sound of "about", Montilladan took aim and zinged a bullet past his ear, the rush so close he felt the heat of its trail. But Axel held his composure and didn't blink, did not budge. "Shut up! You speak only when I tell you to from now on! I am going to love killing you. I got oodles of bullets and they're all for you. Maybe, I'll shoot off some vital parts first and let you cry yourself to death." Montilladan grinned demonically.

"No, something better, you fool, I got a better idea. They won't shoot at me if I use you for a screen. Good move Hawk. I can't kill you yet. Wouldn't want to end your life until I'm out of harm's way in Mexican waters. Use you as a shield, yeah. What a crowning moment sailing into Mexico with you as hostage."

Axel dared to speak as he noticed a discontinuous glimmer of lights, perhaps a cutter heading toward them, but with wave heights, he couldn't tell. He had to distract her lest she see the encroachment to their left. "Life is a stage upon which you have performed. It's hard to know which stage is more satisfying to you- the movies or the civilian stage. Every player has served a deceitful purpose for you in your entire life, haven't they?"

"This place took my life away, you asshole. I didn't intend to be a male performer. Don't you understand? I want my life back. I...want...my...life...back! To screw whomever I want. To perform the most vital part of a female's life. To re-populate, to give birth to my son. The plan that I hatched was so damn exceptionally perfect. Roy impregnated me, Larry Bartlett hand delivered to me the drug of a lifetime, which would allow me and my son to become famous forever. I have conceived a wonder child. I am filthy rich. I designed my own departure from Hollywood and conducted it. It was all so perfect except for Lacey's stupid actions." She was working her way into an emotional frenzy.

"She was so goddam vulnerable. When I look back at it, it was a mistake for me to reveal myself to her. But once in Mexico, with Brissand's last job for me, I can disappear forever with the international papers he provided me. These papers from Brissand are as brilliant as the forged papers of my psychiatry degree, as good as the social security numbers, birth certificates and other documents he crafted."

She boasted. "With my new identity, I can chose my time and place to resurface with my son."

Axel decided to infuriate her. "Wrong! This escapade, excuse me, was never perfect. Your plan is flawed and you are the biggest mistake in it. Thinking that a perfect crime exists is a flaw itself. You introduced flaws into your scheme when you exposed yourself to Lacey Sills, when were dependent on the Appleman, when you lied to Larry Bartlett, when you left the ultrasound and packets of the wonder drug behind. You are so stupid that you have planted the seeds of your own demise along every step of this defective, malfunctioning plan. Christ, it only took Zoe and me five days to find you. You call this plan perfect? I call it complete crap."

"Screw you. I am holding this gun. Who the hell are you to address me that way? I was a Hollywood icon. My films and performances will last eternally. What the hell can you say about yourself, asshole Hawk? It's time for me to radio the Coast Guard and inform them if they come close to this craft, by sea or air, if I see any lights at all, I will blow your fuckin' head off. I'll dissect it and mail it to your sweetheart Zoe, mail it to her bit by cranial bit from Mexico."

Axel now opened his left hand to dangle packets of the purple crystals, which he had withheld from Bartlett. He held them over the side of the Muriel. "Be a shame if I drop these packets into the ocean."

She stared motionless, deciding what to do. "What do I care? Only need enough for my term."

"But you must. Potion for a second child? If you don't have enough elixir? Or maybe the first pregnancy doesn't go well? A miscarriage due to all this stress? Every crystal counts."

As he spoke the word counts, the faint sound of a siren penetrated their space. Axel had concentrated on her eyes since she had first threatened him with the pistol minutes ago. At the sound of the siren, she broke eye contact for the first time, to peer out behind them. It was in that microsecond that he enacted his only possible action.

He catapulted himself through the air, propelling his body horizontally, protecting the front of his face with his bent elbow, venturing to use the thrust of a powerful cross-block to stun her upon impact. They both hit the floor with Axel on top at ninety degrees to her body.

In sync they both leapt up to regain standing positions. Axel gritted his teeth, and charged her from ten feet away, thrusting her against the back railing of the boat, pinning her but not long enough. He searched and spied the pistol sitting in the middle of the floor behind him. Montilladan focused on it, too. She proved to be a strong opponent, suddenly commencing to ram him between his legs with upward thrusts of her right knee. Bolts of pain stabbed at him. He backed away from contact, held one of her arms tightly, and ran at her with three, quick steps, attempting to bump and flip her, succeeding only to the point that she was hurled obtusely onto the floor with no significant damage.

They both soared through the air concurrently to grab possession of the gun. On simultaneous impact, it discharged into the night as their joint lock tugged the trigger. Axel elbowed her hard in the ribs while she ravenously bit his left wrist, which held the weapon; her bite broke his skin and he commenced to bleed. The pistol dislodged again as Axel released his grip completely to kick her wrist hard, the gun falling. Montilladan immediately kicked it to the back of the boat, Axel realizing too late how far he was from the weapon as they broke contact.

He couldn't race to it with her in the way, so he bolted up the stairs two at a time to the top deck and locked himself in the pilot's cabin to execute his next best action.

He stood, stupefied. How to disengage the autopilot? He had only seconds. An idea surfaced. The only one! He waited until he heard her charging up the stairs, probably armed, and caught her off balance by manually taking control of the steering wheel and turning it as suddenly and as hard left as he could, gyrating the craft into a dizzying circle. It worked. Autopilot was broken and the maneuver even sent him into a spin. He prayed that she had tumbled overboard.

Quickly, he rerouted the boat, this time turning a half rotation toward where he thought the shoreline to be, in the direction of the sirens he had perceived earlier. He rammed the throttle to one hundred percent, feeling the excitement of the craft as she tore wildly through waves upon acceleration. For safety, he figured to exit the pilot's cabin by the opposite side that he had entered and away from the side where he had heard Montilladan's last movements.

But in a blink of a second, the glass in front of him shattered as two bullets whizzed into the pilot's room. She stood on the protrusion in front of the command post, seeming barbaric, as a primitive savage. She rammed her body into the weakened glass, mercilessly attacking, bouncing into the cabin, firing shots behind him as he narrowly escaped outside onto the side stairwell sealing the door shut behind him.

Axel's instinct told him to hop up onto the roof, hoping that she would exit so he could tackle her from behind. To his surprise she didn't exit. Rotten luck. The boat was changing course again! She was re-engaging the autopilot route to direct the cruiser back out to sea! What to do?

Axel decided on the only option, dangerous as it was. He crouched above the lip of the broken window, sensing that she was still in the cabin, and in one dramatic motion, he swung his body through the shattered window, driving his feet into her face, with her eyes and neck as targets. As he completed his sortie, he scrapped his back by rubbing against some of the stubs of the broken glass chards still lodged in place.

He collided head into her, and upon impact, he not so luckily ended up on top of her for Montilladan brought her fist up and directly into his damaged cheek. Montilladan now expelled a series of vicious boorish yells, "Yeah! Yeah! Yeah!" as she thrust her tightly wound knuckles up again and again and again and again with highly focused blunt blows on his now reopened facial wound.

He continued to pin down her other arm, the one with the pistol; but, again, powerful blows of her free fist stabbed this time at his left eye while she tried to lunge and bite his throat. Axel summoned his last strength to rise, utilizing her burst of momentum on one of her upward jabs to drag her to her feet, too. The boat suddenly rocked furiously as it intersected high waves at less than optimum angles and tried to find stability. Both bodies swayed in unbalanced motion, but Axel had the advantage on one sway to smash her head into the steering column and used the opportunity to reach into his bowels and surface a power to lunge her upper body into the metal steel column again, but this time with success as he heard bones crack in her upper ribs.

The gun fell on the floor out of her grip. Immediately, Axel grabbed the pistol, realizing the moment and seizing it. Montilladan, bloodied in the nose and mouth, holding her chest with one bent arm, a dazed look on her face, flung herself at him, just as Axel discharged a shot into her chest, only to realize upon her impact, that he had only grazed her thigh. He responded by doing what he thought of initially on the deck floor, that is flinging the pistol overboard into the abyss of the deep waters, creating what he hoped to be an advantage for himself. So he opened the cabin door and he threw the pistol into Pacific waters.

She turned and bashed him from behind with a vicious kick, Axel rebounding off the rail to grapple with her. They arm wrestled in standing position, both wounded, each reaching into their deepest cavities to gasp for breath, twisting and turning back into the pilot's cabin as the cruiser became more unstable.

Axel realized their path was now random, so he decided to taunt her, to provoke a possible irrationality, a focus on him rather than the trajectory of the Muriel. "You should have killed me that night when you so stupidly revealed yourself to me in my own home. You provided Zoe and me with the first concrete proof that you were indeed alive. Another blemish in your fatally flawed plan. Stupid Lacey? No, not as stupid as your move! Not as dumb as a move as you made! We didn't know you were alive until that..."

"I should have killed you! I admit that mistake. But the hell with you as a shield, I will kill you now! I swear it. You will not see the light of tomorrow. The hell with keeping you alive as insurance. I'm going to beat you to death." Montilladan tugged herself free from him with a strong jerk, and breaking the hand lock, spinning herself away from him, she raced to secure an iron bar that rested under the Captain's seat. She turned. She stood tall. She screamed at him. "Say your prayers, asshole! Ah!"

Montilladan turned to thrash him as she gripped the bar with both hands. Axel ducked as she swung wildly and the iron bar crashed into the paneling behind him, the force creating a hole in the wall. He ran out and bounded down the stairwell to the second deck by leaping three steps at a time, recognizing the clear lights of onshore now closer than he could ever imagine. The boat careened onward, she more focused on his destruction, rather than their immediate heading.

As she leaped to the same level in one fluid athletic jump, she grunted as her ribs ached. Now they positioned themselves as two heavyweight wrestlers, assuming the position of legs spread, arms dangling, although she armed with the iron bar, plotting the opportune time to swing and decapitate him.

Axel was content to enter into this pre-ritual of combat, pacing around the floor, stalking each other, recognizing that Montilladan was completely unaware that the Muriel was shortening the distance between the boat and the shoreline with every second. Any radiant nature and charm of Dr. Renee Montoya had completely vanished. Instead, he was confronted with a very dangerous predator, currently consumed with the emotional focus of maiming him, or bludgeoning him to death. His next defense had to be perfect, or she would break all his bones. He tried a distracting tactic again to delay the inevitable.

"Dr. Renee Montoya was a crowning performance."

"Simple, goddam simple. A change of voice; a change of hair and eye color; breast enhancements, a sexy voice, a sexy demeanor, a classy wardrobe, facial makeup, tinted contacts, female body sways. That was so easy playing someone divorced from my real character. Cheek implants, add slight weight around the rotunda from injections, covered elevator shoes. So simple for a professional like me. I fooled you asshole."

She lunged forward with a foolish off-balanced reckless swipe, he remembering Zoe's advice of keeping balance, attacking vital spots and performing unpredictable actions. Thus allowing his upper arm to take the blow, he focused on putting them now in the only position he could think of to neutralize her- a tumble down the narrow stairs into the very lower cabin area. As he guessed, his forearm carried the brunt of the force of her strike by the bar, but as she struck, he grabbed her around the waist to pull her close to him and initiated the simultaneous plunge. Her momentum cooperated and caused them to tumble as Axel had predicted to the bottom of the stairs and to the lower level of the cruiser. He now lay numb with a frightening piercing pain in his right arm and bloody fluids clouding his left eye.

Through the mush, he reacted and choked her with one hand in a suffocating grip, while pinning down her other arm with his injured limb. She in turn thrust her free limb to choke him. With a gurgle in his throat, he gagged, and suddenly decided to enrage her by the most despicable move he could think of, kicking her tender stomach ferociously, again and again, beating the fetus of Adam. She screamed a "No! No! No! You bastard!" and fought to disengage him, releasing her grips to reposition, and chop savagely at his neck. He adsorbed the pain that he was receiving and kneed her hard in the abdomen again. Suddenly, Montilladan chanced the opportunity to now choke him with both her hands. Expelling a vehement roar from her bowels, and acting as if crazed and possessed to strangle him to death, she was smiling, locked nails digging deeper and deeper into his collapsing throat muscles, collapsing his esophagus, shrieking as a cannibal about to conquer the invincible foe, shutting off his air passages, spitting on his face again and again, nails plunging deeper and deeper, jaw jutting upward to try and bite his nose at the same time, she on top in the dominant position.

Axel tried the same maneuver to choke her but, too late, realized that her grip was already depriving him of oxygen, as he felt the initial signs of passing out, his cheeks numbing, and his face becoming flush.

He spied it. To his right he saw the iron bar- his only chance to break her lock. With all his last strength, he toppled them over and with his left arm extended, he grabbed the weapon and whacked her fiercely in the head. Again! Again on the forehead! Now a direct hit on her nose! Why did she not break the strangling grip on his neck? He felt like he was dying.

As he prepared to deliver another blow, she finally released her deadly grip to grasp her nose and protect her face and Montilladan rolled over to protect any other hits against Adam. Axel scurried up the stairs to the second deck and repeated his previous defense by hurling the iron bar into the seas. Exhausted, drained, out of breath, he collapsed at the side rails on his knees.

The silhouettes of the lights of shore were ever so close to them. Axel pulled himself up and realized in fear that the Muriel was now rocketing through the shallow waters to intercept the shoreline at ninety degrees. Paralyzed, he realized their new crisis. The lights of shore were not distant. The Muriel was only feet from the beach! Still locked in full throttle! As he stood stunned analyzing the situation, Montilladan surprised him and strangled him this time from behind in a choking grip. As he twisted his head to try and warn her, he absorbed her crazed demented appearance. She interpreted his thoughts too late.

The boat hit the first sandy bars at full throttle only feet from the true shoreline. The velocity of the impact caused the hull of the boat to rip apart, completely shatter into thousands of small shavings, which showered randomly into the air sideways and upward. The momentum of the craft caused the rest of it to smash and splinter into three large pieces, which were twirled through the air mercilessly.

The upper deck was suddenly disengaged and air bound. It rotated over and over, end upon end, and smashed upside down on the beach. The rest of the craft was dissected into two pieces; a front segment slid through the sandy bars until it disintegrated into numerous disjointed sections. The back piece, with Axel and Montilladan standing upright hit the beach, but instead of plowing into it, it immediately toppled over to become lodged upright, the motion throwing Axel and Montilladan ahead of a shower of sheared projectiles. He landed with a thud on his back in shallow mucky waters.

Axel was fortunate to have his buttocks take the brunt of his rude fall, but the impact rendered him helpless, as he rolled over and over, exhausted, his right elbow dislodged, maybe broken. Axel could only pray that falling debris would not impale him as he was helpless to move. Beside him on the beach, some two hundred feet away, the fuel tanks suddenly exploded in an inferno that fortunately signaled the rescue team of their whereabouts.

In what seemed like a lifetime on the golden lit beach, he dragged himself out of the mud on all four limbs, and in those few moments, the wonderful pulses of sirens penetrated his ears. As he collapsed on his back, he saw her as an apparition, coming to haunt him again. She blocked out the flaming debris, her outline black but disfigured. She was bloodied in her thigh area, probably from when he grazed her, and bleeding profusely from cuts on her left arm and nose and forehead. The determined evil in her face had not been eradicated. Axel was helpless to move and he couldn't believe that she had the strength for another confrontation.

She had a different weapon this time, a very small caliber gun. Bludgeoned, bloody in the mouth, she took aim, standing over him in hunchback position. He savored the justice of the moment as the gun failed to fire. She commenced to wail as she pulled the trigger again and again with the same results. She hurled it into the reeds and cursed.

Saved by the cavalry, Montilladan appeared to want to tangle again, but her attention was drawn to flashing lights, so he watched her disappear into the blackness behind the dunes. He had only two wishes: to see her dead and to see his beloved Zoe once more before he died.

Screaming out his name, tears openly flowing down her cheeks, Zoe Burns was the first to reach him as she collapsed in the sand beside him, cradling his bloodied head in her lap, struggling to speak to him through her grieving. She never let go of his hand, even as the ambulance attendants wrapped him up and carted him off. Even during the ride to the hospital, he heard Zoe say, "I was the homecoming queen of my high school." She kept repeating it over and over through her voice of drenched grief and through her stream of tears. And every time he heard it, Axel Hawk squeezed her hand tighter and tighter, and tighter for dear life, and finally, she heard him say, "Bullshit." She smiled.

SATURDAY AFTERNOON

Awakening from his coma, Axel felt like he had just survived a smash into open mountains of granite. Throbbing pains in his legs and back and head were incessant. His eyes opened. The room was a sterile white except for three interruptions from the décor. One was Tinker sitting on one side of his bed; the other two were Zoe and Speed posed on the opposite side. She was gripping his hand and stroking it gently. She still had that weepy loveable look in her red stained eyes.

"Welcome back." It was Speed who greeted him. "While you were warning me to watch my rear Axel, you forgot to watch your own."

Tinker expelled a deep husky "Ha, ha." Axel forced himself to shape a smile at Zoe and squeezed her hand tighter. It was arduous to talk, but he had to know, so he directed his gaze at Tinker. "Lo...cater?"

"We have combed the shores with no trace of her. She disappeared like a ghost that night Axel. However, we'll find her though. She has lost a great deal of blood and her trail was easy to follow until it intersected the coast road and we lost it. All the hospitals are on alert Axel, and all the small medical clinics in the area have been posted. She can't get far in her present battered physical condition. I got to admit though that I am absolutely amazed at the endurance of that fiend."

Axel had experienced nightmares of her extraordinary strength during his delirious recovery. He wanted to contribute. "Double guard, Bartlett."

Tinker and Zoe bowed their heads on cue. There was no response until Tinker signaled Zoe with body language. Zoe informed him. "Another tragic chapter of Montilladan is complete Axel. Larry Bartlett committed suicide about thirty minutes after we left him Thursday night. He took an overdose of sleeping pills. Tiny Chin kept his part of the bargain for he phoned friends of Larry; he was dead when the ambulance and friends arrived. In his farewell note, he expressed remorse of how he failed to come forward when he knew what illegal deeds and activities Montilladan had committed and he confessed to abetting her and distributing the illegal drugs."

Tinker embellished. "Another life destroyed by the demon."

Dr. Jim Gieske abruptly entered and addressed Axel. "We have to stop meeting like this Axel. If this keeps up you'll be my full time patient." Gieske stood beside him and like a barker opened a scroll and listed the damage and ailments as Axel grimaced. "You are on pain killers now but, when they wear off, you'll read 100 percent on the pain meter. I suggest one of you permanently babysit this child until recovery." With no words spoken, Tink and Speed eyed Zoe. Zee smiled her confirmation back.

"You are free to go. However, I release you only under the care of one, Ms. Zoe Burns. You are to go on sabbatical for three weeks, absolutely no less, and let your dislocated elbow, facial wounds, back lacerations, and five severe body bruises heal. You also have some small cuts on your left leg, and last but not least, you have seriously bruised buttocks. Taking a crap is going to hurt for a few weeks."

Tinker couldn't resist. "Thank God for your ass, Axel because it saved your ass when you hit the beach!" They shared hearty merriment.

Gieske continued. "I dug some glass fragments out of you. It is a miracle that you survived. I'll package these up and send them to you, so you can have some credible props when you recite this incredible tale at Fosse's."

Speed piped up. "Here, here. Jim and I and Tinker and Zee want to be there at the first telling of this tale. I got to hear this whole whopper from the start."

Tink stood and complimented him. "Good job you two, a great piece of bringing a criminal to justice; tracking her down; what can I say? Axel Hawk is a true survivor."

Zoe continued to stare at him. "Your landing place was a high tide drenched mucky spot at Laguna Coast Wilderness Park. You were so lucky." She squeezed his hand. "I mean I was so lucky."

Tinker reminded him. "What an imprint you made upon impact. The Coast Guard's going to fill your body outline with cement to commemorate the spot. But what a mess this case is, Axel. Felix has been briefed and is pissed royally but figures that the beatings you absorbed on this case are lessons enough for bypassing us once again. Although, I assured him that without your help, this whole goddam exciting mess could not have even remotely solved." Even Gieske bellowed.

Axel wondered. "Time?"

Gieske responded as he completed forms. "Four forty-five in the afternoon and its Saturday. Time to discharge you. Sign here with an X. I'll take care of the rest. You have to continue to take these antibiotics as directed Axeman, or you will pay dearly for it."

Zee assured him that the doses would be administered. "I'll see to it. Thanks for responding so promptly early Friday morning Jim."

"It was my duty. I think Axel's cement imprint should be poured and relocated to Hollywood and Vine. I am not privy to the details of this caper like Tinker and Zee, but all I can say about this week is, what a performance. You are lucky to be alive from the details I've heard." With that remark,

Gieske departed. Axel, with assistance from Tinker and Zee, stirred and struggled to ascend.

"Oh, the pain!" As he spoke there was a disturbance in the hallway and with all eyes on the door, Thumper entered with a wheel chair.

Zoe intercepted him to say, "Do not hug him Thump. You'll kill him."

Thumper stood beside the bed to salute Axel and moved closer as the threesome positioned him in the chair.

Zee held him tight under one arm; Thumper had the other. Tinker stood directly in front to catch any collapse; Speed provided directions. Axel groaned as his rear sunk into the chair. He looked at Zee who read his mind.

"I took the liberty this morning to roust Lacey out of bed to explain the events. Unofficially, that is, until the police make their report. She informed me that she was going home- to her parents for a week to recuperate."

"One goal accomplished, Lacey's reconciliation." Axel turned to Tinker. "Your report?"

Tinker took a deep breath and waited until Dr. Gieske had left. "I'm sorry, Axel. I talked to Felix. As far as we know, Dr. Renee Montoya killed Lillian and the Appleman. Dr. Larry Bartlett committed suicide from his recent bouts of depression, which can be substantiated by the loss of his wife, and the reports of his therapist, which we uncovered at his home. The official report is that Montilladan is dead and buried at Forest Haven Cemetery and Roy Spiller is filed as a missing person. Montilladan's burial took place in front of witnesses; so did his death scene. Those are the facts as Felix will sign to. Those are the facts that you and Zoe and Lacey will have to adhere to, and your friend Nikki."

"G-got to be kidding us?"

"Save your strength, Hawk. You want to go to Felix? Demand an exhumation? Explain all this shit? Who in his right mind is going to believe this crap? That a person who died weeks ago, resurfaced from the grave to murder four people and do all this? That a California beachcomber is buried in the grave of a movie star? That the great Montilladan and Axel Hawk took to sea to challenge each other to a wrestling and kick boxing match to the death?" Axel was tired. He did not want to debate the issues.

Tinker squatted in front of him. "It's over, Hawk. That includes what's in your mind. Give it a rest. This was a demented criminal. It is one for your private records. Go home and rest."

Thumper insisted that he navigate. Slowly, Axel Hawk, with his troubadours, Tinker, Speed, Thumper, and Zoe, traversed the pasteurized halls of the hospital, weaving and winding, until they emerged at Zoe's Jaguar, parked curbside. Tink waved goodbye and left with no more advice; Speed promised to check in on Axel's health frequently; he also had tickets for all for an upcoming basketball game; Thumper assured Axel that he would protect him from any ghosts of Montilladan; Axel in and out of consciousness, adsorbed the affections.

The front seat felt so uncomfortable as he jostled about in numerous positions. "I remember someone saying, fasten your seatbelt. We are in for a helluva ride."

Zee looked at him with admiration. "Comfy?"

"No."

"You have to promise to tell me and only me what really happened out there on the Muriel."

"All in good time. Zee?"

"Yes."

"Hurry home d-dear. Zee?"

"What now?"

"Cuddle up tonight?"

"Promise," was her quick response, and they drove to her townhouse where Axel Hawk immediately fell asleep in the arms of Zoe Burns on the infamous living room sofa.

TWO DAYS LATER

"Axel, it really wasn't necessary for you to drag your aching bones to accompany Tinker and I this morning to meet with Lacey. I'd rather you had slept in." She was leaning her head to address him in the passenger's seat.

"I have weeks of sabbatical to look forward to. I want us to bring closure to this case together. Therefore, we will debrief our client together. There are some truths to be withheld; others to be revealed. My aching backside can withstand one road trip and this is it."

The day prophetically warned of rain as they exited the freeway to drive up into the hills. He remembered how Kathleen Whitehurst had turned from enemy to ally. He recalled their embrace. Even so he did not wish her to be present at the debriefing with Lacey, but it might be difficult to exclude her in her own home. *Surely, the Colonel must be absent. A debriefing at the Whitehurst residence would be risky if the Colonel was home. Or perhaps he had this all figured out?*

"Why did Lacey not want to meet us at the office?"

"At first she was vague, and then she blamed it on Doctor's orders. She indicated that she has been heavily sedated. Mrs. Whitehurst warned me that she might not be fully cognizant. The facts as I have conveyed to her have been quite a shock to her system which probably will be Mrs. Whitehurst's excuse to attend our meeting with Lacey, that she needs to comfort her."

"I was sitting here hoping that she and the Colonel would be absent. At least the Colonel must be feeling acheered with Lacey home. I wonder what discussions they have had over this drama."

Zoe added. "The fact that she came running to them in her greatest hour of need must be a victory for the Whitehurst's. Does it hurt to talk?"

"Yes, it hurts to sit, it aches to talk and it is even painful to eat. My rear end is burning up, like a hunk of burning love; can't get comfortable. Drive, Zee, drive. I want to save my strength for the only meeting I need to attend this week."

They twisted their way through woodsy streets, finally turning into the Whitehurst mansion, this time parking directly in the front covered entryway.

Kathleen Whitehurst, anticipating their arrival, sat on the wooden bench and waved as they approached. At the first sight of Axel, she held her arms over her chest and gasped.

"Mr. Hawk, you look worse every time I see you. I knew that you had been in a high speed boat crash from Miss Zoe's information, but I had no idea of how injured you were."

Axel disbanded the crutches and limped toward her in hunchback style. "A dislocated elbow, a few lacerations on my back, cheek wounds with stitches, and a hobble in my gait from an extremely sore derriere. The good news Mrs. Whitehurst is that I can handle it all with the aid of my able assistant." He purposefully looked at Zoe for these last remarks.

Kathleen walked forward to give him a gentle hug; she shook hands with Zoe, welcomed them, and then, surprisingly, grabbed Axel tightly by his arm, motioning Zee to lead the way as she led and assisted him into the house, traversing one step at a time with caution. "I'll help our gallant knight up the steps."

Inside, Kathleen still held Axel and warned them. "Lacey is emotionally in shreds. Please be kind with your remarks and brief in your inquiries. I agreed to this meeting, but please keep it succinct." Suddenly she was shaking.

"I think, Mr. Hawk, you ought to talk to the Colonel first. I know that you probably wanted to avert this, but he is aware of your imminent arrival. There is some business between he and you that he wishes..." her conversation was disjointed, "some discussion to take place between you two that is urgent and he immediately, that is before you converse with Lacey. I'm afraid that this is a condition of entry- he and you alone. I will escort you down the hall. I must ask Zoe to remain here."

The crunchy sounds behind them signaled Tinker's arrival in the driveway as he inched the squad car into the laneway beside Zee's car; his face was emblazoned with the confusing and dramatic events of the past week. He strutted forward without hesitation to greet them with a hearty "Good morning, Mrs. Whitehurst, I am Detective Tinker Lawrence from the Los Angeles Police Department. I am here to attend the briefing with Lacey as Zoe informed you earlier."

The only direct reference to past events was his quip to Axel, "A cat has nine lives. Somehow, Axel Hawk, on my precise count, has lived ten already. I am glad to see you up and around Axel and in the presence of ladies, I shall refrain from further truthful jabs."

Kathleen was disappointed by Tinker's attendance, so Zoe took the lead to explain to Mrs. Whitehurst that Tinker would record the conversation as she and Axel debriefed Lacey on their investigation. Tinker elaborated, "There are unfinished elements of police business surrounding this case which Lacey must answer, Mrs. Whitehurst. I'm sorry if you didn't realize the full implication of my presence."

"Fine, but whatever happens though, Mr. Hawk meets with the Colonel first. Colonel's orders. Do you hear that Mister Tinker? Miss Zoe?" She wasted no time in searching Tinker's body language for approval.

Suddenly, Lacey stood halfway down the grand spiral stairwell in complete view of them. The radiance of her persona was absent. In baggy white pajamas with bare feet, she appeared very ordinary, seemed extremely fragile. Axel noticed the tangles in her hair, the unsteadiness in her walk as she approached, using the rails for guidance; there was a melancholy haze in her eyes.

Her first task was to greet Axel and apologize for all the physical risks that she had exposed him to. By the sound of Lacey's hollow voice and her disheveled appearance, she was in far worse shape than Axel. Up close, the swelling around her eyes was abhorrent; the wrinkles under her eyes projecting her recent bout of trauma.

As she glided to Zoe and Tinker, everyone heard the unmistakable summons of the Colonel. His hails were emanating from his den and he was clearly summoning Axel. After motioning to Zoe and Tinker to remain, he hobbled alone through the gauntlet of grandfather clocks to the entrance of the den, where the distinguished profile of the Colonel was sitting behind his desk, ready to receive Axel Hawk. He sat basking in a solo ray of intruding sunlight. The familiar odor of his sweet cigar smoke filled the room, and in light of the week's events, he appeared to be chipper, waving his hand vigorously for Axel to sit directly in front of him.

Lacey followed quickly down the hallway behind Axel to position herself beside her dad, a grim countenance in contrast to the strong military presence of the Colonel. She placed her arm on his shoulder and stood slightly behind as not to diminish his authority. The Colonel reached over the desk to display his sincere condolences to Axel for the result of his heroic actions. Axel decided to remain standing given the soreness of his derriere and the discomfort of the act of sitting, so he used the back of the chair as a prop to lean on.

"The encounter with an arch adversary has taken its toll," Axel explained. "The good news is that I get three weeks off." The humor was lost as the Colonel remained stern.

"I understand from Lacey that these injuries were suffered as you chased Montilladan, and were involved in a subsequent boat crash. If I had the power I would decorate you with a badge of valor." He admired them, Daddy and Daddy's little girl. Even with her short comings on beauty today, the Colonel and Lacey struck a very handsome couple as they faced him.

"Thank you for your kind comments. It was all in the line of duty." The Colonel's comments took Axel by surprise since, but he did decide that sexual issues and preferences should be avoided. He found that his jaw hinges ached every time he spoke.

"I'm very sorry to inform you that the police have still not captured Montilladan. An L.A. detective is outside. He has assured me earlier that, at least, they are scouring the general Los Angeles area and will continue to do so. Montilladan survived the boat crash and remains at large. While there are recent reports of her sighting, and a trail of blood droppings to confirm this, the severity of her wounds may render her dead. Perhaps that's why they haven't located Montilladan; the body is lying dead in a remote spot." They were both silent as they stared back at him.

"Montilladan and I crashed into a shoreline not far from the search area. There is a great deal more to talk to Lacey about but, in the interim, it would be wise to post sentries around your place if by some freak event Montilladan manages to find her way here!"

Axel, oddly, suddenly, found himself choking on his own words. The phlegm rose in his throat. The Colonel flashed a smile, became animated. "That is enough Mr. Hawk, enough of this foolishness." Axel was confused. "What foolishness?" Like Kathleen earlier now the Colonel was taking about foolishness.

"I understand from your wife that you needed to speak with me, but let me emphasize to you that you must not underestimate Montilladan's tricks of disguise. Look at what that foolish underestimation cost me." Again, he choked, he coughed. Perhaps this sortie was proving too much for him.

The Colonel was firm. "Bloody nonsense!"

After a hearty puff on his cigar, he blew a cloud into the air. Axel found himself gasping for air again, finding it difficult to breath.

"Mr. Hawk, Montilladan is not missing." Axel was stunned at the remark. His head felt dizzy, wobbling on its joints. The air was suffocating. Choking sensations overwhelmed him. Would it be rude to ask the Colonel to extinguish his cigar? It certainly was bothering him in his condition. And now a greater mystery surfaced. The local news and police had confirmed that the criminal of their search was Dr. Renee Montoya. Was the Colonel really unaware of this double life? Now the Colonel stunned him!

"Mr. Hawk, we are glad to receive you and your two friends here today because Montilladan has been here since three-thirty last night. She broke into our house, created a bloody disturbance. My daughter, in some sympathy, proceeded to clean her bloody-crusted wounds. Montilladan told me some sorry, inexcusable, pathetic lies of how you and Ms. Burns had concocted information to destroy her life and how she had been framed for the murders of two of her friends and even a stuntman. How the police, in viewing the murder scene had jumped to erroneous conclusions. How the police have chased her and hounded her for days. How she broke into an infirmary to dress her wounds." Axel was about to faint. Montilladan here? He had to warn Tinker. But there was that feeling of nausea again.

"She inserted a great many empathetic convoluted twists to suit her aims. She begged Lacey to help her. Well, I never saw a more pathetic creature espouse a more pathetic pack of lies to save her. So many sorry excuses." Axel felt dizzy again. Why was Lacey becoming blurred? Was this dream or reality? Had he really arisen this morning? Was Montilladan, the master of disguise, now in front of him disguised as the Colonel? In his state of pain and discomfort, he now only realized the pungent odors of fetid excrement and blood that his body was inhaling. The Colonel stood to point.

"You see, Mr. Hawk, Montilladan is not missing. She is right over there behind you, in the chair in the corner. There she is! Right where I took out my pistol and shot her."

Slowly, Axel turned. The putrid stale stench of plasma filled his nostrils and stung his eyes. The stench of bodily excrements overwhelmed him. Montilladan sat slouched in a high back chair behind him and against the wall under the grand painting of Lacey. The skin on her face was of red and pink and gray blotches. Her eyes were wide open, about to fall out of their sockets, with dead tissue behind no longer serving a mission to hold them in place.

Her bottom lip was disgustingly convoluted to three times its size. Her legs, ala her Montoya character, were crossed one over the other; they were not rocking. Her arms hung limp on each side of her body. Axel could think of nothing else to do but summon Zoe and Tinker with one shrill succinct yell.

The chair was soaked in blood, dripping still, slowly, rhythmically, onto the floor from a neatly administered hole in the middle of her forehead. As Tinker and Zoe entered, they covered their noses, and in awe stared as the Colonel explained. "She bled to death right there in front of us. No one to help her. Not Lacey. Not Kathleen. Certainly not I. What a pathetic site."

Now in a rage he slammed his fist on the desk top while his slender body reached out over the desk in a gesture of contempt. "I forbade it! You understand! I forbade it! As the head of this household, I forbade anyone in this house to lift an ounce of help toward that vile human being," and he pointed his long index finger at her.

Tinker sputtered a "Geez", while Zoe moved forward to examine the body. The Colonel calmly trashed his cigar. "Kathleen!"

Kathleen entered and acknowledged him. "Yes, John?"

"Get my jacket, please. There's a fall chill in the air. I suspect that ah Mr. ah...ah...you there."

"Detective Lawrence, sir."

"Mr. Lawrence of L.A.'s finest here will want me to accompany him to police headquarters to make some sort of official statement on what exactly transpired here last night. He will want to know why I took my revolver out of my desk and shot her dead. I will go on behalf of the three of us." The Colonel turned to his side and hugged Lacey for at least a minute, proceeded across the room to Tinker, and handed him his pistol. He addressed Tinker respectfully. "Shall we go, sir?"

He didn't wait for Tinker's reply but marched forward as a proud military officer would with a sturdy step after step of deliberate paces down the hallway. Kathleen cried heartily. Over her grief, she assured him, "I'll stay here, John, with Lacey."

"Yes, you ladies remain here. I shall not be long."

Axel witnessed the reunion. Lacey moved forward to hold her mother tight in Kathleen's hour of need. They comforted each other. Zoe moved beside Axel and whispered, "Exit, stage left." Tinker politely asked Kathleen and Lacey to vacate the room and returned to seal it with yellow tape from further contamination until the investigative team arrived.

Tinker, Zoe, and Axel walked down the hallway, Tinker shaking his head in disbelief while inciting immediate assistance on his cell phone at the

Whitehurst residence. "I'll require an examination of the body before we move it, officers to examine the death scene and grounds." He continued to deliver orders as he paced down the hallway.

They reached the front entryway. Outside Axel saw Colonel Whitehurst standing at attention at the rear of Tinker's vehicle. Tinker turned to Axel.

"So, what would old Willy say to this mess?"

"I believe that he would say that ambition should be made of sterner stuff." Tinker guessed. "Macbeth?"

"No. Julius Caesar, fallen just as Montilladan. Murdered in false sanctity."

ONE WEEK LATER

The morning fall air was invigorating. "How much farther?"
"Katz, we are almost there." The foursome trudged onward, Axel enjoying his first exercise since the boating accident but still struggling with the nuisance of nettles in his backside and legs. His arm remained in a sling.

"This feels great. This is the first jaunt I've had. I have been confined to bed for days thanks to Zoe and my pal, Dr. Jim Gieske." They carried on for five more minutes, Axel determining the leisurely pace.

"Halt. Here we are. Come and sit over here on this stone bench to achieve the optimum grandiose view." They sat in quiescence. Katz positioned himself in the middle, flanked by Axel and George. Zoe lagged behind to stand guard in the rear, peering back across the clearing.

Katz was confused; George baffled. "We give up. Why are we here?"

"Katz, George, you must honor the confidential pact of ultimate secrecy that you each agreed to before we commenced this hike. You swore to me fifteen minutes ago that you never breathe to a soul about this hike. We have a common bond through that oath."

"Swear to me once again." They did.

Zoe joined them and stood in front on Axel's cue. "George, Katz, let me tell you that Axel and I have been on a case of trying to locate two people. One of those is the actor Montilladan and the other is your friend Roy."

Axel stated firmly. "Guys, Zoe and I found Roy. You are looking at the gravesite of Roy Spiller." George challenged while Katz was still reeling.

"Impossible. It says this is where the movie star Montilladan is buried. I remember reading about his gruesome accidental death. What joke is this?"

"Trust us. The missing persons file that exists on Roy Spiller will never be closed. There is a very logical explanation. He is accidentally buried here under this magnificent tombstone. We swear to it." Katz and George each looked to see Zoe agreeing with Axel by signifying a strong nod.

Zee continued. "Roy was substituting for Montilladan on the day of the accident. Take it from us. Montilladan was very ill that day, did not perform the fatal stunt and did not die that day. Roy did. Please believe us." Katz reinforced the secrecy. "We promise to keep this in confidence, Axel, but this is a sensational turn of events. George and I deserve a further explanation."

"Roy died performing stunts for Montilladan during filming. Because of substantial injuries to the facial area, witnesses just assumed that it was Montilladan who died. They were friends who were very similar in build, and there are people in Hollywood who can testify to their remarkable similar appearances. But as Zoe said, the investigation that Zoe and I recently conducted, lead us to a startling but true conclusion. Roy Spiller is buried here. You are sworn to secrecy."

Katz barked, "But where is Montilladan?"

"Ah! You can't ask that. Remember? That is one of the questions that you are forbidden to ask. Right?"

Katz accepted the reality, stood at attention, and moved toward the gravesite. "It's difficult to believe, but if you say so. Roy would have never guessed that he would have a memorial such as this, a beautiful monument to a great guy."

Axel's mind wandered as Katz spoke. Axel perused, stood, and moved to whisper in Zee's ear, "How ironic, that Roy Spiller should end up here, in this resplendent pocket of nature, and Montilladan in the little known gravesite of Dr. Renee Montoya, buried on the other side of the city before a paucity of attendees."

George challenged them. "What was that you're mumbling?"

"Nothing."

Their attention turned to Katz as he approached the epitaph. "Roy, I know that you can't hear me. Or maybe, you can. This is Katz. I came to pay my respects to you. It seems such a shame that a man with a really big heart such as yours should be taken from us so soon. I miss you, Roy. We all miss you. It is the finality of death that hurts when it occurs so suddenly."

Katz spoke. "In today's world, there are so few who would truly in their hearts share their own good luck and fortune so openly with a lot like us who are honest but down on our luck. I don't know what else to say Roy, except that your memories are all worth treasuring. I shall never forget the way you touched my life with your generosity and your sincerity. I shall never ever forget our friendship. I will keep our memories forever. Farewell, Roy. I promise to visit you again." Tears streamed down his cheeks.

Katz moved forward, and they sank to their knees in silent prayer. George recited lines from a Robert Frost poem and as Katz and George sat there together, an infiltrator broke the touching ceremony.

"That was beautiful." Katz and George were shocked as they bounded to their feet at the sight of the addressee.

Katz spoke first. "Lacey Sills? It is! We're sorry to intrude on your private moments with Montilladan if that's whom you visit."

She sauntered over to stand beside them and provide a shocking comment. "No, I came to visit Roy Spiller."

George looked curiously at Axel. So did Katz. Axel cleared up the uncertainty. "This is not Roy's benefactor if that's what you're thinking. Put that thought out of your mind. Lacey genuinely did know Roy Spiller, stuntman extraordinaire, from the movies. She also knew Roy as a genuine person. Right Lacey?"

Lacey addressed Katz and George. "He was a part time stunt man, little known, but a pleasure for me to have known him. He was a man of generosity and conviction." Katz and George were glued to her beautiful form.

"Axel and Zoe informed me they were dragging you out here today. I took the same oath as you did. Confidentially, I know as you do that Roy's spirit is here."

She carried a bouquet and now placed it at the base of the epitaph. She stepped up to address Katz and George further. "I want to tell you that the man or woman of the week, or the month, or whatever the three of us decide, will live on in the memory of Roy Spiller. Roy Spiller- a really great guy. A bit of a risk taker but, in the end, one who deserved a better fate than death."

Axel thought that both Katz and George were about to join Roy with massive coronaries. With no response, Lacey prompted them. "George, Katz, I want to continue the tradition that Roy began. Axel informed me about it. How about it guys? Do we have a deal?"

"How do you want us to explain the money and gratuities? Roy is...dead." It was George speaking.

"Simple. Roy is missing in action. In Roy's memory, a new transparent benefactor has appeared, Lacey Sills. No need to keep it a secret. We can inform your friends that I knew him. Work with me guys so I'll meet with your group. Transparent actions are called for." Axel recognized they needed encouragement.

"Katz! George! Stop ogling and reply to the lady."

"Miss Sills, on behalf of our rag-tag clan, it would be an honor to adopt you as our new patron." Katz extended his hand to shake. George grew anxious for his turn to touch Lacey Sills as Zoe and Axel laughed at Katz's extended handshake and beaming smile.

"And as a start, I'm treating you to lunch. We can discuss the details. Do the great detectives care to join us?"

"Go ahead, I want to sit and relax here before I start the trek back." He motioned to Lacey to join him away from the tombstone. "How is your father?"

"He has hired a reputable attorney. The police report indicates that the intruder was on the run from police, was dangerous, was guilty of previous murders, and was an intruder named Renee Montoya, died from internal bleeding before the shot was fired. That coupled with the fact that it was clearly breaking and entering should provide an acquittal somehow. We have to go through the process." She turned.

"Katz and George? Ready?"

"Yes, ma'am," Katz answered emphatically for both. Lacey Sills strolled off, accompanied by Katz and George, arm in arm on each side, excitedly babbling. Zoe sat down beside Axel on the granite bench, snuggling up to him, her arm around his waist, his around her shoulder, she curling inward. Behind, and in the distance, they heard Lacey and her new friends bandying about ideas for the group until the din died.

Zoe spoke. "This entire charade unfolded so rapidly, so unpredictably. I was crying like I never did before in my whole life when I saw that boat smash into shore from a distance, witnessed the fireball when the engines exploded, tripped over the fragments hurled in all directions as I raced to you. I prayed and prayed for your safety as I searched for you." Her voice took on soprano tones. Axel drew her closer as he positioned his free arm around her waist to complete the lock. Zoe spoke again.

"I never felt that way before in my whole life. I didn't want you to die," and she burst into tears as she turned to look into his dreamy hazel eyes. "We are definitely not getting married Axel, but I do love you very much." He tightened his grip.

"The true mark of love is to gazest into thoust lover's soul, and discover it is more beauteous than physical appearance itself."

"Hm. Did Shakespeare say that?"

"No, Axel Hawk did. I just made it up!" She giggled.

Axel couldn't help himself.

"You are the sunshine of my life,

And I'll always be arr...ow...ound."

"Axel, be quiet and enjoy the tranquility. Will you?"

"You are the apple of my eye,"

She locked her arms around him, placed her legs over his. Axel, in pain, held her as tight as he could. Zoe hugged him as tight as she could. And there they sat in each other's embrace as he continued his serenade to conclusion.

But she heard him not, for in these moments she closed her eyes and was defenseless in the clutches of Axel Hawk.